Dear Reader:

Summer has arrived in Eclipse Bay and things are definitely heating up between the Hartes and the Madisons. It seems that the mysterious new gallery owner, Octavia Brightwell, is thinking about having a scandalous fling with that rogue Nick Harte before she leaves town. As far as Nick is concerned, a short-term affair sounds perfect. But it isn't going to be easy.

One big obstacle is Mitchell Madison. For reasons of his own, Mitchell has taken it upon himself to play guardian to Octavia. He's made it clear that if Nick fools around with her, there will be a price to pay. And then there's Nick's young son, Carson, who has his own agenda where Octavia is concerned. He doesn't want his father messing up his plans.

Summer in Eclipse Bay is going to be eventful this year. Some long-buried secrets from the infamous Harte-Madison feud are about to surface. The past and the present are on a collision course. I hope you'll join me to watch the fireworks.

Happy reading . . .

Jayne Ann Krentz

*Turn the page for praise for Jayne Ann Krentz's previous novels . . .*

# SUMMER IN ECLIPSE BAY

*Jayne Ann Krentz*

JOVE BOOKS, NEW YORK

### SUMMER IN ECLIPSE BAY

A Jove Book / published by arrangement with
the author

PRINTING HISTORY
Jove edition / May 2002

Copyright © 2002 by Jayne Ann Krentz.
Excerpt from *Light in Shadow* copyright © 2002 by Jayne Ann Krentz.
Cover art by Brad Springer.

Visit our website at
www.penguinputnam.com

ISBN: 0-515-13341-8

A JOVE BOOK®
Jove Books are published by The Berkley Publishing Group,
a division of Penguin Putnam Inc.,
375 Hudson Street, New York, New York 10014.
JOVE and the "J" design
are trademarks belonging to Penguin Putnam Inc.

PRINTED IN THE UNITED STATES OF AMERICA

10 9 8 7 6 5 4 3 2 1

*For Michele Bradshaw—a lady who knows*
*how to stay calm even when we're all late for the wedding!*

# chapter 1

Rejected again.

Sixth time in five weeks.

Not that he was counting.

Nick Harte put down the phone very deliberately, got to his feet, and went to stand at the living room window of the cottage.

Six rejections in a row.

A man could get a complex at this rate. Why was he doing this to himself, anyway?

He looked out into the wall of gray mist that shrouded the landscape. Summer had arrived, just barely, in Eclipse Bay, and with it the familiar pattern of cool, damp, fog-bound mornings and long, sunny afternoons. He knew the season well. Growing up he had spent every summer as well as school vacations and long weekends here. His parents and grandparents maintained permanent homes elsewhere and he and his son lived in Portland most of the time, but that did not change the fact that for three generations the Hartes had been a part of Eclipse Bay. The threads of their lives were woven into the fabric of this community.

Summers in Eclipse Bay meant that on the weekends the town swarmed with tourists who came to walk the breezy beach and browse the handful of shops and galleries. Summers meant the age-old ritual of teenagers cruising in their cars along Bayview Drive on Friday and Saturday nights.

Summers meant the summer people, outsiders who rented the weathered cottages along the bluffs for a few weeks or a month at a time. They shopped at Fulton's and bought gas at the Eclipse Bay Gas & Go. A few of them would even venture into the Total Eclipse to buy a beer or play some pool. Their offspring would flirt with some of the local kids on warm nights near the pier, maybe get invited to a few parties. But no matter how familiar they became, they would remain forever *summer people*. Outsiders. No one in town would ever consider them to be real members of the community with roots here. Eclipse Bay had its own private rules. Around here you knew who belonged and who did not.

The Hartes, like the Madisons, belonged.

But as much at home as he was here, Nick thought, he had long ago given up spending entire summers in Eclipse Bay. Probably because his wife, Amelia, had never really liked the town. After her death nearly four years ago, he had never gotten back into the habit of spending a lot of time in Eclipse Bay.

Until this summer. Things were different this year.

"Hey, Dad, I'm ready for you to look at my pictures now."

Nick turned to see his almost-six-going-on-thirty-year-old son standing in the doorway. With his lean build, dark hair, and serious dark-blue eyes, Carson was a miniature version of himself and all the other males in the Harte family. But Nick was well aware that it wasn't just his physical appearance that marked him a true member of the clan. It was his precocious, frighteningly organized, agenda-driven nature. Carson's ability to focus on an objective with the unwavering precision and intensity of a battlefield commander told you he was a Harte to his toes.

At the moment he had two clearly defined goals. The first was to get a dog. The second was to exhibit a picture in the upcoming Children's Art Show scheduled to take place during the annual Eclipse Bay Summer Celebration festivities.

"I'm no art critic," Nick warned.

"All you gotta do is tell me which one you think Miss Brightwell would like best."

"Got news for you, kid. I'm rapidly coming to the conclusion that I'm the last person on earth who knows what Miss Brightwell likes."

Carson's small face tightened with sudden alarm. "Was that her on the phone just now?"

"Uh-huh."

"She turned you down again?"

"Afraid so."

"Geez, Dad, you gotta stop calling her up all the time and bothering her." Carson thrust out his hands, exasperated. "You're gonna ruin everything for me if you make her mad. She might not pick any of my pictures."

"I don't call her *all* the time." Damn. Now he was on the defensive with his own son. "I've only called her half a dozen times since Lillian's show."

He had been so sure that things had clicked between

himself and Octavia that evening. The proprietor of Bright
Visions, an art gallery business with two stores, one in
Portland and one here in Eclipse Bay, Octavia had staged
a gala reception to display his sister's work. The entire
town had been invited and most of the locals had turned
out for the show. The crowd had included everyone, from
Virgil Nash, owner of Virgil's Adult Books & Video Arcade, to the professors and instructors of nearby Chamberlain College. Several members of the staff at the Eclipse
Bay Policy Studies Institute had also deigned to appear.

They had all crowded into Bright Visions to drink good
champagne, nibble on expensive hors d'oeuvres, and pretend to be art connoisseurs for a night. Nick had walked
into the crowded room, taken one look at Octavia, and immediately forgotten that he was there to view Lillian's
paintings.

The image he carried in his head of Octavia from that
night was still crystal clear. She had worn a pale, fluttery
dress that fell to her ankles and a pair of dainty, strappy
little heels that had emphasized her elegantly arched feet.
Her dark red hair had been brushed back behind her ears in
a style that had framed her interesting, delicately molded
features and mysterious sea-green eyes.

His first impression was that, although she was in this
world, she was not completely anchored to it. There had
been an ethereal, almost fey quality about her; perhaps she
was a fairy queen visiting from some other, magical di-
mension where the rules were a little different.

He had stayed as close to her as possible that evening,
aware of a visceral need to lure her to him and secure her
by whatever means required. He did not want to allow her
to float back to wherever it was she had come from.

The unfamiliar sense of possessiveness had made him

want to bare his teeth and show some fang whenever another man had hovered too long in her vicinity. It was a completely over-the-top reaction, coming, as it did, after nearly four years of practicing what his sisters annoyingly described as commitment-free, serial monogamy. Okay, so he'd had a few discreet affairs. If anything that should have made him all the more immune.

The truth was, he had been stunned and bemused by his own reaction to Octavia. The only saving grace was that he had gotten the distinct impression that she was just as attracted to him as he was to her. Something in her big sea-colored eyes had registered her interest in him.

It had come as a shock at the end of the evening when she had politely turned down his invitation to dinner. He'd convinced himself that he'd heard regret in her voice, so he'd tried again a few days later when they were both back in Portland.

She had declined a second time with the explanation that she had to rush back to Eclipse Bay. It seemed the assistant she had left in charge of the gallery there, Noreen Perkins, had resigned without notice in order to run off with one of the artists whose work was exhibited in Bright Visions.

Octavia had returned to Portland on only one other occasion after that, and her stay had been extremely brief. He had asked her out for the third time, but she had told him that she was there to oversee a reception for one of the artists who showed in her gallery and had no time to socialize. The following morning she had flitted back to Eclipse Bay.

It had become obvious that she was not going to return to Portland any time soon. That had left him a limited number of options.

Two weeks ago he had made the decision to spend the summer in Eclipse Bay with Carson. But proximity was only making Octavia more inventive when it came to excuses for turning down dates.

The thing that should really concern him, he thought, was that he was working even harder to come up with reasons to call her one more time.

As far as he could tell, she did not have a complete aversion to men. She had been seen having dinner with Jeremy Seaton twice this past week.

Jeremy was the grandson of Edith Seaton, owner of an antiques shop located next door to Bright Visions Gallery. The Seatons had roots in the community that went back as far as those of the Hartes and the Madisons. Although Edith's husband, Phil, had died several years ago, she continued to take an active role in local affairs. Her son and daughter had moved away, but Jeremy had recently returned to take a position as an analyst at the Eclipse Bay Policy Studies Institute. The social and political think tank was one of Eclipse Bay's few claims to sophistication.

He knew Jeremy very well from the old days. They were the same age and they had been good friends at one time. But things had changed a couple of years ago. Women sometimes had that effect on a friendship.

He looked at Carson. "Miss Brightwell obviously doesn't think highly of me, but it's pretty clear that she likes you."

"I know she likes me," Carson said with exaggerated patience. "That's because I bring her coffee and a muffin every morning when we go into town to get the mail. But she might change her mind if you make her mad."

The sad fact was that Carson had made a lot more headway with Octavia than he had, Nick realized. His son adored the Fairy Queen of Eclipse Bay. For her part, she seemed to be very fond of Carson. The two of them had developed a relationship that somehow completely excluded him, Nick thought. It was frustrating.

"Don't worry," he said. "She's not the type to hold a grudge against you just because she doesn't want to go out with me."

He was pretty sure that was the truth. Octavia was a great mystery to him in many ways, but when it came to this aspect of her personality, he felt very sure of himself. She would never hold the sins of the father, whatever they might be, against the son.

Carson remained dubious. "Promise me you won't ask her out again until after she chooses one of my pictures."

"Okay, okay, I won't call her again until she makes her selection."

That was a safe promise. He figured it would be at least another three or four days before he could fortify himself to make a seventh phone call.

"Let's see your pictures," he said.

"They're in the bedroom." Carson whipped around and dashed off down the hall.

Nick followed him around the corner and into the downstairs room that his sister Lillian had turned into a temporary studio a few months earlier.

Three large squares of heavy drawing paper were arranged in a row on the hardwood floor. The pictures were all done in crayon, per the rules of the exhibition.

Nick went to stand looking down at the first picture. The scene showed a house with two stick figures standing very close together inside. The taller of the two figures had one arm extended protectively over the head of the smaller figure. A yellow sun shone brightly above the peaked roof.

There was a green flower with several petals in the right-hand corner.

"That's you and me," Carson said proudly. He indicated the stick figures. "You're the big one."

Nick nodded. "Nice colors." He moved on to the next drawing and pondered it for a moment. At first all he could make out was a vague oval shape done in gray crayon. There were several jagged lines around the outside of the oval. He was baffled until he noticed the two pointy projections on top. Dog ears.

"This is Winston, I take it?" he said.

"Yeah. I had a little trouble with his nose. Dog noses are hard."

"Good job on the ears."

"Thanks."

Nick studied the third picture, a scene of five brown, elongated shapes thrusting out of a blue crayon circle. "The rocks in Dead Hand Cove?"

"Uh-huh." Carson frowned. "Aunt Lillian said it would make a good picture, but I dunno. Kind of boring. I like the other two better. Which one do you think I should give to Miss Brightwell?"

"That's a tough question. I like them all."

"I could ask Aunt Lillian. She's a real artist."

"She and Gabe are stuck in Portland for a while because Gabe is tied up with Dad and Sullivan while they hammer out the plans for the merger. You'll have to make the choice without her advice."

Carson studied the two pictures with a troubled expression. "Huh."

"I've got an idea," Nick said smoothly. "Why don't you take all three pictures with you tomorrow when we go into town? You can show them to Octavia when you take her the coffee and muffin. She can choose the one she likes best."

"Okay." Carson brightened immediately, clearly pleased by that suggestion. "I'll bet she goes for Winston. She likes him."

Not yet six and the kid was already displaying an intuitive understanding of the client, Nick thought. Carson was a natural for the business world. *Unlike himself.*

He had hated the corporate environment. His decision to leave Harte Investments, the company his grandfather, Sullivan, had founded and that his father, Hamilton, had taken over had not gone down well. Although his father had understood and supported him, his grandfather had been hurt and furious at the time. He had seen Nick's refusal to follow in his footsteps as a betrayal of everything he had worked so hard to achieve.

He and Sullivan had managed a rapprochement eventually, thanks to the intervention of everyone else in the family. They were back on speaking terms at any rate. But deep down, Nick was not certain that Sullivan would ever entirely forgive him.

He did not really blame his grandfather. Sullivan had poured his blood and sweat into building Harte Investments. He had envisioned the firm descending through generation after generation of Hartes. The company had been a personal triumph for him, a phoenix rising from the ashes after the destruction of Harte-Madison, the commercial real estate development business he had founded with his former partner, Mitchell Madison, here in Eclipse Bay.

The collapse of the company decades earlier had ignited a feud between Sullivan and Mitchell that had thrived until recently. The bad blood between the Hartes and the Madisons was legendary in these parts. It had provided fodder for the gossips of Eclipse Bay for three generations.

But the first crack in the wall that had separated the two very different families had come last fall when Rafe Madison, the bad boy of the Madison family, had married Nick's sister Hannah. Several more bricks had crumbled last month when his other sister, Lillian, had wed Gabe Madison.

But the earth-shattering news that Harte Investments and Gabe's company, Madison Commercial, were in the process of merging had been the final blazing straw as far as the good people of Eclipse Bay were concerned. The newly formed corporation, after all, effectively re-created the company that had been ripped apart at the start of the feud. Life had seemingly come full circle.

"You may be right about the Winston picture," Nick said. "But the house is pretty good, too. The green flower is a great touch."

"Yeah, but there will be lots of houses and flowers in the art show. All the kids I know like to draw houses and flowers. Probably won't be any other dogs, though. Hardly anyone can draw a dog, especially not one as good as Winston."

"Winston is unique. I'll give you that."

Carson looked up at him with a considering expression. "I've been thinking, Dad."

"What?"

"Maybe you shouldn't come with me when I take my pictures to Miss Brightwell tomorrow."

Nick raised his brows. "You want me to wait in the car?"

Carson smiled, clearly relieved. "Good idea. That way she won't even see you."

"You're really afraid I'm going to mess up your shot at getting a picture into the gallery show, aren't you?"

"I just don't want to take any chances."

"Sorry, pal. I've got my own agenda here and I'm not about to waste a perfectly good opportunity to move ahead with it just because you're worried she won't hang your picture."

So he didn't have a lot of interest in the family business. He was still a Harte, Nick thought: He was just as goal-oriented and capable of focusing on an objective as anyone else in the clan.

"If you wait in the car," Carson said ingratiatingly, "I promise I'll tell Miss Brightwell that it would be okay to go out with you."

One of the Harte family mottos in action, Nick thought, not without a degree of sincere admiration. *When you find yourself backed into a corner, negotiate your way out of it.*

"Let me get this straight." He hooked his thumbs in the waistband of his jeans and looked down at his son. "If I agree to stay out of the way tomorrow, you'll put in a good word for me?"

"She likes me, Dad. I think she'd agree to go out with you if I asked her."

"Thanks, but no thanks. I may not have followed in the family footsteps like Dad and Granddad, but that doesn't mean I don't know how to get what I want."

And he definitely wanted Octavia Brightwell.

That, he thought, was the real reason he and Carson were in Eclipse Bay for an extended stay. He had come here to lay siege to the castle of the Fairy Queen.

"Well, okay, but promise you won't wreck things for me."

"I'll do my best."

Resigned, Carson turned back to the dog picture. "I think Winston needs more fur."

He selected a crayon and went to work.

She was an out-and-out coward.

Octavia sat on the stool behind the gallery sales counter, the heels of her sandals hooked on the top rung, and propped her chin on her hands. She regarded the phone as if it were a serpent.

One date.

How could it hurt to go out with Nick Harte just once?

But she knew the answer to that. If she accepted one invitation, she would probably accept another. And then there would be a third. Maybe a fourth. Sooner or later she would end up in bed with him and that would be the biggest mistake of her life. Some thrill rides were just too risky.

They called him Hardhearted Harte back in Portland. Nick had a reputation for confining his relationships to discreet, short-term affairs that ended whenever his partner of the moment started pushing for a commitment.

According to the gossip she had heard, Nick never went to bed with a woman without first having delivered what was known as *The Talk*.

The Talk was said to be a clear, concise position statement that made it plain that he was not interested in any long-term arrangements like marriage. Women who chose to sleep with Nick Harte went into the relationship with their eyes wide open.

They said that even if you lured him into your bed, he would be gone long before dawn. He never stayed the night, according to the stories that circulated about him.

Here in Eclipse Bay, where gossip about the Hartes and

the Madisons had been raised to a fine art, folks were certain that they knew the real reason for The Talk. The local mythology held that Nick, being a true Harte, was unable to love again because he was still mourning the loss of his beloved Amelia. He was under a curse, some said, doomed never to find another true love until the right woman shattered the spell that bound him. His reputation for never staying the night with any of his lovers only fanned the flames of that particular legend.

Of course, that did not stop shoppers in the narrow aisles at Fulton's Supermarket from holding forth on the subject of the importance of Nick marrying again in order to provide his son with a mother. They said the same thing at the post office and in the hardware store.

But Carson didn't need a mother, Octavia thought. Nick was doing a fine job of raising him, as far as she could tell. The boy was the most self-assured, well-adjusted, precocious little kid she had ever met in her life. And there was no shortage of feminine influence available to him. Carson enjoyed the warmth of a close-knit, extended family that included a doting grandmother, a great-grandmother, and two aunts, Lillian and Hannah.

She unhooked her sandals, rose from the stool, and went to stand at the front window of Bright Visions. The morning fog was thinning, but it had not yet burned off. Across the street she could just make out the pier and the nearby marina. The lights were on in the Incandescent Body bakery down the street, and she could see the erratic snap and pulse of the broken neon sign that marked the Total Eclipse Bar & Grill. The tavern's logo, *Where the Sun Don't Shine,* was just barely visible.

The rest of the world was lost in a sea of gray mist.

*Just like her life.*

A shiver went through her. Where had that thought come from? She wrapped her arms around herself. She would not go there, she vowed silently.

But the moody feeling was a warning, loud and clear. It was time to make some new plans; time to take control of her future. Her mission here in Eclipse Bay had been a failure.

Time to move on.

*Her mission.*

For months she had told herself that she had come here to right the wrongs of the past. In the beginning she had established a schedule that had allowed her to divide her time between this gallery and the main branch in Portland. But as the months went by she had found more and more reasons to extend her visits in Eclipse Bay.

Deep down she had actually been elated when her assistant here had run off with the artist. On impulse she had placed the Portland branch in the capable hands of a trusted manager, packed her suitcases, and moved her personal possessions into the little cottage on the bluff near Hidden Cove.

What had she been thinking? she wondered.

It was obvious that the Hartes and the Madisons did not need her help in healing the rift her great-aunt, Claudia Banner, had created so many years ago. The proud families were successfully putting the feud behind them without any assistance at all from her. There had been two weddings in the past few months that had united the clans, and now those old warriors, Sullivan Harte and Mitchell Madison, could be seen drinking coffee and eating donuts together at the bakery whenever Sullivan was in town.

No one in Eclipse Bay needed her. There was no reason for her to stay. It was time to go.

But that was easier said than done. She couldn't just close the door of the gallery and disappear in the middle of the night. Bright Visions was a small business, but it was thriving, and that meant it was worth a goodly sum. She would have to make arrangements to sell up and that might take a while. And then there was the matter of her obligations to the various artists whose work she exhibited and the commitment she had made to the Children's Art Show.

The art show had been her idea. She was the one who had come up with the concept and lobbied the members of the Eclipse Bay Summer Celebration committee to include it as one of the activities associated with this year's event. Enthusiasm for the project ran high. She knew that the children who planned to draw pictures for the event would be crushed if she cancelled it.

All in all, she concluded, what with getting Bright Visions ready to sell and fulfilling her business and civic commitments, she would probably not be able to escape Eclipse Bay until the end of the summer. But by fall she would be somewhere else. She had to find a place where she truly belonged.

# chapter 2

That afternoon she closed the gallery at five-thirty and drove over to Mitchell Madison's house. She got out of the car and waved at Bryce as she went past the open kitchen door. He looked up from the pot he was stirring on the stove and inclined his head in a solemn greeting.

She smiled to herself. Bryce was the strong, silent type. He had worked for Mitchell for years. No one knew much about his past before he had arrived in town, and Bryce had never felt any impulse to enlighten anyone on that subject.

She understood where he was coming from, she thought.

She wandered into the garden and looked around, savoring the little slice of paradise that was Mitchell's creation. She had spent enough time in Eclipse Bay to know that, while everyone in the vicinity was quick to point out his legendary character flaws and remind you of his several failed marriages, no one disputed Mitchell's brilliance as a gardener. Gardening was his passion, and no one came between a Madison and his passion.

She came to a halt on the other side of a bed of gloriously blooming rose bushes.

"I've made a decision, Mitch."

He looked up at her from the padded kneeling bench he was using to work around the plants. He had the face of an aging, beat-up old gunslinger, she thought fondly, one who had only hardened with the years; a guy who could still hold his own against the young toughs if called upon to do so.

"What kind of decision?" Mitchell demanded.

The sharpness of his tone was a surprise. Mitchell never spoke sharply to her.

"I'll be leaving town at the end of the summer," she said.

"You mean you'll be spending more time back in Portland." He nodded, evidently satisfied, and went back to his weeding. "I can see where you might need to give more attention to your gallery there come fall. It's a much bigger operation."

"No," she said gently, "I mean that I will be leaving Eclipse Bay for good at the end of the summer season. I plan to sell both branches of Bright Visions."

He stiffened, eyes narrowing against the fading sun. "You're gonna sell up? Well, shoot and damn. Why the hell do you want to go and do a thing like that?"

"It's time." She smiled to cover the wistful feeling. "Past time, really. In fact, I probably shouldn't have come here in the first place."

"Not a lot of money in the art business here in Eclipse Bay, huh?" He shrugged. "No surprise there, I reckon. Eclipse Bay isn't exactly the art capital of the universe."

"Actually, the gallery here is doing fairly well. We drew clients from Chamberlain College and the institute this past winter, and now with summer here, we're picking up a lot of tourist business. Bright Visions is starting to get a reputation as an important art stop here on the coast."

His brows bunched together. "You're saying your business here is doing all right?"

"Yes, I expect to sell at a profit."

"Then why the hell are you talking about pulling out?"

"As I said, I think it's time for me to go."

He squinted at her. "You don't sound right. You feeling okay today, Octavia?"

"Yes."

"Not coming down sick, are you?"

"No."

"Shoot and damn. What's going on here?" He holstered the trowel he had been wielding, gripped the handholds on the low gardener's bench, and hauled himself to his feet. He seized his cane and turned around to confront her, scowling ferociously. "What's all this talk about leaving?"

"There's something that I want to tell you, Mitch. I don't plan to let a lot of other folks know because I don't want to upset people and cause talk. Lord knows, there's been enough gossip about the Hartes and the Madisons in this town. But you and I are friends. And I want my friends to know who I am."

"I know who you are." He thumped the cane once on the gravel walk. "You're Octavia Brightwell."

"Yes, but there's more to the story." She looked at him very steadily and braced herself to deliver the shocker. "Claudia Banner was my great-aunt."

To her astonishment he merely shrugged. "You think we didn't figure that out a while back?"

She stilled. *"We?"*

"Sullivan and me. He and I have slowed down some over the years, but we haven't come to a complete stop. Not yet, at any rate."

She didn't know what to say. "You *know*?"

"Sullivan spotted the likeness the night you hosted that show for Lillian's paintings down at your little gallery. Soon as he pointed it out, I finally realized why there had always been something sort of familiar about you." He smiled faintly. "You look a lot like Claudia did when she was your age. Same red hair. Something about your profile, too, I think. The way you hold yourself."

"But how did you—"

"Sullivan made some phone calls. Did some checking. Wasn't hard to find the connection."

"I see." She was feeling a little stunned, she realized. Maybe a little deflated, too. So much for her big bombshell.

"Not like you tried to hide it," Mitchell said.

"No, but I certainly didn't want to make a big deal about it here in Eclipse Bay, given what happened in the past and all."

Mitchell reached down and plucked a lush orange-gold bloom. "Funny thing about the past. The older you get, the less it matters."

She fell silent for a long moment, shifting gears as she adjusted to the turn of events. "If Sullivan made some calls, you probably know about Aunt Claudia." She took a deep breath. "That she's gone, I mean."

"Yeah." Mitchell looked up from the rose. His gaze was steady and a little sad. "Heard she passed on a year and a half ago. Heart problems, Sullivan said."

She felt the familiar tightening inside. Eighteen months

but she still had to fight back the tears. "She never managed to give up the cigarettes. In the end, the doctor said it was amazing she made it as long as she did."

"I remember Claudia and her cigarettes. She was always reaching for the next one. Had herself a fancy little gold lighter. I can still see her taking it out of her purse to light another smoke."

"Mitchell, let me get something straight here. Are you telling me that you and Sullivan don't care that I'm related to Claudia Banner?"

"Of course we care. But it's not exactly what you'd call a problem for us."

"Oh." She was not sure how to respond to that.

"Can't say we weren't a bit curious at first, though," he added dryly.

"I can imagine. Why didn't you say something? Ask questions? Demand an explanation? I've stopped by here almost every morning or afternoon when I'm in town to say hello. I must have talked to you dozens of times since Lillian's show. But you never said a word. I've seen Sullivan on several occasions, too. He never gave any indication that he knew who I was."

"It was your personal business. Sullivan and I talked about it some. Figured we'd let you tell us in your own time."

"I see." She thought about that for a while. "Did you, uh, mention your little insight to anyone else?"

"Nope. Didn't figure it was anyone else's affair."

"Believe me, I understand." She wrinkled her nose. "If word got out that Claudia Banner's great-niece was in town and that she had become friends with the Madisons and the Hartes, there would be no end to the wild rumors and speculation. That's exactly why I kept a low profile."

"Yeah?"

"It wouldn't have been fair to you Madisons or to the Hartes. You've all suffered enough over the years because of what happened when you got involved with Aunt Claudia."

Mitchell snorted. "Madisons and Hartes are used to folks around here talking about us. Claudia may have been the spark that started the feud, but you can't blame her for the fact that Sullivan and I kept it going all those years. Hell, Madisons and Hartes have been inspiring conversation here in Eclipse Bay all by ourselves for decades. Got a real talent for it. Sometimes I think the good Lord put us on this earth just to keep this town entertained."

In other words, her concern for discretion and the privacy of the Madison and Harte families had been a complete waste of time and energy on her part. She sighed inwardly. Not only was she not needed here, Mitchell and Sullivan hadn't even cared enough about her presence in town to ask for explanations.

The day was getting more depressing by the minute.

"Well, that's that, then, isn't it?" She straightened her shoulders, preparing to leave. "I just wanted you to know, Mitch." She took a step back. "Guess I'll be going." She retreated another step. "Your roses look incredible, by the way."

Mitchell rapped his cane on the gravel again. "Hang on a minute. I'm the first to admit that you've got a right to keep your private business private, but now that you've mentioned Claudia and what happened in the past, I think maybe I've got a right to know why you've suddenly decided to pull up stakes."

"It's hard to explain."

His hawklike eyes gleamed with shrewd comprehension. "It's Nick Harte, isn't it?"

She was dumbfounded. "I, uh—"

"He's been pestering you, hasn't he? I knew it. I saw the way he moved in on you the night of Lillian's show. When he turned up in town a couple of weeks ago and settled into the Harte cottage for the summer, I got right on the phone to Sullivan."

"You *what*?"

"I warned him that he'd better keep Nick reined in good and tight. Told him I wouldn't stand by and let his grandson play any of his love 'em and leave 'em games with you. I don't care if Nick is still broken up about losing his wife. That's no excuse to fool around with you. Time he got over what happened and straightened himself out. Time he started acting like a real Harte again."

"A, uh, real Harte?" she repeated carefully.

"Damn right. Hartes don't mess around and have affairs. Hartes get married."

"I've heard that theory," she said dryly. "But there are exceptions to every rule. In any event, set your mind at rest, Mitch. This has got nothing to do with Nick Harte."

Even as the words left her lips, she realized she was lying through her teeth. Leaving Eclipse Bay had everything to do with Nick Harte. She just wasn't sure how to explain the connection, not even to herself, let alone to Mitchell.

"Bullshit." Mitchell glowered. "Pardon my language. But you've got to admit that the timing is more than a tad suspicious."

"Look, Mitch, we're getting a little off-topic here. I stopped by to tell you about my link to Claudia Banner.

But since you already know about it, maybe I should tell you why I came here to Eclipse Bay in the first place."

There was a short silence. She could hear the distant clatter of pots in the kitchen. The light breeze off the bay shifted tree branches in the corner of the garden. Birds chattered overhead.

"Sullivan and me, we decided maybe you were just curious," Mitchell said after a while.

"It was more than mere curiosity," she said quietly. "I should probably start at the beginning."

"If that's what you want to do."

She hesitated, looking for the right place to begin. "I was with my aunt a lot during the last couple of years of her life. She needed someone to take care of her and there wasn't anyone else. Aunt Claudia was not the most popular member of the family."

"Hell, I didn't even realize she had a family. She never mentioned the subject."

"She was the renegade. The black sheep. The one who was always a source of acute embarrassment. But I had always liked her a lot. And she liked me. Maybe it was because I looked so much like her. Or maybe she just felt sorry for me."

"Why would she feel sorry for you?"

"I think she saw me as a loner, just as she was. My parents divorced when I was small. They both remarried and started new families. I spent most of my youth shuttling back and forth between them but I never felt at home in either house. Aunt Claudia sensed that, I think."

"Go on."

"Claudia was very special to me. I know she had her faults, and her business ethics left a lot to be desired. But I loved her and she cared about me in her own way. She worried that I was too inclined to play it safe. She said I spent too much time trying to smooth things over and calm the waters. She kept urging me to take a few chances."

"*She* sure knew how to take 'em." Mitchell chuckled reminiscently. "Maybe that was one of the reasons I couldn't take my eyes off her back in the old days."

"She never forgot you, Mitch. When she became seriously ill, I went to stay with her until the end. It took over a year for her to die. We had a lot of time to talk."

"And one of the things you two talked about was Eclipse Bay? Is that what you're saying?"

"Yes. She became increasingly obsessed with what had happened here. Said she didn't have a lot of regrets, but the destruction of Harte-Madison was one of them. She talked about how she wished that she could make amends."

"She should have known she couldn't go back and fix something that happened so long ago," Mitchell said.

"I know. But the subject became more and more important to her. Maybe because toward the end she became a serious student of New Age metaphysics. She talked a lot about karma and auras and such. At any rate, she asked me to come here after she was gone to find out how things stood. She wanted me to see if there was anything I could do to repair some of the damage she had done."

"Well, shoot and damn." Mitchell whistled softly. "So that's why you showed up here in town late last summer?"

"Yes. But shortly after I arrived, Rafe and Hannah returned and fell in love and made plans for Dreamscape. And then Gabe and Lillian started getting serious about each other. I turned around one day and you and Sullivan were having coffee together at the bakery." She smiled slightly. "It has become very clear that the feud is a relic of the past. The Hartes and the Madisons don't need my help mending the old rift."

"Huh," Mitchell said again. Thoughtful now.

She cleared her throat. "So, I feel that it's time for me to go."

"Just like that? You plan to slip out of town and disappear into the sunset?"

"It isn't that simple. As I said, I have to sell the gallery. And then there's the Children's Art Show."

"Loose ends."

"Yes."

"I don't like it," Mitchell said flatly.

"What don't you like?"

"Something doesn't sit right here." He whacked his cane absently against the trunk of a tree and eyed her with growing suspicion. "You sure Nick Harte hasn't been making a pest of himself?"

"No." Another quick dance step back. This was getting sticky. "Really."

"Has he been calling you up since he hit town a couple of weeks ago? Asked you out?"

"Well, yes."

"Hah. I knew it."

"I hardly think that constitutes pestering. Besides, I declined his invitations."

"Obviously."

"Obviously?"

Mitchell grunted. "If you'd had a date with Nick Harte, the news would have been all over town in an hour. Question is, why'd you turn him down?"

She began to feel a little desperate. The last thing she wanted to do was instigate more trouble between the Hartes and the Madisons.

"I've been busy," she said quickly.

"Bullshit. You're avoiding Nick Harte, aren't you?"

"Not exactly."

"Exactly." Mitchell looked fiercely pleased. "It's because you've got him figured out, isn't that right? You know Harte's got a reputation with the ladies. And you're too smart to fall for his tricks."

"Look, Mitch, I've got to be on my way. I would love to stay and chat, but I have some things to do this evening. Business related." She crossed her fingers mentally. She had gotten very good at inventing excuses lately. Aunt Claudia would have approved.

"Hold on here. I'll be damned if I'll let Nick Harte run you out of town." Mitchell aimed the cane at her. "You stay right where you are down there at the gallery. If he gives you any more trouble, let me know and I'll handle it."

"Sure. Right. Thanks, Mitch."

She whirled and fled toward the car.

Damn it, Mitch was right, she thought halfway back to her cottage on the bluffs. In a way she was allowing Nick Harte to run her out of town. It was a humiliating admission to confront but it was the truth.

She was acting like a coward. Madisons didn't run from anything. Neither did Hartes. Aunt Claudia had never run from a risk in her entire life.

Maybe it was time she stopped running, Octavia thought. At least for the summer.

# chapter 3

The ancient mauve Cadillac glided into the small parking lot with the majesty of a massive cruise ship coming into port. Nick had just switched off the engine of his own BMW. He admired the mile-long fins that graced the rear of the vehicle. Chrome gleamed on every curve and angle.

"They don't make 'em like that anymore," he said to Carson.

From his position strapped into the backseat, Carson craned to see out the window. "That's Mrs. Seaton's car."

"So it is."

Edith Seaton's dome of severely permed gray curls was just barely visible. Nick wondered if she could actually see over the top of the wheel or if she had to steer looking through it. Then again, he reminded himself, she had lived in Eclipse Bay all her life. She probably knew her way around blindfolded.

He climbed out of the silver BMW, popped Carson out

of the rear seat, and then went around the long, long fins of the Cadillac to open the door for Edith Seaton.

"Good morning, Nick, dear. My, you and Carson are here bright and early this morning." Edith emerged from the vastness of the big car and dimpled up at him. "Enjoying your stay out at your folks' place?"

"Yes, thanks," Nick said. "How's the antiques business?"

"As slow as ever." Edith reached back into the front seat to collect a white straw purse. "Which is probably a good thing, because I've been so busy lately with my Summer Celebration committee work." She reappeared, purse in hand. "One argument after another, you know. Right now the big issue is whether or not to put up a banner at the intersection where the Total Eclipse is located."

"I take it some folks don't approve?"

"I should say not. There's a strong feeling in some quarters that placing a banner so close to the bar would make it appear that the Total Eclipse is somehow an official participant in the event." Edith made a *tut-tut* sound. "And I absolutely agree. We really don't want the summer people and tourists thinking that dreadful place is considered a respectable business here in town."

Nick smiled. "Come on, now, Edith. The Eclipse has been operating here since my grandfather's day. Hard to pretend it doesn't exist. Fred pays his taxes, like everyone else."

"The Summer Celebration was never intended to promote that sort of tacky establishment and there will be no banner placed near it on my watch." She turned to Carson. "What's that you've got there, dear?"

"I brought my pictures for Miss Brightwell to see," Carson said proudly. He brandished the three rolled-up drawings he held. "She's going to choose one for the art show."

"Ah, yes, the Children's Art Show event. The Summer

Celebration committee is delighted to be including such a wholesome, family-oriented activity as part of the festival this year. The project is a wonderful contribution. We're all so pleased that Octavia is willing to sponsor it."

"I did a picture of Winston," Carson informed her.

"That's lovely, dear." She winked at Nick as they walked toward the row of shops opposite the pier. "Do we have another budding artist in the Harte family?"

"You never know," Nick said.

"Art makes a very nice hobby," Edith said, laying a decided emphasis on the word *hobby*. "Everyone should have a recreational activity of some sort. Jeremy enjoys painting, you know."

"He always did," Nick said, keeping his voice neutral.

"That's true. He doesn't have much time for it now, of course, what with his new position up at the institute." Pride glowed in Edith's face. "I'm surprised the two of you haven't had a chance to get together yet. You and Jeremy were such good friends in the old days."

Nick smiled very casually. "Like you said, he's probably very busy settling into his new job." And dating Octavia.

"I must say, your writing career appears to be going very well. I saw your latest book in the rack near the checkout counter at Fulton's the other day."

Nick wondered if that was a gentle hint. "I'd be happy to sign a copy for you, Mrs. Seaton."

"Thank you, but that won't be necessary," she said airily. "I don't read that sort of thing."

So much for knowing a hint when he heard one. "Right."

"Who would have thought you'd be so successful with your book writing?" Edith continued, shaking her head a few times.

"Not a lot of folks," he admitted. Amelia, for instance.

"And walking away from Harte Investments after your grandfather and your father had poured their hearts and souls into the business." Edith clicked her tongue again. "Really, it was quite a shock to everyone. When I think of what Sullivan went through after that dreadful woman destroyed Harte-Madison all those years ago. I mean, one would have thought that you would have felt some sense of responsibility to the family firm."

Nick realized he was clenching his back teeth a little too tightly together and forced himself to relax his jaw. It was Sullivan who had poured heart and soul into Harte. His father, Hamilton, on the other hand, had taken over the responsibility only because he had felt trapped by a sense of duty and filial obligation. Hamilton had known firsthand how much blood and sweat his father had expended to create Harte Investments. Early on in life he had accepted the fact that he could not reject the company without appearing to reject Sullivan and everything he had accomplished.

But Hamilton Harte had stood firm when it came to passing along the suffocating weight of obligation to his own offspring. He had refused to apply the kind of pressure that had been applied to him to coerce any of his three children into following in their father's and grandfather's footsteps. *Life is too short to spend it doing something you hate,* he'd told his wife, Elaine. *Let them find their own paths.*

The best thing about the merger of Harte Investments with Madison Commercial, Nick thought, was that it had finally freed his father and mother to pursue their own interests. Hamilton and Elaine planned to endow and oversee a charitable foundation. They could not wait to get rid of the responsibility of H.I. And Gabe Madison, fortunately for all concerned, was more than willing to take the helm. Running a business empire came naturally to him.

Nick searched for a way to change the subject. He picked the one he was least eager to pursue, but which he knew was guaranteed to distract Edith.

"How's Jeremy doing up at the institute?"

Edith switched gears instantly, delighted to turn to the topic of her grandson. "Very well, indeed. He says he likes being back in Eclipse Bay again after all those years away in Portland. The divorce was very hard on him, you know."

"I know."

"But he's dating again, I'm happy to say." She lowered her tone to a confidential level and winked broadly. "He's been seeing Octavia Brightwell."

"I heard." He had known this would not be his favorite topic, he reminded himself.

"Such a nice young woman. I think they make a lovely couple, don't you?"

He couldn't imagine a worse couple, Nick thought. Jeremy and Octavia were totally unsuited to each other. Any idiot could see that. But he didn't think Edith Seaton would appreciate being called an idiot, so he dug deep in search of logic and reason. He managed to pull up a vague memory of an article he'd come across in the course of researching his last book, *Fault Lines*. The plot had set his hero, John True, on the trail of a killer who had murdered his ex-wife.

"They say it takes a couple of years to recover from a divorce." He tried to put the ring of authority into his voice. "The trauma, you see. Takes a while to get past it, and experts advise people not to make serious relationship commitments during that time."

"Nonsense." Edith snorted. "What do the so-called experts know when it comes to love and marriage? Besides, it's been a year and a half now, and I'm sure Jeremy doesn't need another six months to recover. He just needs the right woman to help him forget. I think Octavia is doing him a world of good. She's pulling him out of his shell. He's been a little down since the divorce, you know. I was worried about him."

Under any other circumstances, Nick thought, he would have avoided the topic of Jeremy's divorce the same way he would have gone out of his way to sidestep a cobra in his path. But the fact that Edith thought that Octavia looked like a good candidate to take the place of Jeremy's ex was an irritating goad that he could not ignore.

"I'm surprised to hear you say that," he began coolly. "Personally I wouldn't have thought they'd have much—"

He was interrupted by the blare of a horn. He glanced toward the street and saw a familiar battered pickup truck rumbling past. There was no mistaking the driver. Arizona Snow was garbed in her customary camouflage-patterned fatigues. A military-style beret slanted across her gray hair in a jaunty fashion.

He raised a hand in greeting. Carson waved madly. Arizona waved back, but she did not pause. A woman on a mission.

That was the great thing about being a professional conspiracy theorist, he thought. You always had a mission.

The pickup continued down the block and pulled into the parking lot in front of the Incandescent Body bakery.

Edith sighed. "Expect you heard the news about old Tom Thurgarton's will?"

"Rafe said something about Thurgarton having left all his worldly possessions to Virgil Nash, Arizona, and the New Age crowd running the bakery."

"Yes." Edith shook her head. "Of all the ridiculous notions. Just like Thurgarton to do something so bizarre. He was such an odd man."

Nick nodded. "Yeah, he was always a little weird, wasn't he? A real recluse. He lived here in town all the time I was growing up but I doubt if I saw him more than half a dozen times a year."

"They say that Thurgarton's phobia about leaving his house got worse as time went on. Everyone was so accustomed to not seeing him that no one even knew he was dead until Jake down at the post office finally noticed that he hadn't picked up his mail in over two months. When Sean Valentine went out to see what was going on, he found Thurgarton's body in the kitchen. Heart attack, they say."

"Wonder if he left anything valuable to Virgil and A.Z. and the Heralds," Nick mused.

"I doubt it." Edith sniffed as they came to a halt in front of the door of Seaton's Antiques. "The way Chief Valentine tells it, that old cabin was crammed with over forty years' worth of junk. A real firetrap, he said. Old newspapers and magazines stacked to the ceiling. Boxes full of unopened mail. Cartons of things he'd ordered from catalogs that had never been unpacked."

"Going to be interesting to see what kind of conspiracy theory A.Z. will weave out of this," Nick said with a smile. "She's nothing if not inventive."

"I'm afraid A.Z. is one brick shy of a load, and hanging out with the crowd from the bakery isn't improving the situation." Edith turned the key in the lock and stepped into her shop. "Goodbye, you two. Good luck with your pictures, Carson."

"Bye, Mrs. Seaton." Carson was struggling to be polite,

but he was already edging off toward the neighboring shop door.

"See you later," Nick said.

He and Carson continued on to the front door of Bright Visions. Instead of rushing inside, Carson paused.

"Maybe you could stay out here on the sidewalk while I show my pictures to Miss Brightwell," he suggested hopefully.

"Not a chance."

Carson heaved a sigh, resigned. "Okay, but promise me again that you won't say anything to make her mad."

"I already said that I'd do my best not to annoy her." Nick glanced through the window into the gallery show-room. The *Open* sign showed through the glass, but he could not see Octavia. She was probably in her cluttered back room, he decided.

He wrapped his hand around the knob and twisted. The now-familiar sense of anticipation sleeted through him.

The door swung inward, revealing a universe of intense color and light. The artwork that hung on the walls ran the gamut from landscapes to the abstract, but the pictures were grouped in some inexplicably magical fashion that somehow managed to make the whole greater than the sum of its parts. A sense of connection and coherence pervaded the scene. The viewer was drawn from one to another in a subtle progression that took him deeper into the little cosmos.

There was an art to displaying paintings to their best advantage, Nick thought. Octavia knew what she was doing. No wonder she prospered. It was hard *not* to buy a picture when you were in this gallery.

Carson hurried inside, clutching his drawings in both hands.

"Miss Brightwell?" he called. "Where are you? I've got my pictures."

Octavia came to stand in the open doorway behind the counter. The sweeping hemline of a long, full skirt in the palest possible shade of ice blue swirled around her shapely calves. She wore a matching silk blouse. A tiny blue belt studded with small chunks of clear crystal encircled her trim waist. Her fiery hair was held back off her face by a pale aqua scarf that had been folded to form a narrow headband.

People in the art world were supposed to wear black, Nick thought. Until he'd met Octavia, he had always assumed it was a rule.

As always, he felt his insides clench at the sight of her. He ought to be getting used to this sensation, he thought. But the appearance of the Fairy Queen never failed to steal his breath for a few seconds.

When she met his gaze across the showroom, Nick could almost see the familiar, concealing veil slip into place. But when she looked at Carson, she was all smiles.

"Good morning," she said, speaking more to the boy than the man.

"Hi, Miss Brightwell." Carson blossomed in the warmth of her smile. "I brought my pictures to show you."

"You may have noticed that we're here a little early," Nick said dryly. "And we came without coffee and muffins. Carson was in a hurry."

"We'll get you some coffee and a muffin right after you see my pictures," Carson assured her, looking a little worried because of the oversight.

"I can't wait to see your pictures," Octavia said warmly.

"I brought three." Carson tugged the rubber band off the roll of drawings. "Dad said I should let you pick. But I'm pretty sure you'll like the picture of Winston best. I added some extra fur."

"Let's spread them out and take a look."

Octavia led the way to a long white bench at the far side of the room. She and Carson unrolled the drawings and arranged them side by side.

Octavia studied each picture in turn with rapt attention, her expression absorbed and serious—for all the world, Nick thought, as if she were considering the pictures for a real, high-profile, career-making show such as she had given Lillian a while back in Portland.

"The house is very good," she said after a moment.

"That's me and Dad inside," Carson said. "Dad's the big one."

Octavia gave Nick a fleeting glance. He could have sworn she turned a rosy shade of pink before hastily returning her attention to the picture.

She cleared her throat. "Yes, I can see that."

"This is Dead Hand Cove," Carson said, pointing to the next picture. "Aunt Lillian said I should include it, but I think landscapes are boring. Just rocks and water. Take a look at Winston."

Obediently Octavia moved to examine the furry gray blob with the pointy ears.

"You've certainly captured the essence of his personality very well," she said.

Carson was pleased. "I told Dad you'd like this one best. I brought my crayon with me. I can add some more fur if you want."

"No, I think he has precisely the right amount of fur," Octavia said decisively. "I'll hang this one in the show."

Carson bounced a little with excitement. "Will you frame it?"

"Of course. I'm going to frame all of the pictures in the show." She looked at him. "You forgot to sign it."

"I'll do it now." Carson whipped out his crayon and went to work inscribing his first name in large block letters in the right-hand corner of the picture. "I almost forgot," he added, not looking up from the task, "I promised Dad that if you liked my picture, I'd tell you that it was okay to go out with him."

A stunned hush enveloped the gallery. Nick looked at Octavia. Her veiled expression never flickered, but he saw something that might have been speculation in her eyes. Or was that just his imagination?

Oblivious to the electricity he had just generated, Carson concentrated intently on printing the last letters of his name.

"Sorry about that," Nick muttered.

"No problem," Octavia murmured.

There was another short, extremely uncomfortable silence.

"So?" Octavia said.

He frowned. "So, what?"

"So, are you going to ask me out again?"

"Uh—" He hadn't been caught this far off guard since high school. He felt like an idiot. He could only hope that he was not turning red. Something had changed in the situation, but he was at a loss to know what had happened. Only one way to find out, he thought. "Dinner tonight?"

She hesitated; honest regret showed on her face. He'd seen that look before.

"You're busy, right?" he said without inflection. A cold feeling coalesced in his gut. He couldn't believe she'd set him up like that.

"Well, I did promise Virgil Nash that I'd drive out to the Thurgarton house after I close the gallery this afternoon.

He and Arizona Snow want my opinion on some paintings that they discovered stashed in one of Thurgarton's closets. The thing is, I don't know how long it will take me."

He relaxed. Maybe she hadn't set him up, after all.

"Forever," he said.

"I beg your pardon?"

"It'll take you forever to even find the old Thurgarton place unless Virgil gave you really, really good directions. Thurgarton liked his privacy. There's no sign on the road leading to the turnoff, and the drive is hidden in the trees."

"Oh." Her fine, red-brown brows wrinkled delicately in a small frown. "Virgil gave me a little map."

"Forget it," he said easily. "I'll pick you up after you close the gallery this afternoon and drive you out there. Later we can go to dinner."

"I suppose that might work," she said.

She sounded so damn casual, he thought. As if the decision she had just made weren't staggering in its implications. As if it weren't going to alter destinies and change the fate of nations.

Okay, he could deal with the world shifting in its orbit. What really worried him was the question of why it had done so. After six turn-downs in a row, the Fairy Queen of Eclipse Bay had agreed to go out with him.

Lucky number seven.

Be careful what you wish for.

# chapter 4

The little girl with the glossy brown hair and the big, dark eyes was back.

Octavia was discussing the merits of a charming seascape with a middle-aged tourist couple when she caught sight of the youngster on the sidewalk outside. This was the second time this week that the girl had appeared. On the first occasion she had been accompanied by her mother, a pretty but quietly determined-looking woman who wore the unmistakable cloak of single parenthood. The pair had wandered into the gallery and looked at pictures for a long time. The child had been as absorbed in the works of art as her mother—an unusual event. Most kids found the paintings boring in the extreme.

The woman had greeted Octavia politely and made it plain that she was not there to buy, just to look around. She had clearly been braced for a cool reception, but Octavia had assured her that she was welcome to browse.

The woman and her daughter had moved from picture

to picture, talking seriously in low tones about some of them, showing little interest in others. They had been standing in front of a brilliant abstract when the woman had glanced at her watch, frowned in alarm, and hurried out of the gallery with the little girl.

The woman had not returned, but her daughter was here again, standing on the other side of the glass staring at the colorful poster in the window that announced the Children's Art Show.

*I'm not going to lose her this time,* Octavia thought.

"Excuse me," she said to the couple contemplating the purchase of the seascape. "I'll be right back."

She hurried behind the sales counter, reached down, and selected a large box of crayons from a carton that was nearly empty. She took a pad of drawing paper from the dwindling pile.

Crayons and pad in hand, she straightened quickly and looked out the window. The little girl was still there.

Octavia crossed the gallery, opened the front door, and stepped out onto the sidewalk. The child turned, looking a bit startled.

"Hello," Octavia said. "Would you like to enter a picture in the art show?"

The child stared at her. She did not speak.

"Every entrant gets a box of crayons and a pad of drawing paper," Octavia explained. "The rule is that the picture has to be on a piece of paper the size of one of these." She flipped through the blank sheets of drawing paper. "When it's ready, bring it back here."

The girl's anxious gaze shifted from Octavia's face to the pad of drawing paper and the crayons. She put her hands behind her back, evidently afraid that she might lose control and reach out to grab the art supplies.

She shook her head very fiercely.

"Anne?"

The woman who had accompanied the girl into the gallery a few days ago rushed out of Seaton's Antiques. Her head swiveled rapidly as she searched the sidewalk in both directions with the slightly frantic look a mother gets when she turns around and realizes her offspring has disappeared.

"Anne, where are you?"

"I'm here, Mom," Anne whispered.

Her mother swung around. Relief flashed across her face. The expression was followed by stern exasperation.

"You must not disappear like that." She walked swiftly toward her daughter. "How many times have I told you not to run off without telling me where you're going? This may not be Seattle, but the same rules apply."

"I was just looking in the window," Anne said in a tiny, barely audible voice. She kept her small hands secured very tightly behind her back. "I didn't touch anything, honest."

Octavia studied the woman coming toward her. Anne's mother appeared to be in her late twenties but if you had only seen her eyes, you would have added twenty years to her age.

"Hello," Octavia said in her best professional tone. "I'm Octavia Brightwell. You were in my gallery the other day."

"I'm Gail Gillingham." Gail smiled hesitantly. "I'm sorry if Anne was bothering you."

"Not in the least," Octavia said cheerfully. "I noticed that she was looking at the poster featuring the Children's Art Show. I thought she might like to participate. I have room for more pictures."

Gail looked down at Anne. "Thank you, but I'm afraid Anne is very shy."

"Who cares?" Octavia looked at Anne. "Lots of artists are shy. I'll tell you what, why don't you take these crayons and the paper home with you? You can draw your picture in private where no one else can watch you at work. When it's ready, just ask your mother to drop it off here at the gallery."

Anne looked at the crayons and the paper as though they were made of some magical, insubstantial substance that might disintegrate if she were to touch them.

Octavia did not say anything more. She just smiled encouragingly and held out the crayons and the paper.

For a long moment, Anne did not move. Then, very slowly she untwisted her arms from behind her back, reached out, and took the supplies from Octavia. Clutching them tightly to her chest, she stepped back and looked at her mother.

Surprise and a fleeting delight lit Gail's face. An instant later her pleasure was marred by what seemed to be uncertainty. She hesitated and then seemed to brace herself.

"How much do I owe you for the crayons and the paper?" she asked.

"The Children's Art Show has been underwritten by the Bright Visions gallery, which is sponsoring it," Octavia said. "All the entrants receive the same basic supplies."

"Oh, I see." Gail relaxed visibly. "Thank Miss Brightwell for the crayons and paper, Anne."

"Thank you," Anne repeated in the barest of whispers.

"You're welcome," Octavia said. "I'll look forward to seeing your picture."

Anne tightened her grip on the art supplies and said

nothing. She still looked as if she expected the crayons and paper to vaporize in her arms.

At that moment, a familiar silver BMW pulled into the small parking lot at the end of the row of shops. Octavia's stomach fluttered. She glanced at her watch and saw that it was almost five-thirty. Nick was right on time.

Gail gave Octavia a grateful smile. "I don't know if Anne will actually do a picture for your art show, but she loves to draw and paint. She will definitely use the supplies."

"Excellent," Octavia said. She looked at Anne. "But I really hope you'll make a special drawing for the show. If you do, you can choose the color of the frame."

"You're gonna put it in a frame?" she asked in astonishment.

"Of course."

"So it will look like a real picture?" Anne pointed toward the framed paintings hanging inside the gallery. "Like one of those?"

"Yes," Octavia said. "It will look like a real picture because it will be a real picture. Just like one of those inside my gallery."

Anne was clearly dazzled by the prospect.

"Come along, Anne," Gail said. "We have to stop at the store and then we have to go home to help Grandma fix dinner."

"Okay."

Anne and Gail moved off toward the small parking lot. Nick was out of his car now, walking toward the gallery. He wore a long-sleeved, crew neck tee shirt and a pair of jeans. The snug fit of the shirt emphasized the contours of his strong shoulders and flat belly.

He paused to greet Gail and Anne with a friendly nod

and a few words. When the short conversation was finished, Gail and her daughter got into an aging Chevrolet.

Nick continued toward the gallery.

Edith came to stand on the sidewalk next to Octavia.

"Such a sad situation." Edith shook her head and made a *tut-tut* sound when Gail and Anne drove past them down the street.

Octavia waved at Anne, who gazed fixedly at her through the car window. Hesitantly the girl raised a small hand in response.

"I assume you're talking about Gail and Anne?" Octavia said, watching Nick.

"Yes. Gail is the daughter of Elmore and Betty Johnson, the folks who run Johnson's Nursery and Garden Supply. She was such a pretty girl back in high school. Bright, too. Went off to college in Seattle." She paused and smiled at Nick when he came to a halt in front of her.

"Afternoon, Mrs. Seaton. Nice day."

"It is, indeed. I was just telling Octavia how Gail went off to college in Seattle and ended up married to that investor fellow who left her a couple of years ago and ran off with the decorator who redid his office."

"I'm afraid I didn't keep up with the gossip at the time," Nick said in a repressive tone that was clearly meant to change the subject. "I had my hands full in Portland."

"Gail got almost nothing out of the divorce, they say," Edith continued, oblivious to the unsubtle hint. "Word is her husband stashed all his assets on one of those little islands in the Caribbean, declared bankruptcy, and left the state. Never sees his daughter, of course."

"Poor little Anne," Octavia said.

"Ready to go?" Nick said pointedly to Octavia.

She glanced over her shoulder and saw that her potential clients were still contemplating a purchase. "In a few minutes."

"Gail lost her job in Seattle a couple of months ago and now she's back here in Eclipse Bay. She's living with her folks while she looks for work. Money is tight."

"She's job hunting?" Octavia looked down the street. Gail's Chevy had disappeared around a corner. "Is that why she was in your shop?"

"Yes. Unfortunately, I had to tell her that I just don't do enough business to warrant hiring an assistant. I gather she's tried several other places with no luck."

"Hmm," Octavia said.

# chapter 5

The middle-aged couple left a short time later with their newly acquired seascape wrapped in brown paper.

Octavia set the security alarm, locked the door of the gallery, and dropped her keys into the spacious bag that hung from her right shoulder.

Nick gave her an enigmatic smile and put on his sunglasses.

She would have given a lot to be able to read his mind at that moment, she thought. Then again, maybe it was better not to know what he was thinking. The knowledge would only have made her more tense. She was still wondering if this burst of recklessness was going to prove to be a disaster.

They walked together toward the parking lot. When they reached the BMW, he opened the door on the passenger side and held it for her. She searched his face quickly, looking for any concealed signs of triumph. She saw none. If anything, she thought, he seemed as wary as she felt.

Now that was an interesting development.

She collected the folds of her skirt in one hand and slipped into the front seat. "What did you do with Carson?"

"He's spending the evening with Rafe and Hannah out at Dreamscape," Nick said.

"Oh." She realized she had become accustomed to seeing Nick and Carson together during the past two weeks. "Will he be joining us for dinner later?"

He smiled. "This is my date, not Carson's."

He closed the car door very deliberately.

She watched him walk around the front of the vehicle. He moved with an easy, fluid grace that was at once relaxed and purposeful. Probably the way most top-of-the-food-chain predators moved when they were going out to grab a gazelle for dinner, she thought. Fascinating, exciting. More than a little dangerous.

The sense of deep, sensual appreciation that swept through her caught her by surprise. She was still slightly awed by her decision to go out with him. Until tonight, the only big risks she had ever taken in life had involved the buying and selling of art. She trusted her intuition when it came to taking chances on unknown painters. But she had always been cautious when it came to men.

Nick got behind the wheel and closed the door. The interior of the BMW suddenly felt overwhelmingly intimate. She realized she was holding her breath.

"Couple of things you should know," she said carefully when he made to slip the key into the ignition. "The first is that, in case your grandfather hasn't told you, Claudia Banner was my great-aunt."

Dead silence.

Nick did not fire up the engine. Instead, he twisted slightly in the seat and rested his right arm on the back. He watched her very steadily through his dark glasses.

"Want to run that past me again?" he said.

"I'm related to Claudia Banner. The woman who—"

"Trust me, I know who Claudia Banner is."

"Was. My aunt died a year and a half ago."

"I see." Nick waited a beat. "This is for real? Not a joke of some kind?"

"No, it's not a joke." She gripped her bag very tightly in her lap. "Does it change things? Do you want to call off the date?"

"My grandfather knows who you are?"

"Yes. Sullivan and Mitchell both know. They figured it out the night of Lillian's show." She cleared her throat. "Obviously they haven't told anyone else in either family yet."

"Yeah. Obviously." He tapped the key absently against the leather seat back. "Well, hell."

"Is this a problem for you?"

"I'm thinking," he said. "Give me a minute."

"Look, if you're that rattled, I can find my own way out to Thurgarton's place."

"It isn't a problem and I'm not rattled." He took off his dark glasses and examined her with cool, faintly narrowed eyes. "I just find this news a little unexpected, that's all. It raises a few questions."

"I know. I answered some of them for Mitchell and I can do the same for you." She glanced pointedly at her watch. "But not now. We need to get going. I promised Virgil I'd meet him and the others at six."

"Right." He turned back and twisted the key in the ignition. The powerful engine growled softly. "I'm still waiting for the other shoe to drop."

"The other shoe?"

"You said there were a couple of things I needed to

know." He checked his mirrors and reversed out of the parking space.

"I'll be leaving town at the end of the summer."

He shot her a quick glance and she knew that the news had taken him by surprise.

"You're leaving Eclipse Bay?"

"Yes, I'm going to sell the gallery."

He seemed to relax slightly. He gave an understanding inclination of his head. "Not surprised the gallery here isn't working. Makes sense to concentrate on the Portland branch."

She watched the road through the windshield. "Both galleries are successful, as a matter of fact. But I'm going to sell both branches."

"Getting out of the art business altogether?"

"Not that easy." She smiled slightly. "It isn't just a business. More of a calling, I'm afraid. I can't imagine not being involved in art. A couple of months ago I was offered a position in a large gallery in San Diego. I don't have to give them my official decision until next month, but I'm leaning strongly toward accepting the offer."

"San Diego, huh?"

"It's not a certainty. There's also a possibility that I'm looking at in Denver."

"I see."

He drove in silence for a few minutes, piloting the BMW carefully through the small business district, past the pier, the town's single gas station, and the Incandescent Body bakery.

"Sounds like you're cutting a lot of ties all at once," Nick said eventually. "Is that wise?"

"I don't have any personal ties in the Northwest. I

didn't even move to Portland or open the galleries until a couple of months after Aunt Claudia died."

"You've only been in the area a little more than a year?"

"That's right. Not long enough to put down roots. There's nothing holding me here." It was time to accept that truth, she thought. Time to get on with her life.

She looked out over the expanse of Eclipse Bay. The sun was low in the sky. It streaked the clouds gathering out on the horizon with ominous shades of orange and gold.

Nick drove without speaking for a while, concentrating on the road, although traffic was almost nonexistent on the outskirts of town.

"Why did you come to Eclipse Bay?" he asked finally. "Why go to all the trouble of starting up a business in a small town in addition to one in Portland? That was a major undertaking."

"It's not easy to explain. Aunt Claudia talked a lot about what happened here all those years ago. The memories bothered her a great deal toward the end. She felt guilty about her part in the feud. I promised her that I would come back to see if there was anything I could do to put things right."

"No offense, but just what the hell did you plan to do to mend a three-generation rift?" Nick asked dryly.

She winced. His obvious lack of faith in her feud-mending skills hurt for some obscure reason. The worst part was that he was right. She had been a fool to think she could do anything constructive.

"I don't know," she said honestly. "I just decided to give it a whirl."

"I gotta tell you, that sounds damn flaky."

"I suppose it does. The thing is, after Aunt Claudia died there wasn't anything holding me in San Francisco."

"That's where you were living?"

"Yes."

"What about your job?" He flexed his hand on the wheel. "A significant other?"

"I had a position in a small gallery, but it wasn't anything special. And there was no particular significant other."

"Hard to believe."

"I was seeing someone before Claudia got so sick. But it wasn't that serious, and we drifted apart when I started spending more and more time with my aunt. He found someone else and I sort of went into hibernation. By the time I resurfaced after the funeral, I had no social life left to speak of."

"Family?"

"Not in the San Francisco area. My folks are separated. Dad lives in Houston. Mom's in Philadelphia. They've both got other families. Other lives. We're not what you'd call close."

"So you just up and moved to Oregon."

"Yes." She wrinkled her nose. "I suppose that sounds very flighty to a Harte."

"Hell, it sounds flighty for anyone, even a Madison."

That irritated her. Given his track record with women, he had a lot of nerve calling her flaky and flighty.

"I like to think of myself as a free spirit," she said. She rather liked the sound of that now that she thought about it. *Free spirit* definitely sounded better than *flighty* or *flaky*. More mysterious and exotic, maybe. She arched her brows. "Do you have a problem with that?"

"Don't know," he said. "I've never actually met a free spirit before."

He was still pondering all the possible definitions of *free spirit* ten minutes later when he turned into the narrow, unpaved road.

"You know, I think you were right." Octavia leaned forward a little, peering through the window at the trees that loomed on either side of the rutted path. "I might have spent hours searching for this turnoff. Mr. Thurgarton certainly didn't believe in making his place easy to find, did he?"

He shrugged. "Thurgarton was one strange man. Just ask anyone."

She smiled fleetingly. "Sometimes I think that being a bit odd or eccentric is a requirement for renting or purchasing real estate in Eclipse Bay."

"I will admit that the people we're about to meet certainly exemplify the finest in that local tradition."

He eased the BMW deeper into the trees and brought it to a halt at the edge of a small clearing.

Arizona Snow's pickup truck was parked under a nearby tree. Virgil Nash's vintage sports car stood next to it.

A gray, weather-beaten cabin occupied the center of the open space. It was on the verge of crumbling into the ground. The front porch sagged and the windows were caked with grime. There was a worn-out quality to the old house, as if it were content to follow its owner into the grave.

"It doesn't look like Thurgarton took good care of his property," Octavia said.

The touch of feminine disapproval in her voice almost made him smile. He thought about her pristine gallery with its sparkling windows and carefully hung paintings. The interior of her little fairy cottage out on the bluffs probably looked just as neat and tidy.

"Thurgarton was not real big on home improvement projects," he said.

He switched off the engine and climbed out from behind the wheel. Octavia did not wait for him to show off his first-date manners. She got out of the front seat all on her own.

*Free spirit.*

Virgil Nash opened the front door of the cabin as Nick and Octavia started toward the porch steps.

"He certainly doesn't fit the stereotypical image of a porn shop proprietor, does he?" Octavia murmured in a very low voice.

Nick grinned. "Virgil's definitely one of a kind, and you've got to admit that his business offers a unique service to the community. Sort of like a library."

"Well, that is one way of looking at it, I suppose. There is something scholarly about him, isn't there? Maybe it's the frayed sweater vest."

"Could be."

It was true, Nick thought. With his gaunt frame, silver goatee, and preference for slightly frayed sweaters and vests, Virgil would have been at home in an academic environment. There was an old-fashioned, almost courtly air about him. No one knew where he had come from or what he had done before he had arrived in Eclipse Bay. His past was as shrouded in mystery as Arizona Snow's.

For as long as anyone could remember, Nash had operated Virgil's Adult Books & Video Arcade. The establishment was discreetly located a couple of hundred yards beyond the city limits and, therefore, just out of reach of ambitious civic reformers and high-minded members of the town council.

Virgil believed in the old saying that location was everything in real estate.

"Nick, this is a surprise." Virgil walked across the porch. "Good to see you again. Heard you were in town for the summer."

"Needed a change." Nick went up the steps and shook Virgil's hand. "Thought Carson would enjoy the beach."

"Good thing you drove Octavia out here." Virgil smiled ruefully at her. "I got to thinking later that it might not be easy for you to find this place, what with being new to the community and all."

"You were right," she said. "Left to my own devices, I'd probably still be looking for the turnoff."

"Thank you so much for coming all the way out here to look at the paintings. We certainly appreciate it."

"Happy to be of service," Octavia said. "Where's A.Z.?"

"Right here," Arizona boomed through the screen door. "You met Photon, here?"

"Yes, of course." Octavia nodded at the tall man in the long, flowing robes who stood behind Arizona. "Good evening, Photon."

"May the light of the future brighten your night, Miss Brightwell." Photon inclined his gleaming, shaved head in Nick's direction. "Light and peace, Mr. Harte."

"Thanks," Nick said. "Same to you, Photon."

Another resident eccentric, Nick thought. Photon was the leader of the New Age crowd that operated the Incandescent Body bakery. The group styled itself the Heralds of Future History. Their philosophy was a little vague, but their baking skills were outstanding. The incredible muffins, pastries, and cornbread produced at the bakery had gone a long way toward quelling local concerns that Eclipse Bay had been invaded by a cult.

"Come on inside." Arizona thrust open the screen door. "Got the paintings lined up here in the living room."

"We had to clear out two pickup loads of junk to make space to display them," Virgil said dryly.

Nick grinned. "There goes the inheritance, huh?"

"Let's put it this way," Virgil said. "It was nice of Thurgarton to think of us, but it's starting to look like being the beneficiaries of his will is more trouble than it's worth. The furniture is in such bad shape it isn't even worth the effort of putting on a yard sale. Other than the paintings, everything else is just junk. Personally, I'm not holding my breath that the pictures are worth much, either."

Nick ushered Octavia ahead of him into the cramped, dark living room. She came to an abrupt halt.

"Oh, my," she said. "This is really quite amazing."

"That's one word for it." Nick stopped just behind her and whistled softly at the sight of the truly monumental clutter. "The term *firetrap* also comes to mind."

Faded magazines and yellowed newspapers spilled from the tops of row upon row of cardboard boxes stacked to the ceiling. Old suitcases were heaped in a corner. One of them was open, revealing a tangle of old clothes. The surface of the desk near the window was buried beneath piles of file folders and three-ring binders stuffed with notebook paper.

In addition to the desk and its accompanying chair, the only other furnishings in the room were a recliner and a reading lamp.

Octavia gave Virgil, Arizona, and Photon a quick, laughing smile. "And to think that this is all yours now."

Virgil chuckled softly. "You know, this is the first time anyone was thoughtful enough to remember me in his will."

"The property is worth something," Nick said, trying to be optimistic.

"Something," Photon agreed, "but not a lot. No view of the water. The house, itself, is a tear-down. The plumbing is in bad shape and the wiring is decades out of code."

Nick was mildly surprised by Photon's assured assessment of the house and land value. For the first time he wondered what the man had done before he became the leader of the Heralds of Future History. Everyone had a past.

"Hold on, here," Arizona said. "There's more to this than meets the eye. Only one reason Thurgarton would have left us in his will, and that's because he knew we were the only ones he could trust. He must have been working on something mighty big there at the end."

Nick exchanged a knowing glance with Octavia and Virgil. He was pretty sure they were both thinking the same thing he was thinking. Here we go with the ever popular, never dull Snow conspiracy theories.

Virgil cleared his throat. "A.Z. has concluded that Thurgarton stumbled onto a secret operation at the Eclipse Bay Policy Studies Institute." He motioned with one hand to indicate the piles of papers that surrounded them. "She believes that he collected all of this in an attempt to unravel the conspiracy."

"Most of this is just camouflage, of course," Arizona explained. "Thurgarton probably figured that if he piled enough out-of-date newspapers and magazines around the place, folks would write him off as a crackpot. They wouldn't realize that he had hidden the results of his investigation here."

"Camouflage?" Octavia picked up an ancient, tattered copy of *Playboy* and studied the bouncy-looking woman on the cover with grave interest. "That certainly explains some of these magazines. And it definitely beats the old line about just reading them for the articles."

"I resent that remark," Nick said. "In our younger days, my friends and I learned a lot from those magazines."

She gave him an arch look. "I don't think I'll ask you to tell me exactly what it was you learned."

"Examining all of these papers and magazines is gonna take some time, unfortunately," Arizona continued, ignoring the byplay. "Not like we aren't already plenty busy with Project Log Book, eh, Photon?"

"The light of future history will show us the way to accomplish all that must be done in due course," Photon said.

He was out of his real estate assessor's role and back into his fathomless serenity mode, Nick noticed.

He looked at Arizona. "What's Project Log Book?"

"Photon and I talked it over and we decided that the only safe way to ensure that none of the data in my logs gets destroyed by the operatives up at the institute is to put it all online," Arizona said.

"I thought you didn't trust computers," Nick said.

"I don't like 'em and that's a fact. But we've got to move with the times. Got to take advantage of technology if we're going to stay ahead of the bad guys. The Heralds are building a Web site and they're inputting the contents of my logs and journals as we speak. This is all real hush-hush, naturally, but I trust you and Octavia here to keep your mouths closed. And of course Virgil will keep it to himself."

"I won't tell a soul," Virgil promised.

"Loose lips sink ships," Octavia said solemnly.

Arizona nodded. "That's for damn sure."

"You've been keeping those logs and journals for years, A.Z.," Nick said. "You must have hundreds of them."

"The Heralds are working around the clock in shifts on the computer that we set up in my War Room. Logistics haven't been easy, I can tell you. Got to keep things running as usual at the bakery while we put the data online so we don't arouse suspicion. Don't want anyone up at the institute to come nosing around before we're ready to go live with the Web site."

"We expect to have Project Log Book completed by the end of the summer," Photon said.

"And now you've got to sort through all of this junk in addition to putting together a Web site project and operating the bakery." Nick shook his head at the enormousness of the task. "Don't envy you this job."

"We'll get it done," Arizona assured him with her customary can-do attitude. "No choice. Future of the country depends on making sure that the facts in my logs are available to the concerned citizens of this nation. The Internet is the only way to go."

"Uh, where are the pictures you wanted me to examine?" Octavia asked politely.

"Behind that row of boxes," Virgil said.

He led the way, forging a path through the maze of cartons and papers to the far side of the living room. Nick and Octavia followed him.

Four paintings in old, wooden frames were propped against the wall. In the gloom, Nick could see that the first three were landscapes. The fourth looked as if it had been splashed with a lot of dark paint.

Virgil switched on the reading lamp behind the recliner and aimed the beam at the paintings. "I suspect they're all worthless, but I wanted an expert opinion before we dumped them into the yard sale pile."

Nick watched Octavia's face as she studied the paintings. She had the same expression of rapt attention that she'd had when she looked at Carson's pictures. She was taking this seriously, he thought. Given that two of the people who had asked for her opinion were conspiracy freaks and the third ran an adult bookstore, it was going above and beyond the call of duty to show such respect.

She walked slowly past all four paintings and stopped

in front of the one that looked as if it had been painted with a brush that had been dipped in chaos. She looked at it for a long time.

Then she crouched in front of it, heedless of the fact that the change of position caused her long, pale skirts to sweep across the dusty floorboards. She gazed intently at what looked like a scribble in the right-hand corner.

"Hmm," she said.

Everyone went very still. Nick was amused. He could feel the sudden tension that had leaped to life in the room.

"Does anyone know where or how Thurgarton got this picture?" Octavia asked, never taking her attention away from the painting.

Virgil shook his head. "We found it with the others in a closet. No way to tell how he came by it. Why?"

"I hesitate to say anything at this point because I don't want anyone to get too excited."

"Too late," Nick said. "We're excited. Is this thing valuable?"

Arizona frowned. "Looks like the artist dumped the contents of several tubes of paint on the canvas and smeared them around."

Virgil smiled. "That's mid-twentieth-century art for you."

Photon contemplated the abstract painting with a considering air. "The longer one looks at it, the deeper it appears. It is clearly an exploration of the absence of light."

Nick looked at him. "You think?"

"Yes." Photon inclined his gleaming head. "It is a statement of man's craving for light and his simultaneous fear of its power."

Octavia rose slowly to her feet and turned around to face the others.

"I agree with you, Photon," she said quietly. "And if we're right, it may be the work of Thomas Upsall. The signature certainly fits. He always signed his work in a very distinctive manner. And his technique was also quite unique. A very time-consuming method that required layer upon layer of paint."

"Wow," Nick said. "A genuine Thomas Upsall. Who would have believed it? Wait until this news hits the art world."

She gave him a reproving frown. "Very funny. Obviously you don't recognize the artist."

"Nope, can't say that I do."

"Me, either." Arizona looked hopeful. "This Thomas Upsall, was he famous or anything?"

"He produced most of his paintings in the nineteen-fifties," Octavia said. "His pictures were not very popular at the time, but in the past few years they have become extremely collectible. There isn't a lot of his work around because he destroyed a great quantity of it during the last year of his life. He died in the mid-eighties, alone and forgotten."

"What do you think this thing's worth?" Arizona asked.

Octavia looked at the painting over her shoulder. "If, and I stress the word *if,* it is a genuine Upsall, it could easily fetch a couple hundred thousand at auction. Maybe two hundred and fifty."

They all stared at her.

Virgil exhaled deeply. "A couple hundred thousand *dollars?*"

"Yes. The market for Upsall's work is hot at the moment and getting hotter." Octavia gave them all a warning look and held up one hand. "But to be on the safe side, I'd like to get a second opinion from a colleague of mine who specializes in mid-twentieth-century abstract art. She works in a museum in Seattle. Unfortunately, she's on vacation until next week."

"Think we can get her to take a look at the picture when she returns?" Arizona asked.

"Yes, for a fee," Octavia said. "She consults. She may even want to purchase it for her museum."

"That brings up the question of what to do with it until we can get your colleague here to examine it," Virgil said. "Now that we know it's worth two hundred grand or more, I don't like the idea of leaving it here."

"I could take it home with me," Arizona replied. "My security is top of the line. But the spies up at the institute keep a round-the-clock watch on me. If they see me take something from this place into my house, they might get curious. Don't want to draw any attention right now while we're at such a critical point in Project Log Book."

"I've got a security system for the paintings in my gallery," Octavia said slowly. "I suppose I could store the Upsall in my back room for a week."

"Good idea," Virgil agreed. "It should be fine in your back room. Not like Eclipse Bay is home to a lot of sophisticated art thieves."

Photon smiled benignly. "You illuminate us with the radiant light of your kindness."

# chapter 6

The row of shops that lined the street across from the pier was dark and silent at this hour. The last rays of the summer sun were veiled behind the thickening layer of clouds. Whitecaps danced on the slate-gray waters of the bay.

Nick parked in the small lot. When he climbed out from behind the wheel, a snapping breeze tugged at his windbreaker. *Storm on the way,* he thought. Summer squalls were not unusual for this time of year here on the coast.

Octavia was already out of the passenger seat. The bouncy wind whipped her hair into a froth and caused her long, full skirts to billow around her legs. She laughed a little as she grabbed a handful of her skirts to keep them from blowing up around her thighs. Her eyes were bright. He got the feeling that she was savoring the raw energy of the approaching storm. Maybe she tapped into it for her fairy magic or something. Seemed logical.

"We'd better hurry," she said. "The rain will hit any minute."

"Right."

With an effort he wrenched his attention away from her flying hair and skirts and opened the rear door of the BMW. He reached inside and hoisted the painting. Octavia had wrapped the picture in old newspapers before leaving Thurgarton's cabin.

Carrying the painting under one arm, he walked with her to the door of Bright Visions.

"You really think this thing is worth a quarter million?" he asked.

"Between you and me? Yes. But we'll all feel more secure once we've had a second opinion."

She continued to struggle with her skirts with one hand while she withdrew her keys from her shoulder bag. She opened the front door and stepped quickly into the darkened interior of the shop to punch in the code that deactivated the alarm system. Then she flipped some switches to turn on the lights.

"Who'd have believed that old Thurgarton would have possessed a valuable work of art?" He carried the painting into the shop. "He was no collector. You saw how he lived. How the heck do you suppose he got hold of it?"

"I haven't got a clue." She led the way across the showroom to the long counter. "As I told you, there isn't a lot of Upsall's work around. It's amazing to think that one of his pictures has been sitting out here on the coast all these years."

"Who says we're not a bunch of real sophisticated art lovers here in Eclipse Bay?"

"Certainly not me." She opened the back room and turned on more lights. "You can put it there with that stack of paintings leaning against the far wall."

He surveyed the crowded back room. Rows of paintings were stacked five and six deep against every wall. Empty frames of all shapes and sizes were propped in the corner. The workbench was littered with tools and matting materials.

"No offense," he said dryly, setting down the painting, "but this place looks almost as cluttered as Thurgarton's cabin."

"Gallery back rooms always look like this."

He straightened. "The finding of a previously unknown Upsall should make for an interesting story in some of the art magazines."

She smiled. "I can see the headline now. *Conspiracy Buff, New Age Cult Leader and Porn Shop Proprietor Inherit Lost Upsall.*"

"Be interesting to see what they do with the money." He walked back to where she stood in the doorway. "Well, so much for tonight's thrilling adventure in the world of art. Are you ready for dinner? I'd take you to Dreamscape, but Carson is there and we wouldn't be able to talk in peace. How about the Crab Trap? It's not as good as Rafe's place, but it's not bad."

"You do realize that if we dine in any of the local restaurants, there will be a lot of talk tomorrow?"

"So what? Hartes are used to being talked about in this town."

"I know."

Belatedly it occurred to him that she was not accustomed to being the subject of local gossip. "Look, if this is a problem, we can go back to my place. I've got plenty of food in the house. Comes with having a growing boy around. I'm not saying that it will be what anyone would call gourmet, but—"

She cleared her throat. "I bought fresh asparagus and some salmon fillets this afternoon."

Fresh asparagus and salmon were not generally purchased on a whim. He considered the possibilities.

"You planned to invite me back to your place?" he asked finally.

"To be honest, it struck me that it would be more comfortable to eat there rather than in front of an audience composed of a lot of the good and extremely curious people of Eclipse Bay."

He smiled slowly. "Fresh asparagus and salmon sound great."

The atmosphere was making him very uneasy, but for the life of him, he could not figure out what was wrong. On the surface, everything was perfect.

Dinner had gone smoothly. He had taken charge of the salmon while Octavia had dealt with the asparagus and sliced some crusty bread. They had sipped from two glasses of chardonnay while they worked together in her snug, cozy kitchen. They had talked easily, for all the world as comfortable as two people who had prepared a meal together countless times.

It was almost as if they had already become lovers, he thought. A deep sense of intimacy enveloped them and it was starting to worry him. This was a far different sensation than he had known with other women in the past. It was not the pleasant, superficial sexual awareness he had experienced on previous, similar occasions. He did not understand the prowling tension that was starting to leave claw marks on his insides.

Maybe this had not been one of his better ideas. Then again, looking back, he was pretty sure he'd never had much choice. If you went hunting fairy queens, you took a few risks.

He stood at the sink in her gleaming, white-tiled kitchen and washed the pan that had been used to steam the asparagus. Nearby, Octavia, a striped towel draped over her left shoulder, went up on her tiptoes to stack dishes in a cupboard. When she raised her arms overhead, her breasts moved beneath the thin fabric of her blouse.

Damn. He was staring. Annoyed, he concentrated on rinsing the pan.

She closed the cupboard door and reached for the coffeepot. "Black, right? No cream or sugar?"

"Right."

She poured coffee into two cups and led the way into the living room. He dried his hands, slung the damp towel over a rack, and followed her, unable to take his eyes off the mesmerizing sway of her hips.

What the hell was wrong with this picture? he wondered. This was exactly how it was supposed to look, precisely how he had hoped it would look at this point.

She curled up in a corner of the sofa, one leg tucked under the curve of her thigh, mug gracefully cupped in her hands. The fire he had built earlier crackled on the hearth.

She smiled at him and he immediately felt every nerve and muscle in his body shift from Yellow Alert status to Code Red. An almost irresistible urge swept over him to pick her up off the sofa, carry her into the shadowy room at the end of the hall, and put her down on a bed. He flexed one hand deliberately to regain control.

It had been like this all evening, as though he were walking the edge of a cliff in a violent storm. One false step and he would go over into very deep water. It didn't help that outside the rain and the wind had struck land with a vengeance some forty minutes ago.

He crossed the living room to the stone fireplace,

picked up an iron poker, and prodded the fire. The blaze didn't need prodding, but it gave him something to do with his hands.

"I've enjoyed your books," she said. "I've got all four in the series."

"I noticed." He put aside the poker, straightened, and glanced at the bookshelf where his novels were arranged between two heavy green glass bookends. "We authors tend to pick up on little details like that."

The bookends looked expensive, he thought. Dolphins playing in the surf. One-of-a-kind pieces of art glass, not cheap, utilitarian bookends picked up at a rummage sale.

There were other quietly expensive touches in the cottage. An exotically patterned carpet done in shades of muted greens and gold covered most of the hardwood floor in front of the dark-green sofa. The coffee table was a heavy sheet of green glass that rippled and flowed like a wave of clear lava. A couple of framed abstract paintings hung on the walls.

Not the kind of furnishings you expected in a weekend or summer house, he thought. He had the feeling that she had deliberately set out to make a home here. And now she was planning to depart for good.

"Tell me," she said, "was it difficult to make the decision to leave Harte Investments when you decided to write full time?"

"Making the decision was easy." He sat down on the sofa and reached for his coffee mug. "Getting out of the family business was a little more difficult."

"I'll bet it was. You were the firstborn and from all accounts you showed a talent for investments."

He shrugged. "I'm a Harte."

She gave him a fleeting smile. "There must have been a

lot of pressure on you to take over the helm after your father retired."

"My parents were very understanding and supportive." He took a swallow of coffee and slowly lowered the mug. "But Sullivan went off like Mount Saint Helens."

"I believe it. Harte Investments was your grandfather's creation. Everyone around here knows what he went through to recover and build a new company after Aunt Claudia—" She broke off. "After Harte-Madison went under."

He wrapped both hands around the mug. "Dad tried to shield me from the worst of the blast but no one could have suppressed that explosion. Sullivan and I went a few rounds before he finally realized that I wasn't going to back down and change my mind."

"It must have been a difficult time."

"Yeah." He took another sip of coffee. "But we got through it."

"It's a tribute to the strength of your family bonds."

"Uh-huh." He did not want to talk any more about that time in his life. It was tied up too closely with Amelia's death. He glanced around the room. "Looks like you planned to stay here for a while."

She raised one shoulder in a tiny shrug. "Plans change."

He couldn't think of anything to say to that so he tried another topic. "Heard you've been seeing Jeremy Seaton."

"We've had dinner together a couple of times." She sipped her coffee.

He looked at her. "Mind if I ask if there's anything serious in that direction?"

She pursed her lips and tilted her head slightly. Thinking. "I would describe my relationship with Jeremy as friendly."

"Friendly." What the hell did *friendly* mean?

"Jeremy and I have a lot of interests in common."

He nodded once. "The art thing. Jeremy paints."

She gave him polite concern. "Is there a problem here?"

"You tell me." He put his mug down with great care. "Is Jeremy going to have a problem with you and me having dinner tonight?"

"I doubt it." She looked surprised by the question. "But if he says anything, I'll explain the situation to him."

"How, exactly, do you intend to explain it?"

"I'll tell him that we're just friends. He'll understand."

"Just friends," he repeated neutrally.

"What else?" She put down her own mug and looked pointedly at the clock. "Good heavens, it's getting late, isn't it? I have to go into the gallery early tomorrow to frame some of the children's pictures, and I'm sure you're anxious to pick up Carson."

"Kicking me out?"

"It's been a long day," she said by way of an apology and got to her feet.

"Sure." He rose slowly, taking his time.

She handed him his black windbreaker and opened the door for him. Smiling all the while. Friendly.

He went outside onto the front porch. The squall was dying fast, leaving behind crisp, still-damp air.

"Drive carefully," she said.

"I'll do that."

He pulled on his jacket but did not bother to fasten it. He stuffed his hands into his pockets and stood looking out into the night. He could hear the distant rumble of waves crashing against the bottom of the bluffs behind the cottage.

He turned slowly back to Octavia.

In the porch light, her hair glowed the color of the

flames on the hearth inside. He could feel the magic that swirled around her.

He'd had enough. He knew now what was wrong with this picture.

"Something you should understand before we go any further here," he said.

"What's that?"

He took two steps back across the porch, closing the distance between them. He kept his hands in the pockets of his jacket, not trusting himself to touch her.

"Whatever else this turns out to be," he said evenly, "it isn't about being just friends."

She blinked. Her lips parted but no words emerged.

Just as well because he did not want to talk.

He kissed her, hands still in his pockets, leaning forward a little to claim her mouth. She did not flinch or step back but he felt the shiver that went through her.

He deepened the kiss deliberately.

Her mouth softened under his. He got the feeling that she was tasting him; testing him, maybe. Or was it herself she was testing?

She made a tiny, unbelievably sexy little sound and his blood ran hot in his veins. His breathing thickened.

He raised his head slowly. Breaking off the kiss required a serious act of willpower.

"Definitely not just friends," he said.

He turned away, went down the steps, and got into his car.

A short time later he drove into the newly paved, heavily landscaped parking lot at Dreamscape and slotted the BMW into the empty space next to Rafe's Porsche. He glanced at his watch as he got out. It was after eleven. The restaurant had been closed for over an hour. The vehicles that remained in the lot belonged to the overnight guests. There were a number of them.

Dreamscape had been an immediate success from the first day of operation. In addition to tourists, the inn drew a steady clientele from the institute and Chamberlain College.

He walked up the steps of the wide veranda that surrounded the lower floor of the inn. The front door opened just as he reached out to lean on the little bell.

"Heard the engine," Rafe said. "Figured it was you." He stood aside to allow Nick into the front hall. "Want some coffee?"

"No, thanks. Just had some." He nodded at the balding, middle-aged man who emerged from the office behind the front desk. "'Evening, Eddie."

"Hello, Nick. Come to collect your boy?"

"Yes."

"How was the hot date with the charming Miss Brightwell?" Rafe asked.

"No comment."

Rafe gave him a commiserating look and closed the door. "That bad, huh? You know, I wondered if she was really your type."

"No comment means no comment. I thought you Madisons were real big on a no-kiss-and-tell policy."

"Hey, we're family now, remember?" Rafe grinned. "I'm just trying to show a little brotherly interest in your personal affairs, that's all."

"Brotherly interest, my ass, you're just—" He broke off at the sight of Hannah appearing in the opening that led to the central corridor and the solarium.

"About time you got here," she said.

"It's not that late," Nick said, feeling oddly defensive. "Just because you old married folks go to bed early doesn't mean the rest of us are obliged to keep the same boring hours."

"Good point." Rafe raised a brow. "It isn't even midnight, Cinderella. What *are* you doing here this early? I told you we'd be happy to let Carson stay the night if you got lucky."

Hannah turned on Rafe with a withering glare. "You told him that? You actually said something so extremely tacky?"

"He's a Madison," Nick reminded her. "He was born tacky. We can only pray that your classy Harte genes will overpower his unfortunate genetic inheritance when you two decide to start making babies."

Hannah gave him an odd look. Rafe's mouth curved but he refrained from comment. Nick got the feeling he was missing the joke.

"Well?" Hannah said in that tone of voice that meant she was deliberately changing the subject and everyone else had better go along. "How was the date with Octavia? Did you have a nice time? Where did you two have dinner?"

He studied his sister. There was something different about her lately. He hadn't been able to put his finger on it but it was almost as though she harbored a special secret. Marriage definitely agreed with her, he thought. But, then, with the glaring exception of himself, it agreed with Hartes, in general.

"Her place," he said neutrally.

"Oh, man," Rafe muttered. "You went back to her place and she kicked you out before eleven o'clock. Not good." He shook his head. "I'd be happy to give you a little brotherly advice on how to behave yourself on a first date with a nice lady, Harte. Least I could do, you being family and all."

"You can take your helpful dating advice down to the Total Eclipse Bar and Grill and stuff it where the sun don't shine."

"Touchy, are we? Okay, but it's your loss, pal."

He'd had enough, Nick decided. He looked at Hannah. "Got my son?"

"Sound asleep in the library." Her expression softened. "Winston is keeping an eye on him." She hesitated. "He seemed a little concerned about your relationship with Octavia."

"Winston is concerned about my personal life?"

"Not my dog. Your son. He mentioned several times this evening that he was afraid you might make her mad."

Rafe sighed. "Apparently even little Carson is aware of your lack of finesse with the ladies."

"My son is first and foremost a Harte," Nick said dryly. "His chief concern is making sure that nothing gets in the way of his current objective."

"And that objective would be?"

"Getting his picture of Winston exhibited in the Children's Art Show."

"A worthy ambition," Hannah murmured. "And I'm sure the portrait is stunning. Winston, after all, is an excellent subject. But what does your relationship with Octavia have to do with getting the picture exhibited?"

Nick grimaced. "Carson is afraid that if I annoy Octavia she might refuse to hang the portrait in the show."

"A reasonable cause for anxiety under the circumstances," Rafe said cheerfully.

Hannah looked startled. "Oh, I really don't think she'd take out her hostility on a little boy. She isn't the sort of person who would do that. Octavia is very nice."

"So," Rafe said a little too easily, "what, exactly, are you doing to annoy such a *nice* lady, Harte?"

"You know," Nick said, taking another look at his watch, "it really is getting late, isn't it?"

"Yes, it is," Hannah said. She swung around on her heel and disappeared down the long, central hall.

Nick and Rafe followed her. They all came to a halt at the entrance to a comfortable, book-lined room. The dark expanse of the bay filled the space behind the windows. The library lights had been turned down low. Music played softly. A number of the comfortable, overstuffed chairs were occupied by guests who were sipping after-dinner cordials and coffee and talking quietly.

In the corner two small figures sprawled across a mound of pillows. Several children's books were scattered on the rug beside them. Most of the stories featured dogs.

Nick crossed the room and looked down at Carson, who was dressed in jeans, running shoes, and a sweatshirt. The boy was sound asleep, one arm flung across Winston. The Schnauzer raised his head from his paws and regarded Nick with intelligent eyes.

"Thanks for looking after him, Winston. I'll take over now."

Nick scratched Winston behind the ears and then scooped up his son.

Relieved of his nanny duties for the evening, Winston got to his feet and stretched. He snuffled politely around Nick's shoes and then trotted briskly toward Hannah.

Carson stirred a little and settled comfortably against Nick. He did not open his eyes. "Dad?"

"Time to go home."

"You didn't make her mad, did you?"

"I worked very hard not to make her mad."

"Good." Carson went back to sleep.

They all trooped down the hall to the front door and out onto the wide veranda. Winston vanished discreetly into the bushes. Hannah arranged Carson's black wind-breaker—a miniature version of the one Nick wore—around the boy's sleeping form.

"We've got some news," she said softly.

"What's that?" Nick asked.

"We're pregnant."

"Hey, that's great." He grinned and kissed her lightly on the forehead. "Congratulations to both of you."

"Thanks."

Rafe put his arm around Hannah and pulled her close against his side. His pride and happiness were apparent. "You're the first to know. We'll start phoning everyone else in both families tomorrow."

Nick smiled. "Nothing else like it, you know."

"Yeah, sorta figured that," Rafe said.

Nick looked down at Carson lying securely in his arms. "You just wish it was this easy to protect them forever."

They stood there for a moment. No one spoke.

After a while Nick hugged his son a little more tightly to him and went down the steps. At the bottom he paused briefly and looked back. "Almost forgot. I've got a little news of my own."

Hannah smiled encouragingly. "What?"

"Octavia Brightwell is related to our own local legend, Claudia Banner. Turns out that Claudia was her great-aunt."

Hannah's jaw dropped. "You're kidding."

"Nope."

"What the hell is she doing here in Eclipse Bay?" Rafe asked.

"I don't think she knows the answer to that one, herself. She said something about coming here to see if there was anything that could be done to mend the damage her great-aunt did. But I've got a feeling it's more complicated."

"What do you mean?" Hannah replied.

"From what I can tell, she's been drifting since Claudia died a year and a half ago. No close family. No real roots anywhere. Coming here to repair the damage her aunt did gave her a goal. But she tells me that she plans to leave at the end of the summer because it's clear to her that the Hartes and the Madisons have ended the feud all by themselves."

"Yeah, the good times never last, do they?" Rafe said laconically. His expression turned serious. "Does my grandfather know who she is?"

"She said Sullivan and Mitchell have known since the night of Lillian's show. Obviously they chose to keep the information to themselves."

"Figures," Rafe said.

They waited together on the veranda while Winston finished his business in the damp shrubbery. Hannah watched the BMW disappear into the night.

"What do you think is going on here?" she said after a while.

"Damned if I know." Rafe wrapped his hands around the railing. "Maybe it's like Nick said. Maybe Octavia came to Eclipse Bay to carry out her aunt's dying wish and then discovered there was nothing to fix."

"Nick is getting serious about her. I can tell. Octavia is different from the other women he's been seeing in the past few years. He's acting odd, too. I wonder if he's given her The Talk yet?"

"Don't know about that, but one thing we can say for sure. The curse has not yet been lifted. Nick didn't stay the night at her place."

"That business about the curse is absolute nonsense. The reason Nick never spends the night with any of his lady friends is because of Carson. He doesn't like to leave him alone with a sitter all night."

"That excuse doesn't fly," Rafe said flatly. "It's true that Nick doesn't leave Carson with sitters all night, but you know as well as I do that the kid stays overnight with family at times. Trust me, Nick wouldn't have a serious problem arranging to remain in some woman's bed until breakfast if that's what he wanted to do. If you ask me, he's avoiding it."

"I suppose you're right. Waking up with someone in the morning is a little different. More intimate, somehow. He's probably afraid that if he spends the night, the lady in question might get the wrong idea in spite of The Talk. He's done his best to avoid getting entangled in a real relationship since Amelia died."

"It's one thing to have hot sex and leave while it's still dark," Rafe agreed. "It's another thing to face the lady across the breakfast table. Takes the relationship to a whole new level."

Hannah smiled and patted her tummy. "Certainly had that effect on our relationship. But then, you can cook. That made a huge difference."

Winston trotted up the steps and kept going toward the front door. Rafe turned his head to watch the dog disappear inside the hall.

"Uh-oh," he said.

"Something wrong?"

"Just realized that we left the door open."

"So?"

"So Eddie is still at the front desk. He must have overheard everything we said when we talked to Nick a few minutes ago. Got a feeling he now knows just who Octavia Brightwell really is. Probably can't wait to tell everyone down at the post office first thing tomorrow morning."

Hannah groaned. "You're right. Uh-oh."

"What the heck. It was all bound to come out sooner or later. Not like there's any way to keep a secret in Eclipse Bay, after all."

"True." Hannah nibbled on her lower lip for a moment. "All the same, I think I'll give Octavia a call first thing in the morning and warn her. She's an outsider. She won't be prepared for what she's going to walk into tomorrow."

Rafe smiled. He said nothing.

She raised her brows. "What?"

"Just struck me that Octavia isn't that much of an outsider."

"What do you mean?"

"She's related to Claudia Banner, remember?" He tightened his arm around Hannah and steered her back toward the open door. "Her family has been involved in this thing from the beginning. Just like us Madisons and Hartes."

# chapter 7

All eyes turned toward her when she walked into the In-candescent Body bakery shortly before nine the next morning. And just as quickly shifted away again.

Even if Hannah had not been kind enough to give her a wake-up call and a warning, Octavia thought, she had been in Eclipse Bay long enough to know what this peculiar attention meant.

There was fresh gossip going around and she was the focus of it.

She had been well aware of what would happen if she accepted a date with Nick Harte, she reminded herself. And the fact that everyone now knew that she was related to the infamous Claudia Banner just added a whole lot of very hot spice to the stew that was now brewing in Eclipse Bay.

She paused just inside the doorway and drew a deep breath. Hartes and Madisons handled this kind of stuff routinely. Aunt Claudia wouldn't have so much as flinched. If they could do it, so could she.

She gave the small crowd a polite smile and moved forward, weaving a path through the gauntlet of tables. It seemed a very long way to the counter, but she made it eventually.

"Good morning," she said to the brightly robed Herald who waited to take her order. "Coffee with cream, please."

"May the light of the future be with you today." The Herald's ankhs and scarab jewelry clanked gently when she raised her palm in greeting. "Your coffee will be ready in a moment."

The door opened again just as Octavia handed her money to the Herald. She did not need to glance over her shoulder to see who had walked into the bakery. The fresh buzz of excitement said it all.

"Hi, Miss Brightwell," Carson called from the far end of the room. "Dad said he saw you in here."

She turned, cup in hand. A deep sense of wistful longing welled up inside her at the sight of Nick and his son together. In his matching black windbreaker, jeans, tee shirt, and running shoes, Carson was a sartorial miniature of his father. But the resemblance went so much deeper, she thought. You could already see in Carson the beginnings of the strength of will, the savvy intelligence, and the cool awareness that were Nick's hallmarks. There was something more there, too. Carson would grow up to be the kind of man whose word was his bond because integrity was bred in the bone in the Harte family.

Like father, like son.

She squelched the sudden rush of emotion with a ruthless act of willpower. Nick and Carson had everything they needed in the way of a family. And she would be leaving at the end of the summer.

"Good morning," she said to Carson. She looked at Nick and felt the heat in his gaze go straight to her nerve endings, setting off little explosions. "Hello."

"'Morning," he said.

There was an unmistakable intimacy in the low greeting, a dark, heavy warmth that she was certain everyone in the bakery had picked up on. She knew, with a certainty that was so strong she wondered if she'd developed telepathic powers, that he was thinking about that good-night kiss on her front porch.

Not that she had any right to complain. She was thinking about it, too.

Actually, she'd spent far too much of the night recalling it, analyzing it, contemplating every nuance and cataloging her own responses. She had examined that kiss the way she would have examined a painting that had the power to capture her attention and force her to look beneath the surface.

Her reaction had been over the top and she knew it. In fact, the all-night obsession with the details of that encounter on the porch had made her very uneasy this morning. You'd have thought it was her first serious kiss. And that made no sense at all. This was what came of being relationship-free for nearly two years. A woman tended to overreact when the long drought finally ended. She needed to get some perspective here.

Nick and Carson arrived at the counter. There was more than just amusement in Nick's eyes. There was some sympathy, too.

He glanced around with mild interest. "Don't worry about this. The news is out that you're related to Claudia

Banner and that we were seen together in my car last night."

"Yes, I know. Hannah called me first thing this morning to warn me."

"It'll all blow over in a couple of days."

She wasn't so sure about that, but she decided this was not the time or place to argue the point. "Sure."

"Give me a minute to grab some coffee for myself and some hot chocolate for Carson," he said. "Then we'll walk you over to the gallery."

Before she could object or agree, he started to give his order to the Herald.

Carson looked up at her while they waited for the coffee and chocolate. "Have you framed my picture yet?"

"I'm going to do it this morning." She smiled down at him. "Want to help?"

Excitement bubbled through him. "Yes."

Nick collected the cups and a paper sack from the Herald and gave the bakery one sweeping glance as he started toward the door.

"Okay, you two," he said out of the side of his mouth in the stone-cold accents of an Old West marshal. "Let's get the heck out of Dodge."

"Miss Brightwell's gonna frame Winston today," Carson announced. "I'm gonna help."

"Cool," Nick said.

Carson whirled and dashed ahead, completely oblivious to the thinly veiled curiosity that permeated the room.

"A Harte to his toes," Octavia murmured.

"Oh, yeah."

Outside, the remnants of the morning cloud cover were starting to dissipate. The day promised warmth and sunshine by noon.

The shops across from the pier had begun to open for the day. Octavia noticed that the lights were on inside Bay Souvenirs, House of Candy, and Seaton's Antiques.

"Looks like I'm running a little late this morning." She stopped in front of the door of Bright Visions and slid her key into the lock.

Carson and Nick followed her into the gallery and waited while she deactivated the alarm and switched on the lights.

"Where's my picture?" Carson asked.

"In the back room with the others," Octavia said. "But we have to finish our chocolate and coffee first before we start framing. Don't want to risk spilling anything on the pictures."

"Okay." Carson went to work on his chocolate. He seemed intent on downing the contents of his cup in record time.

"Easy," Nick said quietly.

There was no threatening edge to the tone of his voice, Octavia noted; no boring lecture on good manners. Just a simple instruction spoken with calm, masculine authority.

Octavia waited until all three cups were in the wastebasket before she opened the door of the back room.

"All right," she said, "let's see about getting Winston into a suitable frame."

Nick followed as far as the doorway of the back room. He glanced at his watch. "The mail should be in by now. I'll run down to the post office while you two work on the picture. See you in a few minutes, okay?"

"Okay." Carson did not look around. His attention was concentrated on the matting and framing materials that Octavia was arranging on the workbench. "Are you gonna use a gold frame for my picture, Miss Brightwell? I think Winston would look good in a gold frame."

"We'll try gold and black and see which looks best," she said.

"Obviously I'm not needed here," Nick said. "See you later."

The door of the gallery closed behind him a few seconds later. Octavia and Carson, absorbed in their task, barely noticed.

Mitchell Madison ambushed him when he walked into the post office.

"Heard you had a date with Octavia Brightwell last night," Mitchell commented, looming in Nick's path.

"Word gets around."

"You went out to the Thurgarton place together, picked up some old painting, and then you went to her cottage. That right?"

"Yes, sir. You are well informed."

"Now, see here." Mitchell put his face very close to Nick's. "I thought I made it damn clear to Sullivan that I wouldn't stand by while you fooled around with Octavia."

"Whatever arrangements you made with my grandfather are your business, naturally, but I should probably tell you that I don't generally consult with Sullivan before I ask a woman out. I don't think you can blame him for the fact that I had dinner with Octavia last night."

Mitchell squinted in a malevolent fashion. "Is that so?"

"Also, just to set the record straight, I don't call what Octavia and I did last night *fooling around*."

"What the devil do you call it?"

"A date. Mature adults not otherwise involved in a committed relationship get to do stuff like that."

"Sounds like fooling around to me." Mitchell's jaw tightened. "She tell you Claudia Banner was her great-aunt and that Claudia's passed on?"

"I think the whole town is aware of those facts by now."

"I don't give a damn about the town. I'm only interested in what's going on between you and Octavia."

Nick lounged against one of the old-fashioned counters, folded his arms, and studied Mitchell with morbid fascination. "Mind if I ask why you're so concerned with the subject of my social life?"

"Because you've got a reputation for lovin' 'em and leavin' 'em and givin' your girlfriends The Talk so they know up front that you're not serious. I'll be damned if I'll stand by and let you treat Claudia Banner's niece that way. That girl's got no family around to look after her, so I'm gonna do it. You treat her right or you'll answer to me. We clear on that?"

"Very clear. Can I pick up my mail now?"

Mitchell's brows bristled, but he reluctantly got out of the way. "You know something, Harte?"

"What?"

"If you had any sense, you'd get married again. Settle down and give that boy of yours a mother."

"The day I want advice on my personal life from a Madison, I'll be sure to ask."

In the end they went with the gold metal frame. Octavia privately thought that the black did a better job of accenting Winston's gray fur, but Carson was entranced with the flashier look.

When they finished the project, she put the picture together with the others she had prepared for the show.

"Winston looks great," Carson said, satisfied. "I can't

wait for the show. I was afraid maybe you wouldn't want to hang my picture because Dad kept bothering you."

"Are you kidding?" She ushered Carson out of the back room into the gallery and closed the door behind them. "I'd never let my personal feelings get in the way of hanging a beautiful picture like yours. Wouldn't be good business."

"Great-Granddad says all business is personal. People just don't like to admit it."

"Everyone knows that your great-grandfather is brilliant when it comes to business."

"Yeah." Carson looked proud. "He says I'm gonna be brilliant at business, too. He says that in a few years I'll be running my own company."

"Is that what you want to do?"

"Sure."

She hid a smile. There was not so much as a flicker of doubt in the words. "Nice to know where you're going so early in life."

"Uh-huh." Carson's small brow puckered slightly. "Thanks for going out with Dad last night."

"You're welcome."

"He's been acting a little weird lately."

"I'm sorry to hear that."

"It's not your fault." Carson's expression was intent and very serious now. "It's just that everyone keeps telling him that he oughta get a new wife so I can have a new mom."

"Pressure."

"Yeah. That's what Uncle Rafe and Uncle Gabe say. I heard Granddad tell Grandma not to put so much pressure on Dad, but she and Aunt Lillian and Aunt Hannah all say he needs some pressure."

"Hmm."

"They think Dad doesn't want to get married again because he's still sad about my mom being in heaven and all."

"Well, that may be true," she said gently.

"Maybe." Carson was clearly dubious. "I don't remember her, but Dad does. He says she was really pretty and she loved me a lot."

"I'm sure she did love you very much, Carson."

"Yeah, and everyone says Dad loved her. But I don't think that's the reason he doesn't want to get married again. He told me once that if you lose someone, it doesn't mean you won't fall in love with someone else someday."

This was dangerous territory, she thought. Time to change the subject.

"Carson, maybe it would be better if we talked about something else."

He ignored that, intent on making his point. "I think Dad just hasn't found a lady he really, really likes, you know?"

"Quite possible." She went behind the counter and pulled out a sheet of paper. "Now, then, I'm trying to decide how to hang the children's pictures. I've made a little map of the gallery. Want to help me choose a good spot for Winston?"

"Okay." He scrambled up onto the stool. "What about you, Miss Brightwell?"

That gave her pause. "Me?"

"Have you ever found a man you really, really like and want to marry?"

"Not yet." She picked up a pencil.

"Think you will someday?"

"Maybe. I hope so. I'd love to have a son like you someday."

"Yeah?" Carson looked pleased. "You could have a kid of your own if you get married."

"Yes." Way past time to change the subject. She pulled the gallery floor plan closer so that they could both view it. "Now, then, the first thing we have to keep in mind is that the pictures all have to be hung at the right height so that people your age can see them properly."

He studied the floor plan. "Not too high."

"Right." She sketched some pictures on a display panel. "I was thinking of grouping them according to the age of the artists, but I'm wondering if it might be better to arrange them by subject, instead."

"You mean like put all the animal pictures together?"

"Exactly." She made some more notations on the piece of paper. "In addition to your picture of Winston, I received a lot of pictures of horses and one or two cow portraits."

"You didn't get any other dogs besides Winston, did you?" he asked quickly.

"Not yet."

"Good. That means mine will be the best."

"I sense a certain streak of competitiveness here."

"Huh?"

"Everyone knows that Hartes are very goal-oriented. They like to win."

"Great-Granddad says winning is a lot better than losing."

"I'm not surprised to hear that. I suspect it's a family motto. And there's certainly some truth to it. But that viewpoint overlooks the fact that not all situations have to be viewed in terms of win-lose."

"Huh?"

She smiled. "Never mind. I was just thinking out loud.

The point is, the Children's Art Show is not a competition. There won't be any prize for the best picture."

"Oh." He shrugged and let it go. "Mind if I ask you a question?"

"What is it?"

Carson looked up from the floor plan. "Do you like my dad, Miss Brightwell?"

She was amazed when she did not miss a beat in her response. "Yes, I do."

"A lot?"

"I like him enough to go out with him," she said cautiously.

"He likes you, too. A lot. That's why he called you so many times. He didn't mean to make you mad or anything."

"Carson, I really don't think—"

"He never, ever asked a lady to go out so many times after she turned him down once or twice."

She wrinkled her nose, amused in spite of herself. "I suspect that I may have unwittingly aroused those Harte competitive instincts we were just talking about." *Aroused* might not have been quite the right word under the circumstances, she thought. "Make that *triggered*."

"Huh?"

"That attitude about winning that we discussed a moment ago. It's possible that your father decided that persuading me to go out with him was a sort of game. He wanted to win, so he kept calling me until I said yes."

"Oh." Carson gave that some thought and then shook his head. "Nah. I don't think that's how it is with him. Dad says he doesn't like people who play games."

"Neither do I." Resolutely she turned back to the floor plan. "I think that the house pictures would look good on the two panels in the center of the room. What do you think?"

The door of the gallery opened. She looked up quickly, expecting to see Nick returning from the mail run. But it was Jeremy Seaton who strolled into the showroom.

He was good-looking in an angular way. His light-brown hair was cut in a close, conservative style as befitted a member of the institute staff. His clothes were left over from his days in academia: khaki trousers, an open-throated, button-down shirt, and expensive-looking loafers.

"Good morning, Jeremy. Something tells me you've heard about the Upsall."

"Yep. Couldn't resist coming by to see it for myself." He gave her a quick, easy smile and then looked at Carson. "I know you. You're Nick Harte's son, right? You're looking more like your dad every day. I'll bet you don't remember me. We haven't seen much of each other in the last couple of years. I'm Jeremy Seaton."

Carson shook his head. "I don't remember."

"Figured you wouldn't. Well, it doesn't matter. Your dad and I used to hang out together a lot in the old days."

Carson looked intrigued. "You knew Dad when he was a kid?"

"Sure did. We played some baseball together. And when we got a little older we also played a little pool down at the Total Eclipse."

"What else did you do?" Carson asked eagerly.

Jeremy stroked his jaw, looking thoughtful. "As I recall, we spent an inordinate amount of time cruising up and down Bayview Drive on Friday and Saturday nights showing off our cars and trying to get girls to look at us. Wasn't a whole lot to do here in Eclipse Bay in those days."

"Still isn't, as far as I can tell," Nick said from the doorway. "Hello, Jeremy. Been a while."

Octavia could have sworn that the temperature in the gallery plummeted at least twenty or thirty degrees. There was a definite chill in the air.

Jeremy lowered his hand and turned around with a deliberate air and a politely bland expression. "Harte." His tone remained civil, but all the warmth had leached out of it. "Heard you were in town for the summer."

"Heard you've taken up full-time residence and got yourself a job at the institute," Nick said in a voice that was equally lacking in inflection. "Giving up the academic life for good?"

The gallery was flooded with toxic levels of testosterone. Nick and Jeremy might have been good friends in the past, Octavia thought, but something had gone very wrong somewhere along the line.

"Thought I'd try something a little different," Jeremy said. "Everyone needs a change once in a while. How's the writing going?"

"Swell."

"Rumor at the post office this morning is that you're planning to use Octavia here to help with some in-depth research for your next book," Jeremy said coolly.

"You've lived in Eclipse Bay long enough to know better than to listen to post office gossip."

"I sure wouldn't want to think that there was any truth to the rumors I heard today."

"When you get right down to it, it doesn't much matter if there's any truth to them or not," Nick said. "Either way, it's none of your business."

Confusion and something that might have been the beginnings of unease appeared in Carson's small face. She knew exactly how he felt, Octavia thought. This uncomfortable little scene had gone far enough.

"I've got the Upsall in my back room, Jeremy," she said briskly. "Come around behind the counter and I'll show it to you. You know something about art. I'd be interested to get your opinion."

Neither of the two men looked at her. They watched each other with the air of two lions facing off over a downed zebra.

*I definitely do not look good in stripes,* Octavia thought.

She cleared her throat. "Gentlemen, if you wish to continue this conversation, you may do so outside. I would like to remind you that there is a minor present. I would suggest you find someplace private where you can make idiots of yourselves without an audience."

That got their attention. Both men turned toward her. The chill in their eyes would have thawed a frozen pizza in two seconds flat.

"Can't wait to see the Upsall," Jeremy said tonelessly.

"This way." She spun around and walked back into the room behind the counter.

Jeremy followed. Nick came to stand in the opening. He did not enter the room. Carson hovered at his side.

"What's an Upsall?" Carson asked.

Octavia unwrapped the painting with a small flourish. "This," she said, "is an Upsall. I think."

Carson studied the swirling storm of color on the canvas. "Cool. Looks like the painter dropped a big bucket of paint and it splashed all over the place."

Nick's mouth twitched. "Couldn't have said it better, myself."

Jeremy said nothing, intent on the canvas. After a few moments of frowning scrutiny, he crouched in front of the painting and examined the brushstrokes in the corner of the canvas.

"Well?" Octavia asked. "What do you think?"

"It's certainly his style. Upsall had a way of putting paint on canvas that was very distinctive."

"Yes. That's how he obtained such incredible depth of color. It could be a copy, of course, but it looks like there's several decades worth of dirt and grime on it."

"Which means that if it was a copy, it was made years ago."

"Upsall's work didn't become popular until recently," Octavia said. "There wouldn't have been any incentive for someone to take the time and trouble to forge one of his paintings several decades back."

"Could be the work of an admirer or a student," Jeremy said, sounding doubtful. "What are the odds that an original Upsall has been sitting in old man Thurgarton's house all these years?"

"I'm no expert," Nick said from the doorway. "But following your logic, Seaton, what are the chances that Thurgarton would have had an excellent copy of the work of an obscure artist?"

Jeremy did not look at him. "Like you said, you're no expert."

"But Nick does have a point," Octavia said firmly. "It would be just as difficult to explain a fine copy as it would an original. All things considered, I'm strongly inclined to stick with my first instincts. I think this is a genuine Upsall. I'm planning to get a second opinion next week, though, just to be sure."

Jeremy straightened and shoved his hands into the pockets of his trousers. He continued to regard the painting for another long moment. Then he nodded once, abruptly.

"I think you're right," he said. "It's an Upsall. Which means that Arizona Snow, Virgil Nash, and the Heralds are all about to get a very nice windfall."

"Looks like it." Octavia rewrapped the painting.

"Who'd have believed it?" Jeremy shook his head. "A genuine Upsall hidden away in Eclipse Bay."

Nick smiled with icy amusement. "Who says Eclipse Bay isn't the center of the art world?"

# chapter 8

Another summer storm was headed toward Eclipse Bay. Not a yippy little terrier of a storm like the one that had scampered through town last night and left everything damp. This one promised to be a real monster. It prowled and paced, sucking up energy from the sea while it waited for the cover of darkness.

Octavia stopped at the far end of the short stretch of beach and stood looking out over the quietly seething water. The tide was out. The brooding sensation was back.

A couple of days ago she had convinced herself that leaving Eclipse Bay at the end of the season was the right thing to do. Now she was not so certain. The strange feeling that she could not depart until she had accomplished whatever it was that she had come here to do had descended on her again.

Was her imagination going into high gear? Or was she already coming up with excuses to delay the day she

walked away from Eclipse Bay and Nick and Carson
Harte?

A shiver went through her. This was not good. This was
risky rationalization and she did not do risky stuff. According to Claudia, the tendency to play it safe and not
take chances was a major failing. She could still hear her
aunt's words ringing in her head.

*You know what I want you to do after I'm gone? I want
you to go out and raise a little hell. Live it up. Take some
chances. Life is too damned short as it is. You want to get
to my age and have nothing interesting to look back on?*

Okay, so she'd taken a mini-chance last night and what
did she have to show for it? She'd cooked dinner for Nick
Harte. Big deal. She'd kicked him out of the cottage before
she'd even discovered whether or not he was sufficiently
interested in having mad, passionate sex with her to bother
to give her The Talk.

Playing it safe.

She had set out to walk off the restlessness after getting
home from the gallery, but the exercise wasn't working as
therapy. It was tempting to blame her mood on the advancing storm, but she knew there were other factors at
work. One of them was the memory of the tension she had
witnessed between Nick and Jeremy earlier that day.

Why was she allowing the thinly veiled hostility that
had shimmered between those two get to her? It wasn't her
problem if they had issues. She had her own issues. She
had a business to sell. That sort of enterprise required planning and care. And then there was the move away from
Eclipse Bay to engineer. For starters, she had to make
arrangements to ship all of the stuff she had brought here.
What on earth had made her bring so many of her personal

treasures to the cottage? She should have left them at her apartment in Portland.

But the apartment in the city had always had a temporary feel. She had not been tempted to try to settle in there. It was her cottage here in Eclipse Bay that she had tried to turn into a home.

Lots of issues.

Nick Harte.

Yes, indeed. Nick Harte was a big issue.

What was it about him that drew her? He was not her type. She had more in common with Jeremy Seaton, when you got right down to it.

This was getting her nowhere. Brooding was a waste of time and energy and it never, in her experience, resulted in good outcomes. The negative feelings simply fed on themselves and got heavier and more bleak.

It was time to get a grip. Take charge. Act responsibly.

She turned and started determinedly back along the beach.

She had almost reached the bottom of the cliff path when the overwhelming, primordial knowledge that she was not alone jangled her senses.

She looked up quickly and caught her breath when she saw Nick standing at the top of the bluff. The ominous early twilight generated by the oncoming storm etched him in mystery. His dark hair was ruffled by the growling wind. His black windbreaker was open, revealing the black pullover and jeans he wore underneath. Too bad there wasn't a photographer around, she thought. This shot would have been perfect for the back cover photo on one of his books.

For a timeless moment it was as if she'd been frozen by some powerful force, unable to move, barely able to breathe. But an acute awareness arced through her, raising the small hairs on the back of her arms. She ought to be getting used to the sensation, she thought. Nick Harte had this effect on her a lot.

With an effort, she forced herself to move through the oddly charged atmosphere and started up the cliff path. She climbed carefully, conscious of how the wind was whipping her long, white skirt around her legs.

"Looks like the weather people missed the call on this storm," Nick said when she reached the top. He glanced toward the looming chaos that threatened on the horizon. "Going to be a lot stronger than they predicted."

"Yes." She held her hair out of her face. "What are you doing here, Nick?"

"I brought dinner." His tone was casual to the point of careless, but his eyes were anything but casual. A dangerous energy crackled there in the blue depths. "Unless you've got other plans?"

She'd had some plans, she thought. But none of them sounded nearly as interesting as dinner with Nick. Or as reckless.

"You cooked dinner?" she asked, buying herself a little time to analyze the situation before she did something really, really risky like invite him into her cottage.

His mouth curved in a rakish grin that showed some teeth.

"Now, why would I sweat over a hot stove all afternoon when I've acquired a brother-in-law who owns and operates a restaurant?"

She found herself smiling in spite of the invisible lightning in the air. "Good question."

"I brought a picnic basket that is stuffed to the hilt with some of Rafe's finest delicacies. Interested?"

*Live it up. Take some chances. Life is too damn short. . . .*

She breathed deep, inhaling the intoxicating vapors of the oncoming storm. "Are you kidding? If Rafe did the cooking, I'm more than interested. I'm enthralled."

"You know, I always knew that guy would turn out to be useful someday, even if he is a Madison."

"Where's Carson?"

"At Dreamscape."

"Handy built-in baby-sitting setup you've got there."

"I figure I'm doing Rafe and Hannah a favor by giving them a little hands-on practice."

She tilted her head a little. "Do they need practice?"

"Yeah. They're expecting. But don't say anything, okay? They're still in the process of notifying everyone in the family."

"A baby." A sweet, vicarious joy rushed through her. "That's *wonderful*. How exciting. When?"

"Uh, you'll have to ask Hannah. I forgot to check the date."

"How could you forget to ask when the baby is due?"

"I forgot, okay? So sue me."

"Men."

"Hey, I brought dinner. I think that's pushing the envelope of the SG thing far enough, don't you?"

"SG thing?"

"Sensitive Guy."

She arranged the contents of the picnic basket on the glass-topped dining room table while Nick built a fire. Rafe had outdone himself, she thought. There was an array of appetizing dishes including a beautiful vegetable pâté, curried potato salad studded with fresh green peas, cold asparagus spears dressed in hollandaise sauce, little savory pastries filled with shrimp, and cold soba noodles steeped in a ginger-flavored marinade. There were also homemade pickles, Greek olives, and crusty bread from the Incandescent Body. A bottle of pinot noir bearing the label of an exclusive Oregon vintner rounded out the menu. Dessert consisted of tiny raspberry tarts.

"Oh, my," she murmured appreciatively. "This is lovely. Absolutely spectacular. And to think that I was going to fix a plain green salad for dinner. Rafe is amazing."

"Enough about Rafe," Nick said. He struck a match and held it to the kindling. "Let's talk about me."

"What about you?"

"I want full credit for selecting the wine."

"Well, I suppose I can give you that." She glanced at the label. "It's a very nice wine."

"Thanks." He uncoiled to his feet, crossed the room, and took the bottle from her. "I'll have you know that I went through almost every bottle of red in Rafe's cellar looking for it."

"A dirty job, but someone had to do it, right?"

"Damn right."

He carried the pinot noir into the kitchen, found the corkscrew, and went to work with a few deft, economical movements.

A moment later he poured wine into two glasses. He handed one of the glasses to her and raised his own in a small salute.

"To Hannah and Rafe and the baby," he said.

She smiled and touched her glass to his. "And to the end of the Harte-Madison feud. May you all live long and happy lives."

He paused, the glass partway to his mouth, and slowly lowered it. "You sound like you're saying goodbye."

"I am, in a way." She took a sip of the wine. "I've been in a strange place for the past few months—"

"Yeah, Eclipse Bay is a little weird, isn't it?"

"—but I think I've treaded water long enough."

"You're entitled to tread water for a while after you lose someone you love, you know."

"I know. But Aunt Claudia would have been the first to tell me to get on with my life." She did not want to pursue that topic, she thought. She turned away and opened a cupboard to select some of the green glass dishes she stored inside. "Mind if I ask what that scene at the gallery was about today?"

"Any chance I can get away with asking, 'What scene?' "

"No." She looked at him over her shoulder as she took the plates out of the cupboard. "But I suppose you could tell me to mind my own business."

He leaned back against the tiled counter and contemplated the bloodred wine in his glass for a moment. She knew that whatever he was going to tell her, it was not going to be the whole truth and nothing but.

"Jeremy and I go back a ways. We alternated between being buddies and friendly rivals in the old days here in Eclipse Bay. Competed a little with our cars and—"

"Getting dates with fast women?" she finished lightly.

"Fast women, sad to say, were always pretty scarce around Eclipse Bay."

"Too bad. Go on, what happened with you and Jeremy?"

"We had some adventures. Got into some trouble. Raised a little hell. We stayed in touch in college and we both wound up working in Portland. He took a position as an instructor at a college there and I dutifully tried to fulfill my filial obligations at Harte Investments. And then—"

Then, what?"

He shrugged and drank some more wine. "Then he got married. I got married, too. Things changed."

"You lost track of each other?"

"Life happens, you know?"

"Sounds to me like the two of you did more than just drift apart." She carried the plates past him into the living room. "Today I got the impression that there's some serious tension between you two. Did something happen to cause it?"

"Yesterday's news." He prowled after her and settled into a chair near the window. His expression made it clear that he was about to change the topic. "How are things going with the Children's Art Show project?"

Well, it wasn't as though she had any right to push him for answers to questions she'd had no business asking in the first place, she thought.

She gave him her brightest smile and sank down onto the arm of the sofa. The embroidered hem of her long white skirt drifted around her ankles. Swinging one foot lightly, she took a fortifying sip of wine.

"Very well," she said, lowering her glass. "I'm quite pleased. I think I'm going to have nearly a hundred entries. Not bad for a small town like this."

"No." He stole a glance at her gently swinging ankle. "Not bad."

• • •

The casual thing worked right up until the full fury of the storm struck land. She was washing the last of the dishes when the lights flickered twice and went out.

The sudden onslaught of darkness paralyzed her briefly. Her hands stilled in the soapy water. "Oh, damn."

"Take it easy," Nick said from somewhere nearby. "We lose power all the time around here during big storms. Don't suppose you have an emergency generator?"

"No."

"Flashlight?"

She cleared her throat. "Well, yes, as it happens, I do have a flashlight. A nice, big red one with a special high-intensity bulb and an easy-grip handle that I bought last winter after a major storm. It is a model of cutting-edge, modern technology. So powerful that it can be used to signal for help if one happens to be lost at sea or on a mountain."

"I sense a *but* coming."

"But I forgot to buy some batteries for it."

He laughed softly in the darkness and came to stand directly behind her. "Spoken like a real city girl. Don't worry about it, I've got a flashlight in the car."

"Somehow that doesn't surprise me."

He put out his hands and gripped the tiled counter edge on either side of her body. In the shadows she was intensely aware of the heat of his body so close to hers. There was suddenly so much electricity being generated both outside and inside the cottage that she was amazed the lights did not come back on. Probably ought to get her hands out of the dishwater, she thought. A woman could have a major household accident in a situation like this.

Nick put his lips very close to her ear. "I was a Boy Scout. You know what that means?"

"Something to do with being thrifty and neat?"

"Wrong." He grazed her earlobe with his teeth.

"Something to do with getting to wear a cute uniform?"

"Try again." He touched his mouth to her throat.

"Something to do with always keeping spare batteries on hand?"

"You're getting closer. Much closer." He kissed her throat. "Something to do with always being prepared."

"Oh, yeah." She yanked her hands out of the sudsy water and grabbed a dishtowel. "I've heard about the always being prepared thing."

He tightened the cage of his body around her so that her backside was nestled snugly into his thighs. She realized at once that he was aroused. Her senses registered that information and responded with a shot of adrenaline. Her pulse raced. There was a faint trembling in her fingertips. Not fear, she thought. Excitement.

"I take the motto seriously." He brushed his lips along the curve of her throat just below her earlobe. "And not just when it comes to things like flashlight batteries."

She was abruptly grateful for the inky shadows of the kitchen. At least he could not see the flush of heat that was surely setting fire to her cheeks.

"You taste good," he whispered. "Better than those little raspberry things we had for dessert."

There was a new, rougher edge in his voice and she was the cause. All that was female in her rejoiced. Outside, the wind howled. Here in the dark kitchen, power flowed.

He kissed her throat again, his mouth gliding up along the underside of her jaw. She reveled in the intense pleasure and the heady rush of anticipation.

This was why she had tried to keep her distance, she remembered. This was precisely the reason she had been so careful these past few weeks, why she had worked so hard to find so many excuses to decline his invitations. She had known it would be like this: dangerous and unpredictable and very high risk.

And also incredibly exhilarating and intoxicating.

He must have felt her body's response because he shifted again, pressing closer still until she could feel him, hard and muscled, along the full length of her own much softer frame. The contrast thrilled her senses. The mysteries of yin and yang in action.

There was no room to move now inside the cage he had made for her. He had enclosed her in a seductive snare she had no desire to escape.

An urgent, drawing sensation traveled up the insides of her legs and pooled in her lower body. She dropped the dishtowel and clutched at the counter edge for support. Her head tipped back against his shoulder. She savored the strength and power in him and told herself that she would not give in to the almost overwhelming urge to purr.

"I don't think we're going to need that flashlight for a while," he whispered. "We can do this in the dark."

He let go of the counter and put his hands on her at last. His fingers closed around her, spinning her toward him. He pulled her fiercely into his arms. His mouth closed over hers with the inevitability of the steel door of a bank vault slamming shut.

The wild chaos of the storm outside was suddenly swirling here in her tiny kitchen. One glorious rush after another swept through her, leaving her trembling with need and anticipation. She wanted him, she thought. She needed this night with Nick. She owed this to herself.

She almost laughed aloud. Was she good at rationalizing, or what?

"Going to let me in on the joke?" he asked into her hair.

"Trust me, this is no joke."

She put her arms around his neck and kissed him with all of the searing, pent-up hunger and desire that had been making her so restless these past few weeks.

He picked her up and carried her into the living room. The glowing embers of the fire cast an enchanted golden light on the scene. Her head spun a little and her feet left the earth. The next thing she knew, she was lying flat on her back on the rug in front of the hearth.

He followed her down onto the floor, sprawling across her, anchoring her beneath him with one heavy leg flung across hers, his weight pushing her into the thick wool. She pushed her hands up under his pullover until she touched bare skin.

He undid the long row of buttons that closed her white linen blouse and then he unfastened the next set, the ones that sealed her long, white skirt.

"This is like opening a birthday present," he said when he reached her waist. "I've got this nearly overpowering urge to just rip into it."

"I know just how you feel," she said, struggling to free him of his sweater.

He laughed a little and sat up briefly beside her. Crossing his arms at his waist, he grasped the hem of the garment and hauled it off over his head in a single fluid movement.

"Much better." She smiled appreciatively at the sight of his firelit shoulders. "Much, much better."

Deeply intrigued by the ripple of skin over muscle, she reached out one hand and threaded her fingers through the crisp hair that covered his chest. He sucked in his breath and groaned.

He went back to work, unfastening buttons one by one until he reached the hem of her skirt.

"Best present I've had in a long, long time." He put one hand on her bare skin just above the band of her white lace panties. He flexed his fingers gently. "Definitely worth the wait."

The touch of his big, warm palm on her midsection sent shock waves through her. She stirred, feeling sinuous and incredibly sexy beneath his touch.

He leaned over her to take her mouth again. His fingers moved, sliding up her rib cage to rest just beneath her breasts. By the time the kiss had ended she was no longer wearing her bra.

He moved his lips to one nipple and tugged. She gasped and sank her nails into the contoured muscles of his back.

Time became meaningless. The wild night flowed around them, closing them off from the outside world. She was vaguely aware of the winds raging outside the cottage, but here in this intimate, magical place there was another reality, a world where every move brought new wonders and new discoveries.

When Nick found the tight, throbbing nub that was the epicenter of the small storm taking place inside her, he stroked lightly with fingers he had dampened in her own dew. At the same time he slid two more fingers just inside and probed gently.

Without warning, the gathering energy that had created such a delicious tension exploded. She barely had time to cry out in surprise before she tumbled headlong into a bottomless pool.

When she eventually surfaced, she was breathless and joyous with the pure pleasure of it all.

Nick looked bemused by her reaction. His mouth curved slightly. "You okay?"

"Oh, yes. Yes, indeed, I am very okay." She drew her fingertips slowly down his chest and belly until she could cup his heavy erection. "Never better. Yourself?"

He grinned slowly, a sexy, anticipatory smile that sent little sparkling shards of excitement through her.

"Going to be okay real soon," he promised.

He settled heavily between her thighs. In the firelight his face was tight and hard with the effort he was exerting to maintain his control. He used one hand to guide himself carefully into her.

He was larger than she had anticipated. In spite of the unbearable sense of urgency and readiness, she was startled by the tight, full feeling.

*"Nick."*

He paused midway.

"Don't you dare stop now." She grabbed his head in both hands, spearing her fingers into his hair, and lifted herself against him.

He plunged the rest of the way, filling her completely. When they were locked together he levered himself up on his elbows and looked down at her. His expression was one of desire and passion and other forces too strange and wondrous for her to label with words. But she knew the power of those driving, elemental waves of raw energy. She knew them in her heart and soul because they were sweeping through her, too.

Nick began to move, gliding cautiously at first. But when she tightened her legs around his waist, he made a hoarse, husky sound and drove himself into her in a series of fierce, swift thrusts that seemed beyond his control.

She felt the intensity of his climax in every muscle of his body, heard it in his guttural shout of satisfaction.

When he collapsed on top of her she could barely breathe. She stroked his back from shoulder to hip. He was slick with perspiration. He was giving off so much heat you'd have thought that he was in the grip of a raging fever.

All in all, she thought, it was a wonderful way to go.

A cold draft woke her sometime later. She realized it was coming from the front door. Nick was leaving.

The shock of it brought her wide awake. She scrambled to her feet, clutching the chenille throw around herself.

"Nick?"

"Right here." He closed the door. "I just brought the flashlight in from the car. I'll leave it here on the hall table."

"Oh. Thanks." Maybe she'd been a bit hasty in assuming that he was running out on her already.

"No problem." He glanced at his watch. "It's after midnight. I'd better be going."

He *was* leaving. Couldn't wait to be on his way. Outrage and pain knifed through her. Well? What had she expected? This was Nick Harte, after all. He wasn't exactly famous for hanging around until breakfast. It wasn't as if she hadn't known exactly what she was getting into when she went into his arms earlier.

But it still hurt far more than it should. This was why she preferred to avoid risks, she thought. There were good, solid reasons for not opening yourself up to this kind of pain.

Nick crossed the small space that separated them and kissed her lightly.

"Carson and I will stop in at the gallery when we come into town to pick up the mail."

He turned without waiting for a response, slung his jacket over his shoulder, and went back toward the door.

"That would be nice," she mumbled.

He paused, one hand on the doorknob. "Is there a problem here?"

"Aren't you forgetting something?" she asked evenly.

"Such as?"

"The Talk."

A terrible stillness came over him.

"You know about The Talk?" he asked carefully.

She was beginning to wish that she had kept her mouth shut. Maybe she would have had the sense to do just that if she hadn't been jolted out of her very pleasant dreams to find him already dressed and headed for the door.

"Everyone knows about The Talk," she said crossly.

"Is that so?" He sounded irritated. "You shouldn't believe every bit of gossip you hear about me."

"You mean it's not true about The Talk?"

He opened the door, letting in another gust of wet air. "I've got no intention of discussing the details of my private life at this particular moment."

"Why not?" Her chin came up. "None of my business?"

"No," he said grimly. "It isn't. But just so we're clear on this subject, I'd like to point out that we've already had The Talk."

"Is that so?" she asked in icy accents. "I don't recall it."

"Then you've got a short-term memory problem, lady."

"Don't you dare try to wriggle out of this." She strode forward, clutching the chenille throw to her throat, and came to a halt directly in front of him. She jabbed a forefinger against his chest. "You did *not* give me The Talk. I wouldn't have forgotten something like that."

"No," he agreed coolly. "I didn't deliver it. You did."

That stopped her cold.

She stared at him. "I beg your pardon?"

"Don't you remember?" He moved out onto the shadowy porch. "You made it clear that you're a free spirit and that you'll be leaving at the end of the summer. Sounded to me like you weren't looking for anything other than a short-term affair."

"Hang on here, I never said anything of the kind. You're putting words in my mouth."

"Trust me." He flicked on a little penlight and started down the front steps. "I know The Talk when I hear it."

She was too dumbfounded to speak for a moment. By the time she had recovered, he was in the car, driving away into the night.

She abruptly realized that her bare feet were very cold.

# chapter 9

"What do you think is going on?" Lillian asked on the other end of the line.

"I think they've started an affair." Hannah glanced out into the hall to make sure no one was eavesdropping on her conversation with her sister.

Satisfied that she and Winston had the office to themselves, she closed the door and went back to the chair behind the desk. Winston, stretched out on his belly on the rug, watched her alertly.

It was obvious that he sensed her tension.

"You're sure they're involved?" Lillian asked.

"Yes. You should have seen him last night when he came back here to pick up Carson. Whatever is going on between those two, it's serious."

"Did he give her The Talk?"

"I don't think so. I asked him point-blank and instead of making a joke out of it, the way he usually does, he acted pissed off."

"He was mad?"

"Yes. More or less told me to mind my own business. Believe me, he was not in a good mood last night."

"Hmm."

"I know," Hannah said. "I had the same reaction."

They both fell silent for a while, thinking. Hannah looked out the window. The air was crisp and clear in the wake of the big storm. The bay was unnaturally smooth. From where she sat she could see Rafe and the two gardeners working to clear some branches that had been downed by the high winds.

"He hasn't let any woman get to him since Amelia died," Lillian said eventually.

"I know. Give me your professional opinion."

"I'm out of the matchmaking business, remember? I'm an artist now."

"You must still have some instincts. Your intuition when it came to figuring out couples was always amazing."

"My instincts aren't any good when it comes to those two," Lillian said honestly. "I tried to read the situation that night when I saw them together at my show there in Eclipse Bay. I got nothing. A complete blank."

"Does that mean it's a bad match?"

"No, it means I just couldn't tell one way or the other. It's hard to explain, but it was as if there was some sort of invisible glass shield between them and my intuition. I couldn't get past it. Whatever is going on with those two is as much a mystery to me as it is to you."

"Personally, I'm hoping she's the one for Nick. I really like Octavia, and Carson adores her."

That caught Lillian's attention. "Carson likes her?"

"Yes. I've never seen him like this with any of the other

women Nick has dated. You'd think he was trying to do a little matchmaking himself."

"Interesting." Lillian pondered that briefly. "Of course, in all fairness, Carson has never had much opportunity to get to know any of Nick's other girlfriends."

"That's because Nick has always gone out of his way to keep that part of his life compartmentalized and separate from his life with Carson. This time it's different. That's my big point here. The very fact that Nick has allowed Carson to develop a personal relationship of his own with Octavia is a very strong indicator that this is not business as usual. Don't you agree?"

"Maybe. Depends."

"On what?"

"Well, it could be that Nick isn't deliberately allowing Carson to get to know Octavia. It may just be the circumstances. Eclipse Bay isn't a big city. There's no way Nick could have a clandestine affair here. It's impossible to keep one's private life private in this town."

"And nobody knows that better than Nick. Yet he made the decision to spend the summer here and it looks to me as if he has actively encouraged Carson to form an attachment to Octavia. I swear, they find an excuse to stop by her gallery every single day when they go into town to pick up the mail or shop for groceries."

"All right, I agree that isn't Nick's usual M.O. when it comes to women and his personal life," Lillian said thoughtfully. "Could be significant. You're sure he hasn't had The Talk with her?"

"Almost positive. It may mean that he's finally ready to move beyond the loss of Amelia."

"About time," Lillian said.

"Hey, he's a Harte. When Hartes fall in love, they fall hard."

"Mmm."

"What's this?" A flicker of alarm wafted through Hannah. She exchanged a concerned look with Winston, who promptly got to his feet and crossed the small space to put his head on her knee. "You don't believe that Nick has really become Hardhearted Harte, do you?"

"I think," Lillian said carefully, "that there may have been more problems in his relationship with Amelia than he ever let on."

"I know you were never fully satisfied that they were a great match. But there is no absolutely perfect match. And it doesn't mean that Nick didn't love Amelia deeply."

"No. It doesn't mean that," Lillian agreed. "But I've always wondered if it was Nick's decision to leave Harte Investments that exposed the underlying weaknesses in that marriage. If Amelia had lived, they might have worked things out. For Carson's sake, if nothing else. She loved him as much as Nick does."

"Yes. Amelia was a good mother." Hannah touched her still-flat stomach. She had not yet grown accustomed to the sense of wonder that accompanied the realization of the small miracle that was taking place inside her. "No one would ever say otherwise. Especially not in front of Nick."

"True. But if I'm right and there were some serious problems in that marriage, it might explain why Nick has been so careful to avoid a serious relationship in the years since Amelia's death."

"Protecting himself? You think he's afraid of making another mistake?"

"He's a Harte. We're not supposed to screw up when it

comes to love and marriage, remember? We're supposed to get it right every time."

"If he didn't get it right last time, he might be doubly cautious this time."

"Yes, and with good reason. After all, it isn't just himself he has to protect this time around. He's got Carson to consider, too."

Hannah hesitated a moment. "Speaking of children. . . ."

Okay, so she'd over overreacted.

*So sue me,* Octavia thought.

She pulled into the parking lot at the end of the row of shops and switched off the engine. A woman had a right to be angry when she surfaced after a bout of mind-bending sex and discovered that the man with whom she had just shared said mind-bending sex was heading for the door.

The least he could have done was make a bigger show of regretting the unseemly haste of his departure. And how dare he accuse her of giving him The Talk? All right, she had mentioned leaving town at the end of the summer once or twice. That was different.

She got out of the car, dropped the keys into her purse, and slammed the door shut. She was feeling short of both temper and patience, and more than willing to blame everything on Nick this morning. Her emotions were so mixed up and so unstable today that she knew she could not begin to sort them out.

One thing was indisputable, however. She was well aware that she had no one to blame but herself for this untenable situation and that, of course, only made the mess all the more irritating. She had known what she was getting into when she made the decision to take some chances with Hardhearted Harte.

It occurred to her that, in addition to feeling pissed off, she also felt strong and decisive this morning. Energetic. Bold. Powerful. Gutsy.

She stopped in the middle of the sidewalk, struck by that realization.

Everything seemed sharper and clearer today. She was intensely aware of the bright sun and the glare of the light on the bay. She was eager to open the gallery and frame the rest of the children's pictures.

Yes, she was mad as hell at Nick Harte, but even the anger felt good—cleansing in some weird way that she could not explain.

She was almost at the door of the gallery when she belatedly remembered Nick's flashlight. She had left it in the backseat.

With a groan, she turned around and went back to the parking lot to retrieve it. This time she made herself close the car door very gently.

Doing the mature thing.

The power had not failed in the heart of Eclipse Bay, she noticed. The lights inside the gallery worked when she flipped the switch and the security system was still functional. She punched in the code to disarm it and went around the counter to open the door of the back room.

The instant she stepped inside she knew that something was wrong.

It took her a couple of seconds to focus on what it was that seemed different. Then it hit her.

The Upsall was gone.

•   •   •

He could not figure out where things had gone wrong last night.

He was still brooding over the disastrous ending to what had been a great evening when he pulled into the slot next to Octavia's little white compact the next morning and turned off the engine.

"Hey, look," Carson said excitedly from the backseat. "A police car."

Nick turned his head and frowned when he saw the familiar logo of Eclipse Bay's tiny police department emblazoned on the door of an SUV parked at the curb. "That's Chief Valentine's vehicle. Probably had some problems with the security systems in the shops because of the storm."

"Here comes A.Z.," Carson added.

Nick got out of the BMW and watched Arizona park her pickup while Carson scrambled out of the rear seat. When she climbed from the truck and started toward them, he raised a hand in greeting.

"'Morning, A.Z.," Nick said.

Carson waved. "Hi, A.Z."

"'Morning, you two." Beneath the rakish tilt of her military beret, Arizona's expression was that of a battlefield commander readying herself for action. "Expect you already heard we got us some trouble here."

"Problems with the storm last night?" Nick asked.

"Reckon you could say that. Just got a call from Octavia. Looks like the gang up at the institute used the storm as cover to hit us last night."

"Come again?"

Arizona angled her head toward Sean's vehicle. "I see Valentine is on the job, but I doubt that he'll be able to accomplish much. The institute has him and every other official here in town completely bamboozled."

Another car pulled into the lot. Virgil Nash got out and started toward them.

"Good morning, Nick. Carson." Virgil looked at Arizona. "Is Photon here yet?"

"Told him to stay at the bakery and watch things there. The action here last night might be a calculated attempt to draw our attention away from Project Log Book so that they can get at the computer."

Out of long habit, Nick automatically sorted through Arizona's customary conspiracy spin on the situation to get to the single grain of truth at the center.

"What action?" he said abruptly. "Did something happen here last night?"

Arizona angled her chin. "The institute crowd broke into the gallery and snatched our Upsall."

Nick glanced at Virgil for clarification.

Virgil did not look particularly reassuring. "I got a call, too. That's why I'm here. Looks like the Upsall's gone."

*"Octavia."* Nick grabbed Carson's hand and started toward the shop.

"What's wrong, Dad?"

"Don't worry," Virgil called after them. "Octavia's fine. The painting was gone when she arrived this morning."

Nick paid no attention. He kept going toward the shop, moving so swiftly that Carson had to run to keep up with him.

"Is Octavia okay, Dad?" Carson asked anxiously.

They reached the open door of Bright Visions at that moment. Nick halted at the sight of Octavia inside. The first thing he noticed was that she wasn't wearing one of her usual icy-pale fairy queen dresses today. Instead she was dressed in a short jumper in a bright shade of purple. The golden-yellow boatneck tee shirt she wore underneath the dress had sleeves that came to her elbows. There was a wide amber bracelet on her wrist and more amber at her wrists and throat.

When she moved one hand in a small gesture, he noticed that she had painted her nails with a vivid crimson polish that sparkled in the morning light. He looked down and saw her bare toes peeking out from under the red leather tops of a pair of sexy, backless slides. She'd painted her toenails, too. Must have gotten up early, he thought. But then, he'd rolled out of bed at the crack of dawn himself, unable to sleep after a nearly sleepless night.

Octavia looked at him. There was fire in her eyes.

"Yeah," Nick said softly to Carson. "Octavia's okay."

Sean Valentine looked up from the notes he was making on a pad. He gave Nick a brief, friendly nod. "Morning, Harte." His somber face lightened when he caught sight of Carson. "Hey, there, Carson. How are you doing today?"

"Hey, there, Chief Valentine. I'm fine," Carson declared with delight.

Kids always responded to Sean, Nick reflected. He was not certain why. Valentine was no Officer Friendly. He carried a lot of wear and tear on his face. It was true that Sean did project a calm, professional competence, but he always looked as if he expected bad news. Children seemed to look right past the grim stuff and see something else beneath the surface, something they liked and trusted.

Nick noticed that Octavia was also watching Sean greet Carson. There was a thoughtful, reflective look on her face as though she, too, saw something in Valentine that she liked and trusted.

When she switched her gaze to Nick, however, the approval disappeared instantly from her expression.

What he got was cool appraisal. She was looking at him the way she might examine a painting that did not quite measure up to her standards.

Oh, shit. Talk about worst-case scenarios. This was bad. Very, very bad.

"Hello, Nick," she said without inflection. But when she switched her attention to Carson, the warmth returned to her voice. "Good morning, Carson. I like that shirt."

Carson beamed. He glanced down at the dark-green dinosaur emblazoned on his sweatshirt. "Thanks. It's a velociraptor. Dad bought it for me."

"I see."

"A velociraptor can rip you to shreds in seconds," Carson said cheerfully.

Octavia nodded. "I'll bear that in mind."

Nick met Sean's eyes. "What's going on here?"

"Octavia says that the painting Old Man Thurgarton left to A.Z. and Nash and the Heralds has disappeared." Sean rubbed the back of his neck. "Kind of a mystery how it happened. Apparently it was locked up in the back room and the security alarm was set as usual."

Arizona loomed in the doorway. "Getting past a standard security system would be child's play for that gang up at the institute. No offense, Carson."

"Okay," Carson said, clearly not offended.

Sean heaved a deep sigh. "I don't think we can blame anyone at the institute, A.Z. I know you're convinced that those folks up there are bent on subverting the government and running the world from their secret headquarters here in Eclipse Bay, but there's just no good motive for them to steal a painting."

"You want motive?" Arizona stalked toward the counter. "I'll give you motive. They know me and the Heralds plan to use our share of the profits from the sale of that picture to help finance our investigations. The last thing that crowd wants is for us to be able to expand the scope of our operations. If that ain't motive, I don't know what is."

Virgil Nash came through the doorway and nodded politely at everyone. He turned to Octavia. "Was the Upsall the only painting that was stolen?"

"Yes," Octavia said. "It was far and away the single most valuable picture here. Whoever took it must have known what he was doing."

Nick studied the paintings hanging on the wall and then shook his head. "I don't think you can assume that."

They all stared at him.

"What do you mean?" Octavia demanded. "The average person would probably have been more attracted to some of the scenes of the bay. Or that one." She swept out a hand to indicate the painting hanging behind her. "The watercolor with the gulls. To the untrained eye the Upsall looks dark and rather depressing."

"Probably because it is dark and depressing," Nick said.

She gave him a superior smile. "Which only goes to show how much you know about art, but that is neither here nor there."

Sean raised his brows a little at her crisp tone, but he made no comment. Instead he looked at Nick with some curiosity. "What makes you say that whoever took the picture didn't have to be an art expert?"

"The rumor that Thurgarton had left a valuable painting behind and that Octavia was going to get a second opinion on it was all over town by yesterday afternoon," Nick said mildly. "It wouldn't have taken a genius to figure out that she had it stored in the back room, and it would have been easy to recognize. Everyone was talking about how ugly it was."

Octavia did not look pleased with that quick summary. She glared. "How do you explain the thief having a key and knowing the security code?"

Nick glanced at the door. "There are usually several duplicates of a key floating around. And when was the last time the code was changed?"

She drummed her crimson nails on the counter. "It hasn't been changed since I had the Willis brothers install the system when I first opened the gallery."

Virgil frowned. "You had an assistant working here for several months. She would have had the code and the key."

"Of course," Octavia said. "But I don't think we can pin this theft on Noreen. She left town with her artist boyfriend last month, remember?"

Sean looked thoughtful. "Does anyone know where Noreen and the boyfriend are now?"

Octavia shook her head. "She just phoned in her resignation and took off. But now that you mention it, there's, uh, something else."

They all looked at her.

She grimaced. "A few days ago I came across a piece of paper with the code written on it taped inside one of the counter drawers. Noreen had trouble remembering it."

"Which means a lot of people might have had access to that code," Sean said. "Including the artist boyfriend."

Arizona snorted. "Wastin' your time, Valentine. This has the fingerprints of that bunch up at the institute all over it, I tell you."

Sean flipped his notebook shut. "One thing's for certain, Eclipse Bay isn't exactly crawling with experienced, high-end art thieves, and we don't have what you'd call a big market for stolen art, either. Whoever snatched the painting has probably already taken off for Portland or Seattle to try to unload it."

"True." Octavia slouched against the counter, looking very unhappy. "It would be the logical thing to do."

"Our best hope is that the guy trips himself up when he goes to sell the Upsall," Sean continued. "I'll call some people I know in the Seattle and Portland police departments and tell them to keep a lookout for our missing picture."

"That's an excellent idea." Octavia brightened. "I'll contact a few friends in the art world, too, and make them aware that there's a previously unknown Upsall floating around."

"Good thought," Sean said. He started toward the door. "I think that's about all for now. I'll check back later."

"All right," Octavia said. "Thanks, Sean."

"Sure. See you, folks."

A short chorus of goodbyes followed Sean out onto the sidewalk. So did Nick.

They walked together toward Sean's vehicle.

"Something I can do for you, Harte?" Sean asked mildly.

"Just wanted to ask what you think really happened to that painting."

Sean opened the door on the driver's side and paused. "You want my best guess?"

"That would probably be the most helpful under the circumstances, yeah."

"Past experience tells me that whoever stole the painting was probably closely connected to the situation. He knew the picture was valuable, he knew where it was stored, and he knew how to disarm the security system."

"Which means he had access to the code and a key."

"As you just pointed out, how hard would that be? Might not have even needed the key and code. That system the Willis brothers installed for Octavia is good enough for Eclipse Bay, but it isn't exactly state-of-the-art." Sean looked at the window of Bright Visions. "Wouldn't take a rocket scientist to disarm it, especially in the middle of the night during a major storm when no one was around."

Nick followed his gaze and shook his head in a flat negative. "Not A.Z. or Virgil."

"No. Although I gotta tell you that in this situation, any out-of-town cop would be looking real hard at both of 'em. They both have motive. Why split the profits from the painting three ways when you can have the whole pie?"

Nick shrugged. "Guess I'd have to agree that to an outsider they'd both look a little mysterious."

"Try damned suspicious. No one knows anything about either of them before they arrived in Eclipse Bay. I got curious a couple of years ago and did some digging, myself."

Nick looked at him. "Learn anything?"

"Zilch. It's like neither one of them existed before they came to this town."

"For what it's worth, there are some old rumors about them," Nick said. "My grandfather told me once that he thinks Nash may have done some government intelligence work at one time, which could explain why his past has been wiped out of the records. And most folks assume that A.Z. assumed a new identity somewhere along the way because she's so deep into her conspiracy theories. But neither of them are thieves. Rock-solid, upstanding citizens in their own weird ways."

"I'm inclined to agree."

"That leaves Photon and his happy little crew of bakers."

"Yeah. And between you and me, that bunch is right at the top of my very short list." Sean got behind the wheel and closed the door. He squinted a little against the morning sun. "I'm going to run some background checks on some of those Heralds. But keep that to yourself. I want to handle it quietly. If word gets out that the group is under suspicion, some of the locals might turn on 'em real fast."

"I know. There are still a few folks around who think they're running some kind of cult out of that bakery."

"Think I'll also track down Noreen Perkins and her new boyfriend and ask them a few questions, too."

"Why? They aren't even in town any longer."

"Just being thorough."

"Right. Catch you later."

Sean put the SUV in gear and rolled off down the street.

Nick went back into Bright Visions. He stopped just inside. Octavia, Arizona, Virgil, and Carson were all looking at him with expectant expressions.

He surveyed the ring of interested faces. "Did I miss something?"

Carson could scarcely contain himself. "Wait'll you hear A.Z.'s really cool idea, Dad."

Nick managed, just barely, not to groan aloud. He caught Octavia's attention, expecting a little understanding, maybe even some sympathy in spite of the tension between them. After all, everyone knew that any really cool idea that had been concocted by Arizona Snow was an accident waiting to happen.

But Octavia's expression reflected zero commiseration. Whatever this really cool idea was, it was getting serious consideration from her.

In desperation, Nick turned to Virgil.

"Nothing to lose," Virgil said, stroking his goatee.

"Only chance we've got and that's a fact," Arizona stated with satisfaction.

Nick surveyed each of them in turn. "Why do I have a bad feeling about this?"

Octavia cleared her throat. "Virgil's right. It probably won't work, but it's not like we have anything to lose. I say we go for it."

"Yeah!" Carson cheered.

"What, exactly, are you all planning to go for?" Nick asked warily.

"What we need here is a professional private investigator," Arizona announced. "Got to be someone we can trust. The future of Project Log Book may be riding on this."

"You're going to hire a private investigator?" Nick chuckled. "Good luck. I don't think we've got any of those in Eclipse Bay."

Arizona looked crafty. "Got one."

"Is that right?" Nick raised his brows. "Who?"

"Quit teasing, Dad." Carson bounced a little. "A.Z. means you."

"Yep." Arizona rocked on her boot-shod heels. "Far as I can tell, you're the closest we've got to the real thing here in Eclipse Bay."

# chapter 10

"Are you all crazy?" Nick planted both hands on the counter and leaned across it. His tone was low, but his jaw was granite. "I write novels about a private eye. Such books are called fiction. Do you know what fiction means? It means it is *not real.*"

"Calm down, Nick," Octavia said soothingly.

She was very conscious of Carson, who was just outside the front door now talking to a man who had a dog in the back of his truck. She did not want the boy to overhear this argument.

When Arizona and Virgil had left the gallery a few minutes earlier, she had slipped behind the counter. She had deemed it prudent to put a bit of distance between them. Given Nick's simmering outrage, it was clear that he was not thrilled with the idea of having been drafted. But the counter did not seem nearly wide enough.

"Pay attention. I. Am. Not. A. Real. Private. Investigator." Nick spaced each word out very carefully and deliberately, as though talking to someone from another planet who might not have a good grasp of the language. "I do not have a license. I do not investigate for a living. I write *fiction* for a living. And you know that as well as I do. Why did you and Virgil agree to go along with A.Z.'s zany scheme?"

"Because we don't have a lot of choice," she said briskly. "As you pointed out, there aren't any real investigators here in Eclipse Bay, and I agree with A.Z. about Sean Valentine. He's a good man, and he is no doubt a very competent cop. But I'm pretty sure that he intends to waste a lot of time looking in all the wrong places."

"Don't tell me you agree with Arizona's conspiracy theory? You really think Valentine should look for the culprit up at the institute?" Nick spread his hands. "Give me a break. That's nuts and you know it."

"I doubt very much that the painting was stolen by someone at the institute," she said coolly. "But that still leaves a lot of rocks to turn over and I don't think Sean will do that. I've got a hunch he'll concentrate on the Heralds."

Nick was silent.

"I knew it," she muttered. "He *does* think it was someone from the Incandescent Body, doesn't he?"

"He intends to do some background checks on some of them," Nick admitted. "It's a logical place to start. The Heralds constitute the largest group of newcomers and unknowns in town who would have had knowledge of the painting and where it was stored."

"That's not true. There are more newcomers and unknowns up at the institute and Chamberlain College."

"Okay, maybe. Technically speaking. But it's unlikely that many of them would have heard about the painting so soon. With a few exceptions, they're considered outsiders here in Eclipse Bay. Not full-fledged members of the community. Most of them are not hardwired into the gossip circuit. The Heralds, on the other hand, knew everything about the Upsall almost immediately because Photon and A.Z. told them."

"Others could have known, too," she insisted. "You know how word spreads in this town."

"Come to think of it, you're right," he replied curtly. "There are a lot of suspects, aren't there?"

She did not like the way he said that. "Not a lot. Some."

"Jeremy Seaton, for instance. Heck, you showed him right where the painting was stashed. You even let him take a really close look at it. And he's into art. Probably knows some underhanded dealers back in Portland or Seattle who would be willing to take a stolen Upsall off his hands, no questions asked."

Shock reverberated through her. It took a moment to recover. Then she flattened her palms on the counter very close to his own big hands and leaned forward so that they were only inches apart.

"Don't you dare imply that Jeremy took the painting," she said softly. "That is beneath contempt."

"You want a private investigator on the case? You gotta expect some uncomfortable speculation."

"You brought up Jeremy's name only because you don't like him very much," she said through her teeth.

"Just trying to be logical. That's what we investigators are paid to do."

"You know something? When A.Z. came up with the idea to hire you, it struck Virgil and me that there was some merit to the plan. After all, who would know Eclipse Bay better than a Harte? And with your family history and clout here in town, you can talk to anyone. Get through any door. People will take you seriously and open up to you."

He took his hands off the counter. "Because I'm considered one of the locals?"

"Yes. You've got access in a way that Sean Valentine does not." She moved one hand slightly. "And that's why I went along with A.Z.'s scheme. But now I'm having second thoughts."

"Good."

"I agree with you," she went on smoothly. "I think that with your poor attitude, it is highly unlikely that you will be of any use to us."

"Yes, he will," Carson said very earnestly from the doorway. "I'll help him."

"That's very nice of you, Carson, but your father is not interested in working for me, so I'll just have to investigate without him."

"Do you know how to be an investigator?" Carson asked, intrigued.

"I've read all your father's books about John True. How hard can it be?"

Nick's eyes went very narrow. "What's this about investigating on your own?"

She raised one shoulder in a deliberately careless shrug. "I don't see that I have much option."

His mouth thinned. "You're serious, aren't you?"

"Oh, yeah."

"This is a really, really dumb idea, Octavia. Stay out of it. Let Sean Valentine do his job."

She watched him just as steadily as he watched her. Damned if she would let him intimidate her, she thought. She was Claudia Banner's great-niece. She could handle a Harte.

"That Upsall was in my custody," she said. "I feel responsible for the loss and I intend to do whatever I can to recover it."

"You're trying to force my hand and I don't like it."

"I have no idea what you're talking about."

"Sure you do. You can't do this without me and you know it, so you're doing your best to manipulate me into a position where I have no choice but to play private eye for you."

"I wouldn't dream of trying to manipulate you," she said austerely. "I'm sure it would be impossible."

He folded his arms across his chest. He did not try to conceal his irritation.

"Okay," he said at last. "You win. I'll ask your questions for you."

"Thanks, but I really don't want you to do me any favors."

"I'm not doing you a favor," he said. "I'm doing it for A.Z. and Virgil." He glanced at Carson. "Come on, son, let's go. We've got things to do."

"Are we going to be private eyes?" Carson asked eagerly.

"Yep. You can be my assistant, at least until you get bored with the job, which probably won't take long."

"I won't get bored."

"Sure you will," Nick said. "Heck, I already know that *I'm* going to get bored."

"Look, if you don't think that you can keep your attention focused on this problem—" Octavia began.

"I'm a Harte, I can focus. Even when I'm bored." Nick turned on his heel and headed for the door. "Let's go, kid. We'll start at Rumor Central."

"Where's that?" Octavia called after him.

Nick glanced back over his shoulder. "The post office, naturally."

"I heard the Upsall disappeared sometime late yesterday or last night." Jeremy lounged back in his desk chair, cocked one tasseled loafer–shod foot on his knee, and tapped the tip of a pen against the armrest. "True?"

"I'm afraid so," Octavia said.

She sank down into the only other chair in the small office and admired the view through the window. The town, with its marina and pier, was spread out before her in a picture-perfect landscape that would have looked good hanging in her gallery.

The tide was out again. Eclipse Arch, the massive stone monolith that dominated the long sweep of beach framed by the arc of Bayview Drive, was fully exposed. Sunlight sparkled on the water. The air had been scrubbed so clean by last night's storm that she could make out Hidden Cove and Sundown Point, the two rocky outcroppings that marked the southern and northern boundaries of the bay. She could even see the elegant old mansion that Rafe and Hannah had transformed into Dreamscape.

She had gotten into the habit of taking a sandwich in to work with her, but she had neglected to bring one today. Feeling badly in need of a short break, she did something she almost never did: she closed up for the noon hour. She drove up the hillside above town with some vague notion of getting a salad at Snow's Café. Instead she'd steered straight on past to the institute. Luckily Jeremy had been in his office and had invited her to eat with him in the cafeteria. Now they were back, drinking coffee together.

"I assume our noble chief of police is on the case?" Jeremy said.

"Yes. Sean is looking into matters." She decided not to mention that Nick was also investigating.

She was almost certain that Nick hadn't been serious when he had named Jeremy as a likely suspect, but there was so much bad blood between the two men that she did not want to risk pouring gasoline on the fire.

"Got any theories?" Jeremy asked.

"No." She frowned. "I think Sean feels it might be one of the Heralds."

"A real possibility. No one knows much about that crowd down at the bakery. My grandmother still thinks they're some kind of cult. Not that the theory keeps her from buying her favorite lemon squares there, of course."

"When it comes to good lemon squares, you have to do what you have to do."

"Speaking of doing what you have to do, I think I've worked my nerve up at last. Can I persuade you to come up and view my etchings some evening this week?"

"Any time."

"Are you free this evening?"

She thought about how she had hoped that she would not be free tonight. But things had changed.

"As it happens, I am, indeed, entirely free this evening," she said.

Late that afternoon Nick balanced, feet slightly apart, on the gently bobbing dock and looked down at the short, wiry man standing in the back of a boat. Young Boone was dressed in a pair of stained and faded coveralls that appeared to be at least thirty years old. He wore a blue peaked cap emblazoned with the logo of a marine supply firm.

Even on his best days, Young Boone was not what anyone would call chatty. He had inherited the marina decades earlier from his father, Old Boone. Young Boone was somewhere in his seventies and his father had died twenty years ago, but he would probably go to his grave known as Young Boone. If either of the Boones had had first names, they had long since been forgotten in the misty past of Eclipse Bay history.

For two generations the Boones, Old and Young, had made their home in the seriously weathered two-story structure at the edge of the marina. The lower floor housed a bait, tackle, and boating supply shop. The upstairs served as the Boones' living quarters.

"Heard you had a little damage down here last night." Nick surveyed the marina through his sunglasses.

"Some." Young Boone did not look up from the rope he was coiling in the back of the boat. "Nothin' that can't be fixed."

"Glad to hear it. Storm woke you up, I'll bet."

"Couldn't hardly sleep through that racket. Came out here to check on the boats."

"That's what I figured." Nick studied the view of the shops across the street. The front of Bright Visions was clearly visible. "Happen to notice anyone hanging around the art gallery during the storm? Maybe see a car parked in the lot? Should have been empty at that time of night."

"Nope." Young Boone straightened and peered at Nick from beneath the peaked brim of his cap. "Only vehicle I saw was yours. Figured you was headin' back out to your family's place after spendin' time with Miss Brightwell."

Nick kept all expression from his face. This wasn't the first time today that he had been obliged to listen to observations about his late-night drive home.

"Uh-huh," he said. Noncommittal.

Young Boone screwed up his haggard features into a frown that may or may not have been genuine curiosity. "This have anything to do with that picture they say went missin' from the art gallery last night?"

"Yeah. I'd really like to find it for A.Z. and Virgil."

Young Boone nodded. "Wish I could help you but I didn't see a damn thing last night. Course, I was real busy here securing the boats and such like. Might have missed something goin' on across the street."

"You didn't miss my car when I drove past the marina," Nick reminded him dryly.

"No, I didn't and that's a fact. But I finished up down here right after that and went back to bed."

Which meant that there had been long stretches of time during the night when no one would have noticed a car in the parking lot across the street, Nick thought.

Young Boone gave him a knowing wink. "Miss Brightwell's nice, ain't she?"

"Yeah."

"A man like you could do a lot worse."

"A man like me?"

"Raising that boy of yours alone. No wife or mother around. Reckon it's time you settled down and got married again, don't you?"

"I don't think about it much," Nick said.

"Well, you damn well should be thinkin' about it, if you ask me."

"I didn't ask you, but I'll take your opinion under advisement."

"Under advisement?" Boone wiped his hands on a dirty rag. "That a fancy way of sayin' you ain't interested in my opinion?"

"No. Just meant I'll consider it." He watched a familiar,

monster-sized SUV abruptly wheel into the marina parking lot. Mitchell Madison. Bryce was at the wheel.

Damn. He did not need another scene with Octavia's self-appointed guardian, Nick thought. Time to leave.

"You consider it real good," Young Boone said. "Time you found yourself a wife. You're a Harte. Hartes get married and stay married."

"Say, Boone, I've got to be on my way. You'll let me know if you hear anything about that painting, won't you?"

"Sure. But it's probably gone for good."

That gave Nick pause. He turned back. "Why do you say that?"

"Can't see anyone around here hangin' a stolen painting in his house. Sooner or later, someone would be bound to notice the damn thing."

"Okay, I'll give you that. And I'll also admit that this Upsall picture isn't the sort of fine art that you'd expect would appeal to the connoisseurs among us here in Eclipse Bay."

"Heard it looked like something a kindergartner might turn out," Young Boone said.

"Hey, I've got a kindergartner who can do better-looking art. Yeah, the Upsall is sort of ugly. Sure hard to envision someone like, say, Sandy down at the gas station, going to the trouble to steal it just so he could hang it on the wall of the restroom. And it would look a little out of place in the Total Eclipse, too."

Boone thought for a moment. "Still leaves all those fancy types up at the institute and Chamberlain College. They might go for that kinda thing."

"Maybe. If that's the case, we'll have to let Valentine deal with it. I'm just checking out the possibility that someone local might have taken it as a prank or on a dare. I can see some guy who'd had a couple-three-too-many beers down at the Total Eclipse deciding to swipe the painting as a stunt."

"Huh. Hadn't thought of that."

"In which case," Nick said in the same casual tone he'd been using all day long, "if it just shows up again there will be no questions asked."

Young Boone squinted knowingly and snapped his oily rag.

"Gotcha. I'll spread the word."

"Thanks."

Mitchell was out of the SUV. He had his cane in one hand and he was making straight for the dock where Nick stood.

"I'd better get going," Nick said. "Places to go, people to see."

Boone glanced past him toward Mitchell, who was advancing rapidly. "Good luck. Gonna be hard to avoid Madison. He's got a bee in his bonnet about you and that Miss Brightwell gal."

"I know." Nick assessed his chances of escape. He had the advantage of being several decades younger than Mitchell, and he hadn't developed any arthritis yet. If he moved quickly, he might just make it to the car before Madison intercepted him. "See you around, Boone."

"See ya."

Nick went swiftly along the gently shifting dock. He made it through the gate and was halfway across the parking lot when he realized he wasn't going to be able to dodge his pursuer. He could outrun him, of course, but that would have been the coward's way. Hartes did not run from Madisons.

"Hold up right there, Harte." Mitchell thumped his cane on the hard-packed ground as he veered to the right to block Nick's path. His bushy brows bristled across the bridge of his aggressive nose. "I want to talk to you."

Nick halted. Not much choice, he figured.

"'Afternoon, sir," he said politely. "Storm give you any trouble last night?"

"Storms don't give me trouble." Mitchell planted himself in front of Nick and glowered ferociously. "Hartes give me trouble. Just what the hell kind of game do you think you're playing with Octavia Brightwell?"

"I don't want to be rude, sir, but I'm in a hurry here. Maybe we should talk about this later."

"We'll talk right now." Mitchell banged the cane again for emphasis. "I heard you spent the night out at Octavia's place."

"That, sir, is a flat-out lie."

Mitchell was startled into momentary speechlessness.

"You tellin' me it was someone else? You weren't the man who was out there last night?"

"I had dinner with Octavia," Nick said evenly. "I went home afterward. I did not spend the night."

"The way I hear it, you were there until nearly one o'clock in the morning."

"You've got spies on your payroll?"

"Don't need any spies. Young Boone saw you drive past the marina late last night. He told everyone at the post office first thing this morning."

"You know, sir, I hate to break this to you, but nowadays it's not all that unusual for a couple of adults to spend an evening together that doesn't wind up until one in the morning."

"Not here in Eclipse Bay, they don't, not unless they're foolin' around. And you two aren't a couple of adults."

"We're not?"

"Nope."

"Mind if I ask just how you classify us, if not as adults?"

"You're a Harte and Octavia is Claudia's great-niece."

"So?"

"Shoot and damn, son." Mitchell raised the cane and waved it in a slashing arc. "I warned you. If you think I'm gonna just stand by and let you take advantage of that gal, you're—"

"Mitch, wait." Octavia's clear voice echoed across the parking lot. "I can explain everything."

Nick turned his head and saw Octavia coming toward them at top speed. She left the sidewalk in front of her shop and raced across Bay Street, hair flying behind her.

He was amazed that she could actually run in the sexy little slides. They did not look as if they'd provide adequate support or stability for this kind of exercise. But, then, what did he know about ladies' shoes?

A car horn blared. Brakes screeched. Octavia paid no attention. She reached the opposite side of the street and kept moving, heading straight for Mitchell and Nick.

"You don't understand, Mitch," she shouted. "It's okay, really it is."

Mitchell glared at her with concern when she skidded to a halt, breathless and flushed, in front of him.

"See here, you all right?" he asked. "Something wrong?"

"No, no, that's what I'm trying to tell you." Still breathing hard, she shot a quick, unreadable glance at Nick and then turned back to Mitchell. "I just wanted to assure you that you don't have to protect me from Nick."

"I already warned him once that I won't stand by and let him fool around with you."

"That's just it, we are *not* fooling around."

"Well, just what the heck do you call it?" Mitchell demanded.

Nick waited with genuine interest to hear her answer.

Octavia drew herself up with astonishing aplomb. "Nick is working for me."

Mitchell gaped. "What the devil?"

She bestowed an icy little smile on Nick and then looked at Mitchell with cool determination. "He has kindly agreed to investigate the missing Upsall. A.Z. and Virgil and I don't feel that Chief Valentine can handle the case on his own."

"Well, shoot and damn." Mitchell looked bemused for a couple of seconds, but in true Madison style, he recovered swiftly. "That doesn't explain why he was out at your place until all hours last night."

"Relax," Octavia said smoothly. "Last night was no big deal."

Nick felt his insides clench. No big deal?

"It's true we had dinner together, but so what?" Octavia went on in a breezy manner. "The only reason he left as late as he did was because of the storm. My fault, entirely. I didn't want him driving home until the wind had died down a little. I was afraid about stuff like downed power lines and trees falling across the road."

She did not have to sound quite so damned casual, Nick thought.

But her tactics were working. Mitchell was starting to appear somewhat mollified.

"Well, shoot and damn," Mitchell said again. "So you kept him there at your place on accounta the high winds?"

"Violent storms make me a little nervous."

"That one last night was a tad rough," Mitchell admitted. "Worst we've had in a while. You say he's gonna play private eye for you? Just like the guy in his books?"

"Precisely," Octavia said firmly. "From now on whenever you see Nick with me, you may assume that we are discussing the case. Nothing more."

"Huh." Mitchell looked thoughtful now. "If you're sure that's all there is to it—"

"Absolutely certain," Octavia said. "Like I said, last night was no big deal. Just a friendly dinner that lasted a little longer than we anticipated because of the storm."

"Huh." Mitchell looked hard at Nick. "You think you can find that painting?"

"Probably not." Nick shrugged. "But Virgil and A.Z. and Octavia want me to ask around a little so I said I would. If you hear anything useful, let me know."

"I'll do that."

Mitchell nodded to both of them and stalked back toward the waiting SUV.

They watched him climb into the front seat and slam the door. Bryce put the behemoth in gear and drove out of the parking lot.

There was a short silence. Nick folded his arms, leaned back against the BMW, and looked at Octavia.

"Let's get something straight here," he said. "I don't need you to protect me from Mitchell Madison."

Octavia reached into her shoulder bag, removed a pair of sunglasses, and slipped them onto her nose. Leveling the playing field, Nick thought. Now he could not read the expression in her eyes any better than she could read his.

"I think I'm the one who should make things clear," she said crisply. "I have a vested interest in making certain that you are not distracted by Mitchell and his misguided attempts to protect me. I want you to concentrate on finding that Upsall. Do we understand each other?"

"Yeah, sure. We understand each other." He paused a beat. "Last night was no big deal, huh?"

She pursed her lips and tilted her head slightly. Light glared on the lenses of her glasses. "I may not have phrased that correctly."

"I'm glad to hear that."

"After due consideration, I've decided that last night was actually quite therapeutic for me."

Her deliberate, reflective, analytical tone sent a cold chill through him.

"Therapeutic?" he repeated cautiously.

"Don't laugh, but this morning, when I woke up, I felt like the princess in the fairy tale, the one who'd been asleep for a hundred years. Awake at last. Okay, so maybe it was more like having been asleep for a couple of years, but you get the picture."

He relaxed a little but not much. "I'm a little confused here. Are you saying I'm Prince Charming?"

She chuckled. "Hardly."

His belly tightened. "I was afraid of that."

"What I'm trying to explain is that, in a way, I've been living in a different world for nearly two years. I put a lot of things on hold while Aunt Claudia was ill, and I never went back to them after she died. I've been just sort of floating through my life, as it were."

"A free spirit."

"That's how I described it, but it was more like being unanchored or untethered, if you see what I mean."

That fit with what he had figured out for himself, he thought. "Sounds like a form of depression or something."

"Maybe." She snapped her fingers. "But whatever the problem was, it's fixed."

"Because we had great sex last night?"

"The quality of the sex probably wasn't as much of a factor as the fact that I actually did the deed." She smiled coolly. "It has been a while, you see. My social life was one of the things I put on hold when Aunt Claudia got so ill. I never really got back to it."

"Glad I could serve in a useful capacity."

"You were *extremely* useful." She pushed her glasses up more firmly on her nose and cleared her throat. "Since we're having this conversation, I should probably take the opportunity to apologize for that unfortunate little scene last night as you were running out the door. Let's just chalk it up to two years' worth of celibacy, the storm, and the last remnants of my weird emotional condition."

"A nice tidy list of reasons." He shoved his fingers through his hair. "And for the record, I was not *running* out the door. It was late and I had to pick up Carson and get back to the cottage."

"Of course." She glanced at her watch. "I'm glad we've got that settled. You'll have to excuse me. I need to get back to the gallery."

"Now who's running?"

Her mouth tightened. "I've got a business to see to and you've got a missing painting to investigate."

"Sure." He wished he could see her eyes behind those damn sunglasses. "Would you like to come out to my place and have dinner with Carson and me tonight?"

She hesitated. "Thanks, but I'm afraid I'm busy this evening."

The chill returned to his gut. "Seaton?"

"Why, yes, as a matter of fact. How did you know?"

"Lucky guess," he said grimly.

"He wants me to look at some of his paintings." She turned away to start back toward the gallery. "He has never exhibited his work and he wants me to give him a professional opinion on whether it might have commercial possibilities."

"Bullshit. He wants to talk you into bed."

She stopped and looked back over her shoulder. "Would you like to tell me what it is between you two?"

"What the hell. I never told anyone else." He wrenched open the driver's side door of the BMW and got behind the wheel. "Might be *therapeutic* for me."

"Nick, wait—"

He slammed the door and looked at her through the lowered window while he started the engine. "Seaton hates my guts because he thinks that I had an affair with his ex-wife while they were still married."

Her mouth opened but no words emerged. Her speechless condition gave him some satisfaction, but not much.

"One more thing," he added, snapping the car into gear. "What happened last night between you and me wasn't therapy. It was great sex. There's a difference."

He drove out of the marina parking lot, leaving her standing there in her bright purple jumper and ridiculously sexy shoes.

# chapter 11

"What the hell do you expect me to do?" Sullivan snarled into the phone. "I'm trying to put together a merger here."

"Hate to break this to you," Mitchell growled on the other end, "but my grandson and your son don't need any help putting the finishing touches on the Madison-Harte merger. Both of 'em have been running their own companies for years. They know what they're doing. You're just gumming things up, hanging over their shoulders there in Portland. Leave 'em be and pay attention to the larger issues."

"Larger issues? Never heard you use a fancy phrase like that before, Mitch."

"Must have picked it up from one of you silver-tongued Hartes. Look, we've got a problem here in Eclipse Bay."

Sullivan cranked back in the chair and contemplated the view from the window of the temporary office his new son-in-law, Gabe Madison, had provided for him. The headquarters of Madison Commercial, soon to become

Madison-Harte, were located on the top floors of a Portland office tower. From his perch he could see the boat traffic on the Willamette River.

The summer afternoon was sunny and warm. The weather reporters claimed that it was hot down there on the city streets, but he spent most of his time in Phoenix these days. He knew hot, and this was not hot.

"Seems to me that *you* have a problem, Mitch," he said, stalling for time while he considered the *larger issues*. "Not me. You're the one who decided to take on the job of looking out for Claudia Banner's great-niece."

"This problem we're discussing involves your grandson," Mitch shot back. "I told you I wouldn't stand by and let him—"

"Shut up." Sullivan got up out of the chair very suddenly.

Phone in hand, he went to stand at the window. "Don't say it again."

"Don't say what?" Mitchell asked innocently. "That I won't let Nick sucker Octavia into an affair and then dump her when he decides he wants to replace her with some other lady?"

"This is my grandson you're talking about." Sullivan's hand clamped fiercely around the phone, but he managed to keep his voice level. "He is not a philanderer, damn it."

"That so? Then why hasn't he found himself a good woman sometime during the past four years and settled down again? That's what you Hartes do, isn't it? Get married and stay married?"

"Yes, Mitch. Unlike the sterling example of family values you set for your grandsons with your three or four wives and God only knows how many affairs, we Hartes are real big on family values."

"You leave my grandsons out of this."

"Hard to do that, given that they're married to my granddaughters."

"There's not a damn thing wrong with Gabe's or Rafe's family values and you know it. Lillian is Gabe's passion and Hannah is Rafe's. Nothing comes between a Madison and his passion. Those two boys are married for life."

"So was Nick," Sullivan said quietly.

Silence hummed on the line.

"That's the real problem, you see," Sullivan continued. "Nick figured he had married for life. He hasn't adjusted to the loss of Amelia. He's not heartless, he's just trying to protect himself."

"Look, I know folks here in Eclipse Bay like to say that losing her broke Nick's heart." There was a note of gruff sympathy in Mitchell's voice. "Expect it's true, what with him being a Harte and all. But that ain't no excuse for him playin' fast and loose with a nice girl like Octavia. She's had a rough time of it, too, damn it. But unlike your grandson, I don't think she's tough enough to protect herself."

"So you've decided to do it for her?"

"Someone's gotta do it. Not like she's got any family around to take on the job."

Sullivan hesitated. "All right, you've made your point."

"Got another one to make while I'm at it," Mitchell said grimly. "Your grandson spent last night at her place."

That gave Sullivan pause. "The whole night?"

"Well, maybe not the *entire* night—"

Sullivan relaxed slightly. "Didn't think so."

"But it's pretty damn obvious those two are foolin' around."

"Obvious to you, maybe."

"Yeah, obvious to me. You should have seen the way

Octavia jumped to Nick's defense this afternoon when I cornered him down at the marina."

"What the hell do you think you're doing, cornering my grandson?"

"I was just makin' sure he understands he can't have his way with Octavia."

"Damn it, Mitch—" Sullivan broke off abruptly and backtracked to the other part of Mitchell's comment. "What did you mean when you said Octavia jumped to his defense?"

"She claimed he's sort of working for her."

"Nick? Working for Octavia Brightwell? Doing what, for crying out loud?"

"Playing private detective, I hear. Like that fellow in his novels."

Sullivan struggled valiantly to hang onto the few remaining wisps of logic that still dangled from the conversation. "Why does Octavia need an investigator?"

"Long story. That painting Thurgarton left to A.Z. and Virgil and the Heralds got stolen from her shop last night."

"What was it doing in her gallery? Never mind. I assume she notified Valentine?"

"Sure. But he's got his eye on the Heralds and she doesn't think he's looking in the right place. Neither does A.Z. or Virgil."

"So she hired Nick." Sullivan sank down onto the corner of his desk and digested that information. "And he agreed to investigate?"

"Appears that way."

"This is bizarre."

"Like I said, we've got a situation here, Sullivan. I hate to admit it, but I think I'm gonna need some help straightening this one out."

"Now, just a minute—"

"I'll keep you posted."

Mitchell cut the connection.

Very slowly Sullivan reached across the desk and punched in another, very familiar number. He needed advice from the one person whose insight he had come to trust the most over the years.

His wife, Rachel, answered on the second ring.

"Something wrong?" she asked.

"Why do you say that?" he grumbled.

"Because it's the middle of the day and you're supposed to be deep into the intricacies of the merger of Harte Investments and Madison Commercial."

He could hear birds. Somewhere in the background, water splashed. He knew that she was out by the pool of their desert home with his daughter-in-law, Elaine. The two women were holed up together in Phoenix, keeping each other company, while their menfolk worked the merger details with Gabe Madison.

Sullivan summoned up a vision of Rachel in her swimsuit, her body sleek and wet.

She was still the only woman for him, he thought. There had never been another since he had met her all those years ago in the wake of the financial disaster of Harte-Madison. He had been a driven man in those days, completely obsessed with the task of rebuilding his business empire.

But he had learned the hard way that the great strength in the Harte genes was also a potentially devastating flaw. It was the nature of a Harte to be goal-oriented and so focused that other things, important things, sometimes got pushed aside. If Madisons were driven by their passions, Hartes were sometimes inclined to be cold-blooded and relentless in their pursuit of an objective.

Rachel had quietly acted to counter his single-minded obsession with Harte Investments. She had centered him, given him a sense of connection. During the long, hard years when he had thrown himself into the struggle to create H.I., Rachel had been there, sometimes going toe-to-toe with him to remind him that he had other priorities, too. It was Rachel who had taught him the meaning of family. It was Rachel who had saved him from going down a path that would have left him a hollow shell of a man.

"Gabe and Hamilton don't need my help," he said. "They've shunted me off to a corner office on the floor beneath the CEO's suite and made it clear they'll call me if they need me."

"I take it they don't call often?"

"Nope. I'm getting a little bored here, to tell you the truth. I'm thinking of going over to the coast for a couple of days."

"What's wrong in Eclipse Bay?" she asked instantly.

"Nothing's wrong."

"Nick and Carson are there."

"So? Thought I'd spend a little time with my great-grandson. Carson's got a lot of me in him. Going to run an empire one of these days. He needs my guidance during his early, formative years."

"You still haven't told me what's wrong."

The problem with being married to a woman like this for so many decades was that she could read a man's mind.

"Just had a call from Mitch," he said carefully. "Seems like Nick and Octavia Brightwell are involved. Sort of."

"Well, well."

"What, exactly, does that mean?"

"It means it's about time Nick finally got serious about a woman."

"That's the problem, according to Mitch," Sullivan said. "He doesn't think Nick is serious about Octavia."

"Surely Nick wouldn't have an affair with her?" Rachel sounded genuinely concerned now. "Not there in Eclipse Bay. Think of the gossip."

"It's the thought of Mitch trying to manage the situation on his own that worries me."

# chapter 12

"Honest opinion, Octavia." Jeremy looked at the five pictures propped against the walls of the bedroom he was using as a studio. "I can handle it. Really. I think."

She gazed into the depths of the painting in front of her. It was a portrait of Jeremy's grandmother. It showed Edith Seaton seated in her antiques shop, a small, purposeful figure surrounded by the clutter of the past. There was an almost surrealistic quality to the old dishes and small relics housed in the glass cabinets and displayed on the tables.

The painting showed a room crowded with a lifetime of memories. Edith's face was a rich tapestry of emotions and determination layered on each other with such a strong, clear vision that it was possible to see the personality of the woman in every stroke.

"It's really quite wonderful, Jeremy." She did not look up from the painting. "When you said that you wanted to show me some pictures, I had no idea they would be of this quality."

Jeremy visibly relaxed. He looked pleased. "I did that one of my grandmother from a photo I took last year. You know, she's lived her whole life in this town. Hardly ever traveled even as far as Portland. Eclipse Bay is her whole world."

"How long has she been alone?"

"Let's see, Granddad died eight, maybe nine years ago. That's him in the framed picture hanging behind the counter. They both grew up here. Got married the day after they graduated from high school. They were together for nearly sixty years."

She studied the picture-within-a-picture and was able to make out the features of a man with the thin shoulders that often accompanied age. There was a certain self-confident, almost rakish quality to the tilt of the man's head. The viewer got the impression that at one time the senior Seaton had been a good-looking man and knew it.

"Sixty years is quite a marriage," she said. "No one in my family ever managed to stay together that long."

"Mom told me once that Granddad ran around a bit in his younger days. But Grandmother pretended not to know about his little escapades."

"Your grandfather had his affairs right here in town?"

"I guess so. He lived here all of his life and didn't do any traveling to speak of."

She shuddered. "Must have been hard on your grandmother."

"I'm sure it was. She's got a lot of pride in the Seaton name."

"Marriages are always mysterious when viewed from the outside." She turned away from the painting. "I'd love to give you a show, Jeremy. But as I explained, to be important to your career, it would have to be held at the Portland gallery, not here in Eclipse Bay."

"I know. Eclipse Bay isn't exactly on the art world's radar screen."

"No, and I'm afraid that I'm booked solid in the city. I've got shows scheduled every month until the end of summer there and then I plan to sell both galleries."

"I understand," he said.

"But I can certainly hang a couple of your pictures in my gallery here in town and see if they sell. I have a hunch they will. You've got a real commercial talent. What do you say?"

"I'll go with your intuition. You've got the eye, at least when it comes to art."

"Meaning that I don't have it when it comes to other things?"

"Okay, okay, I admit that I have some strong reservations about you seeing Nick Harte."

"I thought so." She folded her arms and propped one hip on the edge of the table. "He told me that you think he had an affair with your ex-wife."

Jeremy looked stunned. Then his expression darkened and his face tightened with suppressed anger. "I can't believe that he actually talked to you about that."

"He didn't discuss it in detail. He just made the statement that you thought your ex-wife had had an affair with him while you were still married."

Jeremy's hand closed into a fist. "So, he admitted it," he said softly.

"No, he did not admit it. He just said that was what you believed."

"It's not a guess, you know." Jeremy looked hard at the

painting of his grandmother. "Laura told me she'd been with him."

"Where is Laura now?"

"Getting ready to marry again, I hear. A lawyer in Seattle."

"When did she meet him?"

"How the hell should I know? I don't keep track of her private life these days."

"You and Laura," she said cautiously, "I assume the two of you were having trouble for a while before you split up?"

"Sure. We argued a lot toward the end. That's usually what happens before you get a divorce, isn't it?"

"That's certainly the way it went in my family." She watched him intently. "Were the quarrels bad?"

"Bad enough."

"The kind of arguments in which both people say things that are calculated to hurt the other person as much as possible?"

Jeremy glanced at her, frowning. "Sometimes. Look, I really don't want to rehash the events surrounding my divorce, okay? It's not my favorite topic of conversation."

"I understand. But I can't help wondering if maybe Laura told you that she'd had an affair with Nick because she knew it would hit you harder than if she said she'd fallen in love with a man you'd never met. Also, it could have been a way of protecting the man she really was seeing at the time."

"What is this? You think you have to defend Harte? Don't waste your time."

"What a terrible position to be in, trying to figure out whether to believe your lifelong friend or your spouse. No one should have to make that kind of decision."

"Look, I'm not after sympathy here," he muttered. "It's over. I've moved on, like they say, okay?"

"Tell me something, did you ever ask Nick directly if he'd slept with Laura?"

"I told him once that I knew about them, yeah," Jeremy growled.

"You accused him. You didn't ask him."

"What's the difference? He denied it."

"Did Nick ever lie to you in the past about anything else that was important?"

"What does the past have to do with this?"

"Did he?" she pressed gently.

"No. But, then, maybe he never had any reason to lie to me in the past."

"You've been acquainted with him since you both were children. Have you ever known him to cheat or steal or betray a friend?"

"Things are different when it comes to sex," Jeremy said with ominous certainty.

"Do you think so? I don't. Cheaters cheat and liars lie. It's what they do whenever things become inconvenient for them or when they can't get what they want in any other way. Most of the people I've known who can lie to your face have had some practice. Aunt Claudia always said that scamming people was an art form that required skill and precision."

Jeremy looked grim. "Your aunt would have known, from all accounts."

"Yes. The only thing I can say in her defense was that she came to regret a lot of the damage she caused. But we're not talking about her. Tell me about Laura. Looking back, can you recall occasions when she lied to you?"

Jeremy started to say something but he closed his

mouth before uttering a word. He just stood there, gazing at one of the landscapes he had painted.

"How long did you know her?" she asked.

"We were married three months after we met. She thought she was—" He stopped.

"She thought she was pregnant?"

Jeremy nodded. "It was okay by me, although my family was a little put off by the rush, and Grandmother was mortified. She's a little old-fashioned, you know."

"Yes. I know."

Jeremy grimaced. "She became my biggest supporter, however, after she found out that Laura came from a socially prominent family in Seattle. But as far as I was concerned, I was excited about starting a family. It felt right, you know? Nick had little Carson and I . . . Well, it didn't happen for Laura and me. Turned out she wasn't pregnant, after all."

"She lied about it?"

He shoved his fingers through his hair, looking hunted. "To tell you the truth, I don't know. I've sometimes wondered. She said it was a mistake at the time. The test didn't work properly or something."

"How long were you married?"

"Eighteen months. Like I said, her family was old Seattle money. Lots of connections. Her parents were never particularly thrilled with me. They felt she could have done better. Once or twice I got the feeling that maybe she'd married me just to defy them and then . . ."

"Came to regret her decision."

"Things got worse in a hurry when I told her that I was thinking of moving to Eclipse Bay. I said it would be a good place to raise a family. She hated the idea so I put it off."

"You like it here. Don't you?" Octavia asked.

He regarded the painting of his grandmother for a while. "It's strange, but I do kind of like it here. Feels like home, you know?"

A wistful feeling drifted through her. "Yes. I know."

Sometimes feelings for places were wrong, she thought, but there was no need to go off on that tangent. Her intuition told her that Jeremy was, indeed, at home in Eclipse Bay. Like the Hartes and the Madisons, he had several generations of family history here.

She had made the mistake of believing that she belonged in Eclipse Bay, too, but that had been wishful thinking on her part. She knew that now. Her search for home was still ongoing.

"Just out of curiosity," she continued, "did Laura have a problem with you spending time on your painting?"

Jeremy jerked slightly, clearly startled by the question. His mouth was a thin, hard line. "She called it 'playing artist.'"

"One last question. Did you see much of Nick while you and Laura were married?"

Jeremy was quiet again for a while. Eventually he shook his head. "No. Things change when you get married, you know? Laura had her own set of friends. We hung around with them for the most part."

"Yet she still found time to have an affair with Nick?" Octavia spread her hands. "Get real, Jeremy."

"What the hell is this? You think you can just walk into this situation and analyze it without knowing all of the people involved?"

"I know something about Hartes. Lord knows, they've got their flaws, but I honestly can't see any of the Harte men fooling around with another man's wife." She straightened away from the desk. "And after looking at your paintings, I know a bit more about you, too. You can see a person's personality and character clearly enough to translate it onto a canvas. Try looking at Nick with your artist's eye. Ask yourself how you would paint him."

"Hell, you really have got it bad for him, don't you?"

"My feelings for Nick have nothing to do with this discussion." She dug her car keys out of her shoulder bag and went toward the door. "But I will tell you one thing, Jeremy. I won't let you use me to punish him for what you think he did with Laura."

# chapter 13

"Hear you're investigating that missing painting." Sandy Hickson drew the squeegee across the BMW's windshield with professional expertise and flipped the dirty liquid off with a flick of his wrist. "Just like that private eye guy in your books."

Nick leaned against the side of his car while he waited for Hickson to finish servicing it. He studied Sandy through the lenses of his sunglasses. It was felt in some quarters that Sandy had been born to work in a gas station. Legend held that as a teenager, he'd had a penchant for collecting phone numbers off restroom walls, the kind that were preceded by the inviting phrase *for a good time call* . . .

Whether Sandy had ever gotten a date using one of the numbers he had found on the grungy white tiles in the station's restroom was still an open question, but one thing was certain: The Eclipse Bay Gas & Go was a nexus point of local gossip.

"You read my books, Sandy?"

"Nah. Nothing personal. I don't read a lotta fiction, y'know? I prefer magazines."

"Yeah, I know the kind of magazines you favor. They've all got centerfolds featuring ladies whose bra sizes exist only in the realm of virtual reality. Talk about fiction."

Sandy did not take offense. He dipped his squeegee into a bucket of water and aimed another swipe at the windshield. "I read 'em mostly for the articles, y'know."

"Sure. Since you know what I'm after, you got anything for me?"

Sandy looked sly. "Been some talk going around about that painting."

"Anything you think I can use to help me find it?"

"Well, now, a few people are saying that you're getting warm." Sandy snickered, evidently enjoying some private joke. "Real hot, in fact."

The snicker became a guffaw.

Nick did not move. Sandy's sense of humor had not matured much since his high school years.

"What have you heard?" Nick asked.

"Heard you were getting it on with the chief suspect, that's what I heard. Whooee. You're hot, all right, my friend. Probably couldn't get much closer if you tried."

Sandy could no longer restrain himself. He laughed so hard he lost control of the squeegee. It dropped into the bucket, splashing dirty water on his shoes. He paid no attention.

Nick watched him for a moment, contemplating his options. The urge to wring Sandy's scrawny neck was almost overwhelming, but he exerted an effort and managed to resist the temptation.

"The chief suspect," Nick repeated. "That would be Octavia Brightwell?"

"You got it." Sandy went into another round of howls.

Nick made himself wait until Hickson's laughter had subsided to a few snorts.

"Who told you that Octavia was the chief suspect, Sandy?"

"Couple of folks mentioned it." Still chortling a little, Sandy retrieved his squeegee.

"Give me a name, Sandy."

"Well, Eugene, for one. B'lieve he mentioned it to me first."

"Eugene Woods?"

"Yeah."

"That would be the same Eugene Woods who is usually between jobs and spends most of his time at the Total Eclipse nursing a beer and associating with his old buddy Dickhead Dwayne and pretending to look for work?"

"That Eugene, yeah." Sandy scrunched up his face into an expression of keen interest. "Why? You wanna talk to him?"

"Yeah. I think I want to talk to him."

Alarm flickered in Sandy's eyes. "Hang on, Nick, I don't know as that's a real smart idea. Eugene ain't changed much since he was a kid. He didn't get that nickname of Mean Eugene for no reason, y'know."

"People change, Sandy. They mature."

"Not Mean Eugene. He's the same as he was back in third grade. Still hold you up for your lunch money if he can figure out a way to do it. And Dickhead's the same, too. Always goin' along with whatever Eugene wants him to do."

"I'll bear that in mind, Sandy."

Nick shoved himself away from the side of the car and walked across the street to the entrance of the Total Eclipse Bar & Grill.

"What does that key open?" Gail asked.

Octavia glanced at the key hanging from the hook inside the storage closet. "I don't know, to be honest. Nothing here in the gallery, that's for sure. I tried it on all the locks. Must have belonged to Noreen. One of these days I'll toss it out. But I hesitate to discard it until I know for certain that it doesn't go to anything important."

"I know what you mean. There's something about a key that makes you think twice before throwing it out, isn't there? Even when you don't know what it unlocks."

"Yes." Octavia shut the closet door and turned around with a smile. "Okay, I think that's it. Any other questions?"

"Not at the moment."

They walked back out into the gallery and went to stand at the window. Outside on the sidewalk several tourists meandered. The day was sunny and pleasantly warm.

Octavia had awakened feeling inexplicably good again today, even though there had been no wild and crazy sex last night and even though she still had the same set of problems she'd had before life had turned so adventurous here in Eclipse Bay.

Gail also looked better today. She seemed cheerful, even a bit enthusiastic.

She was dressed in a dark, lightweight suit with a little scarf at her throat. Her honey-colored hair was brushed sleekly back into a neat knot at the back of her neck. Very formal for Eclipse Bay, Octavia thought. But then, she had come here to apply for a job.

"It's strictly a temporary position, I'm afraid," Octavia

said. "I'm planning to sell the gallery at the end of the summer and there's no way to know if whoever buys it will want an assistant."

Across the street at the end of the block she could see Nick leaning against the side of his car, talking to Sandy Hickson at the town's only gas station. Just the sight of him, even from this distance, did things to her pulse. There was something deliciously compelling about the way the man *lounged*, she thought; a sexy, subtle, masculine grace that made her think extremely erotic thoughts.

Evidently the conversation with Sandy was a riveting one. She wondered if Nick was actively pursuing his investigation or just passing the time of day while Sandy put gas in the tank and washed the windshield. It was impossible to tell from this distance.

"I understand that you can't promise anything beyond the summer," Gail said quickly. "But this will buy me some breathing space to look around and try to line up something permanent up at Chamberlain or the institute. I really appreciate this, Octavia."

"Not as much as I appreciate your agreeing to take the position," Octavia said.

"I'm sure a few more questions will come up, but I think I've got the basics down. As I told you, I've had some experience in retail and I've always loved art. In a way, this is a perfect job for me. I'm going to enjoy it."

"You might as well start this afternoon. If you're free, that is?"

"Yes. Mom is looking after Anne. I'll give her a call and tell her that I've started working. She'll be very relieved."

"Good. I've got a lot of things to do in the next few weeks. I'm planning to move, you know. And then there's the Children's Art Show. Also, I have to get started on making arrangements to sell both branches of Bright Visions." The list of objectives had become her mantra, she realized. She ran through it in her mind whenever she felt dispirited or depressed about her life at the end of the summer. It kept her focused.

Gail hesitated. "I know it's none of my business, but do you mind if I ask why you feel you have to sell your galleries and leave the state?"

"I've been sort of drifting for a while," Octavia said. "Trying to decide what I want to do with my future. I don't have all the answers yet, but I've definitely come to the conclusion that I need to move on."

Gail nodded sympathetically. "Believe it or not, I know exactly what you mean. I felt that drifting sensation for a while after my divorce. It was hard to make decisions. But having Anne to support emotionally and financially did a lot to make me pull up my socks and move forward."

"I'll bet it did." She watched Nick across the street and thought that, whatever else you could say about him, there was no denying that he was an excellent father. "Nothing like being responsible for a child to help you put your priorities in order."

"True. Kids come first."

*I wonder if I'll ever have one of my own,* Octavia thought. A picture of Carson's laughing face danced through her mind. She pushed it aside.

"I've got a question for you," she said to Gail. "Why did you come back to Eclipse Bay?"

"Anne has reached the age where she's starting to ask why her daddy doesn't come see her," Gail said. "I thought it would be good for her to spend more time with my father. The positive male role model thing, you know?"

"Yes," Octavia said softly. "I know."

Down at the station, Nick had straightened away from his car, preparing to leave. Anticipation crackled through her. She wondered if he was getting ready to drive here to the gallery to give her an update on his progress. Maybe she would suggest that they talk over lunch. Yes, that sounded good. A business lunch. She could leave her new assistant in charge of the gallery.

But Nick did not get behind the wheel of his car. As she watched, he started purposefully across the street, heading toward the entrance to the Total Eclipse.

"What on earth?" She stepped outside onto the sidewalk to get a better look. "Good grief, he's going into that dive."

"Who?" Gail came through the opening behind her. She glanced down the street with a puzzled expression. "Nick Harte?"

"Yes. It's almost lunchtime. Maybe he decided to pick up a sandwich there."

"At the Total Eclipse?" Gail wrinkled her nose. "Good way to get food poisoning, if you ask me."

"You're right." Intuition kicked in. "I'll bet he's following a lead."

Gail glanced at her with open curiosity. "It's true, then? Nick Harte is playing private eye for you and A.Z. and the others?"

"He's not *playing* private eye. He's making serious inquiries into the situation."

"Hmm. I don't know how many serious folks he's going to find inside the Total Eclipse, especially at this time of day."

"Good point." She'd been in town long enough to have learned something about the clientele of the Total Eclipse. "You know, I don't like the looks of this. Who do you suppose he's going to talk to inside that joint?"

"Well, there's Fred, the owner," Gail said.

"Of course." She relaxed a little. "He tends the bar. Bartenders always pick up useful tidbits of gossip. The hero in Nick's books often consults them."

"And if memory serves," Gail continued dryly, "you can usually count on finding Mean Eugene and his sidekick Dickhead Dwayne in there most days."

"I know who you mean. I've seen them on the street and in Fulton's occasionally. They're always together. I've heard the Mean Eugene name but I hadn't realized the skinny one was called Dickhead."

"Dwayne and Eugene have been buddies for as long as anyone can remember. They tend to reinforce each other's worst characteristics. Eugene calls the shots and Dwayne goes along. It is generally felt in these parts that anyone who would do whatever Eugene told him to do would have to be a dickhead. Hence the name."

"I can see the logic."

"Back in the big city, folks would probably say that Eugene and Dwayne are the products of dysfunctional families. But around here we just call them bums."

Nick pushed open the door and stepped into the perpetual gloom of the Total Eclipse. He removed his sunglasses and let the smell of stale cigarette smoke, spilled beer, and rancid grease envelop him. The combination brought back a lot of memories.

Some things were a given in Eclipse Bay. A guy bought his first condom from Virgil Nash, not because Grover's Pharmacy didn't stock them, but because it was too damn embarrassing to buy a box from Pete Grover. The pharmacist knew everyone's medical history from date of birth and did not hesitate to make his opinion of your sex life clear. And he always tried to get names. Even if you got up the nerve to risk his beady-eyed scrutiny, you faced the very real threat that he would notify your folks or, worse yet, the girl's folks that the purchase had been made.

Showing up here at the Total Eclipse on the day you were finally old enough to buy a legal beer was another rite of passage for young males in Eclipse Bay. By the same token, if you were still buying a lot of your beers here at age twenty-five or beyond, it was understood that you were never going to amount to much and that you were probably doomed to live out your life at the bottom of the town's social ladder.

Mean Eugene and Dickhead Dwayne were shining examples of the accuracy of that hypothesis. They were in their mid-thirties and still bought their beers here.

Nick gave his eyes a few seconds to adjust to the shadows. The only lights in the Total Eclipse were the narrow spots over the pool tables in the room at the back, the green glass lamp next to the cash register at the bar, and the weak candles in the little red glass holders on the tables. The candles were Fred's notion of ambience.

The place was nearly empty at this time of day. Being seen at the Total Eclipse at any time invited unpleasant comments from the more high-minded members of the community. The comments were always a lot more scathing if you hung out here when there was daylight outside.

But the prospect of societal disapproval did not worry guys like Eugene and his buddy, Dwayne.

Eugene Woods had been born to bully. In high school his size and weight issues had ensured that he went on to become a local football legend and a known thug at Eclipse Bay High. Eugene's post-football years had not gone well, however. The layer of padding that had stood him in good stead on the field had increased in volume, and his brutish ways had earned him an extremely limited circle of friends. Sooner or later his poor work ethic screwed up any job he managed to land.

Dwayne was his constant companion. *Dickhead* was not really an accurate descriptor, at least not when applied to Dwayne's features. He reminded Nick more of an over-sized insect.

Dwayne was thin and brittle with spidery legs and arms. He looked as if he'd crunch if you stepped on him. He twitched a lot, too, like a bug that had been hit with a dose of pesticide.

Bar stools were uncomfortable for a man of Eugene's proportions. Nick looked for his quarry in one of the booths.

Eugene was there, sitting at a grimy table with Dwayne. The big man faced the door, in true Old West gunslinger style. There was just enough light coming from the little candle in the red glass holder to reveal the meanness in his eyes and the ragged tears in the grimy tee shirt stretched over his belly.

Interviewing Mean Eugene was not going to be easy.

Nick went toward the booth. He nodded once at Fred when he went past the bar.

"Fred."

"How you doin', Nick?" Fred did not look up from the little television set he had positioned behind the bar. He was watching a long-running soap opera. Fred was addicted to the soaps.

"Doin' okay, thanks," Nick said.

Civilities completed, he moved on to the booth and stopped. He looked at Eugene and Dwayne.

"Can I buy you gentlemen a beer?" he asked.

Dwayne, who'd been concentrating on a dripping cheeseburger, started and looked up with a startled expression. Clearly the word *gentlemen* had confounded him. And with good reason, Nick thought.

But Eugene, always the faster of the two, chortled. "So we're gentlemen now, huh? Hell, yes, you can buy us a couple of beers. Never say no to a free beer. Besides, it ain't every day a Harte wanders in here and makes an offer like that, now, is it? Sit down."

"Thanks." Nick considered and discarded the prospect of sharing one of the torn, orange vinyl benches with either Eugene or Dwayne. When you dealt with guys like this you did not want to find yourself wedged into a tight place.

He glanced around, spotted a scarred wooden chair at a nearby table, and grabbed it. He reversed it and sat down astride, resting his folded arms on the back.

Eugene swiveled his head, an amazing feat considering that he lacked any sign of an actual neck.

"Hey, Fred," Eugene called loudly. "Harte, here, is gonna stand me and Dwayne to a coupla beers. Give us some of that good stuff you've got on draft."

Fred did not reply, but he reached for two glasses without turning away from the television screen, where someone was dying bravely in a hospital bed.

Eugene squinted malevolently. "You didn't come here to be friendly, Harte. Your type doesn't hang out with guys like us. Whatcha want?"

"Yeah," Dwayne said around a mouthful of burger. "Whatcha want?"

Nick kept his attention on Eugene. "Mind if I ask you a couple of questions, Eugene?"

"You can ask." Eugene polished off the last of the beer

he had been drinking when Nick arrived. He wiped his mouth on the back of his shirtsleeve. "I'll decide if I feel like answering."

"I hear you've been speculating openly on the question of who might have taken that painting that's gone missing from the gallery up the street," Nick said casually.

"Hell, I *knew* it." Eugene uttered a satisfied little snort, savoring his own brilliance. "So you're playing detective, huh? Just like the guy in your books? What's his name? True?"

Nick raised his brows. "You read my books, Eugene?"

"Nah. I don't read much. I'm more into the sports channel, y'know? *XXXtreme Fringe Wrestling* is my favorite program."

"Mine, too," Dwayne volunteered. "That's the one where the women fight almost buck-nekked. They just wear those little leather thong things, y'know? You oughta see those tits flapping around in the ring."

"Hard for a book to compete with that kind of upscale entertainment," Nick said.

"Yeah," Eugene agreed. "But I seen your novels down at Fulton's when they come out in paperback. They got that little rack next to the checkout counter, y'know?"

"Amazing that Fulton's even bothers to stock my books, given that so few people around here are inclined to read them."

"Hey, you're our only local author and besides, you're a Harte." Eugene's voice hardened. "Everyone thinks that gives you special status in Eclipse Bay."

Nick was saved from having to respond directly to that tricky conversational gambit by a loud, jarring crash. Fred had just slammed two glasses of beer down onto the top of the bar.

"Come and get it, Eugene," Fred called, turning back to his soap. "No table service until four-thirty when Nellie shows up for the evening. You know that."

"Allow me." Nick got to his feet and went to the bar to collect the beers. He set them on the table and sat down again.

"Well, well, well." Eugene grabbed his beer and hauled it closer. "Never thought the day would come when I'd get served by a Harte." He gulped some beer and lowered the glass. "How about that, Dwayne? One of the honchos of Eclipse Bay just bought us a beer and served it, too. What d'ya think of that?"

"Weird," Dwayne said. He snickered and downed a hefty swallow from his own glass. "Damn weird."

You couldn't discuss things rationally with these two, Nick reminded himself. It would have been the equivalent of engaging in a conversation concerning the origins and meaning of the universe with a pair of particularly dim-witted bulls. The best you could hope to do was prod them in the direction you wanted them to take.

"Heard you've been doing a little detecting, yourself, Eugene," Nick said. "Sandy over at the station says you've got a theory about just who might have made off with that painting."

Eugene blinked a couple of times and then managed to make the intellectual leap required to grasp the meaning of the sentence.

"Yep, that's me, all right," Eugene said, sounding pleased. "Detective Eugene Woods." He grinned at Dwayne. "Got a ring to it, don't it?"

Dwayne snorted. "A real ring."

Eugene turned back to Nick. "I know who took that painting, but you ain't gonna like it." He put the glass down with a decisive clang and wiped his mouth on the back of his shirt. "Makes you look downright stupid, Harte."

"I've looked that way before," Nick said. "I'll get past it."

Eugene cackled so hard he choked. It took him a while to recover his wind. "Always enjoyed the sight of a stupid-looking Harte."

"I can't help feeling that this conversation is losing its focus," Nick said gently. "Could we return to the subject at hand?"

Eugene stopped grinning. His heavy features twisted into an expression of deep suspicion. Probably worried that he had just been insulted and not quite certain how to react, Nick thought.

Eugene, being Eugene and therefore extremely predictable in some ways, did what he always did in such circumstances. He went on the offensive.

"You wanna know what I think, Harte? I'll tell you. Only solid suspect far as I can see is your new girlfriend, the gallery lady. And you're screwing her. Ain't that a kick in the head? The big-time detective is screwing the prime suspect." He looked at Dwayne. "Ain't that a kick in the head, Dwayne?"

"Yeah," Dwayne said obediently. "A real kick in the head."

Eugene leaned across the table to make his point to Nick. "How do you like them apples, Mr. High-and-Mighty Harte? Looks like the lady has you by the short hairs. How's it feel to be led around by your balls?"

"Before we go into that, maybe you'd like to tell me where you heard this theory," Nick said.

"What makes you think I heard it somewheres else?"

Eugene's features transformed as if by magic, shifting from malicious glee to a twisted glare. "Maybe I came up with it all by myself. You think you're the only smart one around here?"

Nick throttled back his temper with an effort. He was here to gather information, not get into a brawl. "You got any proof that Octavia Brightwell stole the painting?"

"Proof? I don't have to show you no proof. You're the private eye. Find your own proof." Eugene leered. "Just keep digging away. Who knows what you might find?"

"Okay, you don't have any proof," Nick said evenly. "Would you, by any chance, have a motive?"

"Motive?" Eugene glanced at Dwayne.

"He means like a reason why she would steal it," Dwayne said, surprising Nick with his insight and comprehension.

"Oh, yeah." Eugene switched his attention back to Nick. "I can give you a reason, all right. That picture is real valuable and it ain't insured or nothing. Not even mentioned in Old Man Thurgarton's will. There's no record it even exists, get it? No, whatcha call it, prominence."

"Provenance," Nick corrected softly.

"Right. So the way I figure it, little Ms. Brightwell is pulling a fast one on all of you. Works like this, see, she hides the picture, pretends it got stolen and later, when the heat dies down, she leaves town, maybe goes to Seattle or some place like that and sells the damn thing. That way she gets to keep all the money. Now do you get it, Harte?"

"Interesting theory," Nick said.

"Yeah, it is, isn't it?" Eugene quaffed more beer and lowered the glass. Pleased with himself.

"And you say you came up with it all on your own?"

"Yep."

Dwayne opened his mouth, but he closed it again very rapidly when Eugene threw him a warning glare.

"In that case," Nick said, "can I ask you two gentlemen to refrain from spreading it any further until we find out exactly what is going on and maybe get some proof?"

Eugene looked intrigued. "Why should we keep quiet?"

"For one thing, there's a lady's reputation at stake."

"What reputation? Everyone in town knows she's screwing your brains out."

"I was speaking of her professional reputation."

"Who cares about that?" Eugene asked blankly.

"I do, for one," Nick said. "And I think maybe you and Dwayne, being gentlemen and all, should care about it, too."

They both looked at him as if he'd suggested that they should care about quantum physics.

Eugene recovered first. "Hell with her pro-fess-ion-al rep-u-ta-tion," he said, sounding each syllable out with sneering precision. "I don't give a shit about her reputation. You give a shit, Dwayne?"

"Nope," Dwayne said. "I figure the fact that she's screwing Harte's brains out is a lot more interesting than her professional reputation."

Nick rose slowly to his feet. They both watched him, taunting challenge in their faces.

"Let me put it to you this way, gentlemen," Nick said coolly. "If you two cannot manage to refrain from further public comment on either Ms. Brightwell's personal or professional reputation, I have two words of wisdom for you."

"What two words?" Eugene demanded, looking ready to pounce in victory.

*"Lavender and Leather."*

Eugene's face went slack as if he'd just gone completely numb. Maybe he had, Nick thought. With shock.

Dwayne gaped. He looked frozen with horror.

Satisfied that he had made his point, Nick turned and walked through the shadowy tavern. He pushed open the door and went out into the sparkling sunlight.

And immediately collided with Octavia, who had just put her hand on the door to open it.

"Excuse me, I—" She began, stepping hurriedly back out of the way. Then she recognized him. "Oh, it's you."

"Yeah, it's me."

The transition from night to day dazzled his vision. Or maybe it was the sight of Octavia in a dress that was roughly the color of a tequila sunrise and was splattered with impossibly oversized orchids. He took his sunglasses out of his pocket and put them on.

She glanced past him toward the door of the tavern. "What happened in there?"

"I confirmed something that I have long suspected."

"What?"

"No one in this town reads my books."

# chapter 14

"I read them," she said.

"You don't count. You're leaving town in a few weeks, remember?" He took her arm and steered her away from the entrance. "What the hell are you doing here? I hope you weren't planning to eat lunch at the Total Eclipse. You weren't raised in Eclipse Bay, so you probably lack the necessary immunity to survive Fred's cooking."

"I wasn't planning to eat there. I saw you go inside and I knew you had probably gone in to talk to someone about the painting."

"Brilliant deduction." Across the street, Sandy Hickson was watching them with great interest, a dripping squeegee dangling absently from one hand. Nick took Octavia's arm again. "Come on, let's get you out of here. There's enough talk about you going around as it is."

She skipped a little to keep up with him. "Did you learn anything in the Total Eclipse?"

"Always something to be learned in the Total Eclipse,"

he said flatly. "It is never less than an enlightening experience."

She frowned. "What happened in there?"

"Long story."

"It's lunchtime. Why don't we go somewhere and you can tell me this long story."

He looked at her.

"You know," she said with a determinedly bright smile. "You can give me a report."

A report, he thought. First he was therapy and now he was business. This relationship was not improving. On the contrary, it seemed to be going sideways. But an invitation to lunch counted for something.

"Okay," he said. "But you're the client, so you're buying."

She flushed a little and did not seem amused. "Certainly. Where shall we go?"

"I assume you have to get back to the gallery right away. We can grab a bite at the Incandescent Body."

"Well, actually, no, I don't have to get back to the gallery right away," she said smoothly. "I just hired an assistant for the summer. Gail Gillingham. She said she could handle the place for the afternoon."

"Gail?" He thought about that. "Good choice."

"I think so. Unfortunately, I can't offer her anything permanent, but she said that the position will give her some breathing space in which to hunt for a better situation. You know what they say, the best time to look for a job is when you've already got one."

"Yeah, I've heard that." He kept his grip on her arm and angled her across Bay Street, steering toward the gas station, where his car was still parked at the pump.

"Gail has a very professional attitude and she's smart,"

Octavia said, trotting briskly along beside him. "I think that eventually she'll turn up something at the institute or at Chamberlain."

"Probably."

Octavia finally noticed that they were halfway across the street. She frowned. "Where are we going?"

"To get my car."

"Oh."

When they reached the BMW, Nick opened the door on the passenger side and stuffed Octavia into the seat. He closed the door and reached for his wallet.

"What do I owe you, Sandy?"

"Twenty-three bucks." Sandy peered through the windshield, looking at Octavia. "Everything go okay in the Total Eclipse?"

"Sure." Nick handed him the cash and started toward the driver's side of the car. "By the way, turns out Eugene and Dwayne were mistaken about that rumor they were spreading around."

Sandy blinked. "You mean the one about Miss—" He broke off abruptly when Nick gave him a hard look. He swallowed heavily. "Wrong, huh?"

"Yeah." Nick opened the door. "Completely false. Be a good idea if you didn't pass it along. Know what I mean?"

"Right," Sandy said quickly and nodded. "Big mistake."

Nick got behind the wheel. "You got it," he said through the open window. "Big mistake."

He drove out of the station, aware that Octavia was watching him intently.

"What was that all about?" she asked.

"Nothing important."

"Don't give me that. You deliberately intimidated Sandy Hickson. I want to know why."

He turned the corner and drove up the street that led away from the waterfront. "I didn't do a damn thing to Sandy."

"Yes, you did. I saw you. Something about the way you looked at him. I call that intimidation. Why did you do it?"

He contemplated that question for a while. Then he shrugged. "Okay, you should probably know what's going on, seeing as how you're the *client,* and all."

"Absolutely." She put on her own dark glasses, settled back into her seat, and folded her arms beneath her breasts. "Talk."

"There's a rumor going around town that you're the one who swiped the Upsall."

For a couple of seconds she did not move, just sat there gazing blankly through the windshield. Then she whipped around in the seat.

"Someone thinks I stole it?"

"I picked up the story from Sandy. He said he got it from a couple of colorful types who hang out at the Total Eclipse—"

"Mean Eugene and Dickhead Dwayne."

He was a little taken aback. Somehow it was hard to envision her calling anyone *dickhead.* He had to keep reminding himself that the Fairy Queen was not all sweetness and light. Not anymore.

"Uh, yeah," he said.

"Those two are spreading the rumor that I'm responsible for the theft, hmm?"

"Yeah."

"Well, I hate to say it, but you must admit that there is some logic to their theory. I mean, I do have motive, opportunity, and a good working knowledge of the art world. How hard would it be for a slick operator like me to scam a bunch of locals like A.Z. and Virgil and the Heralds? All I'd have to do is make the picture disappear, tell everyone it got stolen, and then, a few months from now when I'm settled in some big city, make it mysteriously reappear. Presto, my name is suddenly legend in the world of modern art."

"Not hard," he agreed.

"And no one back here in Eclipse Bay would have a clue."

"No one but me," he corrected mildly.

"You wouldn't have any way of knowing what had happened, either. Not unless you made it a point to keep up with events in the art world."

He did not take his eyes off the road. "I'd do that, though."

"You would?"

"Let's just say I'd keep up with events concerning you."

"Oh." She mulled that over for a while and then, apparently not knowing what to do with it, let it go. She tightened her arms around her midsection. "Well, it's all moot because I did not steal the painting."

"I explained that to Eugene and Dwayne."

"You did?" Something in her expression lightened. "That was very nice of you."

"That's me. Mr. Nice Guy."

"I'm serious," she said. "That rumor about me taking the painting sounds quite logical when you think about it. I can see where reasonable people might start to wonder if I was the thief. After all, I am related to Claudia Banner and everyone knows what she did here."

He said nothing.

"I appreciate your support."

"Hey, you're the client. I lose you, I lose my fee."

"What fee?" she asked warily.

"Good question. Been wondering about that, myself. What fee?"

"You're not expecting a fee and you know it," she said crisply.

"That right? No fee, huh?"

They were in the woods now, climbing the hillside above the town. The cool, green canopy cut the bright sunlight. He watched for the familiar sign.

"Stop making a joke out of this," she said briskly. "We both know why you're looking for the painting. You want to help A.Z. and Virgil and the others."

"Not exactly," he said.

"What does that mean?"

"Means, not exactly."

The sign inscribed with the faded words *Snow's Café* came into view. The parking lot was crowded with vehicles ranging from bicycles to Volvos. Most of them, he knew, belonged to students and staff from nearby Chamberlain College. Arizona had catered to that particular clientele since she had opened the restaurant.

He turned off the road and parked next to a shiny little yellow Volkswagen.

"You know," Octavia said coolly, "the macho-cryptic private eye talk reads well in your books, but it doesn't go over so great in person."

"I hate when that happens."

He unfastened his seat belt and climbed out before she could pursue that line of inquiry. He was not in the mood to explain that the real reason he was playing private eye was because of her. Something Eugene had said came back to him. *How does it feel to be led around by your balls?*

That was Eugene for you, a real relationship guru. Downright insightful.

He shut the door and started around the rear of the car. By the time he got to her side she was already out of the front seat, moving toward him with a determined stride. She gripped the handbag slung over one shoulder very tightly and there was a dangerous look in her eyes.

Damn. He was getting hard.

He opened the door of the café and ushered her into the pleasant gloom of the comfortably shabby interior. Tough-looking rock stars of another era, thin and angry and wearing a lot of leather, glared down at them from the ancient posters that decorated the walls. The music piped through the old speakers came from the same time warp as the posters, but the decibel level was kept reasonably low so that you could hold a conversation without shouting.

Arizona did not spend much time here these days. She relied on employees she recruited from the work-study offices of Chamberlain. She trained a new crew at the beginning of each academic year and she paid them handsomely. The result was a remarkably loyal staff that, in turn, freed her to concentrate on what she saw as her chief mission in life: keeping tabs on the goings-on at the institute.

"Getting back to the way you *explained* things to Eugene and Dwayne." Octavia tossed her bag into the booth and slid in beside it. "Maybe you'd better tell me precisely what you said."

"Hard to recall *precisely* what I said." He flipped open the plastic-coated menu.

Portions of Arizona's bill of fare were occasionally updated to reflect passing trends such as soy products and veggie patties, but mostly A.Z. stuck with the basic student food groups: burgers, fries, and pizza.

"Talk to me, Nick. I'm very serious here. What did you say to Eugene and Dwayne?"

"Why is that conversation of such great interest to you?" he asked, not looking up from the menu.

"Because the more I think about it, the more it worries me. I don't know those two well, but from what I've heard about them, it would surprise me if they took good advice willingly."

"I tried to provide an incentive."

She went very still on the other side of the table. "That's what I was afraid of."

"Look, don't worry about it, okay?"

"I'm worried." She reached out and plucked the menu from his fingers. "What magic words did you use to make them back off those rumors?"

What the hell, he thought. She would probably find out sooner or later, anyway. He lounged against the padded seatback and contemplated her for a moment.

*"Lavender and Leather,"* he said finally.

"I beg your pardon?"

*"Lavender and Leather* is the name of a gay bar located in the Capitol Hill neighborhood in Seattle," he explained. "About a year ago, Eugene and Dwayne went off to the big city, had a few beers, and decided it would be amusing to hang out in the vicinity of the establishment. They planned to entertain themselves hassling some of the patrons."

She was instantly incensed. "And here I've gone out of my way to be polite to them whenever I see them on the street. I actually felt sorry for those two."

"The interesting part is that, being Eugene and Dwayne, they managed to misjudge their intended victims. They picked on a couple of guys who had studied the martial arts. In short, Eugene and Dwayne got their asses kicked. Literally. It was not, I am told, a pretty sight."

"Oh, good." Octavia brightened. "I love stories that end like that. They confirm Aunt Claudia's theories about karma."

"Eugene and Dwayne apparently got a real jolt of karma that night." He picked up the menu she had taken from him and opened it again. "As you can imagine, however, it is not an incident they wish to have widely publicized here in Eclipse Bay."

"Ah, so that's it. Now I understand. No one here knows about their humiliating experience in Seattle?"

"Trust me, it is, perhaps, the best-kept secret in Eclipse Bay. If it ever got out that two gay men had used Eugene and Dwayne to mop out an alley, I doubt if the dynamic duo would ever be able to appear in public around here again."

She propped her elbow on the table and rested her chin on her hand. "In other words, you threatened Eugene and Dwayne."

"That's pretty much what it comes down to, yeah. Subtlety does not work well with those two."

"Hmm."

He looked up at that. "What?"

"If no one here in Eclipse Bay knows about Eugene and Dwayne's excellent adventure in Seattle, how did you learn the details?"

"Virgil Nash."

"Virgil? What does he have to do with Eugene and Dwayne?"

"As little as possible, like everyone else. It's another long story but I'll give you the short version. Several years ago, back in our wilder days, a bunch of us used to get together with some other guys out on a road near the bluffs to race our cars."

"I thought drag racing was illegal."

"Hey, we were nineteen-year-old guys with cars. What else could we do?"

"Right. Guys with cars. Go on."

"At the time, Eugene's pride and joy was a Ford that he boasted could beat anything else on the road. He was winning regularly but one night I beat him. He didn't take losing well, to put it mildly. After the race he followed me home. It was one o'clock in the morning."

"Go on."

"He had Dwayne with him, naturally. They probably egged each other on. At any rate, Eugene started playing games on the road that runs along the low cliffs just south of town."

"I know it. There are a lot of tight curves. What kind of games?"

"Coming up fast from behind, nipping at the bumper of my car, pulling up alongside and swerving toward us just as we went into a curve."

"Us?"

He shrugged. "Jeremy was in the car with me that night."

"I see." She looked thoughtful.

"We didn't know if Eugene was really trying to force us off the road or merely attempting to scare us. He was more than just annoyed because he had lost to me that night. He was crazy mad."

"What happened?"

"I figured I had two choices; I could either try to outrun Eugene, which would have been dicey on those curves, or try to fake him out. I went for faking him out. Jeremy watched him while I concentrated on driving. When Eugene made one of his moves to pull up alongside, Jeremy gave me the word. His timing was right on the mark. I braked hard. Eugene kept going and lost control. His car went over a low bluff and down a short incline, and landed in some shallow water."

"Whew. Well, obviously he and Dwayne weren't killed."

"No. The only thing that saved them was the fact that the tide was still partially out. I stopped at the top of the bluff and Jeremy and I went down to see how bad things were. Eugene was slumped over the wheel. At first we thought that he was dead but then we realized he was just badly dazed. Dwayne was frozen with shock. There was no time to get help because the tide was coming in fast. Jeremy and I hauled them both out of the car and dragged them out of the water. We wrapped them in some blankets I kept in the back of the car."

"In other words, you and Jeremy saved Eugene and Dwayne."

"And neither of them ever forgave us for the humiliation," Nick concluded dryly.

"Where does Virgil Nash fit into this story?"

"Virgil lives out near where the accident happened. After we got Eugene and Dwayne out of the car, we went to Virgil's house to get help. He was there when Eugene made some threats to Jeremy and me."

"Threats?"

"Eugene was really pissed, like I said. Blamed us for wrecking his beloved car. But mostly he was just furious because he had screwed up and we'd had to rescue him. Anyhow, Virgil took us aside later and said that we should watch our backs for a while. We did, but Eugene never made any moves. The years went by and we figured every-one involved had forgotten about what happened that night."

"But Virgil didn't forget?"

"No. Virgil's been watching Eugene ever since, and that means watching Dwayne, too, since for the most part they're inseparable. When they got into trouble last year in Seattle, Virgil heard about it from a colleague who runs a sex toy shop there. He e-mailed both Jeremy and me and told us the story. Reminded us that guys like Eugene don't change and that someday it might pay to have some am-munition on hand, just in case."

"And today you used your ammunition."

"You could say that."

She watched him with an odd, unreadable expression. "For my sake."

"Yeah, well, I didn't want them spreading that story around."

"It's the kind of thing your hero, John True, would do."

He should have been flattered, he thought. But for some reason it irritated him that she was making a connection between him and the character in his books. He wasn't John True. He was Nick Harte. He closed the menu a sec-ond time and looked at her very steadily.

"Don't," he said grimly, "get me mixed up with John True. He's pure fiction. I'm real."

The interesting expression on her face disappeared im-mediately behind a cool veil. She took her chin off her hand and sat back. "Got it. Trust me, I won't make that mistake."

"Good." He was more annoyed than ever now. What the hell was wrong with him today?

A young waiter appeared, saving him from getting too

deep into the introspective thing. Octavia ordered a salad. Nick realized that he was hungry. The confrontation at the Total Eclipse had given him an appetite. He chose the oversized tuna sandwich and fries, knowing from past experience that it would do the job.

When the waiter had disappeared, Octavia looked at him.

"Don't get me wrong, I appreciate what you did today," she said. "But do you think it was wise to threaten Eugene and Dwayne?"

"I'm not worried about those two," he said.

"Okay, so what *are* you worried about? I can see that you've got something else on your mind."

"Eugene and Dwayne are not the sharpest knives in the drawer, if you know what I mean."

"I sort of got that impression. So?"

"So, while they are both the type to spread false and malicious rumors, neither of them has the brainpower to concoct the one going around about you."

She elevated her brows. "I believe I see where you're going here."

"When you stop and think about it, that story Eugene and Dwayne were spreading about you is a fairly sophisticated piece of gossip. They gave you motive and opportunity and they've added a few inside bits about how the art market works. Eugene even tried to use the word *provenance.*"

"Not the sort of word you'd expect a guy like him to have in his vocabulary."

"No."

"From what I've heard about those two, they aren't likely to know much about the art market, either."

"Highly doubtful," he agreed.

"Which means that they are probably not the source of the rumors."

"Probably not."

She was quiet for a moment. Her expression turned somber. "What do you propose to do next?"

"I'm going to try to find out who started the gossip about you," he said. "I figure whoever is responsible for the rumors might have had a motive for implicating you."

"Like, maybe, to cover up his own involvement in the theft of the painting?"

"Yeah." He hesitated and then decided to give her the rest of it. "There's something else that bothers me about that elaborate story, too."

"What?"

"It would have been a lot simpler to point the finger of blame at the Heralds. They already seem a little suspicious to most folks. Instead, whoever concocted it chose you for the fall guy."

"You think this may be personal?"

"Yeah," he said. "I do. I've come to the conclusion that someone isn't just looking for any scapegoat. Whoever took the painting wants to make you, in particular, look guilty."

# chapter 15

Anne came into the gallery with Gail the following morning. She clutched a carefully rolled-up sheet of drawing paper in both hands.

"I brought you my picture," Anne said in her whispery little voice. She held it out to Octavia.

"Thank you." Delighted, Octavia came around from behind the counter to take the rolled artwork. "I'm so glad that you decided to enter a drawing in the show, Anne."

Before she could unroll the picture, Nick and Carson walked into the gallery. Nick carried a paper sack bearing the Incandescent Body logo. Carson had a cup of hot chocolate in one hand.

"Morning, Gail," Nick said. "Hi, Anne."

"Hi," Gail replied. "Say hello to Mr. Harte, Anne."

"Hello, Mr. Harte."

"This is Carson," Nick said.

"Hi," Carson said cheerfully. He looked at Anne and

then at the rolled-up drawing in Octavia's hand. "Is that your picture?"

"Yes," she said.

"I did one, too. Miss Brightwell put mine in a gold frame." He looked at Octavia. "We brought you some coffee and a muffin."

"Thanks," Octavia said. "That sounds good."

"Let me see Anne's picture," Carson said.

"I was just about to look at it myself, and then Anne can select her frame."

Octavia carefully unrolled the drawing and put it down on a low table. She looked at the picture, ready with admiring words. Then she took a second look, awed by the remarkable talent displayed in crayon.

The form, color, shading, and expression were astounding, especially given the age of the artist. In some ways it was clearly a child's picture, but in others it vibrated with the raw power of a gifted and as yet untrained artist.

"Anne," she said very gently, "this is a beautiful picture. Incredible."

Anne looked thrilled. "Do you really like it?"

Octavia took her gaze off the picture with some reluctance and looked at her. "Yes." She caught Gail's attention. "It is quite remarkable, to be honest."

"I told you she was good," Gail said with quiet pride.

"Brilliant is more like it," Octavia murmured.

Carson was alarmed now. "Let me see." He hurried closer and examined the picture with an expression of mounting outrage. "It's a *dog*."

"It's Zeb," Anne told him. "He's my dog. Well, partly mine. He belongs to Grandpa, but Grandpa says I can share him."

Carson rounded on her. "You can't do a dog for the art show. I did Winston."

"Carson." Nick spoke quietly. "That's enough."

Carson turned to him. "But, Dad she can't do a dog. I already did one."

Anne started to look uncertain. She glanced from her mother to Octavia for reassurance and then glowered at Carson. "Miss Brightwell said I could make any kind of picture I wanted."

"That's right," Octavia said calmly. "No two dog pictures are the same, so we can have any number of them in the art show, just like we can have any number of house pictures and flower pictures."

Carson was not appeased, but he obviously knew that he was fighting a losing battle. "It's not fair."

"Take it easy, Carson," Nick said. "You heard Miss Brightwell. No two dog pictures are the same, so there can be lots of them in the show."

"Each one is special," Octavia assured him. "Each one is unique. Your picture of Winston doesn't look anything like Anne's picture of Zeb."

Carson's face tightened but he did not argue further.

Octavia smiled at Anne. "Come with me and we'll pick out a frame for your picture of Zeb. You have a choice of black, red, or gold."

Anne brightened instantly. "I want a gold one, please."

Carson clenched his hands into small fists at his sides.

Nick took Carson out of the gallery. They went across the street and walked out onto the pier.

Nick stopped at the end and braced a foot on one of the wooden boards that formed the railing. He peeled the top off his cup of coffee.

"You want to tell me what's wrong?" he asked.

"Nothing's wrong." Carson took a desultory swipe at one of the railing posts with the toe of his right running shoe. "It's just not fair."

"Why isn't it fair?"

"It just isn't, that's all. My picture was the only dog picture until now. That's why Miss Brightwell liked it so much."

*So that's what this is all about,* Nick thought. He took a swallow of coffee while he considered how to handle the situation. He understood Carson's position better than his son realized. Every time he thought about Jeremy and his artistic talent and how much Jeremy had in common with Octavia, he was flooded with a wholly irrational jealousy, too.

"Miss Brightwell made it clear that she likes both dog pictures," Nick said.

"She likes Anne's better than mine," Carson muttered.

"How do you know that?"

"Anne's is better," Carson said.

It was a simple statement, uttered in the tone of voice of a guy who knows his hopes are doomed.

"Mind if I ask why you care so much what Miss Brightwell thinks about your picture of Winston?" Nick asked. "Is this just a simple manifestation of the Harte competitive instinct, or is there something else going on here?"

Carson frowned. "Huh?"

Sometimes he had to remind himself that Carson wasn't quite six yet. He was smart, but words like *manifestation* and *competitive instinct* could still throw him.

"Remember, the Children's Art Show isn't a competition. Miss Brightwell isn't going to choose a winning picture. All the drawings will be exhibited. There won't be any losers."

"Doesn't mean Miss Brightwell doesn't like Anne's picture best," Carson grumbled.

"Why do you care? I mean, let's face it, you've never shown a lot of interest in art until you decided to draw a picture for Miss Brightwell's show."

"I want Miss Brightwell to like my picture best."

"How come?"

Carson shrugged. "She likes artists. If she thought I was a good artist, maybe she'd like me better."

"Better than what? Better than she likes Anne?"

Carson kicked the post again. The blow was not so forceful this time. More of a gesture of frustration. "I dunno."

"She likes you a lot," Nick said. "Trust me."

Carson took another halfhearted shot at the post with the toe of his running shoe. Definitely losing steam now. *A little boy struggling to deal with complex emotions that he doesn't comprehend,* Nick thought.

They stood there in silence for a while, morosely watching the sunlight dance on the waters of the bay. Nick finished his coffee.

*I want her to like me, too. I don't want her to think of me as therapy or business. I want her to want me, the way I want her.*

He heard a crumpling sound and looked down, vaguely surprised to discover that he had crushed the empty coffee cup in his hand. Irritated, he tossed the remains into the nearest trash bin.

*An adult male struggling to deal with complex emotions that he doesn't comprehend,* he thought. Well, at least he wasn't going around kicking fence posts. A definite sign of maturity.

"So," he said, "what do you say we ask Miss Brightwell to have dinner at our house tonight?"

"Think she'd come?" Carson asked with sudden enthusiasm.

"I don't know," Nick said, determined to be honest. "But we're a couple of Hartes. That means we go after what we want, even if we lose in the end."

"I know," Carson said, "she likes salads. Tell her we're gonna have a really big salad."

"Good idea."

"Salad, hmm?" Octavia said a few minutes later when they presented her with their proposition.

"With lots and lots of lettuce," Carson assured her. "As much as you want."

Nick leaned back against the counter and folded his arms. "Maybe a couple of radishes, too," he promised.

She gave him that mysterious smile that left him in limbo. "I could hardly pass up an offer like that," she said. "It's a date."

Nick turned to Carson. "Guess we'd better hit Fulton's before they run out of the best lettuce."

"Okay." Carson whirled and rushed toward the door.

Nick looked at Octavia. "Thanks. He's dealing with his first-ever case of professional jealousy. Anne's picture of Zeb hit him hard."

"I noticed."

Outside, Jeremy drove his Nissan into the little parking lot. Nick watched him climb out of the car and start toward the row of shops.

"Carson realized right away that Anne's picture was much better than his," he said to Octavia.

"The art show isn't a competition."

"Yeah, I reminded him of that." He crossed the showroom to the open door. "But he's a Harte. He had an agenda when he entered his picture of Winston in your show. He wanted you to think his drawing was the best. Now he's worried that he's been outclassed by a better artist."

She nodded. "I understand."

Outside on the sidewalk, Jeremy had paused at the entrance to Seaton's Antiques. He glanced at Nick, his face impassive. Then he opened the door and disappeared into his grandmother's shop.

"I'm really glad to hear that you understand," Nick said softly. "Because I'm having a similar problem."

She leaned her elbows on the counter. "You're worried that you've been outclassed by a better artist?"

"Professional jealousy is tough to deal with at any age."

He went outside to join Carson.

At six that evening she stood on the top of the bluff with Carson and looked down at the five finger-shaped stones that thrust upward out of the swirling waters at the base of the short cliff.

"It's called Dead Hand Cove," Carson explained, cheerfully morbid. "Dad named it when he was a kid. On account of the way the rocks stick up. Like a dead hand. See?"

"Got it." The day had been pleasantly warm but there was a mild breeze off the water. Octavia stared down into the cove. "The stones really do look like fingers."

"And there's some caves down there, too. Dad and I

went into them yesterday. We found some marks on the walls. Dad said he put them there when he was a kid so that Aunt Lillian and Aunt Hannah wouldn't get lost when they went inside."

"That's a Harte for you," she said. "Always planning ahead."

"Yeah, Dad says that's what Hartes do." Carson's mood darkened into a troubled frown. "He says sometimes all the planning doesn't work, though. He says sometimes stuff happens that you don't expect and things change."

"You mean stuff like Anne's picture of Zeb?" she asked gently.

He gazed up at her quickly and then looked away. "Yeah. It was better than my picture of Winston, wasn't it?"

She sat down on a nearby rock so that their faces were level. "Anne has a marvelous talent. If she decides to work hard at her drawing and if she has a passion for it, I think she could someday be a fine artist."

"Yeah." He kicked at a clump of grass.

"Different people have different kinds of talents," she said. "It's true that Anne has a gift for drawing. But the fact that you could see that her picture was so good means that you have another kind of talent."

He glanced at her, still scowling but intrigued now. "What kind?"

"It isn't everyone who can take one look at a picture and know that it is very good."

"Big deal."

"Yes, it is a big deal," she said matter-of-factly. "You have an eye for excellence, and that talent will be an enormous asset to you in the years ahead."

"How do you know?" he grumbled.

"Because it's the same talent I've got."

That stopped him for a few seconds. Then he looked appalled. "The same kind?"

"Yes."

"But I don't *wanna* run an art store. I wanna run a big company like Granddad Hamilton and Great-Granddad Sullivan. Dad says that's probably what I'll do on account of it's in my genes or something."

"The talent to recognize quality and beauty when you see it will be useful to you no matter what you do with your life," she said.

"You're sure?"

"Positive."

"Cause I don't wanna have to run a little art gallery like yours."

"Don't worry, I doubt if you'll end up doing that for a living. But you may decide to buy art to hang in your home or on the walls of your office someday, and with your talent you'll be able to buy really excellent art. You won't have to pay a consultant to tell you what's good and what's not so good. You'll be able to make your own decisions."

"Huh." But he was clearly somewhat mollified by the prospect of making decisions.

"Who knows?" she said. "Maybe someday you'll be in a position to buy one of Anne's paintings."

"I'm not gonna buy any pictures of her dumb dog, that's for sure."

Dinner went well, Nick thought later. He was unaccountably relieved, even pleased. It had, after all, been a new experience for him. Not that he couldn't do salad and boil a pot full of some of Rafe's ravioli stuffed with gorgonzola cheese, spinach, and walnuts. He had, after all, been cooking for himself and Carson for quite a while now.

But when he had resumed a social life a year or so after Amelia's death, he had consciously or unconsciously confined himself to women who, he was fairly certain, would not have been comfortable sitting at a kitchen table with a precocious kid.

Maybe the women of the Harte family had been right all along, he thought. Maybe he just hadn't wanted to see any of his dates in a domestic light. You looked at a woman differently after you'd seen her hanging out in your kitchen, carrying on an intelligent conversation about dogs and dinosaurs with your son.

Whatever the case, one thing was certain. When he looked across the old kitchen table this evening, a wooden table that had been scarred and scuffed with the marks of three generations of Harte family meals, it had hit him with shattering clarity that Octavia looked perfect sitting here with Carson and himself.

They played all of the ancient board games that had accumulated in the hall closet over the years until Carson reluctantly fell asleep on the sofa. Nick carried him upstairs to bed. When he returned to the living room, Octavia was in her coat, fishing her keys out of her pocket.

"It's getting late," she said, smiling a little too brightly. "I'd better be on my way. Thanks for dinner."

She was the one running away this time, he thought.

"I'll walk you out to your car."

He collected his jacket from the closet and put it on without buttoning it. When he opened the front door he smelled the sea and saw the trailing wisps of a light fog.

"Good thing I'm going now," Octavia said. She stepped

out onto the porch and looked around. "This stuff looks like it's going to get heavier."

"Probably." He followed her outside, leaving the door ajar. "Thanks for what you said to Carson earlier. He's feeling a lot better now that he knows you're not going to judge him solely on his art."

"No problem."

"The kid's a Harte, what can I say? He wants you to like him and he'll do whatever he thinks will work."

"He doesn't have to worry. I like him. A lot. He's a pretty terrific kid."

He gripped the railing with both hands and looked out into the gathering mist. "What about me?"

"You?"

"I'd better warn you that this is a case of like son, like father."

She went still on the top step and gave him a politely quizzical look. "You want me to like you?"

"I want you to like me a lot."

She jangled her keys. "If this is about sleeping with me again—"

"It *is* about sleeping with you again," he said deliberately. "But it's also about explaining why I left in such a rush the other night."

"I know why you left in a rush. You panicked."

He released the railing and swung around abruptly to catch hold of her by the shoulders. "I did not panic."

"Sure you did. You're obviously dealing with a lot of unresolved issues connected to the loss of your wife, and when you get too close to a woman, you panic."

"Bullshit."

She gave him a gentle, sympathetic pat on the arm. "It's all right, I understand. I spent some time going through the grieving process after Aunt Claudia died. I can't even imagine how hard it would be to lose a beloved spouse."

He tightened his hands on her now. "It was hard, all right. But not for the reasons you think. I'm going to tell you something that no one else, not even anyone in my family, knows."

She stiffened. "I'm not sure I want to hear it."

"Too late, I'm going to tell you, whether you want to hear it or not. You probably know that the man at the controls of that small plane that crashed with Amelia on board was a family friend."

"Yes. Everyone knows that."

"Yeah, well hardly anyone else except his wife and me knows just what a very good friend he was of Amelia's."

"Nick, please stop."

"I found out after the funeral that they had been lovers at one time. They'd quarreled and each of them wound up marrying someone else. A couple of months before that plane crash, they had reconnected. It seems they'd both reached the earthshaking conclusion that they had married the wrong people."

She touched his cheek and said nothing.

"They were going off to spend the weekend together at a ski resort that day. His wife thought he was out of town on business. I thought Amelia had gone to visit her sister in Denver."

Octavia said nothing, just shook her head sadly.

"After the funeral his widow and I talked. We both decided that, for the sake of her son and mine, we would let the story stand about her husband having given my wife a lift to Colorado. Everyone bought it."

"I see." She lowered her fingers. "I'm sorry, Nick."

"I don't want you to feel sorry for me." He took his

hands off her shoulders and cupped her face between his palms. "I just want you to understand why I've been a little reluctant to rush back into a serious relationship."

"You're scared."

He set his jaw. "I am not scared."

"Yes, you are. You made the kind of mistake that Hartes aren't supposed to make. You screwed up and married the wrong woman once, and you're absolutely terrified of screwing up again. So it's easier to play it safe."

"I made a mistake. I'll give you that much. And it's true that Hartes don't usually make those kinds of mistakes. But I'll never regret it."

She comprehended immediately. "Because of Carson."

"Amelia gave me my son. I will always be thankful to her memory for that."

"Of course you will, and that is as it should be. But that doesn't mean that deep down you're not afraid of trusting your emotions again."

"I am not afraid," he said evenly, "but I am damn careful these days. Amelia and I rushed into marriage because we both thought passion was enough. It wasn't. Next time around, I'm going to take my time and make certain that I know what I'm doing."

"Know what I think? I think you're being so careful that you get nervous when there's even a hint that a relationship might cross the line between casual and serious." She searched his face. "Is that what happened the other night? Did you panic because you thought our one-night stand might turn into something more than that?"

"For the last time, I did not panic. And for the record, I never intended it to be a one-night stand."

"I beg your pardon, did you freak out because you were

worried that *our little summer fling* might get too heavy and too complicated?"

He refused to let her push him into losing his temper. He was trying to accomplish an objective here. Hartes never lost sight of their goals.

"Correct me if I'm wrong," he said, "but I was under the impression that you weren't looking for anything more than a short-term arrangement either, Miss Free Spirit."

She flushed. "I wasn't the one who ran for the door that night. I was doing just fine with the summer-fling thing."

"I did not run for the door. I left in a hurry, but I did not run."

"Details."

"Important details. And I'd like to remind you that I showed up at your gallery the next morning," he said. "It's not like I didn't call. And how the hell do you think I felt when you told me that the sex had been therapeutic? You made it sound like a good massage or a tonic, damn it."

She bit her lip. "Well, it was, in a way."

"Great. Well, do me a favor. The next time you want physical therapy, call a masseuse or a chiropractor. Or buy a vibrator."

Her eyes widened. She was starting to look a little unnerved, he thought. For some reason, that gave him an unholy amount of satisfaction.

"Don't push me," she warned.

"I haven't been pushing you." He hauled her close. "*This* is what I call pushing you."

He kissed her, using everything he had to seduce her into a response. He was not sure what he expected, but he knew what he wanted. He had his agenda. He was going to make her admit that the sex hadn't been merely a therapeutic tonic.

He was vaguely surprised and somewhat reassured when she made no move to free herself. After an instant's hesitation, her mouth softened under his. Her arms went around his neck and her fingers sank into his hair. Heat swirled through him, igniting his senses.

He had been right about this much, at least, he thought. She still wanted him. Nothing had changed on that front. He could feel the passion quickening within her.

When she shivered in his arms and tightened her hold on him, his triumph was tempered by the sheer enormousness of his sense of relief.

He dragged his mouth away from hers and nibbled on her earlobe. "It was good between us. Give me that much at least."

"I never said that it wasn't good." She tipped her head back, giving him access to her throat. "It was great."

"Then why not enjoy it?" The taste of her skin and the herbal fragrance of her hair combined into an intoxicating perfume. He knew that he would never forget her scent as long as he lived. "We have the rest of the summer."

She tensed in his arms. Her fingers stopped moving through his hair. Very slowly she pulled away and raised her lashes. "Maybe you're right."

He kissed the tip of her nose. "No *maybe* about it."

"It's possible that I overreacted the other night."

"Understandable," he assured her. "You were coming off a difficult year. A lot of emotional stuff going on in your life. You're making some major decisions about your business and your future. Lot of stress."

"Yes."

"Maybe you were right about one thing," he offered, feeling generous now. "Okay, it's not easy to think of myself as a sort of physical therapist, but I have to admit that there is a therapeutic side to really good sex."

"Probably releases a lot of endorphins, and then there's the exercise aspect."

"Right. Exercise." He was not sure this was going the direction he had intended, but it wasn't like he had a lot of alternatives.

"Rather like taking a brisk walk on the beach, I think," she mused.

He made himself count to ten and forced a smile. "No need to analyze it too much. Sex is perfectly natural and there's no reason that two healthy, responsible adults who happen to be single and uncommitted shouldn't enjoy it together."

She did step back then, slipping out from under his hands. "I'll think about it."

He did not move. "You'll *think* about it?"

"Yes." She turned and went down the steps. "I can't give you an answer tonight. I'm not thinking clearly right now, and I don't want to make another rash decision based on overheated emotions. I'm sure you can understand."

"Now who's panicking?" he asked softly.

"You think I'm afraid of having an affair with you?"

"Yeah. That's exactly what I think."

"Maybe you're right." She sounded regretful but accepting of that possibility. "As you said, I've been under a lot of stress lately. It's difficult to sort out logic and emotions."

He followed her down the steps, shadowing her to the car. When she stopped beside the vehicle he stopped too, very close behind her. He reached around her, letting his fingers skim across the lush curve of her hip, and opened the door.

"I'll see you in the morning," he said. "Meanwhile, try to get some sleep."

She slipped into the front seat. "I'm sure I'll sleep just fine, thank you."

"Lucky you."

She started to put the key into the ignition and then paused. "One more thing I wanted to say."

He gripped the top of the car door. "What's that?"

"I think you should give Jeremy a call. Invite him out for a beer or whatever men do when they want to talk things over."

"Now, just why in hell would I want to do that?"

"Because you were once good friends and there's no reason why you can't be friends again. Deep down, he knows that you didn't have an affair with his wife."

She turned the key in the ignition, pulled the door shut, and drove away into the night.

# chapter 16

Nick knew it was going to be a bad day when he drove into the parking lot of the Incandescent Body bakery the following morning shortly after ten and saw the black limo sitting near the front door. The driver was behind the wheel, sipping coffee and reading a newspaper.

"I don't need this," Nick said to himself while Carson scrambled out of the backseat. "I definitely do not need this."

Carson looked up at him. "What don't you need, Dad?"

"You'll find out in a minute." He closed the rear door and started toward the entrance to the bakery.

"I'm gonna have hot chocolate and an orange muffin this time," Carson announced with relish. "And we can get some coffee and a muffin for Miss Brightwell, too, okay?"

"I'm gonna have to think about that." He was still feeling pretty pissed off by her parting remarks last night, he thought. She'd had a lot of nerve suggesting that he take the lead in repairing his shattered friendship with Jeremy.

Carson looked startled. "How come? We always bring her some coffee and a muffin."

"The situation is getting complicated."

"But we gotta take her coffee and a muffin. We always take her that stuff. She 'spects it now. Dad, you promised you wouldn't do anything to make her mad."

"Okay, okay, we'll get her coffee and a muffin."

He opened the door of the bakery. Carson spotted the two men sitting at the small table immediately. Excitement galvanized him into motion. He raced forward at full speed.

*"Great-Granddad."* Carson looked back over his shoulder. "Dad, it's *Great-Granddad.* He's here."

"I noticed," Nick said. He met Sullivan's eyes over the top of Carson's head. Then he flicked a glance at Mitchell, who was looking smug. "What a surprise."

He took his time following Carson to the table where the two men sat together over coffee. Two canes were propped against one of the chairs. Misleading, those canes, Nick thought. At first glance you might make the mistake of assuming that they indicated weakness. Nothing could be further from the truth.

He had seen photos of Mitch and Sullivan when they had been in the military together decades earlier. They had been young men in their prime at the time, strong and competent, ready to take on their futures. But the picture had been taken shortly after they had survived the hell of combat in a far-off jungle, and the experience had left an indelible imprint on them. If you looked closely, you could still see it in their eyes today. These were two very tough men, the kind you wanted at your back if you decided to walk down a dark alley.

They were also both stubborn as hell and downright

bloody-minded when it came to getting their own way. But in fairness, Nick thought, those traits ran through every generation of both the Madison and the Harte families.

Sullivan grinned at Carson when the boy barreled to a halt at his chair. He gave Carson a hug and ruffled his hair affectionately.

"Hello there, sport, how are you doing?"

"Hi," Carson replied. "Did you come to see my picture in the art show? Cause if you did, you'll have to wait for a few days. The show isn't until next weekend. I did a picture of Winston."

"I won't miss the show," Sullivan assured him. He gave Carson a gentle push toward the front counter. "Go get yourself a muffin on me."

"Okay." Carson hurried away.

Nick looked at Mitchell. "This is your doing, I assume?"

"Just thought your grandfather oughta be made aware of what was going on here in Eclipse Bay," Mitchell said with malevolent good cheer.

"I hear you've been busy lately, Nick." Sullivan picked up his coffee. "Trying to find a painting that used to belong to Thurgarton and seeing Octavia Brightwell on the side."

"Not necessarily in that order, but, yeah, that pretty much sums up my summer vacation so far." Accepting the inevitable, Nick grabbed a chair and sat down. "But I've got hopes that the situation will improve."

After lunch at Dreamscape and some hurried conversation with Rafe and Hannah, who were busy with a crowd in the restaurant, Nick and Sullivan took Carson and Winston down to the beach below the old mansion.

Sullivan watched his great-grandson dart all over the

landscape, following Winston from one tide pool to another.

"One of these days you're going to have to get that boy a dog of his own," he said.

"When he turns six," Nick agreed.

"That's next month."

"Yeah, I know. Carson reminds me just about every day."

"Six years old." Sullivan shook his head in wonder. "Where the hell did the years go? I remember when I used to walk on this same beach with you and Hamilton and a dog named Joe."

"If this is another one of those little grandfatherly chats on the subject of how the years are slipping away and how Carson needs a mother and how it's time I got married again," Nick said, "could we just skip to the end? I've heard it so many times that I've got it memorized."

"Take it easy. We're all worried about you and Carson. Harte men are family men, you know that."

"Carson and I have plenty of family. Every time I turn around, I'm running into family. Take this morning, for example. I walk into the local bakery to get a cup of coffee and what do I see? Family."

"Not like a Harte to be playing the field at your age."

"I do not play the field."

"What do you call it when you have relationships with several different women?"

"I call it a social life. And for the record, I did not have those relationships simultaneously. Hell, I've only dated maybe a half dozen different women in the past three years. I don't think that's excessive."

"Your mother and your grandmother and your sisters do."

"They're all obsessed with the idea of getting me married again."

"They think you've got some kind of psychological block. They've all decided that you've got a problem with getting serious about another woman because you're afraid of losing her the way you lost Amelia."

Nick watched Carson poke at a hole in the sand with a long stick while he tried to decide how to respond to that. "What do you think?" he said at last.

"Me?" Sullivan seemed surprised to be asked for his opinion. He halted beside a rock. "I think you just haven't found the right woman."

Nick realized he had been braced for a lecture. He allowed himself to relax slightly. "Yeah, that's sort of how I see it, too."

"But Octavia is different, isn't she?"

So much for letting down his guard. "Mitchell sent for you, didn't he? That's why you're here."

"Mitch feels protective toward Octavia Brightwell."

"Octavia can take care of herself."

"What about you?" Sullivan asked quietly.

It took Nick a beat or two to grasp that. "Don't tell me that you're afraid that I'm the one who might be in trouble here."

Sullivan's gaze rested on Carson and Winston, who had moved on to explore the entrance of a shallow cave. "Got one question for you."

"What?"

"Did you give Octavia The Talk?"

"Damn. I'm starting to think that everyone in the Northwest knows all the details of my social life. A guy could get paranoid."

"You didn't answer my question. Did you give Octavia

your patented lecture on the subject of keeping things light?"

"You know what? I'm not going to answer that question."

Sullivan nodded. "Things went wrong this time around, didn't they? Mitch was right."

"I think we'd better change the subject, Granddad."

"Probably a good idea. Relationship counseling isn't exactly my forte. But for what it's worth, I came here to see what was going on, not to put pressure on you. I figure you can handle your own love life without my interference."

Nick raised his brows. "I'm stunned. Since when did anyone in our family ever hesitate to apply pressure whenever the opportunity arose?"

Sullivan exhaled heavily. "I put enough pressure on you when you were growing up. Always figured you'd take over Harte Investments, you know."

"I know."

"I didn't handle it well that day when you came to me and told me that you were leaving the company. Lost my temper. Said some things I shouldn't have said."

"We both did," Nick said quietly.

"Hamilton cornered me in my office that same afternoon. He was mad as hell. Angrier than I'd ever seen him. Told me to back off and leave you alone. Told me that you and Lillian and Hannah all had the right to make your own choices in life the same way I'd made mine and that he wasn't going to stand by and let me pressure any of you into doing what I wanted you to do. He really let me have it that day."

"Dad said all that?" Nick was surprised. He had known that he'd had his father's support when he made the decision to leave the company but he hadn't realized that Hamilton had gone toe-to-toe with Sullivan over the issue.

"Yes. Looking back, I can see that he was trying to protect you and your sisters from the kind of pressure I'd put him under when he was growing up. I didn't mean to force anyone into a mold, you know. It's just that I had always had this vision of H.I. descending down through the family. I couldn't believe that my grandson didn't want what I had spent so much of my life creating."

"The thing is," Nick said, groping for the words he needed, "Harte was your creation. I needed something that was all mine."

"And you found it in your writing. I understand that now." Sullivan's jaw tightened. "Something I've always wondered, though."

Nick glanced at him warily. "What?"

"Was it your leaving Harte after your first book was published that put the strain on your marriage?"

Nick sucked in a deep breath. "How did you know?"

"I didn't. It was your grandmother who guessed that things weren't going so well between you and Amelia there at the end. She had a hunch that the problems started when you decided to quit Harte. She always felt that, for Amelia, the company was part of the deal."

He did not know what to say, Nick thought. He had never realized that anyone had known about the fault line in his marriage.

"Grandmother is right," he said after a moment. "Amelia was having an affair with the man who was flying the plane that day. I think that, if she had lived, there would have been a divorce. She wanted out."

"And you wouldn't have been able to handle her cheating. You're a Harte."

"Yeah."

"Figured it was something like that." Sullivan kept his attention on Carson and Winston. "That's the real reason why you've been so cautious about getting serious with another woman. Got burned once and you're a mite nervous about sticking your finger back in the fire."

"Shit. Seems like everyone is trying to psychoanalyze me these days."

Sullivan's brows bristled into a sharp frown. "Who's everyone? Far as I know, only Rachel figured out the problems between you and Amelia. We never mentioned them to anyone else in the family or outside, for that matter."

"I told Octavia about how it was between Amelia and me. She leaped to the same conclusion that Grandma did."

"Huh. Women. Always trying to analyze what makes a man tick."

"Yeah."

"If only they knew how simple we really are."

"Better to keep 'em guessing," Nick said. "Probably makes us appear more interesting."

"True." Sullivan dug the tip of his cane into the coarse sand and started walking again. "Well, I think we've exhausted that subject. Tell me about this missing painting. You really trying to play private eye like that guy, John True, in your books?"

"I got into it because Virgil, A.Z., and Octavia asked me to look around a bit." Nick fell into step beside him. "They didn't think Valentine was looking in the right places, and they may have had a point. He suspects one of the Heralds probably took it and arranged to unload it in Seattle or Portland. He figures it's long gone."

"Mitch told me that much."

"I got a lot more serious about the situation after I heard

the rumor that Octavia had been voted Most Likely Suspect."

"Octavia?" Sullivan scowled. "Now, that's interesting."

"I thought so." Never let it be said that the old man was losing it mentally, Nick thought. Sullivan had grasped the implications immediately. "Especially when you consider that she's well-liked here in town. It would have been a lot easier to cast suspicion on the Heralds, who are viewed as the local weirdos and outsiders."

"You figure it's personal, don't you? Someone is out to pin the blame on Octavia for some specific reason."

"That's how it looks to me."

"You sure she hasn't managed to piss off someone here in town? Maybe refused to market some artist who's decided to get even?"

"I don't think so." Nick shot him a searching glance. "I'm starting to wonder if this could be coming out of the past."

"Claudia Banner."

"Yes."

"But the only folks who got hurt when Claudia pulled off her scam all those years ago were Mitch and me. And we're both a little too old for revenge, even if we had a notion to go after it."

"I doubt if anyone gets too old for revenge if the motivation is strong enough, but I agree that you and Mitch are not the ones behind this. What I want to know is, do you think there's anyone else in Eclipse Bay who might harbor a grudge against Claudia Banner that would be big enough to make him go after Octavia?"

Sullivan contemplated that in silence for a while.

"If there's one thing I've learned about business in the past sixty years," he said finally, "it's that it's always personal. And when the deal involves as much cash as Claudia's scam did, there's usually a fair amount of collateral damage."

"Meaning maybe someone besides you and Mitchell Madison got hurt?"

"Could be. It's possible. I can't give you any names but I'll tell you what I'll do. I'll go over this with Mitch. You know, he and I never really talked about the details of what happened when Claudia put us into bankruptcy. We were too busy blaming each other and firing up the feud. But maybe we can discuss it calmly now. Put our heads together and reconstruct events, so to speak."

"Thanks. Let me know if you come up with anyone who might still be so pissed off at Claudia Banner that he would go after her niece."

"All right. It's a long shot, though. You do realize that?"

"Sure. But that's all I've got at the moment. Long shots."

"I can see that." Sullivan came to a halt and stabbed the cane into the sand a few times. He gave Nick a beatific smile. "Now that that's settled, how about I do you a favor and give you some time to yourself?"

"You offering to babysit?"

"Figured I'd take Carson back to Portland with me for a few days. Lillian and I can look after him while Gabe and Hamilton argue about the details of the merger. You'll have time to work on finding that missing painting."

"Sure. If he wants to go, you're welcome to take him with you, but don't pretend that you're trying to do me any favors. You just want another opportunity to mold him in your image. You think you can turn him into the next major empire builder in the family."

"You've got to admit, the boy's got a flair for business."

Sullivan chuckled. "Remember how much money he made off that lemonade stand he set up in front of the house a few months ago when you brought him down to Phoenix? Talk about a natural aptitude."

Nick regarded his son playing with Winston and felt a rush of pride. "We'll see."

"We will, indeed. By the way, don't tell me that I'm not doing you any favors by removing young Carson from the vicinity for a while. I'd think you'd appreciate me giving you a little space in which to do your courting."

"*Courting.*" Nick stumbled over a rocky outcropping. He caught his balance and glowered at Sullivan. "What the hell are you talking about?"

"I figure I owe you that much," Sullivan continued smoothly, "after the way I tried to coerce you into taking over Harte Investments. And I've got to say, I think you've made a fine choice. I'm rather fond of Octavia."

"Damn it, who said anything about me courting Octavia Brightwell?"

"Gives me a good feeling to be helping you out like this. I do believe I'm getting downright sentimental in the twilight of my life."

"Twilight, my ass. You're not getting sentimental, you're still trying to run things, the way you always have."

"What can I say? It's in the blood."

They set out for Portland two hours later. Sullivan waited until they passed the *You Are Now Leaving Eclipse Bay* sign before he picked up the cell phone and punched out Mitchell's number.

"Well?" Mitchell demanded. "Did you get Nick straightened out?"

Sullivan glanced at Carson seated beside him. The boy

was immersed in a book about dogs. "There's no need to worry about my grandson's, uh, association with Miss Brightwell."

Mitchell snorted loudly on the other end. "So you say."

"You'll have to take my word on that subject, Mitch. Meanwhile, something has come up in regard to that missing painting. Nick's got a hunch that there's a personal angle here. He thinks the thief might be someone who is still holding a grudge because of what happened when Claudia took Harte-Madison apart."

"But you and I were the ones who went bankrupt all those years ago. As far as I know we were the only people who got ripped off. Why the hell would anyone else still hold a grudge?"

"I don't know. I suggest we start with a list of everyone we knew at the time who might have had anything to do with Claudia and Harte-Madison."

"That's gonna take some thinking."

"I know. Tell you what. You put your list together and I'll make up mine. Then we can talk and compare notes. Maybe something will hit us."

"I'll see what I can do." Mitch paused. "You're sure Nick is gonna get his act together with Octavia?"

"Count on it."

Sullivan ended the call and looked at Carson. "Picked out the kind of dog you want?"

"I want one just like Winston."

"Can't go wrong with another Winston." Sullivan ruffled the boy's hair, then reached into his briefcase. "That reminds me, I brought a printout of your investment portfolio with me. Want to see how those lemonade profits are doing?"

Carson slammed the dog book closed. "How much money did I make?" he asked excitedly.

"You did very well with those ten shares in Fast Toy, Inc."

"I told you they made good toys."

"So you did." Sullivan put the brokerage statement on the seat between them. "Take a look at that bottom line. You made three hundred dollars."

"Oh, wow." Carson snatched up the statement and immediately started asking questions about the various entries.

Sullivan settled back against the seat and prepared to indulge himself in one of his favorite hobbies: teaching his eager great-grandson the finer points of investment strategies.

Life was good, he thought. He had Carson, and two hours ago Hannah had informed him that he was soon to become a great-grandfather for the second time. Judging by the intimacy and the joy he witnessed when he was with Gabe and Lillian, he was almost certain there would be more good news coming from that quarter one of these days.

All he had to do was get Nick and Octavia on the right track and life would be damn near perfect.

# chapter 17

An eerie green light emanated from Arizona's War Room. Octavia studied the glow seeping around the edge of the heavy steel door with great interest.

"Think maybe she's thawing some of those frozen space aliens she claimed the institute was trying to hide a few months ago?" she asked.

"When it comes to A.Z. and her conspiracy theories, nothing would surprise me." Nick pushed open the door and stood back to allow Octavia to enter the room.

In any normal house, the space would probably have been described by the architect as a study. But Arizona didn't live in a normal house. Her cabin was fortified with locking metal shutters on all the windows. The doors had been reinforced with steel bolts. Rumor had it that Arizona had six months' worth of supplies and food stored on the premises.

Octavia had lived in Eclipse Bay long enough to know that the reason no one in town got nervous about Arizona was because it was a fact that she had no interest in weapons of any kind. In her bizarre fantasy world, her mission was to collect and analyze intelligence data on the various conspiracies she was certain lay just below the surface at the Eclipse Bay Policy Studies Institute. The fact that the institute dismissed her as a quaint, local eccentric suited Arizona just fine. As she had explained to Octavia on one occasion, the disdain from the institute staff only made her job of spying on them simpler.

Octavia stepped into the War Room and saw that the mysterious green light radiated from a computer screen. Three people garbed in flowing robes and wearing a lot of the vaguely Egyptian-style jewelry favored by the Heralds sat hunched over the table. Two of them were going through heavy, leather-bound log books. The third was pounding away on the keyboard. They barely glanced up when Octavia and Nick entered.

There was a spartan, military-spare look to the furnishings. A large topographical map of Eclipse Bay was laminated to the surface of a massive desk. Rows of log books were arranged on the metal shelving that lined one wall.

Arizona, dressed in her customary camouflage-patterned fatigues, occupied the aging wooden chair behind the desk. A chubby, unlit cigar stuck out of the corner of her mouth. The narrow beam from the desk lamp was aimed low to illuminate the topo map. Most of Arizona's face was in shadow.

"About time you two got here." Arizona motioned toward the chairs that sat opposite her on the other side of the desk. "Have a seat. Coffee?"

Octavia glanced toward the machine in the corner. She could detect the unmistakable odor of burned coffee from where she stood. The glass pot had been sitting on the hot plate for a long, long time.

"No, thanks," she said politely. She took one of the chairs. "I've had enough today."

"I'll pass, too." Nick dropped into the chair beside her. He angled his chin toward the three Heralds. "How's Project Log Book going?"

"Right on schedule, and I intend to keep it that way." Arizona permitted herself a small moment of intense satisfaction. "Those bastards up at the institute aren't going to stop us. But we've got a problem."

"What's up?" Nick asked easily.

"The institute crowd has started a rumor. Heard it at Fulton's this morning," Arizona stated, clearly agitated.

Octavia sighed. "That would be the rumor that I'm the one who stole the painting and faked a break-in at my gallery to cover my tracks?"

"Bingo." Arizona snorted. "So, you've heard it, too, eh?"

"Yes," Nick said. "Seemed to be coming from Eugene and Dwayne. I took steps to keep them quiet, but I had a hunch that they weren't the original source."

"I reckon that the institute tried to use them to spread it for obvious reasons," Arizona said. "Not like those two blockheads would question the source of a story. They'd just happily blab to anyone who would listen. Whoever used them knew that was their nature."

Nick thought for a minute. "You said you heard the rumor at Fulton's?"

"Checkout counter," Arizona said. "Overheard Betty Stiles talking about it to Marjorie Dunne."

An unpleasant whisper of unease went through Octavia. Marjorie Dunne was the mother of little Katy Dunne, one of the children who had entered a picture in the Children's Art Show. Gordon Dunne served on the town council and had made it clear that he intended to run for mayor in the next election cycle. The family took its role as pillars of the community seriously.

"Betty and Marjorie, huh?" Nick leaned back in his chair and thrust his legs out toward the desk. He steepled his fingers. "What we need to do is trace this rumor back to the source."

"We know where it got started," Arizona snapped. "That crowd up at the institute concocted it. I'll bet they've got that painting stashed somewhere up there, too. Now, I've come up with a plan—"

"No." Nick unsteepled his fingers and held up one hand, palm out, to silence her. "Don't even think about it. You are not going to send Octavia and me into the institute to search for that painting."

"Got to go in," Arizona declared. "Don't see any other way to find the picture."

"Give me a few more days," Nick said. "I'm working on some angles."

Arizona looked skeptical. "What angles?"

"It's a little complicated and I'm not ready to talk about it yet. Let's just say that I think this thing has roots in the past. I've asked my grandfather to help. He and Mitch Madison are doing some deep background research. When I get the results I'll contact you."

"Deep background, huh?" Arizona chewed on her cigar while she pondered that. "When do you expect a report from 'em?"

"Soon," Nick promised. He got to his feet. "Any day now. Hold off on your plans to go into the institute until I get back to you, okay? If you move now, you may alert the folks who are behind this and they'll probably move that painting. Maybe ship it to California. We'll never find it if they take it out of town."

Arizona munched on her cigar a couple of times and then nodded decisively. "All right. I'll give you a few days to finish your deep background. But if you don't get anything useful out of Sullivan and Mitch, we're gonna have to go in. It's our only option."

"Right. I'll be in touch." Nick took Octavia's arm and hauled her up out of the chair. "Come on, we've got work to do, honey."

The *honey* bemused her a little. She got the feeling that he wasn't even conscious of having used the endearment. She thought about that while she allowed herself to be dragged from the War Room.

Outside, a light summer rain was falling. The woods surrounding the fortified cabin were cloaked in a gray mist. Nick hustled her into his car, and then went around the front and got in beside her.

She looked at him as he quickly reversed and drove back along the thin, rutted path that served as Arizona's driveway.

"Deep background?" she said dryly.

"I thought it sounded good. Had a nice military ring."

"It did seem to impress Arizona, but you only bought us a little time. What do you expect to accomplish?"

"Beats me. But I didn't have much choice. I had to come up with something fast. I definitely do not want to get tangled up in one of Arizona's little clandestine recon projects at the institute."

"From what Mitch told me, it's sort of a family tradition. Hannah and Rafe carried out a mission for Arizona and so did Lillian and Gabe."

"And it was just damn good luck that none of them got picked up for illegal trespass." Nick turned the wheel and drove out onto the main road. "I've got no intention of following in their illustrious and heroic footsteps, thank you very much. Especially when there's no reason in hell to think that the painting has been hidden up there at the institute."

Her small flash of amusement faded. "But you do believe that it's still somewhere in town, don't you?"

"Yes." He did not take his attention off the road. "I think whoever took it did it for personal reasons, not for profit. That means it's probably still somewhere in town. We need to find the source of those rumors."

A few minutes later Nick drove into town, turned onto Bay Street, and parked in the lot at the end of the row of shops. He got out and walked with Octavia to the door of the gallery.

The flicker of unease she had experienced a short time ago when Arizona had recounted the scene at Fulton's returned. Inside the gallery, Gail stood at the counter. She was engaged in an intense conversation with Marjorie Dunne.

"That's a ridiculous rumor, Mrs. Dunne," Gail said forcefully. "I can't imagine who started it, but it has absolutely no basis in fact."

Marjorie was clearly not about to be reassured or placated. Clad in tailored slacks and a fashionable cream silk blouse and wearing a lot of gold jewelry, she was, as usual, overdressed for Eclipse Bay. Her blond hair was cut in a short, sophisticated bob that Octavia was pretty sure had not come from Carla's Custom Cut & Curl. The local beauty shop specialized in two distinctive looks: Very Big Hair and the Senior Citizen Helmet.

"I'm sorry," Marjorie said, not looking particularly remorseful, just very determined, "but regardless of whether or not the rumors are true, I must insist that you give me my daughter's picture. I can't allow Katy to participate in the art show so long as there's a cloud hanging over Octavia Brightwell and this gallery. I have to think of my husband's position in the community."

Octavia felt Nick go very still beside her. Alarmed by the anger she sensed humming through him, she stepped forward quickly to defuse the situation.

"I assume this is about the gossip that is going around concerning me," she said calmly.

Gail and Marjorie both turned quickly. Gail's expression was every bit as resolute as Marjorie's.

Marjorie looked momentarily taken aback at the sight of Nick standing next to Octavia. She started to speak to him, but Gail overrode her.

"Katy will be crushed if her picture isn't in the show," Gail said to Octavia. She gave Marjorie a brief, pointed look. "I'm sure Mrs. Dunne wouldn't want her daughter to feel left out because of some stupid gossip. You know how sensitive children are."

Marjorie flushed a dull red, but she was resolved. "I'm sorry about this, Octavia. Katy may not understand why I'm doing this, but it's for her own good. I'm sure you can see my position here. Dunnes have been respected members of this community for three generations."

"You must do what you feel is best for your daughter," Octavia agreed. "It's unfortunate that you believe the rumor that I stole the Upsall, but that is your choice. I'll get the picture for you."

Marjorie's mouth tightened. "I didn't say I believed the gossip. I'm sure there's nothing to it. But it just wouldn't look good for Katy's picture to be in the show."

"That's ridiculous," Gail fumed. "The best way to help us squelch that gossip is to allow your daughter's picture to be exhibited with the others. If you pull it, you'll just add fuel to the fire and you know it."

Octavia was touched, but she was not about to let Gail fight this battle for her. "It's all right, I'll get the picture."

She circled the counter, opened the door of the back room, and went inside.

"I'm sorry about this," Marjorie said coldly, "but it really is not my problem, is it?"

"Depends how you look at it, Marjorie," Nick said.

In the back room, Octavia winced. Nick was in a dangerous mood.

Marjorie, however, apparently did not recognize the razor-sharp edge of the blade buried in the too-soft words.

"Nick." She was suddenly overflowing with warmth and cordiality. "I heard you were in town for the summer. Nice to have you back in Eclipse Bay for a while."

"Thanks," Nick said.

"I saw your latest book on the rack at Fulton's," Marjorie said. "A very intriguing cover."

"Think so?"

"Yes, indeed. I have an excellent sense of color and design, you know. I'm sure the story is very good, too. I understand you've become quite popular. Unfortunately I don't have much time to read these days."

"Why am I not surprised?" Nick murmured.

Octavia stifled a groan and hurriedly went to work sorting through the framed paintings to find Katy's picture. If she didn't get out there fast, there would be blood on the floor of the gallery.

"Gordon is getting ready to run for mayor, you know," Marjorie continued in a blithe, chatty fashion, evidently unaware of the ledge she was walking. "And what with all the campaign work and Katy's summer activities schedule, I haven't had a chance to read anything other than a newspaper for months."

"I know what you mean," Nick said. "I've been a little busy myself lately. I'm working on finding out who started those rumors that are circulating about Octavia."

"Oh, yes." Marjorie sounded nonplussed, as if she hadn't intended the conversation to go in this direction. "Yes, I did hear that you were asking around about the painting. Uh, any luck yet?"

"Yes, as a matter of fact. I'm getting close."

"That's wonderful," Marjorie said vaguely.

"I'm working on this theory, you see. I figure that when I find out who started the rumors, I'll have the thief."

Marjorie cleared her throat. "Is that so? I don't see why there would be any connection . . . ?" She let the remainder of the question dangle in thin air.

"There's a connection, all right," Nick assured her with the grave authority of an expert in his field. "It's obvious that someone is promoting the gossip in order to divert attention from himself." He gave it half a beat before adding very deliberately, "Or *herself,* as the case may be. It's an old tactic."

"It is?" Marjorie asked warily.

"Sure. Thieves and bad guys use it all the time. That's why the first thing law enforcement types do is check out the rumors surrounding a crime. They call it following leads."

"I see." Marjorie cleared her throat again. "I didn't know that."

"Probably because you've never read one of my books," Nick said very politely.

Octavia gritted her teeth. Things were getting nasty out there. She tried to sort more swiftly through the pictures. She was pretty sure Katy had done a drawing of a house. And she thought she recalled a big yellow flower, too.

"I'm making a list of everyone who repeats the gossip," Nick explained. "Checking out the sources. See who's trying to spread the rumors."

"That doesn't sound very helpful." Marjorie sounded a little desperate now.

"When I'm done, I'll give the list to Sean Valentine so that he can take a closer look at some of the people on it. I figure it's safe to say that someone on the list will prove to be the guilty party."

"I don't think you can make that assumption." Alarm registered in Marjorie's voice. "I mean, that's ridiculous. Everyone in town is spreading that gossip."

"Not quite everyone," Nick said. "For instance, I'll bet Gail, here, hasn't repeated the rumors."

"Nope, not me," Gail assured them with ferocious glee. "I wouldn't spread that kind of outrageous nonsense. I've got my position in the community to consider. After all, my family is third-generation here in Eclipse Bay. Same as yours, Marjorie."

"Well, I heard the story from Betty Stiles down at Fulton's," Marjorie said. Defensive now. "I have no idea where she got it."

"Thanks, I'll talk to Betty," Nick said smoothly.

"Why waste your time?" Marjorie asked. "It's Sean Valentine's job to find that painting."

"I'm doing this as a favor," Nick said. "Octavia is what you might call a close friend of the family."

There was another short pause.

"I see," Marjorie said cautiously.

Octavia spotted Katy's picture and snatched it out of the stack of framed drawings. She hurried toward the door.

"Here's your daughter's picture." She thrust it across the counter toward Marjorie. "It's a lovely drawing. Nice feel for color. Tell her she can keep the frame. Compliments of the gallery."

"Thank you. I truly do regret this. But I have to consider Gordon's position." Marjorie took the picture somewhat uncertainly and turned back to Nick. "Good luck with your little investigation."

"I'm sure we'll find out who took the painting," he said with astounding confidence. "My list is almost finished."

"Yes, well, I certainly hope you get the situation resolved soon." Marjorie summoned up a polished smile. "By the way, since you're in town for the summer, I'll be sure to send an invitation to Katy's birthday party to Carson. Katy's turning six in August, you know."

"I appreciate the thought," Nick said, "but it would probably be better not to bother with the invitation. I'm sure you can understand my situation here. I can't allow Carson to attend a birthday party given for a child whose mother's name is on my list. Got to consider Carson's position in the community, you see."

Marjorie's jaw dropped visibly. Shock and horror blended in her expression.

Octavia had a sudden urge to cover her face with both hands. Beside her, Gail did not make any attempt to conceal a satisfied grin.

Marjorie pulled herself together with commendable

speed. "How dare you imply that I . . . that I'm on your list."

"Don't worry about it, Marjorie," Nick said. "When this is all over, I'm sure everyone will eventually forget who was on the list and who wasn't."

"Of all the—" Marjorie was overcome with outrage. Unable to speak, she simply stood there, glaring helplessly.

"You know," Nick went on as if nothing awkward had been said, "if you'd like to assist in the investigation, I'd be very grateful. In fact, everyone in my family would really appreciate the favor. Given your position in the community, you could be very helpful."

Marjorie's mouth worked once or twice before she managed to speak. "Well, of course, I'd love to help you but I honestly don't see how I could be of any more assistance. I told you, it was Betty Stiles who is spreading the story."

"I'll be talking to Betty next," Nick assured her. "But, since you've offered to help, there is one thing you could do that would go a long way toward narrowing my list."

"What's that?"

Nick glanced at the picture Marjorie clutched in her beringed hands. "Leave Katy's drawing here with the others. It will send a strong signal to the community that you don't think the rumors are true."

Marjorie was trapped and they all knew it. She shot a fulminating look at Octavia, and then she put the picture down on the counter and turned back to Nick with an earnest smile. "Well, if you really think it would help—"

"Oh, yeah," Nick said. "No question about it. Like I said, I really appreciate it."

"About your list," Marjorie added delicately.

"Obviously I won't have to add you to it," Nick said.

That seemed to cheer Marjorie slightly. She went quickly toward the door. "I hope it won't take you and Sean long to end this matter."

"It won't," Nick said.

They all watched in silence as Marjorie fled out the door and down the sidewalk toward the parking lot.

Octavia rested both elbows on the counter, propped her chin on her hands, and looked at Gail and Nick in turn. "Don't get me wrong. I am deeply touched. But I'm not sure that coercing Marjorie into leaving Katy's painting here was smart."

"Who cares about smart?" Gail said. "It felt good."

"That was Marjorie Dunne, for heaven's sake," Octavia reminded her dryly. "She's the wife of a member of the town council. Probably the wife of the next mayor of Eclipse Bay."

"So what?" Gail said with a chuckle. "This is Nick Harte. His family can buy and sell the entire town council and the mayor, too. In point of fact, if old legends are to be believed, they have done just that on a number of occasions."

"Be fair," Nick said to her. "It's not our fault that the council and the mayor have historically shown a certain willingness to accommodate us Hartes in exchange for contributions to their library building funds and pier renovation projects."

Octavia studied him with fresh appreciation. "My, my. I believe I have just witnessed an exhibition of what is commonly called throwing one's weight around."

"Relax, Marjorie deserved it," Gail said. "She has a history of behaving badly to lesser mortals. She was the same in high school. I don't suppose it escaped your notice that she didn't offer to send one of those birthday party invitations to my Anne."

"I did notice the oversight," Octavia admitted.

"If it's any consolation," Nick said, "Anne will get an invitation to Carson's party next month."

Gail smiled. "Thank you. She'll be thrilled. She hasn't had a chance to make any friends yet here in town."

"She'll have plenty of opportunity to meet other children her age at Carson's party," Nick said. "Every kid in town will get invited. Even Katy Dunne."

# chapter 18

Later that afternoon Octavia was in the back, framing the last of the entries in the Children's Art Show, when she heard Jeremy's voice in the other room.

"Gail?" Jeremy sounded surprised and somewhat incredulous. "Gail Johnson?"

"Gail Gillingham these days. Hello, Jeremy. It's been a long time."

"You can say that again. The last time I saw you, you were just a kid."

"Not quite. I was in college the last time our paths crossed. I'm surprised you even remember. You had finished grad school and were getting ready to accept a position at a college in Portland, as I recall."

"That's right. My grandmother mentioned that you were back in town. Said you were looking for a job."

"I found one, as you can see. It's temporary because Octavia plans to sell her business at the end of the summer, but it will give me some time to look around. I'm hoping something will open up at the institute or at Chamberlain."

"I'm working at the institute," Jeremy said. "I'll keep my ears open for you, if you like. There's bound to be some turnover before the fall."

"Thanks. I'd really appreciate it."

There was a short pause.

"I guess you probably heard about my divorce last year," Jeremy said.

"Your grandmother mentioned it," Gail said gently. "I can empathize. I went through one a couple of years ago. That's the main reason I came back to Eclipse Bay. I wanted my daughter to have more family around her."

"Sounds like a smart move. Kids need a sense of belonging. Maybe everyone does."

"Is that why you came back?" Gail asked. She sounded genuinely curious.

"Maybe. In a way, Eclipse Bay will always be home. When the institute offered me the position, it just felt like the right time to make a move."

Octavia went to the door. Jeremy and Gail stood on opposite sides of the counter. They were looking only at each other, she mused. Neither of them noticed her. She could have sworn she felt vibrations in the air.

She cleared her throat discreetly. Both of them jumped a little and turned toward her with expressions of surprise. She nearly laughed. You'd have thought she'd been hiding in a closet and leaped out unexpectedly.

"Hi, Jeremy," she said. "Did you bring in your paintings?"

"Are you kidding? Of course I did." He gestured toward a wooden crate leaning against the counter. "Got two of them right here."

Gail leaned over the counter. "Octavia said you painted. Let's have a look."

"I just brought the landscapes with me today." Jeremy went to work opening the crate. "Octavia thinks that's my most likely market here in Eclipse Bay."

He hauled one of the pictures out of the crate and propped it against the closest wall. Gail and Octavia came out from behind the counter to examine it.

Gail reacted immediately, her approval evident in her excited tone. "The Arch at sunset. I love it. What's more, I can sell it. It'll be gone by the end of the week."

Jeremy and Octavia exchanged amused glances.

"Tell you what," Jeremy said to Gail. "If you sell this sucker in a week, I'll buy you dinner at Dreamscape."

Gail did not take her eyes off the painting. "It's a deal."

He ran Betty Stiles to ground outside Carla's Custom Cut & Curl. Betty emerged from the beauty shop with a stiff, cotton-candy cloud of pink hair. The hairdo had been frozen in place with so much lacquer that Nick was pretty sure it could have withstood a nuclear blast. She wore a jaunty denim skirt with a matching vest over a red blouse.

Betty was a widow in her late seventies. She had made a hobby of following every nuance of local gossip for as long as Nick could remember.

"'Afternoon, Mrs. Stiles." He came away from the fender of his car and walked toward her. "How are you doing?"

"Why, Nick Harte. How nice to see you. I heard you were in town for the summer."

"Yes, ma'am."

"Saw your new book down at Fulton's the other day."

"Did you?" He would not ask if she had read it, he promised himself.

"I would have bought it because I read a lot of mystery and suspense. But when I read the back cover it didn't say anything about a serial killer."

"Probably because I didn't put one in the story."

"I only read books about serial killers."

"Figures," Nick said.

"Who would have thought you'd have made a success-ful career as a writer? You know, the day I heard you'd quit Harte Investments I told Edith Seaton that you were mak-ing a big mistake. 'Edith,' I said, 'that young man is going to ruin his life and break his grandfather's heart.'"

"We all survived, interestingly enough. Mrs. Stiles, I wondered if I could ask you a few questions."

"You're trying to find that missing painting, aren't you?" Betty sighed. "Of course you can ask me some ques-tions, but if what I've heard is true, I'm afraid you're wast-ing your time."

"Why is that?"

She lowered her voice. "Well, dear, as everyone knows, the most likely suspect is Octavia Brightwell."

"Funny you should mention that, Mrs. Stiles. I've heard the same thing and I'm trying to find out who started that rumor. Thought maybe you could tell me."

"You want to know who *started* it?" Betty asked in-credulously.

"That's right."

"But why does it matter, dear? I mean, it's perfectly ob-vious when you think about it that Miss Brightwell is the person most likely to be the thief."

"It's not obvious to me," Nick said.

"Oh." Betty seemed baffled by that news. Then she

gave him a pitying look and patted his arm. "Well, I suppose it's understandable that you would want to think the best of her under the circumstances. But for what it's worth, my advice is to find another girlfriend."

Nick smiled coldly. The hard part about being a real private eye, he decided, was that sometimes it was extremely difficult to avoid losing your temper. But there was nothing to be gained by telling Betty Stiles that she was an interfering busybody.

"I don't plan to take your advice, Mrs. Stiles. So that leaves me with no choice except to find the real thief."

"But if Miss Brightwell took the picture—"

"Octavia didn't take it."

She made a *tut-tut* sound. "You seem very sure of that."

"I'm sure, Mrs. Stiles."

"Really, Nicholas, I wouldn't have thought that you were the type to be so easily taken in by a woman's wiles."

"And here I thought you were too smart to be conned by a thief."

Betty bridled. "I beg your pardon?"

"Isn't it obvious? Whoever started the rumor is the person who stole the painting."

"But that's ridiculous."

"Where did you hear it first, Mrs. Stiles?"

Betty drew herself up with great dignity. "I heard it right here at the beauty shop."

Nick looked past her through the window and saw two women sitting under the hair dryers. They had magazines on their laps but neither was reading. Both were focused intently on the scene taking place outside the shop. The owner of the salon, Carla Millbank, was watching him in the mirror as she wrapped a client's hair in little pieces of aluminum foil.

His conversation with Betty was going to be all over town by nightfall.

His new problem loomed large. The gender divides in Eclipse Bay were still firmly entrenched. There were some places a man could not go. Carla's Custom Cut & Curl was terra incognita for every male in the community.

Fifteen minutes later he walked into Bright Visions, still fine-tuning the details of his new scheme.

The place appeared to be empty except for Octavia, who was sitting on the high stool behind the counter. She looked up from some notes she was jotting down on a sheet of paper.

"There you are," she said. "I was getting worried. Did you find Betty Stiles?"

"For all the good it did me." He studied the two framed paintings leaning against the wall. "I don't remember those. Are they new?"

An odd expression crossed her face. "Yes, as a matter of fact."

"I'm no expert, but I like them."

"So do I."

"Nice view of the Arch. The scene of the pier at night is great, too. Sort of moody with the fog and the dark water and that little light on the boat. Who's the artist?"

There was a movement in the doorway behind the counter. Jeremy appeared from the back room. He looked at Nick with a veiled expression.

"That would be me," Jeremy said.

Gail came to stand beside him. "Isn't he terrific?" She was bubbling with enthusiasm. "I've already got a client in mind."

*Of course it would be Jeremy,* Nick thought. What the

hell was the matter with him? How could he have forgotten Jeremy and his *considerable commercial talent.* If he'd been paying attention instead of concentrating on how to get someone inside the beauty shop, he would have put it all together instantly as soon as he saw the pictures. Now he was stuck with doing the polite, civilized thing in front of Octavia and Gail.

"Congratulations," he said to Jeremy, keeping his voice absolutely level. "Nice work."

"Be even nicer work if it pays," Jeremy said. His tone was just as level as Nick's. "But I'm not going to quit my day job anytime soon. I mean, what are the odds of actually being able to make a living by painting? A million to one, maybe?"

"I'm sure Nick knows exactly how you feel," Octavia commented. "He must have had the same doubts when he put his first manuscript in the mail. Isn't that right, Nick?"

She had him neatly cornered, he thought.

"Sure," he said. "And every time I've put a manuscript in the mail since that first one. It always feels a lot like jumping off a cliff."

Obviously it had been a mistake to tell her what lay beneath the surface of this little feud he and Jeremy had going. What was it with her, anyway? Why couldn't she let the two of them conduct their private war without outside interference?

Jeremy looked serious. "The jumping-off-the-cliff thing never goes away?"

Nick shrugged. "Not that I've noticed. My advice is to get used to it. It'll give you an edge." He switched his gaze to Gail. "How would you like to play undercover agent?"

"Do I get to wear a trench coat?" Gail asked.

"Not unless you want to get the collar wet in the shampoo bowl."

Octavia hopped off her stool. "Carla's Custom Cut & Curl? You want Gail to see what she can pick up in the way of gossip in the beauty shop?"

"Yeah. Betty Stiles says that's where she first heard the rumors."

"You're really serious about this detective thing, aren't you?" Jeremy asked Nick.

"No, I just needed something interesting to put down in my journal under the subject of what I did on my summer vacation," Nick retorted.

"Okay, okay, I get the point," Jeremy muttered. "You're serious." He glanced at Octavia. "Is there anything I can do to help?"

"You'll have to ask Nick," she said smoothly. "He's in charge of the investigation."

Jeremy did not look happy with that, but he dutifully turned back to Nick. "Let me know. My roots in this town run as deep as your own. I might be able to save you some time."

"That's very kind of you, Jeremy," Octavia said. "What do you say, Nick?"

She was not going to let up, Nick thought. She wouldn't be satisfied until he bit the bullet and invited Jeremy out for a beer. Maybe the easiest way out of this mess was to make the offer in front of her. Jeremy would turn it down and then they would both be off the hook.

He glanced at his watch and then at Jeremy. "It's nearly five. I want to talk to Gail about what I need her to do at the beauty shop tomorrow. Then I'm going to have dinner with Octavia." Out of the corner of his eye he saw her raise her brows at that news. But she kept silent as he expected.

She knew where he was going with this and she wasn't about to put up any roadblocks. "I figured I'd hit the Total Eclipse later this evening to pick up the latest gossip. You want to join me? I'll buy you a beer and we can play a little pool, keep our ears open, and see what we come up with."

Jeremy's jaw went rigid. But to Nick's astonishment he moved slightly. It was a single, robotic inclination of the head, but it was a definite nod of acceptance.

"Why not?" Jeremy said.

Damn. Now they were both trapped, Nick thought.

Octavia looked quietly pleased. She gave him a warm smile of approval.

An electrifying jolt of awareness shot through him. It was as if the floor of the gallery had opened up beneath his feet and he had plummeted into the abyss.

Oh, shit. He had been asking the wrong question all along, he thought. He had been wondering why Octavia insisted on meddling with his life. The really important question here was why was he allowing her to do so?

They ate at the Crab Trap, surrounded by tourists, summer people, and a sprinkling of locals.

"You won't regret this," Octavia said earnestly.

"Uh-huh." He cracked open a crab leg and went after the tender meat with a vengeance.

"Jeremy wouldn't have agreed to have a drink with you if he still believed that you'd had an affair with his wife."

"Uh-huh." He reached for another leg and assaulted it with grim enthusiasm. The sound of crunching shell was good.

"It's obvious that he wants to mend the rift."

"Uh-huh."

"He was just looking for an opportunity and now you've provided it."

"Uh-huh." He looked around for another crab leg to destroy.

"It was the right thing to do, Nick."

"I don't like being manipulated."

"I didn't manipulate you."

"Yes, you did."

"I just made a suggestion."

He looked at her, not speaking.

She swallowed. "Okay, it was a forceful suggestion."

"You nagged me into this meeting tonight."

She reddened. "I'm sorry if you feel that way."

"I do feel that way."

She sat back and folded her napkin very deliberately, her expression troubled now. "You're really mad, aren't you?"

"Yes. I'm really mad. But mostly at myself."

"Because you're allowing me to strongarm you into this meeting with Jeremy?"

"Uh-huh."

"I see." Her voice was steady but when she put down the napkin, her fingers shook slightly. "Well, if you feel that way about it, why don't you cancel the arrangement?"

He smiled humorlessly, staring into the abyss. "It's too late." *In more ways than you can possibly know,* he added silently.

"I don't understand."

"Yeah, I can see that."


Establishments like the Total Eclipse had their place in the universe, Nick thought. It was, for instance, the one venue in Eclipse Bay where two guys involved in a private feud could meet on neutral territory.

The tavern was starting to fill up for the evening, but the buzz of conversation was muted in the back, where the pool tables were located. Only one other green-topped table was in use at the moment, and mercifully no one was smoking, so the air was still relatively clear. The gloom hung in thick curtains interrupted only by the narrow bright spot over the center of each table.

If the bar was the place for this conversation, Nick thought, pool was the game. Attitude was everything.

Nick adjusted his stance slightly, made a bridge with his fingers, and leaned into the shot. He stroked the cue gently. Going for a little spin. Concentrating on the follow-through, the way his grandfather and father had taught him. The way he would one day teach Carson. He stayed down until the ball dropped into the pocket.

"You do realize that we've both been set up," he said, straightening.

On the other side of the table, Jeremy watched him from the shadows. "I got that impression. But, hey, she's going to hang my paintings in her gallery. Shooting a little pool with you and letting you buy me a beer doesn't seem like such a high price to pay for my chance at money and immortal fame."

"Uh-huh." Nick chalked his cue. "I figured that was the real reason you agreed. Octavia's got this compulsion to make things right, you know. Has to do with what her great-aunt did to Harte-Madison all those years ago."

"I figured that much out. She says she's leaving town at the end of the summer."

"Yeah." He studied the position of the balls on the table, doing the strategy thing. "That's what she says."

Jeremy studied him across the green felt. "She also says that you didn't have an affair with my ex."

"She's right. I didn't."

Jeremy did not respond to that. But he didn't hurl any more accusations, either.

They played for a while, not speaking. The only sounds were the click and snap of the balls striking each other and the gradually rising noise from the front of the tavern. Someone had turned on the music. A country-western rocker was wailing away about a good woman gone bad.

Nick dropped another ball into the pocket. "You know, you're not the only guy in the world whose wife had an affair." He wasn't sure why he said it. It just seemed the right time.

Jeremy went still on the other side of the table. "Amelia?"

"The man who was at the controls of that plane."

"Jesus. I didn't know."

"Not many people do. I'd like to keep it that way."

"Sure. Believe me when I say I understand your feelings on that particular subject." Jeremy paused a couple of beats. "Octavia said I should ask myself whether you or Laura had ever lied to me about other things."

"Come up with any answers?"

"Yeah. Laura lied to me about a couple of other matters. Important stuff. Guess we had a communication problem." Jeremy used the chalk on the tip of his cue. "Couldn't think of any times when you had lied to me, though."

Nick studied the table. "No offense, but I didn't even like Laura very much. Always had the feeling that she figured she'd married beneath herself when she married you."

"No offense, but I didn't care much for Amelia. Figured

she was more in love with Harte Investments than she was with you."

"You may have been right." He took his shot and waited until the ball dropped. "But she was a good mother."

"That counts," Jeremy said quietly.

"Counts for a lot."

"At least you have Carson. I found out the hard way that Laura didn't want kids. At least she didn't want them with me."

"Carson made it all worthwhile," Nick agreed.

The sound of the growing crowd in the other room got louder. Someone cranked up the music system another notch. The hard-driving song playing now was about guys getting drunk on cheap whiskey and engaging in bar fights over good women gone bad.

"And to think that we both thought we knew what we were doing when it came to the female of the species." Jeremy drank some beer while he watched Nick take another shot. "Guess we had a lot to learn."

"Yeah."

The atmosphere around the table was more comfortable now. A lot of the tension was leaking out of it. Maybe it was the beer.

"So," Jeremy said, "who do you think took the Upsall?"

"Whoever is trying to pin the blame on Octavia. This is personal. I can feel it."

"Doesn't make sense. Octavia hasn't hurt anyone here in town."

"No, but her great-aunt did."

"According to the old stories, Claudia Banner's victims were Hartes and Madisons." Jeremy made a bridge and angled his cue stick. "You think maybe there were others?"

"My grandfather used the term *collateral damage*."

Jeremy banked a shot. "You know, my grandmother was a woman in her twenties when Harte-Madison fell apart. She grew up in this burg and knew everyone. Plays bridge every week with three other women who also have a lot of history in this town. They might remember something useful about the good old days. Want me to talk to her? See if she can get anything out of her bridge group? I'm sure she'd enjoy playing Mata Hari."

"I'd appreciate that," Nick said.

The music got louder and so did the crowd. Other players drifted into the back room and took over the remaining tables. Smoke from the cigarettes of neighboring players started to foul the air.

"Getting late," Nick said.

Jeremy shrugged. "One more game?"

"Why not?"

Nick had just racked the balls for another round when a familiar voice rumbled from the opening that divided the pool room from the bar area.

"Well, if it isn't the SOB who thinks he's the king of Eclipse Bay." Eugene slurred most of the *s*'s and there were a lot of them in the sentence, but his meaning was clear. "And will you look at that, Dwayne? He's shooting a little pool with his good buddy Jeremy. Isn't that sweet?"

The players at the other tables did not look toward the pair in the doorway. Everyone pretended to concentrate on their games. But Nick knew that the crowd was listening intently to every word. The tension was suddenly so thick he could have carved it into topiary shapes.

"You were right," Jeremy said quietly. He did not bother to glance at Eugene and Dwayne either. "Time to go."

"What are you doin' here, anyway, Harte?" Eugene bellowed. "Shouldn't you be with that little redheaded suspect of yours? Everyone knows she's been screwing your brains out so's you'll overlook the fact that she stole that painting."

Nick set the cue down very slowly. On the other side of the table, Jeremy did the same. This time they both looked at Mutt and Jeff.

The dark room fell silent. None of the other players moved so much as a finger. Everyone waited for the other shoe to drop.

Nick looked at Eugene. "You don't want to say anything more, Eugene."

But it was obvious that Eugene was too drunk to worry about consequences.

"You think you can threaten me?" Eugene stalked closer, hands clenched at his sides. "You really think I'm gonna put up with that kind of shit from a Harte?"

"He's right, Eugene," Jeremy said softly. "You don't want to do this."

"I'm not takin' any crap off you, either, Seaton. You think you can come back to town after all these years and start actin' like you're better than the rest of us again just because your mama married a Seaton and you hang with Nick Harte? Got news for you."

"Let's go," Nick said to Jeremy.

"Fine by me." Jeremy started around the table.

"Something me and Dwayne, here, been wondering about, Harte." Eugene came to a halt, blocking the path to the door. He leered. "Is she a *natural* redhead? She as red *down there* as she is up on top?"

Nick moved around the corner of the table.

"Take it easy," Jeremy said out of the side of his mouth. "The plan is to get out of here, remember?"

"The plan," Nick said, coming to a halt directly in front of the pool table, "is to tell everyone here a little story about Eugene and Dwayne's excellent adventure in Seattle a while back."

"Shut your mouth, Harte," Eugene roared. "Just shut your damned mouth. Say one more word and I'll rip your head off your shoulders and use it for a cue ball."

"Think so?"

"Hey, nobody cares if you're screwin' the redhead. Nobody gives a shit about your sex life, Harte."

"Except you, apparently, Eugene," one of the other players offered helpfully. "But maybe that's because Harte's sex life is a lot more interesting than yours."

Eugene turned purple, drew his head into his shoulders in the manner of a large turtle, and lumbered forward. He was surprisingly fast for a man of his size and bulk. The old football training, Nick figured.

"Hell," Jeremy muttered. "So much for a quick exit."

Nick did not move until the last instant. Then he sidestepped the ferocious charge. Eugene still had speed, but his maneuverability was shot. He blundered straight on, past the point where Nick had stood a second earlier, and crashed into the table. He folded over and went facedown on the green felt.

"Okay," Jeremy said. "Now we leave, right?"

Nick ignored him. He grabbed hold of one beefy shoulder. There was no need to try to haul Eugene erect. The big man came up off the table, one massive fist already arcing through the air.

Nick ducked the blow and slammed both clenched hands into Eugene's midsection. It was like hitting a very solid pillow. The impact felt good, but it didn't do much damage. Nick stepped back hurriedly, shaking his numbed hand.

Okay, maybe that had been a mistake.

Fortunately Eugene was off balance, thanks to too many beers and the collision with the table. When he charged a second time, flailing wildly, Nick stuck out a foot. Eugene obligingly tripped and went down with a crashing thud that shook the floor.

Dwayne squealed, grabbed the nearest pool cue, and launched himself at Nick. Jeremy snatched the stick out of his hands as he went past.

"You know," Jeremy said, "if you'd ever bothered to read one of Nick's books, you'd know he never gets into a fight without his trusty sidekick, Bonner."

Robbed of his ersatz rapier, Dwayne scrambled to a halt and turned to throw a short punch at Jeremy. He caught one of the other pool players on the shoulder, instead.

"Hey, watch it, you little creep." The player took a swipe at Dwayne and sent him tumbling into one of the men who had come from the bar area to see what all the excitement was about.

A man standing behind Nick chuckled. "Man, the little redhead must be one hot number, huh? So what's the deal? Is she, or isn't she a natural—"

Nick swung around and punched the commentator in the chest. The man fell back against a table. His cue stick went sailing and struck someone else.

The poolroom exploded in a firestorm of shouts and flying fists.

Nick turned back, searching for Eugene amid the swarm of sweating, heaving bodies.

"Son of a bitch, Harte." Eugene had managed to get up off the floor. He threw himself at Nick.

Nick moved out of the way and came up against Sandy Hickson, who had wandered into the poolroom. The two went down together and rolled under a table.

Jeremy bent over to look at the pair beneath the table. "Everyone okay down here?"

Someone hauled him up and swung at him. Jeremy took the blow on the side of his jaw and reeled back against a table.

Nick untangled himself from Sandy and came out from under the table in a low rush. He tackled the man who had just hit Jeremy and they both went down, rolling in a small river of spilled beer.

Fred picked up the phone. Sean Valentine and two other officers arrived ten minutes later.

# chapter 19

Shortly before midnight Nick and Jeremy stood with Rafe in the parking lot that fronted the Eclipse Bay Police Department.

"I gotta say, this is a real red-letter occasion for me." Rafe tossed his keys into the air and caught them. "Never thought I'd see the day when a Madison had to bail one of you fine, upstanding, pillar-of-the-community Hartes out of jail. To say nothing of a Seaton."

"If you're looking for undying gratitude, try the Yellow Pages." Jeremy put a cautious hand to his jaw.

"One thing I really hate," Nick muttered, "is a guy who bails you out of jail and then gloats."

"You two are going to look very colorful tomorrow," Rafe said, amused.

"You know, neither of us is in the mood for this." Nick gave him a sour look. "The only thing we want from you right now is a lift back to the Total Eclipse so that we can pick up our cars. Think you can manage that without further comment?"

"No," Rafe said. "You want a ride, you've got to put up with the witty remarks."

Nick exchanged glances with Jeremy. "We could beat him up now or we could do it later."

"I vote for later," Jeremy said. "To tell you the truth, I'm not really up for any more physical activity tonight."

"Okay, later." Nick turned back to Rafe. "Drive."

"My pleasure." Rafe led the way across the parking lot to where he had left Hannah's car.

At that moment another vehicle swung into the lot, briefly dazzling Nick's eyes with its headlights. It came to an abrupt halt nearby. Octavia's fairy-tale coach.

"The perfect end to a delightful evening," Nick said to no one in particular. "It just doesn't get any better than this, does it?"

They all watched the door on the driver's side snap open. Octavia shot out of the front seat. Her red hair was a wild, fiery tangle in the yellow glow of the street lamp.

"No," Rafe said. "It sure doesn't. Oh man, am I ever glad I'm not in your shoes, Nick. All I can say is good luck."

Octavia rushed toward them around the hood of the white compact. She wore a gauzy, ankle-length, flower-patterned skirt and a snug-fitting tee shirt with a deeply scooped neckline. When Nick glanced down, he saw that she was wearing slippers. She had dressed in a hurry.

"I just had a phone call from Hannah. Something about a tavern brawl. Tell me there's been some terrible mistake."

"There's been a mistake, all right," Nick said. "You forgot to put on your shoes. You know, the importance of proper footwear is often overlooked."

"Are you both all right?" she asked.

"Sure," Nick said. "We're fine. Aren't we, Jeremy?"

"We're fine," Jeremy said obligingly.

"They're fine," Rafe assured her.

Nick saw some of her tension ease. The slight shift in the set of her shoulders caused her breasts to move beneath the tee shirt. The thin cotton fabric clung briefly to her nipples and he realized that she was not wearing a bra.

He was suddenly intensely aware of Rafe and Jeremy standing there with him. They were looking at her, just as he was. Probably also noticing that she wasn't wearing a bra.

Annoyed, he yanked off his windbreaker and held it out to her. "Here. Better put this on. It's chilly out here."

She frowned at the jacket, as if she'd never seen one before. He moved closer, putting himself between her and Jeremy and Rafe, and tugged the jacket forcibly around her shoulders. It was so large on her that it fell like a cape in front. He wasn't entirely satisfied, but at least her nipples were no longer visible.

She ignored the jacket to glower at him. "What happened? How did the fight start?"

"Eugene Woods started it," Nick said. He glanced at Jeremy. "Isn't that right?"

"Definitely," Jeremy said. "Eugene Woods was the cause."

Rafe nodded. "Eugene Woods."

"You weren't even there when it happened, Rafe. How do you know?"

"You got a situation involving Mean Eugene and Dickhead Dwayne and you know who started it," Rafe explained.

"Just the way things are in Eclipse Bay," Nick said.

Jeremy opened his mouth to give his two cents' worth. She hushed him with a raised palm and turned back to Nick.

"What was the fight about?"

Nick shrugged. "Bar fight. They happen. Jeremy and I were just in the wrong place at the wrong time."

Suspicion gleamed in her eyes. She turned to Jeremy.

"Tavern brawls are sort of like whirlwinds and tornadoes," Jeremy said seriously. "Forces of nature. They erupt out of nowhere for no known cause."

She moved on to Rafe. "Do I get an answer from you?"

He held up both hands, palms out. Innocent as a lamb. "I wasn't there, remember?"

She looked at Nick again.

"Hey, it was your idea that I buy Jeremy a drink," he reminded her.

She planted her hands on her hips. The movement parted the edges of the windbreaker and stretched the tee shirt across her unconfined breasts. "So this whole thing is my fault? Is that what you're trying to say? Don't you dare blame this on me, Nick Harte."

Nick moved forward again to block his companions' view. "You can take me back to where I left my car."

"Wait a minute, I'm not finished here," she said.

"Yes," he said. "You are."

He put his arms around her shoulders, turned her smartly around, and shoehorned her into the front seat of her car before she could say another word.

He followed her back to her cottage and got out of the car to see her to her front door.

"There was no need to follow me home." She shoved her key into the lock.

"It's after midnight and this cottage is pretty isolated out here on the bluff."

"This is Eclipse Bay." She turned the key. "Probably has the lowest crime rate on the entire West Coast."

"It's still late. I'd have worried." But mostly he would have gone crazy alone in bed tonight, thinking about her. Maybe it was some kind of testosterone hangover, a residual effect of the brawl. Or maybe he was in worse shape than he had realized.

She got the door open, stepped inside, and switched on a lamp. Turning, she studied him from the opening. With the light behind her, it was impossible to read her expression. Her red hair formed a fiery aura around her face. She was doing the enigmatic Fairy Queen thing again. He wanted to put her down on a bed and bury himself so deep inside her that she would never be able to forget that she was as human as he was.

"Thank you," she said, ever so polite. "As you can see, I'm home, safe and sound. You may leave now."

He wanted her so badly he'd probably go out into the woods and howl at the moon if she forced him to leave tonight.

He reached out and gripped the door frame. "Invite me inside."

"Why should I do that?"

"How about because I've had a hard night and it was, as you have already noted, your fault."

"I told you not to blame that tavern brawl on me." She tipped her head a little. "By the way, you never told me how things went between you and Jeremy this evening. Were you able to work through some of your issues before the brawl erupted?"

"Oh, yeah, we definitely rebonded."

Her expression softened. "I'm so pleased."

He saw his opening and put one foot over the threshold. "Now can I come inside?"

"Nick—"

He leaned forward and shushed her with a slow, deep kiss, careful not to touch her. If he put his hands on her, he thought, he might not be able to take them off again. Not before morning, at least.

She did not retreat. He felt a little shudder go through her. Progress, he told himself. When he lifted his mouth he saw that her lips were soft and parted.

"You know what?" he said. "I am not in the mood to talk about my issues with Jeremy tonight."

"I understand." The tip of her tongue appeared at the corner of her mouth. "Are you sure you're all right?"

"You already asked me that earlier."

"Yes, I know, but you sound a little weird."

"Possibly because I am feeling a little weird." *Also a little wired,* he thought. As if he were running on high-voltage electrical current.

"Maybe you're having some sort of delayed reaction to the violence."

"Maybe."

She raised her hand. He thought she was going to touch his face, but at the last instant she hesitated, fingertips an inch from his jaw. "Did you take any blows to the head?"

"I can't remember." He caught the drifting fingertips in one hand and raised them to his lips. "Could be that I did and it gave me amnesia."

"Nick." Softer now. And there was a broken edge on his name.

He drew one of her fingertips into his mouth and bit gently. She drew in a sharp breath.

He took that as an invitation and glided over the threshold. She moved back to allow him inside. He closed the door behind himself and reached for her.

*"Oh, Nick."*

And then she was in his arms, clinging wildly, her lips against his throat.

"I was so worried when Hannah told me there had been a fight," she whispered urgently against his neck. "And then she said you were at the police station and that you'd called Rafe to come bail you out and I got mad. But I was still scared, too. It was awful."

"It's okay," he said into her mouth. "Everything is okay."

"Are you sure you're all right?"

"I will be soon."

He scooped her up and carried her toward the hall. There was enough light from the single lamp she had switched on a moment ago to guide him past the darkened bathroom into the shadow-drenched bedroom.

His first thought when he saw the bed was that it was surrounded with ghosts. Then he realized that he was looking at a lot of pale, gauzy draperies. The hangings spilled from a wrought-iron frame that arched overhead.

*The hidden bower of the Fairy Queen,* he thought.

He let Octavia slide slowly down the length of his body until she was on her feet once more and then he peeled off the tee shirt. He'd been right about the lack of a bra. Her elegantly curved breasts fit perfectly into the palms of his hands. He moved his thumbs lightly across her taut nipples. She closed her eyes. Another little tremor went through her. He felt his own body shudder in response.

He lowered his hands slowly down her sides, savoring the feel of warm, soft skin until he found the elasticized waistband of the long, flowing skirt. Sliding his palms beneath the band, he pushed the garment down over her hips.

And discovered that a bra was not the only item of underwear that she had neglected that evening.

He let the skirt drop to her ankles. Then he threaded his fingers through the triangle of curling hair. Damned if he would ever tell Eugene or any other man that Octavia was, indeed, a natural redhead.

"You're not wearing any panties," he said against her bare shoulder.

"I was in a hurry when I left the cottage tonight."

"I may go crazy here."

A smile played at the edges of her mouth. She started to unfasten his shirt. "Because I forgot to put on a pair of panties?"

"Doesn't take much to drive me over the edge when I'm this close to you."

"I'm glad."

She separated the edges of his shirt and flattened her palms against his chest. "I'm not feeling wholly sane myself at the moment."

He eased her backward, kissing her with every step, until she came up against the high bed. The ghostly bed curtains drifted gently behind her, guarding the interior of the secret bower.

He did not take his mouth from hers when he reached behind her to pull the hazy fabric aside. Grasping the quilt, he pulled it straight down to the foot of the bed, exposing pristine white sheets.

He picked her up, put her down on the pale bedding, and stepped back to finish undressing himself. The wispy bed hangings drifted closed. On the other side of the veil Octavia watched him through the misty material. She lay on her side, knees slightly bent, hips curved in graceful, seductive lines.

He stood there for a few seconds, every muscle rigid with the effort it took to exert some control over the aching, raging need that was uncoiling rapidly throughout his body. It had never been like this with any other woman, he thought, baffled and bemused. He could not seem to wrap his mind around this sensation. It was not just physical. He was old enough and sufficiently experienced to take the physical effects in stride.

There was something else going on here. He knew that in the depths of his soul. He'd been trying to ignore it, work around it, deny it, but there was no possibility of avoiding the reality. Octavia was different.

He looked at her through the drifting veils that surrounded the bed, and for a moment he wondered if she really was a sorceress who had somehow managed to enchant him.

He had no time to wonder about his predicament. The heaviness of his erection made it impossible to think clearly. He fought his way out of the rest of his clothing.

When he pulled the bed hangings aside the second time, Octavia reached for him, drawing him down onto the snowy sheets. He put one hand on the sweet, round curve of her hip and she twisted urgently against him.

"Nick."

"Not so fast," he whispered.

But she was moving, sliding, slipping along the length of him. He felt her mouth on his chest and then her tongue touched his belly.

When her fingers curled around him and her lips moved lower, he thought he disintegrate.

He rolled her onto her back, pinning her with one leg

thrown across her thighs. "I meant what I said. We're going to take this nice and slow."

"Are we?" Her voice was both mischievous and sensual. A woman who knows she's in control of the situation. She wriggled a little beneath his weight. "Do you really want to go slow?"

"Most definitely," he said. "I want to go slow tonight. And what's more, I'm going to make sure that we do."

She drew her fingertips down the length of his back. "Wanna bet?"

"Oh, yeah."

He bent his head and covered her mouth with his own. When she was absorbed in the kiss, giving herself completely over to it, working her sorcery, he reached out and snagged one of the trailing bed hangings.

He looped the fabric around her left wrist and tied a quick knot in it.

"Ummph?"

She wrenched her mouth away from his. Her eyes snapped open.

He grasped a wispy hanging on the opposite side of the bed and anchored her other wrist.

"Oh, my." She looked up at him, sexy laughter sparkling in her eyes. "This is interesting."

He leaned over her, bracing his weight on his elbows. "I thought so."

"All this just to slow me down?"

"I'm a desperate man."

She could pull the airy bed hangings down and free herself with a couple of quick tugs, but somehow he didn't think she would do that. He sensed that she was in a mood to walk on the wild side tonight. He could tell because he was inclined in the same direction. A shining example of synchronicity at work.

"What happens next?" she murmured.

"I don't know." He slid one hand between her legs and found the pearl in the oyster. He smiled when he felt her move beneath him, seeking more. "Shall we find out?"

"Oh, yes." She licked her lips and looked up at him through veiled lashes. "Let's do that."

He stroked her slowly, dampening his hand in her dew.

She lifted her hips against his fingers, tempting him with her body. She could have lured an angel into trouble. And he was no angel.

He moved down her body with his mouth, going lower until her scent enveloped him. He was so hard now he dared not brush his erection against her skin for fear of losing the fragile grip on his self-control. This was going to be a test of endurance and he was determined to make sure that he won tonight.

Eventually, when she was moaning and restless, he found the small, sensitive nubbin with his mouth. She caught her breath and tensed.

"Nick."

He used his tongue until she was gasping and writhing.

"Yes, please, *yes*. Now, damn it."

He slid a finger into her, searching for the spot; pressed upward. She gasped.

"*Yes*. Right there. Oh, yes. Oh, yes, oh, yes, oh, yes. *Nick*."

She came in shuddering little waves of raw, feminine energy that took his breath away. He barely made it back up her body in time to sink himself fully into her before his own climax ripped through him.

She jerked her arms abruptly and then her nails were in

his back and her legs were wrapped snugly around his hips. The last thing he remembered was the feel of the bed hangings floating down like so many silken cobwebs, tangling him in a snare he did not think that he would ever be able to escape.

He came back to his senses a long time later. For a moment he did not open his eyes, preferring to savor the satisfaction that hummed through him. He was content to drift forever in the aftermath of the lovemaking.

Then he felt the soft touch of gauzy fabric twining around his right wrist. He opened one eye. Octavia's breasts brushed across his chest when she leaned over him to secure his other wrist to the bedpost. He opened his other eye.

"What's going on here?" he asked with lazy interest.

She straddled him and smiled slowly. "My turn."

"Oh, wow."

She felt him leave the bed again shortly before dawn. Dismay and regret and a strange resentment whispered through her. She opened her eyes and stared at the wall, listening to him pad barefooted across the floor.

Of course he was leaving. What had she expected him to do? Stay until morning? What would be the point? This was a summer affair.

But she was not about to let him just slide out like this. He could say a proper goodbye when he left her bed, damn it.

She turned on her side, searching for him in the shadows, expecting to see him making for the bathroom with his clothes. But he wasn't creeping across the carpet.

He stood at the window, one hand braced against the

sill, and looked out at the moonlit bay. The pale glow streaming through the glass etched his shoulders in steely silver and cast his profile into deep shadow.

"Nick?" She levered herself up on her elbows. "What are you doing?"

He turned his head to look toward the bed. "I was just thinking."

"About what?"

"About what happens at the end of the summer."

She did not move. She did not even breathe. "This isn't The Talk, is it? Because if you're trying to sneak it in now—"

"It's not The Talk," he said, his voice roughening abruptly.

She stared at him. "Are you angry?"

"Maybe. Yeah. I think so. I'm trying to have a rational discussion here and you're throwing that crap about The Talk in my face."

He was angry, all right. Fair enough. She was rapidly losing her temper, too.

"Okay, sorry," she said stiffly. "I just wanted to be sure you weren't going to try to deliver that stupid talk now. Because it's much too late."

He did not move for a few seconds. Then he came away from the window and walked back to the bed to stand looking down at her.

"Too late?" he repeated neutrally.

"Whether you like it or not, we are involved in a relationship. It may not work out for a variety of reasons, but I'll be damned if I'll let you put some arbitrary limit on it."

"There seems to be some confusion here," he said coldly. "You're accusing me of trying to specify the time and date when this thing between us ends, but I'm not the one who keeps talking about leaving Eclipse Bay in a few weeks."

She opened her mouth to argue and then closed it quickly.

Okay, he had a point.

She cleared her throat. "That's different."

"Like hell."

She glowered. "I have to be pragmatic. I've got a business to sell. That takes time and planning. And then there's the move. A person can't make those sorts of arrangements on a last-minute basis."

He put one knee on the tumbled bedding. "You're the one who's running scared here."

"That's not true."

"Hell, maybe we've both been running scared for a while." He came down on top of her, pushing her back onto the pillows. "But I think it's time we both stopped."

"You do?"

"If you want to sleep with me, lady, you're going to have to take a few chances."

"Is that so?"

"Yeah."

"What about you?" she managed. "Are you willing to take a few risks, too?"

His smile was slow and enigmatic in the shadows. His eyes had never been more dangerous. Or promised so much.

"I've been taking chances since the day I met you," he said. "Want to know why I didn't give you The Talk back at the beginning of this affair?"

"Yes."

"I forgot about it, that's why. Never even crossed my

mind to give you The Talk." He brushed his mouth across hers. "You see? Taking chances."

"Oh."

He bent his head again and put his mouth to her throat. She felt the edge of his teeth against her skin and excitement stormed through her. She wrapped her arms around him and stopped thinking about the end of summer.

# chapter 20

Gail rushed through the door of the gallery shortly after ten-thirty the next morning. "You won't believe this."

"What's that?" Octavia came around the corner of one of the display panels and stopped, staring in amazement. "You're right. I don't believe it. Good grief, what happened? You've got Very Big Hair."

"What? Oh, yeah, my hair." Gail grimaced and put up a hand to touch the crisply starched mountain of hair on top of her head. "You owe me for this, boss. Big time."

Octavia shook her head slowly in disbelief. She could not get over her hair. "That's amazing."

"Carla wanted to color it, too, but I drew the line at that."

"Let me guess. Blonde?"

"Probably. I didn't get into a discussion of shades. I told her I needed to think about such a major move." Gail waved that aside. "But that's not important. What's important here is what I heard while I was trapped in the chair."

"Ah, yes." Octavia propped a scene of Hidden Cove at dawn against the panel. "Your undercover assignment. I almost forgot. Well?"

Gail drew herself up proudly. "Laugh if you will, but I found out something you really ought to know."

Octavia reached up to remove a picture of the marina from a panel. "Okay, Madam Spy. What did you find out at the beauty shop?"

Gail leaned against the counter and examined her nails. "Not much."

"I'm not surprised." She set the marina scene aside and hoisted the picture of Hidden Cove.

"Just two tiny little snippets of information that you might find interesting."

Octavia hung the Hidden Cove picture on the panel in the space that had been previously occupied by the painting of the marina. "And those two tiny little snippets would be?"

"Well, for starters, I found out what caused the big fight at the Total Eclipse last night."

"It was a bar brawl." Octavia stepped back to study the position of the picture she had just hung. "I have it on excellent authority that such events are random acts of nature. They don't need a cause."

"This one apparently had a very specific cause," Gail murmured dryly.

"Really?" Octavia made a tiny adjustment to the frame. "And what was it?"

"You."

Octavia's fingers stilled on the frame. "Someone said that I was the cause?"

"Actually, *everyone* is saying it this morning."

Octavia turned slowly. "That's very irritating."

"Irritating? Is that the best you can do? I expected a more forceful reaction."

"Well, it's also extremely annoying and a complete misrepresentation of the facts."

Gail slumped back against the counter. "I don't believe it. I am doomed to go through a Very Big Hair day and all you can say is that the information I brought back from my mission is irritating, annoying, and a misrepresentation of the facts?"

Jeremy came through the open door of the gallery. He had three cups of coffee cradled in the wedge formed by his hands.

"What's irritating, annoying, and a misrepresentation of the facts?" He stopped abruptly, staring at Gail. "Oh, jeez. I see what you mean. They really did a number on you down at the beauty shop, didn't they? I hope the information you got was worth the torture you had to go through to get it."

"Unfortunately the torture has only begun." Gail sighed in exasperation. "I have to live with this hair for the rest of the day. But for the record, the information I picked up is downright fascinating."

"I sure hope so. Any news on the Upsall?"

"Unfortunately, last night's excitement dominated the conversation. No one was talking about anything else this morning." She studied him as he came toward the counter. "Good heavens, you've got a shiner."

"I've already looked in a mirror today." Jeremy put the cups down beside her. "Tell me something I don't know."

"It's from the brawl last night, isn't it?" Gail stepped closer, concern darkening her expression. "I knew you were at the Total Eclipse with Nick, but I didn't realize you got hurt. Have you seen a doctor?"

"I don't need a doctor. I'm okay." He peeled the lids off the coffee cups. "Here you go, sugar and cream."

"Thanks." She took the cup from him without glancing at it, still studying his black eye with a troubled air. "Did you put ice on it?"

"For a while. Don't worry about it. Looks a lot worse than it is." Jeremy handed the second cup to Octavia. "Cream, right?"

"Yes. Thank you." She took the cup in both hands and stared at his bruised face. "Are you sure you're all right?"

"I'm sure." He chuckled. "You oughta see the other guy."

"What other guy?" she asked swiftly.

"Nick. I've got a hunch he looks a lot worse than I do this morning. He was in the middle of most of the action last night, as I recall. Just my bad luck to be standing around in the vicinity when it all went down. Yeah, I expect old Nick has a couple of beautiful shiners this morning."

Octavia concentrated on removing the lid from her cup. She became aware of an acute silence. When she looked up she saw that both Gail and Jeremy were watching her with rapt attention.

"Something wrong?" she asked politely.

"Uh, no." Jeremy raised his brows. "Just wondered why you weren't a little more concerned about Nick, that's all."

"He looked fine last night when I saw him outside the police station."

"I looked okay last night, too. Bruises take a while to color up. I figure he's probably a real mess today."

"He's not," she said shortly.

"You're sure?"

"I saw him earlier." Octavia dropped the lid into the trash bin.

"Earlier," Jeremy repeated. "That would be earlier this morning?"

"Yes." She took a tentative sip of the coffee. It was still a little too hot for comfort. She blew on the surface of the liquid a few times.

"Precisely how early this morning would that be?" Gail asked with great interest.

"I don't recall the exact time. Why? Is it important?"

"Could be." Gail exchanged glances with Jeremy. "Especially if it was, oh, say sometime around dawn or thereabouts."

"That would be critical," Jeremy agreed.

"And it would confirm the second tidbit of information I got this morning," Gail added smoothly.

Octavia peered at each of them in turn. "Am I missing something here?"

"You can tell us, honey," Gail answered. "We're your friends."

"Sure," Jeremy said. "You can tell us everything."

"Out with it," Gail said. "We're on pins and needles here. The suspense is killing us. Did Hardhearted Harte really spend the whole night with you last night? Was he actually there for breakfast? Did you or did you not break the curse?"

Too late Octavia recalled the second part of the Nick Harte legend. *He always leaves before dawn.* She felt herself turn red. "I really don't think that's any of your business."

"Oh, gosh," Gail said. "Both of the rumors I heard at the beauty shop are true. Nick got into that brawl because of you *and then he spent the night with you.* You've done it. You've broken the curse on Hardhearted Harte."

Octavia choked on a mouthful of coffee. She sputtered and dabbed madly at her lips. "*That's* what they're saying at the beauty shop?"

"Yep."

"I've never met anyone who broke a curse before," Jeremy said. "How does it feel? Do you get a little rush when it happens? Or do you have to wait for results?"

"Yes, tell us every little detail," Gail said.

"Hold it right there." Octavia slapped the coffee cup down on the counter. Drops of coffee shot over the rim and splattered the wood surface. "Let's get something straight. Apparently Nick is having fun telling people that he got into the brawl because I suggested he have a drink with you, Jeremy. Big joke. Ha ha."

"Well—"

"Okay, okay, maybe it *was* my idea for you two to have a beer together and talk things over. But it's quite a stretch to say that the bar fight was therefore my fault. I certainly never intended for Nick to take you to the Total Eclipse for that beer and chat."

"Where else could a couple of guys go to talk over old times in this burg?" Gail asked innocently.

"You misunderstand, Octavia," Jeremy said gently. "Nick's not spreading the story that he got into the fight because of you. It's all over town this morning because it's the flat-out truth and everyone who was in the Total Eclipse last night knows it. There are witnesses. Lots and lots of them. They're the ones who are doing the talking."

"But all I did was suggest that you two have a drink." Her voice was rising. That almost never happened. "It's not fair to blame me."

"There's a little more to it than that," Jeremy said.

"And what's with this nonsense about breaking the curse?" She no longer cared that she was getting loud. "Are there witnesses to that, too?"

Nick appeared in the doorway at that moment, three

coffee cups in his hands. He studied the trio in the gallery through the lenses of his dark glasses and appeared to make an executive decision.

"Maybe I should come back later." He started to step back out onto the sidewalk.

Octavia rounded on him. "Don't you dare leave. Get back in here right now. Do you hear me, Nick Harte?"

"Oh, yeah." Nick went to the counter and set down the three cups. "I definitely hear you."

She crossed her arms and faced the three of them. "Let's try to get some clarity on this issue."

"Damn." Nick removed his dark glasses with obvious reluctance and dropped them into his pocket. "Do we have to do clarity? I hate the clarity thing." He looked at the cup Gail held and the one that sat on the counter. "You've already got coffee."

"I brought it," Jeremy explained.

Nick glanced at him. "You look like hell."

"Which is extremely unfair," Jeremy said, "given that I was just an innocent bystander."

"Innocent bystanders have a very high accident rate," Nick informed him with an air of authority. "Look it up."

"I'll remember that. But, you know, you might want to show a little gratitude here, Harte. I'm the one who took that cue stick away from Dickhead before he could ram it where the sun don't shine."

Nick nodded. "I am, indeed, grateful for that. By the way, that reminds me. You mentioned True's sidekick, Bonner, last night. Do you read my books?"

"What can I say? A divorced man has a lot of spare time on his hands."

"Is that how you got the black eye?" Gail asked Jeremy. "Did Dickhead hit you with the pool cue?"

"Actually, it was a little more complicated than that," Jeremy said.

*"Excuse me,"* Octavia said very loudly.

They all looked at her with polite expectation.

"As I was about to say before I was so rudely interrupted," she went on, not even trying to lower her voice, "I want to know why everyone in town believes that I was the cause of that stupid bar fight last night."

"Probably because, as I just told you, it's true." Jeremy took a swallow of coffee.

"It is *not* true," she shot back.

"According to the ladies down at the beauty parlor, it is," Gail offered. "That's all anyone could talk about. That and the fact that Nick spent the night at your place, of course."

Nick paused in the act of taking a sip of coffee. "Folks are discussing that, too?"

"With relish and zest," Gail assured him.

"Huh." He shrugged and drank more coffee.

Octavia threw up her hands. "Okay, so I suggested that you two have a drink together. How was I to know you'd be dumb enough to have that drink at the Total Eclipse?"

"It wasn't the fact that Nick bought me a beer that started the fight," Jeremy said with grave precision. "The fight started when Mean Eugene announced to the entire bar that you had bestowed your favors upon Nick for certain agenda-driven reasons."

She stared at him. "I beg your pardon?"

"Eugene implied that you had commenced an affair with Nick, here, with the goal of causing him to become so bemused and befuddled that he would be unable to think clearly. The net result would be that our intrepid investigator would be unable to detect that you were the person most likely to have stolen the Upsall."

Octavia made it to the end of the counter and grabbed hold of it to steady herself. "Good lord."

"Of course, Eugene didn't put it in precisely those words." Jeremy glanced at Nick for confirmation. "Don't think he used the words *bemused* and *befuddled,* did he?"

"No," Nick said. "I believe what Eugene said was that Octavia was *screwing me senseless.*"

Jeremy shook his head. "Don't think he said *senseless,* either. Maybe it was *screwing your brains out.*"

"Right." Nick raised a cup in a small salute. "That was it. He said that Octavia was *screwing my brains out* in an effort to distract me from my investigation."

Jeremy turned to Octavia. "There was also some question about the naturalness of your red hair. Naturally, Nick could not let Eugene and Dickhead get away with talking about a lady in such crude terms. Hence the bar brawl."

Octavia clutched the counter, feeling dazed and disoriented. She looked at Nick, hoping he would tell her it was all just a big joke. "The brawl really did start because of me?"

"Don't worry about the gossip," Nick said, dismissing the entire event with another shrug. "It'll blow over in a few days."

"Are you kidding?" Jeremy asked. "Folks around here still talk about the big fight between your grandfather and Mitchell Madison that took place outside of Fulton's decades ago. What makes you think that forty or fifty years from now, they won't be telling the story of what happened last night at the Total Eclipse?"

"Jeremy's right," Gail said. "You're a Harte, Nick, and Octavia is related to the woman who sparked the original Harte-Madison feud. Trust me, the legend of the big brawl at the Total Eclipse will live on forever."

Jeremy nodded in agreement. "Mostly because there's so little to talk about in a small town like this."

"Well, it's only to be expected, I suppose. You do know she is related to that Claudia Banner woman. The one who started the Harte-Madison feud all those years ago."

Octavia froze in the act of putting the six-pack of bottled spring water in the basket of the supermarket cart. The voice came from the next aisle over, the one labeled *Canned Veg & Beans.*

"My Hank said there hasn't been a brawl like that at the Total Eclipse in ages. Not since that biker club came through town three years back. Fred claims that there was a couple of thousand dollars worth of damage done in the pool room last night."

She recognized the voices now. Megan Grayson and Sandra Finley. Both women had come into Bright Visions to browse on occasion and both served on the Summer Celebration committee.

"If you ask me, Fred's just taking advantage of a golden opportunity," Megan said. "One of the Willis brothers told my husband that Fred has been thinking about repainting the Total Eclipse for years. He put it off because he was too cheap to pay for the job. But he knows he can get the money out of Nick Harte and Jeremy Seaton now, so why not go for it?"

"You have to wonder why Nick and Jeremy were playing pool together in the first place. Those two haven't had much to do with each other in a couple of years. Not since Jeremy's divorce, in fact. Everyone assumed they'd had a falling out of some kind."

"And then they both went and dated Octavia Brightwell here in Eclipse Bay." Sandra made a disapproving noise that sounded a lot like the clucking of a chicken. "That can't have helped the situation. In fact, you'd have thought that those two would have been at each other's throats by now. Nothing like a woman coming between two men to cause trouble."

"Well, from all accounts they were on the same side in that bar fight last night. Sounds like they must have settled their differences."

"Who would have thought a Harte and a Seaton would get into a barroom brawl? Oh, sure, you expect that sort of thing from a Madison, but I always thought the Hartes and the Seatons were a lot more refined."

"Don't you believe that for one moment," Megan said. "Remember, it was Sullivan Harte who got into that fist-fight with Mitch Madison all those years ago and launched the feud. And from what I've heard, the Seatons aren't all saints, either. I can imagine how poor Edith must feel today. They say she's absolutely beside herself this morning because of what happened last night. Didn't even open her shop. Probably can't face the gossip."

"More likely she can't stand to be civil to Octavia Brightwell," Sandra said. "I mean, everyone knows that Octavia was the cause of the fight that involved Edith's precious grandson."

"Edith has always been so proud of Jeremy. I swear his divorce hit her harder than it did him. She was so thrilled that he'd married into such a *fine* family, remember? Not that the *fine* family ever gave her the time of day, as far as I could tell. Word had it that they encouraged the divorce."

"And now he's involved in a free-for-all at the Total Eclipse. No wonder she doesn't want to show her face in public today."

"By the way, you did hear that Nick Harte spent the night with Octavia Brightwell?"

"I certainly did. His car was seen leaving her place at eight o'clock this morning."

Megan giggled. "Word is, she may have broken the curse."

"I think it's a lot more likely that Nick Harte is having himself a little fun this summer. It'll end when he goes back to Portland."

"If you ask me, it's Octavia Brightwell who ought to go into hiding. She should be ashamed of herself. When you stop and think about it, she's the real problem here."

"A real troublemaker," Sandra agreed. "Back in high school we had a name for women like that."

*That does it, I've had enough,* Octavia thought. She wheeled her cart around the corner and started down Canned Veg & Beans.

"Good morning, Sandra. Megan." She gave both women a brilliant smile. "Lovely day, isn't it?"

Sandra and Megan hushed instantly. They gripped the handles of their shopping carts and stared at her as though she had materialized out of thin air.

"I couldn't help overhearing your conversation." Octavia jerked her own cart to a halt a short distance away and blocked the aisle with it. "And I am very curious to find out exactly what word you had for *women like me* back in high school, Sandra."

Sandra Finley turned an unpleasant shade of red. "I don't know what you're talking about. You must have misunderstood."

"She's right," Megan said quickly. "You didn't hear her correctly." She looked triumphant. "It never pays to eavesdrop, you know."

"Hard to avoid hearing you two, since you insist upon discussing me in the middle of a grocery store aisle."

"You'll have to excuse me." Megan glanced at her watch. "I've got a committee meeting at three."

"So do I," Sandra said. She tightened her grip on the cart handle.

Octavia did not shift her shopping cart out of their path. "You know, speaking of names that we used back in high school, I remember one that fits both of you perfectly. Rhymes with rich."

Sandra got her jaw back into place. "Did you just call me a bitch?"

"I really don't have time for this," Megan said.

Having concluded that she could not go forward, she swung her shopping cart into a tight U-turn. And promptly banged into Sandra's cart. The baskets jammed together. The wheels snagged, making it impossible for either woman to maneuver out of the aisle.

Octavia surveyed her captive audience. "Now, then, I have a suggestion. Since the two of you are obviously going to spend the rest of the day spreading gossip, what do you say we take a few minutes to get one particular fact straight?"

"I don't know what you're talking about," Sandra said stiffly.

Octavia ignored that. "For the record, Nick Harte did *not* leave my cottage at eight o'clock this morning. That is a flat-out lie."

Megan and Sandra looked at her, suddenly rapt. Neither said a word.

"He left at precisely seven thirty-five," Octavia said coolly. "I remember, because we had just finished breakfast together and I turned on the radio to catch the morning news."

Megan and Sandra blinked.

Octavia smiled. "Hey, you know what? I'll bet that *women like you* are the sort who will appreciate a few of the more intimate details about my relationship with Nick. I'm sure there are probably all kinds of stories going around about us and the techniques I used to break the curse."

Megan and Sandra's jaws dropped.

Octavia leaned forward, bracing her arms on the handle of her cart, and assumed a confidential air. "I imagine you'd like to hear just how I did it, wouldn't you? Are you ready for this? I made poached eggs and toast for Nick's breakfast."

A thunderous hush fell on the adjoining aisles. It seemed to Octavia that the whole of Fulton's had suddenly gone silent.

"My secret is a little Dijon mustard on the toast under the eggs." She winked. "Trust me, it really adds some zip. You should have seen Nick's face when I put that plate down in front of him. Talk about a man who looks like he thinks he's died and gone to heaven."

Megan and Sandra were no longer watching her. Their gazes were riveted on a point just beyond her shoulder.

*I'm getting an audience,* Octavia thought. Terrific. Another little scene, the details of which would be all over town by sundown. The really interesting thing was that she did not give a damn. Not right now at any rate. Right now she was on a roll.

"If you think that the thing with the mustard is kinky, wait until I tell you how Nick got his coffee this morning," she said in a gossipy tone. "Talk about getting down to the good stuff. So, there we were, sitting at the breakfast table and I can tell that he's ready for a second cup, you know? I mean, he's *really, really* ready for it. Wow. This man is *hot* for another cup, if you get my drift."

"Might be a good idea to give everyone some time to cool off before you tell them about the coffee thing," Nick said behind her. He sounded amused, but there was the barest hint of a warning in his voice. "I'm not sure Eclipse Bay is ready for the details of my second cup of coffee."

She spun around. Reality came back with a jarring thud.

"I think it might be a good idea to check out now," he said.

She wondered just how big a fool she had made of herself. He was right. This was a very, very good time to check out.

"Okay." She whipped the cart around and headed for the checkout counter, leaving Sandra and Megan still tangled up in Canned Veg & Beans.

"I hope you don't mind me interrupting back there," Nick said, falling into step beside her. "It's just that some things are personal, you know? That stuff about the second cup of coffee? That's special to a sensitive guy like me."

"Oh, for heaven's sake, Nick, you didn't even have a second cup of coffee this morning and you know it."

"Are you sure?"

"Of course I'm sure. Can't you remember what you had for breakfast?"

"It's all a blur after the eggs and mustard."

# chapter 21

At four o'clock that afternoon he went back to the gallery to check on Octavia. She had looked good during the scene with Sandra and Megan at Fulton's, but underneath he thought he had detected some additional strain.

"She's not here," Gail said the instant he walked through the door. "She went home early."

"She never goes home early," Nick said.

"She did today."

He was getting more concerned by the minute. "Is she okay?"

"I don't think so." Gail exhaled deeply. "She's lived in town off and on for over a year and she's been hanging out a lot with Hartes and Madisons, but that doesn't mean she's completely acclimated to our quaint little traditions here in Eclipse Bay. In spite of the way she handled Sandra and Megan, I think she's a lot more upset about the gossip that is going around than she's letting on."

Nick frowned. "You really think it's bothering her? Seemed like she was dealing with it fairly well earlier."

Gail watched him very steadily. "The brawl last night was bad enough. But the fact that everyone is talking about how you spent the night at her place is a real problem, I think."

"Why? Everyone knows that we're seeing each other. It's no secret. She's aware of that."

"No offense, but I do believe that you're missing the point here," Gail said. "You were seen driving away from her cottage at eight o'clock this morning."

"Seven thirty-five, and so somebody noticed my car coming from the direction of her cottage early this morning. So what? Not the first time."

"Yes, it is, as a matter of fact."

"You're right, I am missing something here. You want to run that by me again?"

Gail picked up a stack of brochures announcing the Children's Art Show and made a pretense of straightening them. "Eight o'clock or, to be precise, seven thirty-five, is well after dawn at this time of year."

"What about it?"

"Pay attention, Nick." She slapped the brochures back down on the counter. "The word has gone out that Octavia has broken the curse."

"Yeah? So?"

"You do know about the curse, don't you?"

"That idiotic story about me that claims that I never spend the entire night with a woman?" He waved that aside. "I've heard about it, sure."

"Well?" she demanded.

"It probably got started because I've never left Carson with a sitter overnight. But it doesn't follow that I never have any nights to myself. Carson stays with family once in a while. He's with his grandfather and his great-grand-father and Lillian and Gabe at the moment. Leaving me free to do as I please at night."

"So, does that mean that you *do* sometimes spend the entire night with a woman with whom you're romantically involved?" Gail asked with disconcerting interest.

"Guys don't get *romantically* involved."

"What do they get?"

"Involved, period."

"Oh, sure, I knew that. So, do you sometimes spend the entire night with women with whom you're *involved, period*?"

"You know, I didn't come here to discuss my love life with a woman who has Very Big Hair."

"That was a low blow." Gail patted the rigid outer layer of her voluminous hairdo. "I was only carrying out my assignment."

"Yeah." Nick went toward the door. "Too bad you didn't learn anything useful about that damned painting."

Gail straightened her shoulders and held her chin high. "In the long run, I feel that I discovered something infinitely more important."

"Such as?"

"The name of the woman who broke the curse on Hard-hearted Harte."

He went out onto the sidewalk and slammed the door closed.

Twenty minutes later he stood on the bluff above the small, crescent-shaped beach, looking down. She was sitting on a rock, knees drawn up under a long, geranium-red skirt, her face hidden beneath the wide brim of a big straw hat. The now-familiar flicker of intense awareness crackled through him, tightening his belly and heating his blood.

It was a deeply sensual feeling, but he could not slap the label *great sex* on this and let it go at that. He had known that from the beginning.

He watched her there in the sunlight, her skirt fluttering a little in the breeze, her gracefully rounded arms wrapped around her knees, and he finally understood.

This strange, bone-deep sensation that he always experienced when he thought about her or when he was in her vicinity wasn't merely desire or anticipation. It was a sense of connection. In some manner that he knew he would probably never fully comprehend, he was linked to her now.

He had never known this particular kind of bond, he realized. Perhaps it would have developed eventually with Amelia if they had had more time and if he had not screwed things up by quitting Harte Investments and if she had not turned to an old lover when the chips were down.

No. It would never have been like this with Amelia. It could never be like this with anyone else.

Maybe the rumors were right. Maybe he had been under some kind of curse.

But what was the point of being freed if he lost the lady who had the magic touch?

She turned slightly, obviously aware that someone was on the bluff behind her. The straw brim of the hat tilted at an angle and he caught a glimpse of her face. She had on a pair of dark glasses. He could not read her expression but he got the distinct impression that she was not overly thrilled to see him. She was certainly not waving.

He found the path that led to the beach and went down it swiftly. Tiny pebbles scattered before him.

When he got to the bottom he walked toward Octavia

feeling as if he were walking toward his destiny. She did not take off her sunglasses. It occurred to him that he was still wearing his, too. Neither of them could tell what the other was thinking, he realized.

"Are you all right?" he asked.

"Yes."

"Gail was worried about you. She said you'd left the shop in a hurry."

"There's nothing to be concerned about. I just wanted to get away for a while. I need to think."

He sat down beside her on the broad, sun-warmed rock. Close enough to be intensely conscious of her nearness; not quite touching. A curious kind of panic started to gnaw at his insides. She really was upset. He was not sure how to deal with it.

"I'm sorry the three of us gave you so much grief this morning," he said. "We were just teasing you."

"I know."

"I realize these past few days have been rough on you. You're not accustomed to being the subject of local gossip."

"It's not that."

"People were bound to talk after it got out that we were seeing each other," he said. "But the gossip will fade when folks get used to the idea."

"I don't particularly care what people think of our relationship."

That did not sound good, he thought. He turned his head to get a better look at her profile. She remained enigmatic behind the shields of her dark glasses.

"You don't care that everyone's discussing our relationship down at the beauty parlor and in the aisles at Fulton's?" he asked carefully.

She unclasped her knees and braced her arms behind

her, flattening her palms on the rock. "Well, it feels a little strange to be the subject of so much local interest, but I've had plenty of opportunity to see how the Hartes and the Madisons handle that sort of situation. I thought I was dealing with it very well."

"You are," he agreed immediately. "You're handling it beautifully."

"And, as you just said, the talk will fade in time."

"Sure." He mentally crossed his fingers. "Eventually."

She said nothing else; just sat there, gazing thoughtfully out over the bay.

"So," he said when he could no longer stand the suspense. "If it's not the fact that everyone is chatting about how I spent the night at your place that's bothering you, what, exactly, is the problem here?"

"The bar fight last night."

He exhaled slowly. "I was afraid it might be that. Look, I'm sorry it happened, but it was just a case of a bunch of guys who'd been drinking some beer and got carried away. Not the first time it's happened at the Total Eclipse, and it sure as hell won't be the last."

"I realize that." She finally turned her head to look directly at him. "But it is the first time anyone has ever gotten into a fight on account of me."

Dread settled heavily in the pit of his stomach. "Okay, so you're accustomed to dating a classier sort of guy. The type who doesn't get into bar brawls. Would it help if I told you that I don't make a habit of that kind of thing?"

She just looked at him for a small eternity. Her mouth twitched a couple of times.

And then she was laughing so hard that tears started to run down her face beneath the rims of her dark glasses.

He watched her for a while, fascinated. "Did I say something funny?"

"Yes." She yanked off the dark glasses and dried her eyes on the sleeve of her gold shirt. "Yes, you said something very, very funny."

"You know you're losing it when you don't get your own jokes."

She pulled herself together with a visible effort. The laughter faded into giggles and then shrank into a wide smile. Her eyes were warm and clear and bright with the remnants of her amusement.

"You're not losing it," she said. "We're just not quite in synch here. What I was trying to tell you is that I have never considered myself the type of woman who is capable of launching a barroom brawl."

"You're not."

"You're wrong. Clearly I must be that type because I did ignite that fight last night. The facts are on the record from dozens of witnesses, apparently."

He winced. "This is one of those no-win situations, isn't it? Any way I respond, I screw up big time."

She ignored that. "I like it."

"What? That I'm trapped in a lose-lose scenario?"

"No, that I'm the type of woman who has what it takes to spark a tavern brawl."

"Huh."

"I also like being the type of woman who inspires gossip in the beauty shop and creates great excitement in the supermarket aisles."

"Uh-huh."

"The type who ties men up in bed."

"And the type who lets herself be tied up in bed," he reminded her.

"That, too. Aunt Claudia would be so proud."

"Yeah?"

"Definitely. She was always telling me that I had to stop trying so hard to smooth things over and fix things. She said I should learn to raise a little hell. I'm starting to wonder if maybe that's the real reason she sent me here to Eclipse Bay. Not to repair the damage she did but to discover this other side of myself."

"Interesting theory."

"The thing is, how could she have guessed that I'd get into so much trouble if I got tangled up with you Hartes and those Madisons? You think maybe there really was something to all that stuff about auras and New Age metaphysics that she studied during the last years of her life?"

He folded his arms on his knees and savored the sense of relief that was washing through him. Octavia wasn't sunk in depression. She wasn't even pissed off. There was still hope.

"Wouldn't take a lot of metaphysical intuition and aura reading to figure out that sending you here to get involved with Hartes and Madisons would get you into trouble," he said. "A woman as smart as Claudia Banner would have been able to predict exactly what would happen."

The following morning Nick scrawled his name on a check and pushed it across the bar. Beside him, Jeremy signed his check with an artistic flourish and put it on top of Nick's.

"Thank you, gentlemen." Fred snapped up both checks and put them into the cash register drawer. "Always a pleasure doing business with you. You're welcome back to the Total Eclipse any time. I like to encourage a high-class clientele."

"I don't think we'll be able to afford to come back often," Jeremy grumbled.

Fred contrived to look hurt. "This is the thanks I get for dropping all the charges?"

"You know damn well we didn't do two thousand dollars' worth of damage here the other night." Jeremy waved a hand to indicate the shabby surroundings. "Hell, the joint doesn't look any different than it did before things got exciting."

"You ruined my walls."

"Right, the walls." Nick lounged on a bar stool and folded his arms. He glanced toward the far end of the room, where the Willis brothers were busy with a tape measure and a clipboard.

The brothers were fixtures in town. For as long as Nick could remember, they had worked as general contractors, doing everything from plumbing to roof repairs. They were identical twins, but no one in town had any trouble telling them apart.

From his cleanly shaved skull to his crisply laundered overalls, Walter Willis was as precise and polished as one of the gleaming tools he wore on his belt. Torrance, on the other hand, wore his thin, straggling hair in a greasy pony-tail. His work clothes were stained with everything from paint splatters to pizza sauce.

"What color are you going to paint the place?" Jeremy asked.

Fred pursed his lips. "I'm thinking taupe."

"Taupe?" Jeremy stared at him. "You're kidding, right? Taupe isn't the color you use for a bar."

"What color is taupe, anyway?" Nick asked.

"Who knows?" Fred said. "Walt over there suggested it."

"Forget taupe," Jeremy advised. "I'd go with dark green and maybe a warm brown on the baseboards and trim."

"Listen to him," Nick said. "The man's an artist."

"Green and brown, huh?" Fred pondered that for a while. "Walt said he'd give me a special on the taupe. Said he had some left over from a job he and Torrance did for one of the summer people."

"Don't suppose it much matters what color you use," Nick said. "No one will be able to see it in here, anyway, what with the low lighting and all."

Fred scowled. "Gotta keep the lights low."

"Why?" Jeremy asked. "So folks won't notice the size of the roaches?"

"Gives the place ambience," Fred said.

The door opened. For a few seconds the glare of daylight silhouetted the distinctive figures of Eugene and Dwayne. Then the door closed again.

"Don't think you need a lot of ambience to attract those two," Nick said. "Just spray a little stale beer around the place and sprinkle some aged French fries under the tables."

Eugene came to a halt halfway across the room and staggered a bit, feigning astonishment. "Well, as I live and breathe, Dwayne, if it ain't our good buddies, Harte and Seaton."

Dwayne, who had been tailgating his companion, collided with Eugene's backside and ricocheted off a couple of feet. He regained his balance and peered at Nick and Jeremy.

"Oh, yeah," Dwayne said. "It's them, all right."

"Dwayne and me was just over at the station talkin' to Sandy," Eugene explained. He lumbered into gear again, making his way through the maze of empty tables. "Saw you guys come in here. We want to buy you a drink."

Jeremy straightened warily. "Much as we'd love to stay and chat, Nick and I have appointments today. Isn't that right, Nick?"

Nick did not take his eyes off Eugene. "You want to buy us a drink?"

"Sure. After all that fun we had together, it only seems fair." Eugene reached the end of the bar and gestured expansively. "Beers all around, Fred."

Fred shrugged and set out four glasses.

"Gee, Eugene," Jeremy muttered. "We don't know what to say, do we, Nick?"

"Speechless," Nick agreed dryly. "What's this all about, Eugene?"

"Hell, me and Dwayne figure we owe you two something for covering the damages Fred, here, claims he's owed for the other night. Ain't that right, Dwayne?"

"Right." Dwayne perched on the stool next to Eugene. "Mighty generous of you."

Fred put a full glass down in front of everyone.

Eugene hoisted his glass. "Here's to good times."

"Good times." Nick picked up his glass and drank some beer.

Jeremy hesitated and then followed suit.

Eugene beamed. "Never thought I'd see you in a bar fight, Harte. Or you, either, for that matter, Seaton. Who'd have believed that you two would turn out to be just a couple of regular guys, after all? You ever believe that, Fred?"

"Wonders never cease." Fred walked out from behind the bar. "I'm gonna go talk to Walt and Torrance. I kinda like the idea of green and brown on the walls."

Eugene waited until he had moved off into the pool room where the Willis brothers were now working. Then he looked down the bar at Nick and Jeremy. He stopped smiling.

"You know, Dwayne and me, we never thanked you two

for getting us out of the car that night we went into the water," he said.

"Forget it," Nick said. "That was a long time ago."

"Yeah." Eugene took a long pull on his beer. "A long time ago."

No one said anything for a while. Eugene and Dwayne worked steadily on their beers.

"After it happened," Eugene said eventually, "we figured you'd go straight to Chief Yates, you know? Maybe tell him about that little game of chicken we were all playing."

"You mean, tell him how you tried to run us off the road?" Jeremy asked neutrally.

"Maybe things got a little outta hand," Eugene said. "Me and Dwayne were really pissed after you showed us up at the races that night. If you'd gone to Yates and told him your version of events, he'd have believed you on accounta you and Harte, here, come from such fine, upstanding families and all."

"I don't want to belabor the issue," Jeremy said, "but our version of events would have been the truth."

"We were just foolin' around," Eugene insisted. "Like I said, things got outta hand. But that ain't the point. Point is, Yates and everybody else would have believed you guys. Nobody would have even listened to our side of the story on accounta everyone around here figures me and Dwayne for trash."

Nick glanced at Jeremy. Eugene was right and they both knew it. Nobody in Eclipse Bay would have taken Eugene's or Dwayne's word over the word of a Harte or a Seaton, regardless of the circumstances.

Eugene looked at Nick. "The other night, I'd had a few

beers. I maybe said some things about your girlfriend that I shouldn't have said."

Nick inclined his head. "True."

"You know, that Miss Brightwell always says something nice when she sees us on the street," Eugene continued. "Ain't that right, Dwayne?"

"Yeah." Dwayne drank more beer. "Always says somethin' like, *Good morning,* or *How are you?* or *Beautiful day, ain't it?*"

Nick looked at Dwayne. "She says, *Beautiful day, ain't it?*"

"Nah, that ain't right." Dwayne's thin face twisted into a tight little knot with the effort of trying to think. "She says, *Beautiful day, isn't it?* Yeah, that's it. *Isn't it.*"

"Sure glad we got that straight," Jeremy said under his breath.

"Anyhow," Eugene went on with a doggedly determined air, "point is, she's a nice lady, even if she did swipe that painting. Me and Dwayne shouldn't have said that stuff about her deliberately screwing your brains out just so you wouldn't figure her for the thief. I mean, so what if that's the reason she's sleeping with you? It's a damn good reason, if you ask me. Goes to show she's smart."

"It takes a real man to apologize," Nick said. "Far as I can tell, you were among the first to hear the rumors at Fulton's. If you really want to settle things between us, you can tell me the name of the person who gave you the story."

Eugene and Dwayne exchanged nods. "It was that prissy old bitch, Mrs. Burke, wasn't it? Remember, Dwayne, she was talking to Carla from the beauty shop? I was in the ice cream section getting a couple of quarts of chocolate fudge swirl and they were right across from me in frozen orange juice. Acted like they never saw us."

"Sure," Dwayne said. "I remember. Old Lady Burke and Carla from the beauty parlor."

Nick saw Jeremy's eyes narrow a little at the names. He put down his unfinished beer and got to his feet.

"Thanks, Eugene," he said. "You, too, Dwayne. I appreciate the information. And the beer, too."

"Same here." Jeremy set his unfinished glass down on the bar next to Nick's.

"Ain'tcha gonna finish your beers?" Eugene asked, looking offended.

"The thing is," Nick said, "you've given us a hot new clue and we've got to get to work on it immediately."

"A clue, huh?" Eugene sounded pleased. "How about that, Dwayne? We gave 'em a clue. If they find that missing picture it'll be on accounta us."

"You'll have our undying gratitude," Nick said.

"I like the sound of that," Eugene said. "You sure you don't want the rest of your beer?"

"I wish I could hang around to finish it, but time is of the essence," Nick said. "Help yourself."

"Don't mind if I do." Eugene picked up Nick's unfinished beer and dumped it into his own nearly empty glass.

Dwayne did the same with the remaining beer in Jeremy's glass.

"That strike you as sanitary?" Jeremy asked as they went through the front door into the sunlight.

"The alcohol probably kills all the germs," Nick said.

"Sure. Eugene and Jeremy would have considered that."

The sunshine was blinding after the endless night of the Total Eclipse. Nick reached for his dark glasses. "What's with Mrs. Burke? You know her well?"

"No, but my grandmother does. Mrs. Burke is a member of her bridge group," Jeremy said. "They've been playing together every Wednesday and Saturday for nearly forty years."

"Which means your grandmother might be able to tell us where Mrs. Burke got the story."

Jeremy exhaled heavily. "There may be a little problem with me interrogating Grandma at the moment."

"She's still upset about you being hauled off to the police station after the big brawl?"

"Yeah. I stopped by to see her again this morning. I wanted to explain things and then ask her some questions about her recollections of what happened in the past. But I didn't get far. She was just sitting there at her kitchen table looking more depressed than she did after my divorce. Evidently I am proving to be just one major disappointment after another."

"Want me to talk to her? Tell her it was all my fault?"

"She's already decided whose fault it is," Jeremy said. "Like everyone else in town, she blames Octavia."

The door of the Total Eclipse opened again behind Nick. He glanced over his shoulder and saw Walter Willis emerge from the gloom. Something clicked.

"Hey, Walt, got a minute?"

"No problem." Walt changed direction and veered away from the van at the curb. He went toward Nick, sunlight gleaming on his meticulously shaved head. "I need to get some tools but I'm in no rush. What can I do for you?"

"You and Torrance installed the security alarm system in Octavia Brightwell's gallery, didn't you?"

"Sure did. She asked us to put it in when she opened for business. Why? Got a problem with it?"

"No. I just wondered if anyone besides Octavia and her former assistant might have access to the code."

"This is about the missing painting, isn't it?"

"Yes. Any ideas?"

"Well, Torrance or I could override the system if need be. But we've never had to do it. A real solid alarm system. Hasn't failed yet, not even during that big storm the other night." Walter's expression clouded. "See here, you thinking maybe one of us used the override code to sneak in and steal that painting?"

"Never crossed my mind," Nick said with absolute sincerity.

Walter snorted and relaxed. "Should hope not."

"But can you think of anyone else who might be able to override that system?"

Walter stroked his square chin, reflective and willing to be helpful now that he had been assured that he and his twin were not suspects. "Torrance and I never gave out the code to anyone except Miss Brightwell. I know she gave it to Noreen Perkins, but that's about all I know. You'd have to find Noreen to ask her if she gave it to anyone."

"Sean Valentine is working that angle," Nick said. "Don't think he's tracked her down yet, but he will eventually. Thanks, Walt. I just wanted to make certain I wasn't overlooking something obvious."

"You bet." Walter winked broadly. "I figure it's the least I can do for you after what you and Seaton, here, did for me and Torrance. Told Fred years ago the place needed a new coat of paint but he kept putting it off on account of he was too damn cheap. But now he says he wants a first-class job. Bottom line, on behalf of the Willis brothers, I'd like to say thanks."

"It was nothing," Nick said. "Just doing our part to improve Eclipse Bay. Hartes and Seatons have got a deep sense of civic responsibility, you know."

# chapter 22

"Way I figure it," Mitchell said into the cell phone, "getting into a bar fight over a lady like Octavia is as good as a marriage proposal. You'd damn sure better speak to that grandson of yours or I'm gonna have to do it for you."

"Stay out of it, Mitch," Sullivan said. "Things will get sorted out a whole lot easier if you don't interfere."

"Shoot and damn." Mitchell stabbed at some weeds with his trowel. He could hear the muted background noises of a vehicle in motion. Sullivan was calling from the backseat of the limo. "The whole blamed town is talking about her."

"Presumably the whole town is also talking about Nick."

"Well, sure, but that's different. He's a Harte. Around here everyone talks about you Hartes and us Madisons."

"If she's going to marry Nick, she'd better get used to being a subject of conversation there in Eclipse Bay."

*Progress at last,* Mitchell thought. The tough old bastard had at least used the word *marry* and Nick's name in the same sentence. He stopped assaulting weeds and tapped the trowel absently against a stake. "Just so long as he doesn't cut and run."

"You ever known a Harte to cut and run?"

"Nah. You're all too damn stubborn."

"Sort of like you Madisons, eh?"

"I reckon."

There was a short silence on the other end.

"Just got to hang on until dawn, Mitch," Sullivan said quietly.

The trowel went still in Mitchell's hands. The words echoed in his mind, bringing back the old memories. *Just got to hang on until dawn.*

He pocketed the trowel and pushed himself up off the low gardener's bench. Grabbing his cane, he made his way along the graveled path that wound between the richly planted flowerbeds, heading toward the greenhouse.

But it wasn't the glorious blooms of his roses that he saw in his mind now. Instead he was suddenly hit with visions of the ominous, eerie green of a jungle plunging inevitably into darkness. It would be a night in which death stalked at every hand. There would be no hope of rescue until dawn.

Survival that night had depended on silence and not giving in to the panic. Most of all, it had depended on being able to trust the man who guarded his back and whose back he, in turn, had guarded.

*Just got to hang on until dawn* were the last words that he and Sullivan had spoken to each other before they had settled in to keep watch in silence for the duration of that night.

The words had become a private code, a vow made between two young men who had gone through hell together. Neither he nor Sullivan would have made it until dawn if it hadn't been for the other and they both knew it. *Just got to hang on until dawn* meant *You can count on me. I'm with you here. We'll get through this together. You can trust me, buddy.*

He shoved the old images back into the furthest corners of his mind and concentrated on the present. He opened the door of his greenhouse and stepped inside.

"You got your list finished?" he asked.

"Yes, but it's damn short. You?"

"Same here. Most of the folks who were involved in Harte-Madison at the time have either moved away or died. There was our secretary, Angie, remember her?"

"Sure," Sullivan said. "But she died ten or twelve years ago. We both went to the funeral."

"Her son still lives here in town. Took over the hardware store."

"I can't see any connection. He wasn't even born when Claudia was with us. Besides, Claudia didn't do his mother any harm other than indirectly put her out of a job when the company went under. Angie wasn't all that upset about losing her position, as I recall. She went to work for George Adams and later married him. Who else have you got on your list?"

Mitchell fished the little notebook out of his pocket and flipped it open. He rattled off the names of the handful of other people who had been directly or indirectly connected with Harte-Madison in the old days. He paused when he came to the last person on his list.

"There is one more," he said slowly. He read the name aloud. "Remember him?"

"Hell, yes. He's on my list, too."

"You know, for a while I thought maybe he was the one who had screwed us."

"That's because you were so dazzled by Claudia that you couldn't see straight. You were willing to blame anyone else except her."

"Yeah, well, later when I got to thinking straight again."

"Think she cut him in on some of the action? Made him an offer he couldn't refuse so he'd cover up for her?"

"Something like that," Mitchell said.

They talked for a while longer, comparing notes, going over different scenarios, and eliminating other possibilities. At last they were both satisfied that they had a possible answer.

Neither of them was very happy about it.

"I'm not gonna take this to Nick and Octavia on my own," Mitchell said. "What if we're wrong?"

"I don't think we're wrong, but either way this is going to be very unpleasant for everyone concerned. Sit tight. Carson and I will arrive sometime around noon. What do you say we keep this to ourselves until after the Children's Art Show tonight? I don't want to go upsetting everyone and spoil the big event. No reason this can't wait until tomorrow morning."

"Yeah," Mitchell said. "No reason to ruin the fun tonight."


Nick sat in the old wooden porch rocker, heels stacked on the railing, and watched the gleaming black limo coast slowly toward him down the long drive.

He did not like the conclusions he had reached after his conversation with Mrs. Burke that afternoon, but he had to admit that when he put the pieces together, everything fit.

The only problem now was how and when to confront the suspect.

It was going to be an extremely delicate operation, he thought. The reputation of an upstanding member of the community was at stake. And much as he would like to do so, he couldn't see any way to hush things up, not if Octavia was to be completely vindicated. And she was his top priority in this affair.

The truth would have to come out, he thought, watching the limo pick its way along the unpaved drive. He sure as hell was not going to let the cloud of rumor and suspicion hang over Octavia indefinitely. Someone had to take the fall and it wasn't going to be her. Which meant that there was no way around the unpleasantness that lay ahead.

The limo drifted to a halt in front of the cottage. The rear doors snapped open before the driver could extricate himself from behind the wheel.

"Dad." Carson pelted toward him at a hundred miles an hour. "Dad, we're back."

Sullivan levered himself out of the other side of the vehicle, cane in hand, and started around the rear of the car.

Nick looked at Carson running toward him. *My son.*

And then Carson was in his arms and he was swinging his boy around in the familiar greeting ritual.

When he set Carson back on his feet, he caught Sullivan watching them. There was fierce love and pride in the old man's face. He did not speak, but there was no need for words. Nick knew exactly what he was thinking. *I didn't do everything right along the way but by God, one thing you can count on, I'd go to hell and back for you two, no questions asked.*

Nick met Sullivan's eyes. *I'd do the same for you,* he thought. *No questions asked.*

Sullivan smiled slightly and Nick knew that he understood.

The limo driver put two suitcases down on the porch and looked at Sullivan. "Anything else, sir?"

"No, thanks, Ben. We're all set for a few days. I'll give you a call when I need you. Take it easy on the way back to Portland."

Ben nodded. "Will do."

"Bye, Ben," Carson said.

"So long, pal. I'll look forward to meeting your dog when you finally get him."

"Okay," Carson said.

Ben nodded to all of them and went back down the steps. He got behind the wheel of the big car, put it in gear, and drove off toward the main road.

Nick ruffled Carson's hair. "How was the trip?"

"We stopped along the way and I got ice cream and Great-Granddad and Ben got coffee and then we looked at some caves. Really big caves. Bigger than the ones we have in Dead Hand Cove," Carson reported with excitement.

"We stopped to stretch our legs," Sullivan said, coming up the steps, "but we made good time." He raised his brows. "Didn't want to risk being late for the art show."

Carson looked at Nick. "Has Miss Brightwell hung my picture yet?"

"When I stopped by the gallery a couple of hours ago it was closed to the public, so I didn't go inside," Nick said. "Octavia and Gail were very busy getting things ready for this evening. They're probably hanging your drawing of Winston as we speak."

"Oh, boy." Carson whirled around and raced into the house.

Sullivan stopped beside Nick. They watched the screen door swing shut behind Carson.

"Had a long talk with Mitch today when we set out from Portland," Sullivan said. "We came up with a name for you. But we think we ought to go with you when you confront the person. If we're right, this goes all the way back to the days of Harte-Madison. Mitch and I feel some responsibility for the situation."

"That collateral damage you mentioned?"

"Afraid so."

"What's the name of your suspect?" Nick asked.

Sullivan told him.

"That pretty well cinches it," Nick said. He picked up one of the suitcases. "I came up with the same name."

Sullivan hoisted the other suitcase. "No reason this can't wait until tomorrow, is there? When word gets out no one's going to be able to talk about anything else. Gonna be rough."

"If Octavia agrees, it can wait until tomorrow," Nick said. "But no longer. I'm sorry about what's going to come down when this becomes public knowledge, but I've got Octavia to think about."

Sullivan nodded. "And she comes first now, is that it?"

"That's it."

At six o'clock that evening every parking lot was full. A large crowd of locals, Heralds, tourists, and summer people thronged the street and sidewalk.

Colorful balloons bobbed from the open doors of the shops and gallery. The temperature had been above average during the day, a balmy eighty-two, and the late sum-

mer sun was fending off the evening chill. The Annual
Eclipse Bay Summer Celebration was in full swing.

Octavia breathed a sigh of relief when several kids,
dragging their parents, surged into Bright Visions the
minute the door was opened.

"It looks like the show isn't going to be a disaster after
all," she said in a low voice to Gail, who was supervising
the punch-and-cookies table.

Gail chuckled. "Told you not to worry. Did you really
think anyone would stay away? Every kid with a picture in
the show will be here tonight, and everyone else in town
will come just to get a look at you and Nick together. After
all, you're the lady who shattered the curse."

"And then, of course, there is the fact that I am a noted
local art thief," Octavia said dryly.

"Hey, a little notoriety never hurts when it comes to
publicity."

"Just goes to prove the old publicity axiom, I guess. 'I
don't care what you call me so long as you spell my name
right.'"

Gail's amusement faded. "It's true that people are very
curious about your relationship with Nick. And I won't say
that the rumors about the missing Upsall haven't piqued
everyone's interest. But the bottom line is that a lot of people really like you, Octavia. You're a nice person."

Octavia made a face. "You mean, for an art thief?"

"Gail is right." Hannah appeared out of the crowd and
helped herself to a chocolate chip cookie. "You and the
Bright Visions gallery are part of this town. Folks wouldn't
be talking about you if you weren't considered a legitimate
member of the community. Local folks never talk about
outsiders. They're not interested in the summer people or
the casual visitors."

"Like it or not, you belong here," Gail said.

Hannah glanced toward the door. "And here come a couple of your biggest admirers."

Octavia followed the direction of her gaze and saw Eugene and Dwayne enter the gallery. They looked different. It took her a few seconds to realize that both men had shaved and put on clean shirts and pants for the occasion. Eugene's hair was slicked down with some sort of shiny pomade, and Dwayne had tied his in a ponytail.

The pair came to a halt just inside the entrance, blocking traffic. Although they had walked into the gallery with a certain air of bravado, they now appeared uncomfortable. She got the feeling neither of them knew what to do next.

"Will you look at that," Gail murmured. "They've actually buttoned their shirts."

"Sort of ruins the image when you can't see Eugene's hairy belly through the holes in his undershirt, doesn't it?" Hannah mused.

Gail frowned. "I hope they're not here to start trouble."

"Don't worry," Hannah said. "Sean Valentine is just outside talking to Nick and A.Z. and Virgil. Eugene and Dwayne won't create any problems with the chief nearby."

"I agree, there's no cause for alarm." Octavia picked up two paper cups filled with punch. "They wouldn't have gone to all the effort to get cleaned up if they'd planned to start another brawl."

She made her way through the crowd to where Eugene and Dwayne hovered uncertainly.

"Hello," she said brightly, handing a cup to each man. "I'm glad you could make it tonight. Please come in and have a look around."

"Thanks." Eugene seemed to relax. He took one of the

cups of punch. "Dwayne and me figured it was about time we educated ourselves about art, y'know?"

"Of course." She gestured toward the buffet table. "Help yourselves to cookies."

"Look, Dwayne, they've got free food."

He started toward the table.

"Excellent." Dwayne downed the contents of his punch cup and set off in Eugene's wide wake.

Nick sauntered through the door at that moment. His gaze tracked Eugene and Dwayne's progress. "Everything okay in here?"

"Yes, indeed," she said. "I was just welcoming a couple of other legitimate members of the community."

He raised his eyebrows. "Do I detect a trace of irony here?"

"Probably." She glanced at Carson, who stood with Anne in front of the picture of Zeb. The two children appeared to be deep in conversation. A couple of miniature art connoisseurs, she thought. "Tell me the truth, Nick. Would you say that I'm a real member of this community?"

"Are you kidding? You've got everyone from Mean Eugene and Dickhead Dwayne to the wife of the future mayor here tonight. You've also got representatives of both the Harte and Madison clans. Trust me, in Eclipse Bay, it doesn't get any more legitimate."

"You're teasing me, aren't you?"

"I'm dealing the truth here. And there's another thing that guarantees you a place of honor in our fair town."

"What's that?"

"You broke the curse."

She made a face. "If you mention that stupid curse one more time, I swear, I'll—"

"I'd appreciate it if you would not refer to the condition of my former sex life as stupid," he said with grave dignity.

"At least you had a previous sex life. When I look back, I've got to wonder if I was the one under a spell. Two years is a long time to go between dates."

He gave her a smile that curled her toes.

"But it was worth the wait, right?" he said.

"I am not going to respond to such a leading question. Not in public, at any rate. Now, you'll have to excuse me, I'm trying to host a show here." She made to move off.

"By the way," he added, lowering his voice, "there is one more thing I wanted to tell you."

She paused and looked at him inquiringly. "Yes?"

He glanced around, apparently checking to see if there was anyone within earshot. Then he grasped her arm and urged her into a quiet corner of the room.

"Mitch and Sullivan and I think we've got a lead on the Upsall."

Stunned, she just stared at him for a couple of seconds. He was standing very close, one hand braced against the wall behind her. There was something utterly, dangerously masculine in the way he leaned into her slightly, cutting off her view of the room with his broad shoulders. His body language spoke of possession and a silent claim that she knew every other man in the room could probably read.

A sense of déjà vu swept through her. This was the way he had stood with her at Lillian's gallery show, she thought. He had put himself between her and the crowd that evening, too, cutting her out of the herd, making her intensely aware of him and then asking her out on a date. She had known in her heart where a date with Nick would lead and her nerve had failed her that night.

Oh, sure, later she had come up with lots of really good

reasons for avoiding the risk of getting involved with him, but the stark truth was that her courage had failed at crunch time that first night. She had run from him that evening and several more times after that.

But tonight was different. Tonight, because she had finally taken the risk, she knew him far more intimately and deeply and she could see what lay beneath the surface. In addition to the intensely sensual threat he posed, there was strength and honor and integrity. *Dear God, I'm in love.*

Automatically she lowered her own voice to a whisper. "Who? What? Where? Tell me what's going on here, Nick."

He looked at her very steadily. "No one's got more of a right to answers than you do. But this afternoon Sullivan and Mitchell asked me to ask you to give them until noon tomorrow to confirm our hunch."

"Why the delay?"

"We need to be sure. We're talking about someone with deep ties throughout the community. People are going to be hurt. We can't afford to be wrong."

She searched his face. He was genuinely concerned about what might happen when it all came undone.

"And if you're right?" she asked gently.

"There will be a lot of fallout. And it won't all come down on the person who took the painting. There is someone else who will probably get dumped on, too. An innocent bystander."

"Collateral damage."

"Yes."

She shivered. "I hate those words. Translated, they mean that real people will get burned."

"Yes," he said again. But this time his eyes went cold. "I told Sullivan and Mitch that, although I'm willing to give them some time, I'm not going to let this thing get hushed up or swept under a rug. One way or the other, by tomorrow afternoon, your name will be cleared, no matter who gets hurt. I'm not going to let you take the rap."

He meant every word, she thought. He was making it blazingly clear that she was his first priority. The realization gave her an odd feeling. No one had ever fought any battles for her and now, in the space of less than a week, Nick had gotten involved in a barroom brawl and was about to expose an upstanding member of the community as a thief. All in her name.

"All right," she said. "Tell Mitch and Sullivan I'll wait until tomorrow."

"Thanks. They'll be grateful."

"I owe them that much," she said. "For Aunt Claudia's sake, if nothing else." She peeked around his shoulder. "I'd better go. This crowd is getting bigger and it looks like the cookies have disappeared."

She made to slide around the broad shield of his shoulders.

"One more thing I wanted to tell you before you run off," he said quietly.

She looked back at him, her mind on the cookie supply issue. "Yes?"

"Something I should have said that first night at Lillian's show. Something I knew at the time. Something I've known all along. Just didn't quite recognize it until recently. Probably because I'm a little out of practice."

"What's that?"

"I love you."

She stared at him, open-mouthed. Bereft of speech.

He gave her a sexy, knowing smile. "Better go check on the cookies."

He pushed himself away from the wall and strolled off into the crowd.

"When are you gonna get your dog?" Anne asked.

"Right after my birthday," Carson said. "That's when the puppies will be old enough to be 'dopted. Dad says we'll drive to Portland so I can pick out one. It's the same place where Winston was born."

"What are you going to name him?"

"I don't know yet. I'm still thinking."

"When you bring him back here to Eclipse Bay can I see him?"

"Sure," Carson said, feeling magnanimous. "You can come to my birthday party, too."

"Okay. Do you want to come to mine?"

"Yeah," Carson said. "When is it?"

"August fourteenth."

"I'll bring my dog with me," Carson promised. He looked across the room to where Jeremy stood talking to Hannah and Anne's grandparents. "Is he gonna be your new dad?"

"Maybe." Anne took a bite of her cookie. "Mom likes him a lot, I think. Grandma and Grandpa like him, too. Mom says they have good taste in men and this time she's going to listen to 'em."

"I like him, too. Do you?"

"Uh-huh." Anne nodded enthusiastically. "He came to our house for dinner last night and everybody laughed and we played games and stuff. He liked my pictures. It was fun." She looked at Octavia, who was moving across the room toward the cookie table. "Is Miss Brightwell gonna be your new mommy?"

"I think so," Carson said. Then he frowned, still a little

troubled about some aspects of the situation. "Unless Dad screws up again."

Octavia spied the Willis brothers shortly before the end of the event.

She was about to bid them a pleasant good evening and thank them for attending the show when she suddenly remembered the mysterious key she had found in the back room closet.

"Torrance? Walter? Have you got time for a quick question?"

"Thinking of doing a little remodeling in here?" Walter surveyed the gallery with a speculative expression. "A new paint job wouldn't hurt. We can give you a good price on a few cans of taupe."

"I'm not planning on doing any painting for a while. This is more of a hardware issue. I found a key in the closet. It doesn't fit either of the doors. You two did the security and locks here and I thought I'd see if you recognized it. If not, I'll toss it."

They followed her into the back room and looked around with interest while she took the key off the closet hook.

"Sure is cluttered in here," Torrance said. "We could build you some shelving or maybe some racks for stacking all these paintings."

"That's not a bad idea," she said. "I'll think about it." She held out the key.

Walter took it from her and gave it a quick, cursory glance. "No problem. Reckon we know what this goes to, don't we, Torrance?"

"Sure do," Torrance said. "Leastways, it's the same brand we used for that job. I remember we ordered it in special after the problems with that little rash of break-ins we had a couple years back." He looked at Octavia. "Turned out to be some kids fooling around. Summer people, you know. Sean Valentine took care of the situation, but a few folks around here got nervous and asked us to upgrade their locks and such."

"Won't be hard to check and see if this key fits where we think it does," Walter said.

# chapter 23

Octavia parked in the drive in front of the old, two-story house, turned off the ignition, and got out of the car. It was six-thirty in the morning, but fog veiled the early light and cast a damp pall on the entire town.

Or maybe it was just her mood, she thought as she went up the steps and crossed the front porch. She had not slept much last night.

She banged the brass knocker on the front door. When there was no response, she banged it a second time.

Eventually the door opened a crack.

"What on earth are you doing here at this hour of the morning?" Edith Seaton demanded.

"I think you know why I'm here," Octavia said gently. "I came to get the Upsall."

Edith stared at her through the narrow opening for a long moment. Without warning her face suddenly crumpled. In the space of five or six seconds she seemed to age at least a decade.

"Yes." She stood back and held the door open. "Yes, I suppose you'd better take it."

Octavia stepped into the shadowy foyer.

Edith turned, not speaking, and led the way toward the living room. She wore a long, faded dressing gown and slippers.

Octavia took a quick look around as she followed Edith. The house was decorated with what appeared to be left-overs from Edith's shop. There was a display of carnival glass in a case that stood against one wall. Small porcelain figures were arranged on the end tables. The furniture was heavy and old-fashioned.

Edith sat down very stiffly in a rose-patterned rocking chair. Octavia went to stand at the window that overlooked the garden.

"How did you figure it out?" Edith asked in a resigned voice.

"I came across a key in my back room. Last night I asked the Willis brothers if they recognized it. They said they had installed a special lock in the door of your shop. We checked. The key fit. Last night I got a phone call from Noreen Perkins. Sean Valentine had tracked her down to ask her about a missing painting and she was worried that I might think she'd had something to do with the theft."

"And you asked her about the key, I suppose," Edith said dully. "She no doubt told you that several months ago we exchanged keys and that she also gave me the security code to the gallery."

"Yes. She said that both of you had occasionally gotten accidentally locked out. She had trouble remembering the security code for the alarm system so she made sure you had it in case she ever needed it."

"We thought it would be a convenience for both of us,"

Edith said. "But after she left, I forgot all about having the code and a key in my desk. Just never gave it another thought."

"Until the day you and everyone else in town discovered that Claudia Banner was my great-aunt."

"I couldn't believe it." Color rushed back into Edith's face. Her gnarled, spotted hands knotted into fists. "It was as if her ghost had come back to haunt me. Worse yet, it was happening all over again, just like it happened all those years ago. But this time it was my grandson she, I mean *you,* seduced."

"I did not seduce Jeremy."

"All that talk about putting his pictures on display in your gallery. Encouraging him to do more paintings for you. It was seduction, all right, and well you know it."

"It was business, not seduction."

"You went out to dinner with him several times, too."

"We are friends, Mrs. Seaton. But not lovers."

"Only because something better came along," Edith shot back hoarsely. "You dropped my Jeremy like a hot potato when Nick Harte started to date you. Don't deny it."

"I do deny it. Every single word. You're putting your own spin on this, Edith, but I think deep down you know that it isn't the truth."

"You caused trouble between Jeremy and Nick the same way Claudia Banner did with Mitchell Madison and Sullivan Harte."

"So you took the painting the night of the storm and tried to destroy my good name in a noble attempt to defend Jeremy from my wiles?" Octavia shook her head. "I'm not buying that, Edith."

Edith sat in rigid, stubborn silence.

"Do you know what I think?" Octavia sat down in the

chair across from the older woman. "I think you used Jeremy as an excuse to take revenge for something that Claudia Banner did to you all those years ago. She is beyond your reach and maybe you told yourself you had put it all behind you. But when you realized that I was her niece, the old anger came rushing back, didn't it?"

Edith flinched. "She got away with it. But then, Claudia Banner got away with everything. She never paid for the trouble and pain she caused."

"Tell me what my great-aunt did to you, Edith."

"She seduced my husband." Edith surged up out of her chair. "And then she used him."

Octavia was on her feet now. "How did she use him?"

"Phil was the accountant for Harte-Sullivan. She got him to doctor the company books while she carried out her scam. That was the reason Mitchell and Sullivan never saw the bankruptcy coming until it was too late."

Octavia drew a deep breath and let it out slowly. "I see."

"It was as if she was some sort of sorceress," Edith whispered. "She put my Phil under a spell for a time. The poor fool never realized how she'd manipulated him until he woke up one morning and discovered that she had vanished. He actually thought that she would contact him after the heat died down. He really believed that she loved him and wanted him to run off with her. It was months before he finally understood that he'd been used."

"Was that when you discovered his role in the bankruptcy?"

"Yes. I'd suspected he was having an affair with her, but I never dreamed that she had seduced him into helping her drive Harte-Madison into bankruptcy. I was stunned. He was a Seaton, after all. How could he do something like that?"

"But you kept the secret."

"I had no choice. I had to think of the family name. I had the children to consider. Just imagine what they would have had to face here in Eclipse Bay if it had come out that their father had had a hand in the destruction of Harte-Madison."

"It would have been rough on them."

"And then there was the financial situation. If the truth had surfaced, my husband's career as an accountant would have been destroyed. At the very least the shame and humiliation would have forced us to leave town. Where would we have gone? This was our home."

"So you buried the past as best you could. Your husband never told Mitchell and Sullivan what he'd done."

"Of course not. I pointed out to him that there was nothing to be gained by confessing his part in their disaster and everything to lose."

"You succeeded in protecting your husband and the Seaton name, but you never forgave him or Aunt Claudia."

"I swear she was some sort of witch. She never paid for her wicked works. Probably never even gave her victims a second thought."

"You're wrong there, Edith. Aunt Claudia thought about the past a lot toward the end. In a way, she was obsessed with it."

There was no need to get into the specifics, Octavia thought. No point bringing up the fact that Claudia had never even mentioned the name Seaton during those times when she had talked about her adventures in Eclipse Bay. The only people who had concerned her at the end had been the Hartes and the Madisons.

"I have no right to ask you to forgive me for what I did," Edith said. "My only excuse is that, for a while after

I discovered who you were, I went a little mad. It was as if a curtain had opened and I was looking at the past again. It all came crashing back and the only thing I could think about was punishing that dreadful woman."

"It's called visiting the sins of the father on the son, or in this case, visiting the sins of the great-aunt on the niece."

"I told myself I was doing it to show Jeremy and Nick the truth about you, but you're right, of course. I did it to avenge myself."

"So you took the Upsall and started the rumors that I was the thief."

"When I finally came to my senses, it was too late. It will all come out now, won't it? What Phil did in the past and what I tried to do to you. This time I won't be able to keep the stain off the family name. Jeremy will be embarrassed. The rest of the family and most of the people in town will think I've gone senile. And as for my friends—" Edith trailed off, bowing her head.

So much for nearly four decades of Wednesday and Saturday bridge games and civic committee meetings, Octavia thought. Even if the community and her friends were willing to forget the affair, Edith would never be able to hold her head up high in Eclipse Bay again.

She put a hand on one of Edith's thin shoulders. "You know, it was Aunt Claudia who urged me on her deathbed to come to Eclipse Bay. She said she wanted me to see if perhaps I could repair some of the damage she had done here. I assumed that she was referring to the Harte-Madison feud, and I have to tell you that I was feeling pretty useless because the Hartes and the Madisons took care of that issue all by themselves."

Edith took a hankie out of the pocket of her old robe

and dabbed at her eyes. "Yes. Those two stubborn men seem to have become friends again."

"They didn't need me," Octavia said. "But maybe I was looking in the wrong place. Maybe this was the damage I was supposed to repair."

"I don't understand," Edith said.

"I know. I'll explain it to you while you get dressed. Hurry, we don't have a lot of time."

"It's very kind of you to want to help me after what I did to you, but it's too late, my dear. The truth will be all over town by nightfall. It's only right after all this time."

"You're going to have to trust me on this, Edith. For Jeremy's sake and the Seaton family name."

"But—"

"Aunt Claudia owes you this much," Octavia said.

She unlocked the gallery an hour earlier than usual and went straight to work reorganizing and tidying up the shop.

She took down drooping balloons and swept the cookie crumbs off the floor. It required three trips to the Dumpster to get rid of all the used paper cups, plates, and napkins.

When the trash had been dealt with, she concentrated on the display panels. One by one she took down the framed drawings that had been done by the children and replaced them with the usual pictures. She stacked the kids' pictures in one corner in the back room, ready to be collected by the proud artists.

She was coming through the door that separated the back room from the showroom, a large seascape in her hands, when she caught a glimpse of Nick's car. He was just pulling into the parking lot. Directly behind him was Mitchell's big monster of an SUV.

Nick, Carson, and Sullivan, accompanied by Mitchell,

came through the front door two minutes later. They all looked at her, concerned and serious and a little baffled.

"Okay, we're here," Nick said. "What's this all about?"

"Hang on," she said. "I'll be right back."

She darted into the other room to scoop up the painting that she had left propped against the leg of the worktable.

She walked back out into the main room holding the picture aloft for all to see. "Look what I found when I started cleaning up after the art show this morning."

They all dutifully stared at the painting. None of the men said a word.

"Hey," Carson said gleefully, "I remember that picture. It's the one that belongs to A.Z. and Mr. Nash and the Heralds. The one everyone said had been stolen."

"It is, indeed," Octavia agreed. "You really do have a good eye for art, Carson."

He beamed.

She put the Upsall very carefully on the counter. "Evidently it got pushed behind a stack of pictures that was leaning against the wall. Heaven only knows how long it would have stayed back there if it wasn't for all the rearranging I had to do in here this morning."

"Well, shoot and damn," Mitchell said. The somber look evaporated from his eyes. A knowing expression took its place. "It was in your back room all along. How about that."

"Thank the good Lord we didn't rush off to confront our suspect last night," Sullivan said dryly. He grinned at Octavia. "Could have been more than a little awkward."

"Naturally, I feel like a complete idiot," Octavia said. "But at least this fiasco is finished and Nick no longer has to play detective."

Nick smiled slowly. He did not take his eyes off Octavia. "I was just starting to get the hang of it."

That evening Nick drove her back to the cottage after dinner with Carson and Sullivan at Dreamscape. There was obviously a conspiracy at work to give them some time together, Octavia thought, amused. No one had even been particularly subtle about sending them off by themselves this evening.

She made coffee and put two large, leftover chocolate chip cookies on a plate. When she carried the tray out into the living room, she found Nick slouched deep into her sofa. Looking comfortable, she thought. At home. Like he had every right to be there.

*Something I should have said that first night at Lillian's show. Something I knew at the time. Something I've known all along. Just didn't quite recognize it until recently. Probably because I'm a little out of practice . . . I love you.*

A deep sense of joy welled up inside her and shimmered through her senses.

Nick watched her set the tray down on the coffee table. "Alone at last," he said.

"Mmm." She put one of the cookies on a napkin and handed it to him.

He took a healthy bite. "Okay, let's have the real story," he said around a mouthful of cookie.

"You refer to the case of the missing Upsall, I presume?"

"What else? It's the only thing this town is talking about at the moment." He stretched out his legs and sank deeper into the sofa. "With the exception of you and me, of course."

"Mmm."

He sounded so matter-of-fact about the *you and me* part.

"You can skip the version in which you miraculously discover the Upsall when you tidy up your back room, by the way. I'm not buying it for a second."

She curled one foot under her leg and took a tiny sip of coffee. "The other version is a little complicated."

"Let's start with the fact that Sullivan, Mitchell, and I all know that Edith Seaton took the picture."

"She had her reasons."

"Sullivan and Mitchell figured that out. Phil Seaton was their accountant in the old days. Can one assume that your great-aunt seduced him into covering her tracks for her?"

"I'm afraid so. And afterward Edith was so horrified at the thought of being caught up in the scandal that she covered up for Phil."

"But never forgave your aunt, I take it?"

"She blamed Claudia for everything, not without considerable justification, I might add. When word got out that I was related to her old nemesis, Edith freaked. After all, I was having dinner with Jeremy, encouraging him to paint, and then I started sleeping with you. Clearly history was about to repeat itself. It was just too much for her to handle."

"So she stole the picture and spread the rumors. Piss-poor sort of revenge, if you ask me."

"It was the only kind that was left to her," Octavia said simply. "And she could justify it to herself for a time because she truly believed that I was turning out to be a bad influence on Jeremy."

"Because you encouraged him in his painting?"

"Yes."

"Huh." Nick ate the last of the cookie. "She didn't have any qualms about taking the easy way out, did she? Obviously she went along with your scheme to make the Upsall magically materialize in your back room."

"To be fair, she was reluctant at first. But when I told her that we were doing it for Jeremy's sake and for the sake of the Seaton name, she went for it. I also told her that I was sure that was the way Aunt Claudia would have wanted it."

Nick raised his brows and reached for his coffee. "Think it's true?"

"To be honest, I'm not sure Claudia even remembered Phil Seaton, let alone worried much about the damage she did to his family. But even if that was the case, one thing is certain—she definitely owed the Seatons. And now the debt has been paid in some small measure."

"Thanks to you."

She put her empty cup down on the coffee table. "It was the least I could do, given that I never got the chance to fulfill my mission of repairing the Harte-Madison feud."

"I thought you had concluded that the real reason Claudia sent you here was so that you could get wild and crazy."

"Yes, well, if that's true, all I can say is, mission accomplished."

"Not quite." His mouth quirked in sexy promise. He reached for her and started to pull her close. "But you know what they say, practice makes perfect."

She spread her hands against his chest, holding him off for a moment longer. "Before we get to the wild and crazy stuff, there's something I want to tell you."

"And that would be?"

"It may have been Aunt Claudia who sent me here to Eclipse Bay but you're the reason I decided to stay on even after it became apparent that the feud was ending."

"Is that right?"

"I love you."

He smiled slowly. The look in his eyes was so dazzling she could hardly catch her breath.

"I was hoping you'd say that," Nick whispered against her mouth. "Now can we get to the wild and crazy stuff?"

"Of course," she said demurely. "I'm sure Aunt Claudia would have wanted it this way."

"Do me a favor." He pushed her gently down onto the sofa. "Don't mention your aunt again for a while, okay?"

"Okay."

She put her arms around his neck and kissed him with all the love and passion that she had discovered within herself here in Eclipse Bay.

*Wherever you are, Aunt Claudia,* she thought, *thank you.*

# chapter 24

On a sunny afternoon in the fall, Mitchell stood with Sullivan at the end of the long veranda that wrapped around Dreamscape. Each of them held a glass of champagne in one hand. Their canes hung, side by side, over the railing. From their vantage point they had a clear view of the newlyweds, who were dutifully working their way through a seemingly endless reception line.

The entire town, from the current mayor and his likely successor and his wife to Mean Eugene and Dickhead Dwayne, had turned out for Nick and Octavia's wedding.

"Knew all along Octavia belonged here with us," Mitchell said.

"You won't get any argument from me." Sullivan smiled to himself at the sight of Nick standing so close to Octavia, one arm wrapped protectively and possessively around her waist, the other outstretched to shake hands with the next well-wisher in line. "She and Nick and Carson are a family already."

Mitchell glanced at Rafe and the now obviously pregnant Hannah. The pair was busy supervising the buffet tables.

"And there's more family on the way," he said proudly. "I'm gonna have me a great-grandkid, real soon now."

"Probably more than one," Sullivan said dryly. He motioned toward Gabe and Lillian, who stood with Jeremy and Gail. "I think I recognize that rosy glow on Lillian's face."

"Yeah?" Mitchell followed his gaze and grinned. "Think so?"

"I do, indeed."

Mitchell swallowed some more champagne and grimaced at the taste. "I think Rafe said he stashed some beer in the solarium. Want to go see if we can find it?"

"Good idea. This stuff tastes like fizzy water, which is a real shame, given what I happen to know it cost."

They gripped their canes and made their way around the corner of the veranda to a side entrance. A bright red ball shot past in front of them. A small bundle of silver and gray exploded out of the open door. The young Schnauzer seized the ball in his jaws and kept going, heading for the open lawn at full speed.

Carson and Anne burst threw the door, chasing after the dog.

"Come back, Tycoon," Carson shouted. "You're supposed to get the ball and bring it to me when I throw it for you. You're not supposed to run off with it."

"Zeb always brings back whatever I throw," Anne said with cheerful superiority. "He's a really smart dog."

"Tycoon is smart," Carson informed her as he dashed down the steps in pursuit of his dog. "He's still learning how to do stuff, that's all. Winston's teaching him."

Winston trotted sedately out of the doorway, following in the wake of Tycoon, Carson, and Anne with an air of patient authority and attentive vigilance.

Sullivan watched the pack of dogs and children race across the lawn in pursuit of the renegade Tycoon. "I'd swear that dog of Hannah's must have been a butler or a nanny in his past life, the way he keeps an eye on those kids."

"That's a fact."

They went into the lobby of Dreamscape and made their way to the solarium. The beer was there, as promised, resting comfortably in a chest filled with ice.

Mitchell handed a bottle to Sullivan and opened one for himself.

They each took a long pull.

"Sure beats the hell out of champagne," Mitchell said.

"It does."

They went to the window and looked out at the happy scene.

"You know something," Mitchell said, "it wasn't always easy, but in the end, we did okay, you and me."

"We did just fine," Sullivan agreed. "We hung on until dawn."

*Turn the page for a sneak preview of Jayne Ann Krentz's
new novel,*

## LIGHT IN SHADOW

*Coming soon from G. P. Putnam's Sons*

# CHAPTER ONE

The walls screamed at her.

"Oh, damn," Zoe Luce whispered. She halted in the doorway of the empty bedroom and stared at the white walls. *Not now. Not today. Not this time. I really need this job.*

The walls sobbed. Terror pulsed through layers of Sheetrock and the fresh coat of stark white paint that covered it. The silent shrieks ricocheted off the floor and ceiling.

She put her fingers to her temples in a purely instinctive, utterly useless gesture. She squeezed her eyes shut, bracing herself against the ragged bolts of icy lightning that were shooting through her and pooling into a glacial pond somewhere in the vicinity of her stomach.

Davis Mason had followed her so closely down the hall that he was only a pace behind her when she came to a sudden stop. He bumped awkwardly against her.

"Oops, sorry." He caught his balance. "I wasn't paying attention."

"My fault." With what she hoped was an unobtrusive movement, she eased out of the doorway and back into the hall. Things were much better out here. She could cope. She gave Davis what she hoped was a bright, assured smile. It wasn't easy, what with the muffled cries still leaking out of the bedroom.

She wanted out of this house. Fast. Whatever had happened in the bedroom had been bad.

"Hey." Davis touched her shoulder lightly. "Are you all right, Zoe?"

She gave him another shaky smile. It was relatively easy to smile at Davis. He had elegant lines and clean styling with just the right touch of roguish flair. If he'd been a car, he would have been a sleek, European roadster. Judging by the spacious home, the hand-tailored shirt and trousers and the onyx-and-diamond ring he wore, he was also wealthy. In short, she thought sadly, until that moment, she had considered him the ideal client.

Everything had changed now, of course.

"Yes, I'm fine." She did a little on-the-spot deep breathing using the techniques she had learned in her self-defense class. Summoning up her teacher's instructions, she sought the calm, stable center that was supposed to be somewhere deep inside her. Unfortunately she had not yet mastered that part of the program. All she could feel was a bad case of the jitters coming on.

"What's wrong?" Davis was looking seriously concerned now.

"Just the start of a headache," Zoe said. "I often get one when I forget to eat breakfast."

The lies came so easily these days. But, then, she'd had

a lot of practice. Too bad she wasn't yet clever enough to convince herself, she thought. A little self-delusion would be very welcome right now.

Davis watched her intently for a few seconds and then he relaxed. "Missed your morning shot of caffeine?"

"And food. It's a blood-sugar thing. I should know better." Feeling an urgent need to change the topic of conversation, she looked back into the bedroom and blurted out the first thing that came into her mind. "What happened to the bed?"

"The bed?"

They both looked at the large, empty stretch of uncovered section of hardwood floor between two massive, Mission-style bedside tables.

Zoe swallowed uneasily. "The rest of the residence is fully furnished," she said. "I couldn't help but notice that there's no bed in here."

"She took it," Davis said grimly.

"Your ex-wife?"

He sighed. "She loved that damned bed. Spent months shopping for it. I swear, it meant more to her than I did. When she left, it was about the only thing she insisted on taking with her in addition to her personal stuff."

"I see."

"You know how it is in a divorce. Sometimes the biggest fights are over the smallest, dumbest things."

Whatever else it had been, Zoe thought, the missing bed had not been small.

"I understand."

Davis searched her face. "Headache getting worse?"

"It'll be all right once I've had lunch and a cup of coffee," she assured him.

"Tell you what. You've seen the rest of the house. I'm

sure you've got the general picture. Why don't we take a break and get something to eat at the club? It will give us a chance to talk over your initial impressions."

The thought of eating made her stomach churn. She knew from experience that she would not be able to keep any food down until the chills stopped. That could take a while. This had been a really bad experience and it had caught her totally off guard.

It was her own fault. She knew better than to enter a room so recklessly. But she had been caught up in her plans for the interior; completely focused, and the rest of the spacious residence had seemed so new, so *clean*. She simply had not been expecting trouble and, as often happened, she had paid the price.

"I'd love to join you for lunch but I'm afraid I'll have to take a rain check." She made a show of glancing at her watch. "I've got another appointment this afternoon and I need to prepare for it."

Davis looked hesitant. "If you're sure—"

"I'm afraid so." She tried to inject a note of apology into her tone. "I really do have to run, and you're right, I've seen all I need to see for now." *And sensed far more than I ever wanted to know, thank you very much.* "I've got the floor plan you gave me earlier. I'll make some copies and do some sketches that will give you an idea of what I have in mind."

"I'd appreciate the drawings." Davis glanced into the bedroom and shook his head somewhat ruefully. "I'll admit I'm not what you'd call a visual person. It's easier for me to grasp the concept when I can see a picture."

"It's always easier when you can look at a drawing. Hang on while I check my calendar."

She reached into her voluminous tote, one of six similar bags in different colors that she owned. Each functioned as a combination briefcase and purse. She had chosen the chartreuse-green one today because she liked the way it contrasted with her deep-violet pantsuit.

Groping in the vast depths, she pushed aside the small camera, a sketchbook, measuring tape, a clear plastic box containing an array of colored pens and felt markers, a folder of fabric samples and the large, antique brass doorknob attached to the ring that held the keys to her apartment.

The appointment calendar was at the bottom. She hauled it up to the surface and flipped it open.

"I'll get some ideas down on paper," she said briskly, "and I'll try to have some preliminary layouts ready for you by the end of the week. What do you say we meet in my office Friday morning?"

"Friday?" Davis was clearly disappointed. "That's a week off. Do we have to wait that long? I'd like to get started as soon as possible. The truth is, this house has been damn depressing since my wife walked out."

*Yeah, I'll bet it has,* she thought.

"I understand," she said aloud, trying to sound sympathetic. It wasn't easy, given the fact that the fine hairs on the nape of her neck were still tingling and there were goose bumps on her arms beneath the sleeves of her lightweight jacket.

"I'm trying hard not to be bitter," Davis said. "But the divorce is costing me a bundle. Got a feeling I'll be getting bills from the lawyers for a long time."

All the available evidence indicated that Davis Mason had come out of the divorce in excellent shape, financially. From what she could see, he possessed a very expensive residence—the interiors of which he was prepared to pay her handsomely to have redesigned—as well as a membership in a pricey country club. But she did not raise those points aloud.

She was rapidly learning to be diplomatic with the newly divorced, having discovered that they constituted a hot market niche for interior designers such as herself. People emerging from shattered marriages frequently yearned to redo their living spaces as a form of therapy to help them get past the negative emotional fallout caused by the breakup.

She flipped through the pages of her calendar pretending to study her schedule. Abruptly she snapped the leather-bound volume closed with a decisive air. "I'm afraid I'm booked solid. Friday is the only day I can give you the time this project deserves. Will two o'clock work for you?"

"Looks like I don't have much choice." Davis was not pleased. He was used to getting what he wanted. "Friday it is. Didn't mean to sound so impatient. It's just that I'm very anxious to get moving on the project."

"Of course. Once you've made the decision to redesign a personal living space, there's a natural urge to rush into the job." She spoke quickly, trying to inject a professional, businesslike quality into her voice. "But redoing an entire residence is a major undertaking and mistakes at this stage can be extremely costly."

"Yeah, I found that out the hard way." He took one more look at the bedroom. "I got as far as repainting this room and realized I needed expert help. I didn't think I could go wrong just putting a coat of white paint on the walls but as soon as I finished I realized it didn't look right. I wanted to make it seem light and airy in here and instead—" He shrugged and let the sentence trail off with a *who knew* expression.

And instead, the bedroom had all the cozy ambience of an autopsy room or an embalming chamber, Zoe concluded silently. No amount of the bright Arizona sunlight dancing on the surface of the sapphire pool outside could counteract that effect. Some of the unpleasant sensation was attributable to the stark white paint but she knew that the real problem had been treated by whatever it was that had happened in this bedroom. Some things could not be covered with a coat of paint.

She also knew that Mr. Ideal Client was not consciously aware of the emotions trapped in the walls. To her everlasting regret, she had never encountered anyone else who picked up on that kind of stuff the way she did: as pure, raw energy. But she had seen enough instances of others reacting in subtle, unconscious ways to the atmosphere of a particular room to be convinced that a lot of people responded to a space on some deep, psychic level.

She had also learned the hard way to keep her inner knowledge to herself.

"You chose a stark, bright white." She took another step back, putting more distance between herself and the bedroom doorway. "I know it seems like pure white should be simple and straightforward but it is actually very difficult to work with because it reflects so much glare, especially here in the desert. It also tends to create very cold shadows when you add furnishings. Ultimately that makes for a lack of harmony and tranquility. You were right to stop painting after you finished this room."

"Knew it wasn't the right direction." Davis made a casual gesture that invited her to go ahead of him down the hall. "I have to tell you, Zoe, when I decided I needed a professional designer, I didn't really put much stock in this feng shui thing that you do."

"A lot of people have doubts about it until they experience the result."

"I knew it was trendy and all. The women at the club are really into it. When Helen Weymouth gave me your name, she went on and on about how you had completely transformed her home after she got her divorce. She said she'd been on the brink of putting it up for sale because of all the bad memories. She credits you with changing the whole atmosphere of the place."

"The Weymouth project was an interesting one." Not much farther to the front door. A couple more minutes and she would be out of here. "Mrs. Weymouth gave me a free hand."

"She advised me to do the same thing. A few months ago, after Jennifer left, I would have said that all this business of arranging the furniture to regulate the flow of negative and positive energy was way too far-out for me. But the longer I live here alone with everything just the way it was when she was here, the more I'm convinced that there may be something to your design theories."

"I don't practice one particular school of feng shui." To her horror she realized she was talking much too fast. *Act normal. You know how to do this.* "I use elements of several different approaches combined with organizational principles from other classic design traditions such as Vastu."

"What's that?"

"An ancient Hindu science that sets out principals for architecture and design. I also incorporate what I consider the most useful elements from contemporary theories of harmony and proportion. My style is really quite eclectic."

*Actually, I pretty much make it up as I go along,* she added silently. But clients did not like to hear that.

She walked swiftly toward the front of the house, desperate to escape into the fresh air. Now that she had been sensitized by the experience in the bedroom, she was picking up wispy tendrils of dark, unwholesome emotions from other walls in the residence. She had to get out of this place fast.

She reached the terra-cotta foyer at last. Davis was right behind her. He opened the front door and she escaped into the reassuring warmth of the early November day.

"Are you sure you're feeling well enough to drive back to your office?" Davis asked.

*Act normal.*

"I've got an energy bar in the car." Another lie. Was she getting good at this or what?

"All right. Well, take care. And I'll see you on Friday."

"Right. Friday."

She gave him what she hoped was a bright, professional-looking smile, tightened her grip on the chartreuse tote and went briskly toward her car. She tried not to appear as if she was rushing away from the screaming house.

She breathed a sigh of relief when she reached the vehicle. Yanking open the door, she tossed the tote onto the passenger seat, slid behind the wheel, put on her dark glasses and fired up the engine, all in what felt like a single motion.

Her hands were still trembling. Aftershocks from the surge of adrenaline, she surmised. This wasn't the first time. She could handle it.

But she had to grip the wheel very tightly in order to steer her way out of the exclusive community. To her left was the long stretch of impossibly green fairway that served as the approach to the sixteenth hole of the Desert

View Country Club. Elegant homes similar to the Mason residence were scattered artfully around the golf course.

Beyond the vivid green links stretched the rugged expanse of the Sonoran desert and low, rolling mountain foothills. The golf club community and the adjoining town of Whispering Springs were a little more than an hour's drive from Phoenix, close enough to catch some of the spillover from the tourist trade but far enough out to avoid the traffic and congestion of the city.

The harsh, dry landscape had seemed a strange and alien place to her when she had moved here a year ago but somewhere along the line her new environment had begun to feel familiar, even comfortable. She had discovered an unexpected beauty in the desert, with its spectacular sunrises and sunsets and the astounding depths of light and shadow. She had always been drawn to contrasts and there was nothing subtle about this place.

The decision to move to Whispering Springs had been a good one, she mused, but maybe she should reconsider the career move she had made at the same time. Interior design had seemed like a natural, logical way to go. After all, she had a background in the fine arts, a good, trained eye and she certainly knew how to get the feel of a living space. Best of all, she hadn't needed any additional degrees or qualifications in order to set herself up in business legally. But today's encounter was enough to give her some second thoughts.

A uniformed guard came out of a small building located at the gated entrance. The emblem on his snappy khaki jacket declared him to be an employee of Radnor Security Systems. He greeted her politely, wished her a good day and went back inside his air-conditioned sanctuary to make a note on his log.

Security was tight here in this carefully planned enclave of wealth and status but someone in the Mason residence had not benefited from it.

She waited until she was clear of the gates and on her way back toward the downtown section of Whispering Springs before she picked up her phone. She punched in the only number that she had coded into her speed dial.

Arcadia Ames answered on the third ring, giving the name of her gift shop in her low, throaty voice. "Gallery Euphoria."

Arcadia sold unique, expensive gifts to an upscale clientele but Zoe was pretty sure her friend could have sold sand here in the desert with that voice.

Arcadia was her best friend; make that her *only* friend. She had once had other friends, Zoe thought. But that was a long time ago; back when she had had a real life and had not been living in the shadows.

"It's me," Zoe said.

"What's wrong? Something happen with Mr. Ideal Client?"

"You could say that."

"He decided not to hire you after all? That idiot. But don't worry, there will be other good clients like him. The divorce rate doesn't seem to be going down very much."

"Unfortunately, Mason didn't change his mind," Zoe said evenly. "I wish he had."

"Did the creep make a pass at you?"

"He was a perfect gentleman."

"He must be rich because everybody who lives in Desert View is, by definition, a high-roller," Arcadia said patiently. "So what went wrong?"

"I think Mr. Ideal Client may have murdered his wife."

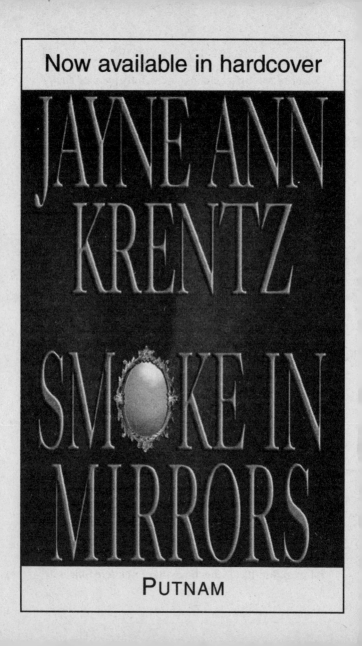